Dying on Second

a Marie Jenner mystery

E. C. Bell

The Marie Jenner Series

Dying on Second
Stalking the Dead
Drowning in Amber
Seeing the Light

Dying on Second

a Marie Jenner mystery

E. C. Bell

TYCHE BOOKS LTD.

Dying on Second
Published by Tyche Books Ltd.
www.TycheBooks.com

Copyright © 2017 E.C. Bell
First Tyche Books Ltd Edition 2017

Print ISBN: 978-1-928025-72-6
Ebook ISBN: 978-1-928025-73-3

Cover Art by Guillem Marí
Cover Layout by Lucia Starkey
Interior Layout by Ryah Deines
Editorial by Rhonda Parrish

Author photograph: Ryan Parker of PK Photography

All rights reserved. No part of this book may be reproduced or transmitted in any form or by any means, electronic or mechanical, including photocopying, recording or by any information storage & retrieval system, without written permission from the copyright holder, except for the inclusion of brief quotations in a review.

The publisher does not have any control over and does not assume any responsibility for author or third party websites or their content.

This is a work of fiction. All of the characters, organizations and events portrayed in this story are either the product of the author's imagination or are used fictitiously.

Any resemblance to persons living or dead would be really cool, but is purely coincidental.

This book was funded in part by a grant from the Alberta Media Fund.

Alberta
Government

To the Edmonton Ladies Softball Association,
and to sixty more years.

Prologue

IN 1974, THE City of Edmonton built five diamonds at the Southside Industrial Park, which backed onto Palm Dairy on the southern edge of town. They were built so the Ladies Fastball League could be moved, quickly and quietly, out of the McCauley neighbourhood and the city could build a stadium for the Commonwealth Games in 1978. The Commonwealth Stadium was going to be one of the city's crowning achievements, and after the Games, the Edmonton Eskimos, the local football team, was going to use it. But before that could happen, the city had to move the women and their softball out of the way.

All the diamonds at the Southside Industrial Park were originally supposed to be for women's softball. The park was also supposed to have a concession and bathrooms. It was supposed to be fantastic, so the women wouldn't feel so angry about having to move.

Of course, none of that panned out, exactly. Goldstick Park and men's baseball got the concession and washrooms, and two of the diamonds at Southside were designated for men. Diamond One was for baseball and Diamond Three was for men's softball. Diamonds Two, Four, and Five were built for the Ladies League. A league that fielded one hundred teams a year, and they got three diamonds.

I was dead, but even I knew a rip-off when I heard one.

MY BODY WAS buried just behind second base on Diamond Two in the spring of 1974, before the diamonds were finished. Before the city of Edmonton named the ball park John Fry, after a local politician and do-gooder. Before the lights and the shale were put in. Before everything.

The park was a cold, quiet place that year. All I could do was watch the workmen as they finished the diamonds and added the bleachers. Then, I sat in those newly built bleachers and wished that somebody would find me and get me the hell out of there.

I even had dreams, in those early days, about finding my family and somehow letting them know what happened to me. My parents must have been going out of their minds, wondering. It would have seemed to them that I'd fallen off the face of the earth. Like I hadn't cared how much I'd hurt them. Like I'd just walked away, without a backward glance.

But I couldn't find the gumption to leave that spot, and the dreams about my family faded. The living women showed up in the summer of 1975 and started to play softball, and my nightmares about how I died slowly faded, too.

Then the dead came, and all I thought about was softball . . .

I hadn't played softball growing up. Lots of girls did, but my parents didn't see what use a game like that would give me later in life.

"You need to learn how to type, and how to keep a clean house," they'd say to me. "So you can get a man."

That bit of advice is kind of what got me stuck at Diamond Two, if you want to know the truth. But that was ancient history. Better left buried. Just like me.

I learned to play from the other dead who came to the diamond after me. They'd known the game, loved the game, and wanted it to keep going. The diamonds were only used by the living twice a night for most of the spring and summer. We had the rest of the year to play our own games, whenever we wanted.

Until Marie Jenner wandered onto Diamond Two.

Then, it all blew up.

Stage One
Learning the Game

Marie:
Oh Yeah, Sunshine and Fresh Air Will Fix Me Right Up

"You got your glove. Right?"

That was James Lavall. It was the third time in as many hours that he'd asked me about that stupid glove he'd found for me in the back of his closet when I first mentioned that I might be thinking about playing softball. I answered him for the third time. As sweetly as I could. Like he wasn't driving me absolutely bonkers.

"I already answered that stupid question! It's in that bag thingy you gave me. With my sneakers and hat. Are you going senile or something?"

Okay, so maybe I wasn't being as sweet as I could have, but wow, James. Take a pill.

All James did was smile that patronizing, condescending smile that could drive me right around the bend as he pulled the Volvo out of the parking lot behind the Jimmy Lavall Detective Agency, where we worked.

Millie the comfort dog was curled up in the back seat. She'd been my mother's dog. After Mom died, my sister Rhonda had offered to take her, but Rhonda had three kids, which made her place way louder than Millie liked so I was very glad when James scooped the little dog up into his arms after the funeral. "She's coming home with me," he'd said. And that had been that.

I didn't look at her, but knew that if I did, she'd be giving me the same condescending smile as James. Comfort dog, indeed!

"Relax, Marie," James said. "I just want to make sure you show up for your first game with all the equipment you'll need. You know?"

"I know."

"You're going to have fun."

"Sure."

We were heading to John Fry Park, on the south side of town, so I could play my first softball game of the season. I stared down at my hands and wished desperately that the phone on my cute little receptionist's desk had rung before we'd left the office. If it had rung, and there had been a big enough case, I could have convinced James to forget about coming to the game. Heck, I might have even been able to miss out myself.

It hadn't, of course. So there we were, driving to my first official softball game in what felt like a million years.

"Besides," James continued, as he wove the Volvo through the stop-and-go traffic on Ninety-Ninth Street, heading south, "Dr. Parkerson says that sunshine and exercise will help."

"Yes," I hissed through clenched teeth. "She did say that, didn't she?"

I'd taken self-defence classes as my first foray into the exercise thing, but my shrink, Dr. Parkerson, hadn't been convinced that self-defence was the best way for me to work through my issues.

That was what she called nightmares and panic attacks and not being able to sleep for more than five hours a night after my mother died. Issues.

I wonder what she'd call them if she knew about the ghosts?

I'd been able to see ghosts—and interact with them—forever. Didn't like it much, but I'd let my mom talk me into helping them move on to the next plane of existence.

That might have been all right if Mom hadn't abandoned me shortly after I'd made that promise. All right, so she hadn't really abandoned me. She'd died. But for people like us, dying was hardly ever the end, so I'd fully expected her to show up after her funeral and follow me around for a few years, driving me crazy as she taught me everything I needed to know about moving spirits on.

She should have. I wasn't prepared. I'd barely decided to join her in the family business before she died. But she didn't come back to me. Not once.

And I couldn't even talk to my shrink about it.

"Maybe I should have picked golf or something," I said. "Then you and I could play together. You know?"

"Golf would drive you crazy," James said, shortly. "And besides, softball's fun. Once you get to know the rest of your team, you'll have a good time. And you've played before, so you'll get the hang of it quick enough. I know it."

Personally, I doubted that very much.

When I was twelve, Dad had decided to help coach my softball team. I'd lasted three seasons. I'd liked the game, but Dad never got off my back the whole time, so the idea of playing again left a bad taste in my mouth.

So, if I didn't like playing softball, and didn't want to play softball, how had I ended up playing softball? It was all Sergeant Worth's fault.

She'd "invited" James and me back to her office at the downtown police station once we'd returned from Fort McMurray. She wanted to confirm—with her own eyes—that James had actually passed his private investigator's test and had his licence to practice, so he could reopen the PI office his uncle had willed to him.

That was when she'd seen that I wasn't in very good shape, emotionally. She was the one who'd suggested I go to a shrink, and she was the one who'd suggested I play softball when James told her I needed to get out and exercise "for my mental well-being."

She'd given me the name of a coach who was looking for players. "Don't worry," she said as she handed me the scrap of paper with Greg Robertson's name and number on it. "We won't see each other. Much."

Yeah. She played softball, too. Which meant I was going to see her out on the diamonds, at least twice that season. Which made golf seem even more appealing, but James had been so enthusiastic about me playing, I got caught up in the whole "let's sign up" thing.

So, there I was, on my way to my first official softball game since I was fifteen. What had I gotten myself into?

"Do you want a coffee?" James asked.

My nerves were jangling, and I could feel an absolute river of nervous sweat running down my back. Probably the last thing in the world I needed was a coffee.

Whatever.

"Sure," I said. "Why not?"

He pulled into a Tim's and got into the line of cars waiting for the drive-through.

"I'm not going to be late, am I?" I looked at the spot where the clock had been on the Volvo's dash, but it was still black, like a dead eye. I'd managed to knock a cup of coffee onto it on my way to Fort McMurray eight months before, effectively killing it. There was no point in looking at the Timex on my wrist, either. It had been my mother's and when the battery ran down I hadn't had the heart to change it, so now it was a reminder of her, not a timepiece. "What time is it?"

"We have lots of time," James said. "Don't worry. I'm keeping track."

"Wonderful."

It actually didn't take too long to snake our way through the drive-through, and then we were back on Ninety-Ninth Street, heading to the ball diamonds.

"I should have practiced a bit," I muttered. "This is going to be just horrible."

James stopped at the corner, waiting for the traffic to clear so he could make his turn. "I told you I'd practice with you," he said. "But you said you didn't want to."

Screamed it was more the truth, I thought, and sipped the coffee.

"I'm just nervous," I said.

"Everything will be fine," he replied. "You did bring your glove, didn't you?"

"Yes!" I yelled. "I already told you that!"

We didn't speak again as we passed the first two diamonds. Vehicles were huddled around them on both sides of the street, and women streamed out of the cars, pulling equipment bags and carrying bats. A couple of women had kids in tow, but mostly, they were alone. There was a lot of hugging and chatting as they began warming up. It looked like they were having fun.

James and I had Googled John Fry Park that afternoon, and we knew these were Diamonds Four and Five. We were looking for Diamond Two.

"I don't have a bat," I muttered.

"Your team will have some," James said. "You can use one of those." He still sounded snippy about me yelling at him, so I left him alone until we pulled into the big parking lot edging Diamonds Two and Three.

I watched the cars streaming into the lot and felt woozy. Then I stared at the big set of bleachers surrounding the diamond closest to the parking lot, and felt like maybe I was going to throw up. There was enough room for a thousand people in those bleachers. Did people actually come and watch these games? Why hadn't I been warned about any of this? Why?

"You'll be fine," James said.

"Yeah." The bile was really rolling around, and I was afraid if I said one more thing, I would actually vomit.

"Don't forget your glove," he said then leaped out of the Volvo and strode across the gravel toward Diamond Two.

He had to come back to get Millie, and I felt a small mean bit of humour watching him try not to make eye contact with me as he pulled the dog out of the back seat. He walked away as I opened my ball bag and checked to make absolutely certain that I had been telling him the truth about the glove.

There it was, in all its faded, beat-up, second-hand glory, lying in the bottom of the dusty bag along with my brand-new hat.

"All right," I muttered, slamming the door of the car shut and crunching through the gravel to Diamond Two. "Here we go. Fresh air and sunshine. This is going to be great."

Yeah. Right.

Karen:
First Game of the Season

A GOOD SOFTBALL game needed decent weather and two teams. Oh, and a ball and bat. In that order. But in early May in Edmonton there could be snow just as easily as there could be rain. Either one would ruin a game.

Back in the mid-70s, most diamonds still had dirt infields and when it rained the mud was horrible. The only diamond that had shale—Diamond Four—was set up as an experiment to see if shale was better to play on than dirt. It was, of course—a game could be played on Diamond Four even while it was raining, for heaven's sake—so eventually, all the diamonds were redone in shale. I'd half expected my body to be found when they shaled Diamond Two, but it wasn't. It had been buried too deeply, and so, I was able to stay.

Even with the shale it was always interesting to see if the living games were actually going to be played, early in the season. Often teams would get to the diamond, only to find out the game had been cancelled. But that night, the weather was clear and warm, and all the games were going to play.

I watched from my spot by second base as the living teams assembled, each to their own side. They dragged sleeping bags and blankets into the dugouts, because it got cold when the sun went down—and in May, the sun went down early. I recognized most of the girls, because, like I said before, I've been here forever.

There were lights on both the diamonds, but the guys who maintained them always seemed reluctant to turn them on. That made it tough for the living to finish their games, and when they complained, the maintenance guys would mutter under their breath about the women being bitches, or lesbians, or on the rag. As if that explained everything.

The dead didn't bitch about the dark, of course, and it wouldn't have helped if we had. None of those idiots could hear or see us. Thank goodness.

I glanced up into the bleachers to see if Andrew was there yet. I should be used to it, after all these years, but as I looked my stomach tightened, that old familiar fist in my gut. He was there up near the top of the bleachers behind the backstop. He looked old. Used up. But not dead. Not yet.

I looked away, willing myself to ignore him. Just ignore him. *You knew he'd be here. He wouldn't miss the first game of the year. He wouldn't miss any of the games.*

He never did.

I'd never told the rest of the girls about Andrew because he'd been coming to the diamond longer than most of them had been dead. Some of them knew him from before—when they were alive and thought of him as just one of the old coots who liked to watch softball. A fixture at the diamond. Like the shale, or the bases. To me, though, not so much. But over the years, I'd managed to ignore him. Mostly.

He'd missed two seasons in the early eighties, and I was certain he was dead himself. Half of me wanted to track his spirit down and beat it into the ground, but the other half was just glad he was finally gone.

He came back and never missed another game after that. No one talked about what had happened to him those two years and, because I didn't want anyone to wonder why I'd care about a guy who just liked watching softball, I never asked. But the fist in my gut returned when he came back. And it never, ever went away. It lessened after time, of course—even a nightmare can get boring if you have the same one night after night forever—but the fear was always there.

Just like him.

The living women rolled in and arranged their gear down the

fences on either side of the diamond. A lot of the women were tugging at their uniforms like they grabbed in the wrong spots. It was the winter expansion thing. Happened every year.

There were a few new faces on each team. No surprise, because every year, people dropped out—some were pregnant or had recently had kids, and some of them just gave up on the game. And every once in a while, somebody died. So those ones—plus the ones playing college ball—had to be replaced.

The replacements were usually easy to pick out. They looked like deer in the headlights. They'd probably been dragged up from Division Three or Four—the beer leagues—with promises of more playing time and the possibility of going to Nationals. But some of them hadn't played since high school—or earlier—and didn't have a clue. Those newbies stood out like they were covered in bright pink paint, every one of them.

One of the new women was wearing running shoes and blue jeans. She looked like she was trying to find a place away from the others to puke.

A newbie, for sure. She wasn't going to last one game, I was certain of that.

A big guy with black hair and an easy smile waltzed up and put his arm around her shoulders. He said something to her, and when she hitched her shoulder, knocking his arm away, and snapped something back at him, his face crumbled. He turned away from her and wandered over to the mostly empty bleachers, where he sat and morosely sipped at the drink he'd brought in a paper cup.

The girl in the jeans and inappropriate footwear watched the good-looking guy leave, and her shoulders sagged. When he didn't look at her again, she dug around in the old bag she carried. Out came a hat, which she pulled resolutely over her ponytailed hair. Then she grappled out an old glove and pulled it onto her left hand. She stared at it like she'd never seen it before in her life, then pulled it off, tucked it under her arm, and wandered over to the Jolene Transport team.

The rest of the team stopped warming up and stared at her.

"Is she supposed to replace Leslie?" one of them asked. "Does she even look like she can play second base?"

The rest didn't answer. They didn't need to. Everybody knew that she wasn't replacing anyone important. She didn't have a clue what she was doing there.

Greg Robertson, the coach, leaped out of the dugout with a big smile on his face. "You Marie Jenner?" he asked.

The girl in the jeans nodded, and Greg handed her a uniform top and a couple of sheets of paper.

"Glad you could make it," he said. "You fill these out, and we'll get you registered before the game." He glanced at his watch. "You got fifteen minutes before the office closes, so get on it, please."

She blinked a few times, like she was trying to comprehend his words, then took the sheets of paper and sat at the bleachers behind the dugout. She dug through her bag, then pushed it aside, and looked around at the rest of the girls, sheepishly.

"Anybody got a pen?" she asked.

They all stared at her for a few moments, silently. Then the pitcher—Lily Roloson, who had played on the team for at least ten years—reached into her bag and retrieved a dusty pen. She handed it to Marie, with a half-smile. "Remember where you got it," she said. "It's the only one I have."

Marie nodded without a smile, barely making eye contact. She sat down and scribbled her information on the sheets of paper, then handed back the pen.

"Thanks," she said.

"You play much?" Lily asked.

Marie blinked again, several times, rapidly. "You mean softball?" she finally asked.

Lily's smile tightened. She didn't do so well in the suffering fools department. "Yeah," she said. "Softball."

"Not in a while," Marie said.

"Ah well," Lily sighed. "It's like riding a bike. It'll come back."

Marie nodded, but Lily didn't see her, because she'd turned her back and called to another player walking across the cropped grass to the dugout.

"Jamie!" she cried. "Get your ass over here, girl! Let me give you a squeeze!"

Jamie—Jamie Riverton—was the back catcher. She hoisted her huge bag of equipment more securely on her back and jogged over to Lily. She tapped her arm twice, perfunctorily, and dropped the equipment on the ground at her feet.

"Have a good winter, Lill?"

"Good enough," Lily said. "Went to Puerto Rico for three weeks."

"Oh, to be a teacher with all that time off," Jamie replied, pulling her face mask and glove from the pile of equipment and walking onto the diamond proper. "You ready to warm up?"

"Ready as I'll ever be."

Lily had been playing softball since she was seven, and had been pitching almost as long. She was one of the lucky few who'd gone to the States to play college ball on a scholarship. When she came back, she took a year off to right her head, and then she'd settled in with Greg's team, playing twice a week with the occasional tournament for good measure. Secretly, I think she would have loved to go to Nationals, but it wasn't really that kind of a team even though they played Division One. And she wasn't that kind of a pitcher. Not anymore.

I didn't bother listening to their chatter as they warmed up. Lily worked on her curve ball, her signature pitch, trying to get it to actually curve. Then her fast ball. And then her two changeups. It was the usual stuff, and I wasn't that interested in listening to the living natter on about their lives. I wanted to see how the new girl would handle her own warm up.

She'd finished the paperwork, and Greg's long-suffering wife dashed out to her car and drove off, to get Marie registered before the game. Luckily, the Ladies League office was just a couple of blocks away.

Greg—who had coached for as long as I've been here—called the team over to the dugout, and made the introductions.

"We've got a new player," he said. "To fill one of the spots that opened up over the winter."

There was a ripple of unease through the rest of the players, and I perked up. Had someone died?

I looked around, like I was expecting to see whoever it was who had passed to my side of things, but could only see the living. Didn't surprise me, because it usually took the dead a year or two to make their way here. So, I looked back at the team, to see who was missing.

Robin Vickers, who played short stop and centre field. And Leslie Hunter, who played second base.

I hoped it was Robin who had passed on. My team could have used a utility player like her. For sure, they didn't need a second baseman. Second base was my position, and I had it all locked up. Everybody knew that.

"How was the funeral?" somebody asked. "Anybody go?"

"I did," Greg said. "It was nice. Robin got a real good send off."

So it was Robin, then. Good. Like I said, my team could use a good utility player.

The new chick—the one wearing the jeans—gasped. "Did someone die here?"

Greg frowned at her like she'd suddenly grown another head. "Robin Vickers. Cancer got her. But she's in a better place."

"I hope so," the new girl said. Kind of a strange thing for her to say. And then, she looked around like she was expecting to see Robin pop up right in front of her.

"Don't worry, new girl," I called from my spot by second base. "She won't be here for a year, at least."

Sometimes, I talked to the living, even though it never did any good. Usually I called out useless advice when someone booted the ball, just like everybody else did. And when someone hit the ball out of the park—it happened. Not often, but it did happen—I'd join the rest in congratulating the player. That kind of thing. And they never, ever responded.

But the new girl—Marie, her name was Marie—looked right at me and blinked rapidly, like she was thinking about fainting right there on the field.

"Oh no," she said, her voice a weak whisper. She dropped her glove to the ground, and turned to Greg. "I quit," she said. And then she walked off the field.

I knew she wouldn't last.

Marie:
But She's looking at Me!

DAMMIT! IT NEVER ceased to amaze me how the dead could wreck things without even trying.

I walked over to the fence separating the bleachers from the diamond on legs that felt frozen. "Take me home," I said to James, who was sitting with his coffee halfway to his mouth.

"What happened?" he spluttered, setting the cup aside and scrambling out of the bleachers. He pushed his fingers through the diamond shaped fencing that kept us apart. "The game hasn't even started yet."

"I just want to go," I whispered. I clung to his fingers like they were a lifeline and glanced over my shoulder at the dead girl. She was gaping at me just like, I imagined, my team was. "There's—a dead girl here. Please take me home."

My throat tightened up at that point—stupid throat—and I couldn't speak anymore.

I hadn't had to work with a ghost since my mother died, and I didn't know if I had the guts to take another one. Not without Mom.

James, who had recently learned that I could see the dead, and generally handled that fact a bunch better than I ever had, looked out at the diamond like he thought he'd actually be able to see the ghost which, of course, he couldn't. Then he sighed and dropped his head so he could look right into my eyes, through the fence.

"Any chance you can ignore her?"

"What?" I couldn't believe what I was hearing. Didn't he understand? There was a dead girl on the diamond. How the hell was I supposed to play a stupid game with a stupid dead girl on the stupid diamond?

"Try to ignore her," he said. "Just for this game. Please."

He looked around, even though there was no one near enough to hear us, then turned back to me. He clutched my fingers, hard, through the fence. "You have to do this, Marie. Remember what Dr. Parkerson said."

"But she talked to me, James." I felt my mouth work and was afraid I was going to burst into tears. "I don't think I can do this."

I heard crunching in the shale behind me, and James glanced past my left shoulder. "It's your coach," James whispered. "Please give it a try, Marie. Please. He's counting on you."

That was the real kick to the head about team sports. All those people behind me needed me to stay—and play—or they wouldn't have enough people to field a team. I'd wreck the whole game, and not just for my team, but for the other team, too.

All those people counting on me, so that we could all get a little sunshine and exercise. Just like the doctor ordered.

"Fine," I said, though it wasn't fine at all. Not even a little bit. "I'll stay."

I turned and looked into the coach's weary blue eyes and tried to smile.

"You okay?" he asked.

"Yeah," I said.

"I thought I heard you say you quit."

"No." I thought as fast as I could, under the circumstances. "I didn't say that. I said I'd be back in a second. I just forgot to give James my watch."

"Oh." The coach's eyes brightened, and he huffed out relieved laughter. "Good. I was worried that we'd have to forfeit the first game. And that would be bad, now wouldn't it?"

"That's not happening," I said. "Don't worry, I'll be right back."

I worked at the leather strap holding my mother's old Timex on my wrist, and wished the coach would leave so I could spend a few more seconds letting James convince me that this would all work out just wonderfully. That I'd somehow imagined I'd seen a dead girl when I hadn't. That everything was sunshine and roses behind me, and all I had to do was turn around and see.

But the coach didn't leave. Just stood, staring at me with his confused, earnest eyes as I scrabbled the watch from my wrist and pushed it through the mesh to James.

"Don't lose it," I said.

"Back at ya," he replied, half smiling.

Hilarious.

"I'm ready," I said to Greg.

"Good," he said and took me by the arm. He was going to make absolutely certain that I wasn't going anywhere but back on that field. "It'll be fine, you know. Playing ball is just like riding a bike. It'll—"

"All come back to me," I said. I glanced out at second base, and there was the dead girl, still staring in shocked silence at me. "Yeah, I heard."

THE FUNNY THING was, James's advice worked. All I had to do was ignore the dead girl, and everything went just fine.

All right, not fine. Not actually. That "it'll all come back to you," crap everybody kept flinging at me was just that—crap. I flailed around out in right field and tried to remember everything I'd learned about softball those three summers I'd played.

Right field was where the incompetent were hidden, for the most part. That was because most batters were right-handed. When they came up to bat, a left field hit was naturally more powerful for them. Which meant, hitting to right field should have been a little harder for them, and an easier out for us.

With me there, not so much.

I spent most of the first inning trying to remember where to stand. There's a sweet spot out in the field where you can track a ball that's going to fall in front of you—or behind you—and actually get to a ball before it hits grass. But I didn't quite have the spot yet, which meant I had to run like a fool with every crack of the bat. On top of that, I was trying to ignore the dead girl. That part actually was quite easy, because she was ignoring the heck out of me too. She didn't even track the ball when it was hit out to my field. Just stood with her back to me, waiting for the ball to come infield.

The pitcher—I think her name was Lily—figured out pretty

quickly that I didn't have a clue what I was doing out there, so she altered her pitching so that more balls were hit on the ground and to the left than to the right. Thank God. The left fielder made two quick outs, and then second base—the living girl, not the dead one—played the final ball of the inning for the third out.

The other team scored two on hits that I'd missed. I didn't want to go to the dugout and face my team, but I couldn't exactly stand out in right field with the other team either, so I trudged in and tried to act all light and airy about my errors.

"Thanks for saving my ass," I said to the pitcher. Lily looked surprised that I'd noticed, and then shrugged.

"No problem," she said. "Let's get 'em back."

Luckily, I didn't have to bat that inning, or the next. Three up three down both innings. But inning three, it was finally my turn to attempt to hit the ball.

I stared at the bats lining the fence in front of the dugout, trying to decide which one to use. I picked the purple one, mainly because no one else had used it.

I heard twittering behind me when I grabbed that bat. The rest of the women on my team definitely had something to say about my choice. Oh whatever. I figured that the three up three down pattern was going to continue now that we were down to our final batter—me.

As I strode up to home plate, I could feel all eyes on me, including the eyes of the three people in the bleachers who'd come to watch the first game of the season. One of them—of course—was James. He'd found some guy to talk to, but smiled and waved as I walked past him. I tried to smile back, but my lips and teeth were so dry, I couldn't manage anything past a sneer. Luckily, he didn't seem to notice.

"Hit it out of the park!" he yelled. I thought I heard snickers from my dugout but decided to ignore the noise and just give it my best shot.

I glanced down the third base line at the coach. He gestured, touching his hat, and then his right arm. Then he made a slashing motion across his chest and clapped his hands together three times.

Oh God, he was giving signals. Trying to tell me where to hit the ball, for maximum effect. He'd told me his signals before the game started, but I couldn't remember one of them. I stepped out of the batter's box.

"I need to talk to my coach," I said to the umpire.

"That's your one," he replied, and pointed down the third base line. I skittered over to Greg.

"I can't remember the signals," I whispered. "Just tell me what you want me to do."

He blinked, and then chuckled. "Try to get on base."

"Oh, all right." I half smiled at him and he smiled back.

"You'll do fine," he said.

I didn't answer. Just walked resolutely back to home plate, and stepped into the batter's box.

I stared at the pitcher, trying to focus on her and not look past to the dead girl, who was, I could see, actively avoiding my gaze. I wondered who she was and how she'd ended up in the middle of a ball diamond.

"Strike one," the ump called.

Focus, I thought, and licked my dry lips with my equally dry tongue. Watched the pitcher, and heard the back catcher slide her feet in the shale behind me. She was setting up to have the pitcher throw an inside pitch on me, and for a second I thought what a waste it was. All the pitcher had to do was keep throwing hard, right down the middle, and I'd never catch up.

The second ball flew past me, inside, but not by much. Obviously, the pitcher thought the same way I did about my chances of touching her fastball with that purple bat.

"Strike two," the umpire called.

The pitcher looked bored, and I could hear my teammates gathering their equipment, readying themselves for the inevitable third strike. That pissed me off.

I narrowed my focus until all I could see was the pitcher's hand and the ball. I waited for the release. It came. She'd thrown me a drop ball and it was slow. A changeup. She'd thrown me a changeup.

I sucked in breath, waited a microsecond longer, and then I swung.

And, holy crap, I actually hit the ball! A line drive, right over second base. Right through the dead girl, who looked as shocked as everybody else out in the field.

"Run!" somebody—might have been James—yelled. So I ran. And I beat the throw to first base by a full pace.

"Safe!" the ump cried. He sounded kind of surprised.

I stood on first base listening to the cheers from my dugout, from my team, and through the disbelief, felt a thrill of pure joy. It had been so long since I'd felt anything even close to that emotion, I barely understood what I was feeling. But as I settled my foot beside first base and faced second, I saw the dead girl standing there, waiting for me even as she ignored me. The joy abruptly drained away, leaving the oh so familiar feeling of dread.

Luckily, Lily the pitcher, who batted next, popped up, and the other team's right fielder didn't screw up. Lily was out. The third out. I didn't have to face the dead girl that inning.

Actually, I didn't have to face the dead girl for the rest of the game. My next at bat I popped out to centre, and then our time was up, and our game was over. We'd lost, two to nothing.

"Pretty good game, ladies," Greg said. "Maybe a practice tomorrow night wouldn't hurt."

"Oh Greg, you know I don't practice," somebody, I think it was the left fielder, said. "I got slow pitch every other night."

"Well, what about the rest of you?" Greg asked. Most of the women avoided eye contact, suddenly busy with putting away equipment and finding keys, until he sighed and gave up. "All right," he said. "Try to get to the batting cages, at least. We play Thursday, eight thirty. Right here."

If I decided to keep playing I was going to have to face the dead girl in two days.

Here was the thing, though. In spite of the dead girl, I actually did feel better. I decided that it would probably be a good idea to keep coming, at least for a while, for more of that sunshine and exercise. Which meant I was going to have to face that dead girl sooner rather than later.

I packed up my hat and my glove, turned back to the diamond, and strode out to second base.

"Hey, Marie!" I heard Greg call. "Get off the diamond. The other game's about to start."

I glanced at the women warming up on the field, and smiled broadly. "Just checking for my hair tie," I said. "I think I dropped it out here."

I pretended to scan the ground as I walked over to second base and stopped in front of the dead girl. Then, I waited for her to stop pretending she couldn't see me.

She stared at her feet. At her old-fashioned platform shoes. I could see scuffs on the mock leather, and one of the straps was nearly ready to break.

Not that it ever would because all I was seeing was a mystic representation of the dead girl's shoes, but whatever.

Her hair, long and curly, was pulled up in a rough ponytail, held by what looked like an actual rubber band.

Nobody used rubber bands to hold their hair back. Not anymore. She was an old ghost, I was sure of it. She'd been here a long time.

I looked at her clothes. A peasant shirt with cheap-looking embroidery around the scoop neck, and a short, heavily gathered skirt. I frowned. When had they gone out of style? Forever ago?

Then I realized she was looking at me. I felt my face heat, embarrassed that she'd caught me staring at her clothing.

"Who are you?" I whispered. I carefully kept my back to the living second baseman, who was just three steps away from me. "And don't act like I can't see you, because I can."

"What do you want?" she asked.

"I want to talk to you," I whispered. And, hopefully, figure out a way to quickly move her on to the next plane of existence so I could keep playing softball without the dead interrupting me. "I think I can help you."

The dead girl's face turned to stone. "Leave me alone," she said, her voice angry. "I don't want your help. Just leave me alone."

"How long have you been here?"

"It's none of your business," she cried. "Leave me alone! Now!"

Then she turned away from me, quite pointedly.

Huh.

I walked away from second base and the living girl called out to me. "Did you find your elastic?"

"No," I said. "Good luck with your game."

"Thanks," she said. "We're up against the Blues. We need all the luck we can get."

I smiled at her and walked off the field. Looked like we were both going to need some luck.

JAMES WAS POSITIVELY giddy as he drove me home.

"You did really well," he said, "After the first inning, anyhow. And you can hit!"

"Who knew?" I said.

"I can help you with your fielding—" he said.

"I need to practice batting—" I said at the same time. Then we both stopped speaking. The classic Canadian stand-off. Nobody wanting to be impolite. Finally, James broke the silence.

"If you want, I can take you to the batting cages," he said. "Tomorrow. After work."

"Sounds great."

"And about fielding—"

"Just let me focus on the positives, for a bit," I said. "Please."

"Sure. Sure." He nodded, and pulled out into traffic. "No problem." We were both silent as he maneuvered down Ninety-Ninth Street.

"So, you've decided to keep playing?" he finally asked.

"I think so," I said.

"What about the ghost?"

I shrugged. "She wants me to leave her alone."

James glanced at me. "Can you do that?"

"I don't know," I said. "I had fun tonight, for the most part. And I can't let the dead wreck everything, now can I?"

"No," he said. "I guess you can't."

We sat in silence for a few moments while I thought about whether or not I could actually leave the dead girl alone. I didn't know if I could. Mom had taught me that eventually all ghosts want to move on.

"Talk to them, Marie," she'd said. "Find out what's holding them here and help them to come to terms with their issues. Then, they'll want to move on."

"Are you sure?" I'd asked, every time.

Every time, she'd replied, "I'm sure. It might take some time, but be willing to commit. Help them see what they need to see, and they will always want to move on."

The girl on second base seemed pretty convinced that she wanted to stay, but if Mom was right about her eventually choosing to move on, I needed to know her deal, even if she wasn't willing to tell me.

But I wasn't going to talk to James about any of this at the moment. He was on a need to know basis when it came to ghosts, and as far as I was concerned, he didn't need to know.

"Looked like you made a friend at the diamond," I said. "Who was the guy you were talking to?"

"Oh, you mean Andy. Seemed all right, I guess. He knows Sergeant Worth." He laughed. "I think he knows everybody."

"Sergeant Worth?" I said, then shrugged. "Everybody probably does know everybody else. It's a small world. Was he watching his wife play?"

"No." James glanced over at me. "His wife never played. His daughter used to, but I don't think she does anymore. He said he'd just come out to see the new recruits. Like you, I guess."

We were comfortably silent for the rest of the ride to Jasmine's place. I was still couch surfing there, even though I had a full-time job and could afford to live on my own. We—meaning my always meddling shrink, Dr. Parkerson—had decided that it was better for me if I lived with someone. At least for a while. Until I steadied emotionally, she said.

To be honest, I was glad of the company. Jasmine's three kids were always entertaining, and Jasmine didn't seem to mind when I woke her up in the middle of the night, covered in nightmare sweat and needing to talk.

At least it wasn't every night, anymore. It had been, when I'd come back from Fort McMurray. Fort McMurray was my home town. I'd gone to visit my mom, and ended up being kidnapped and almost killed by my crazy ex-boyfriend's even crazier girlfriend. That kind of homecoming would make anybody go just a bit bonkers, wouldn't it?

Seriously, though, after I got back I'd had some dark damned nights, and I wouldn't have blamed Jasmine at all if she'd thrown me out. But she hadn't. She was one of the good ones, that was for sure.

"Before we go to the batting cages tomorrow, we need to get you some better footwear," James said. "You need cleats. And some sweats." He clicked his tongue. "I can't believe the coach didn't give you a complete uniform."

"He said he'd have pants and socks for the next game," I said. "I think he was trying to decide whether or not he was going to keep me on the team."

"Well, that's good," James said. "But we'll get you some sweats anyhow. For practices."

"I don't think this team practices much," I said.

"But you need some," James said.

Surprisingly enough, that didn't make my sunny disposition disappear. "All right," was all I said, as he pulled up in front of Jasmine's neat little bungalow and stopped the car. "You're right. I need shoes—"

"Cleats."

"All right. Cleats. And sweats."

"And practice?"

"Yes," I said. I felt my jaw tighten, but tried to ignore it. "I need practice, too."

"Excellent." He smiled. "And tomorrow—"

"We'll go to the batting cage," I said. My voice tightened and I realized I was grinding my teeth.

"Ha! No!" James laughed. "Well, yeah, but after. I was talking about work. We've got the Bensons coming in at ten, and then I have to surveil at the Bluebird Motel. Remember?"

"Absolutely!" I said. Talking about work was easy because since James got his licence he actually had some. Hence my full-time job and being able to afford a shrink.

"Because until you can figure out how to make this 'seeing the dead' thing pay off, we need the living to keep the lights on." He laughed again, and I tried to laugh too, but it was a bit harder this time.

My mother had looked after the spirits of the dead her whole life, and had never figured out a way to make it pay. I suspected that she thought that filthy lucre would sully her art, or something.

Maybe it would. I didn't know. All I knew for sure was, I liked working with James. And I liked working for the living, most of the time. Even when they were conniving jackasses, like our ten o'clock appointment, the Bensons.

"Sounds good," I said, and leaned over to peck him on the cheek. "Thanks for coming with me tonight, and talking me off the cliff."

"You are more than welcome," he replied.

I could smell the sunlight on his skin and leaned closer, wishing I could bathe in it. Just for a moment. He put his hand to my hair and pulled me closer. Then my mouth was on his, and for a while, his sunshine flooded my soul.

Yeah, we were doing all that, too. What can I say? It had been an interesting eight months.

Karen:
Apparently, We Are Doing Something About the Girl

I WENT UP to the bleachers after that Marie girl left because a couple of the old umps had shown up and I wanted to talk to them about her speaking to me. They were ten rows down from Andrew which caused my stomach to tighten more, even though he couldn't see me. I had to talk to them, though, even with Andrew sitting where he was.

The conversation didn't go the way I'd hoped it would. At first, they didn't even want to talk about my problem—just wanted to take in the lights, and the action, and forget about being dead for a couple of hours. But there were a lot of errors on the field, which pissed them both off to no end, so they finally turned to me.

"Tell us about this girl," Isaac Middleton said.

"Who you think sees you," Samuel Kelly said.

They both looked like they didn't believe me, which didn't surprise me but did tick me off. I pointedly turned away from them to watch the lack-lustre second game of the season being played under the bright white lights.

"Forget it," I said. "You're right. I was probably deluded." I emphasized the word deluded, because Mr. Middleton used that word at me when I'd first tried to tell him about the girl. "Let's just watch the game."

They glanced at each other. Mr. Kelly shrugged, but Mr. Middleton wasn't about to let it go.

"Come on, Karen," he said, using his wheedling little old man voice. "You know I was kidding. Tell me about the girl."

"You don't want to know," I said.

"What girl?"

Joanne Watson, who'd died in a car crash near Leduc on her way to the Early Bird Tournament here in 1978, slid onto the bleacher next to me. "What girl you talking about?" she asked again.

I shrugged but Mr. Middleton turned around and beamed at her. She was a fine shortstop and he'd always had a soft spot for her. "Karen says a live girl saw her," he said. "At the early game."

"Saw you?" Joanne asked. She stared at me as though she was trying to drill holes into my head with her gaze. "You mean, she actually saw you?"

"Talked to her, too," Mr. Kelly said. "Apparently." Then he clicked his tongue and shook his head as the living woman at third base booted the ball all over the infield, allowing all runners to proceed safely to their various bases. "What is Gillian thinking out there?" he muttered. "She was steady as a rock last year."

"Maybe she's knocked up," Mr. Middleton said. "That can throw off their timing."

Mr. Kelly nodded, and then shrugged. "Is she married?"

"I don't know," Mr. Middleton replied. "But that don't stop them, now. Maybe it happened over the winter."

"Well, her game's gone to hell in a handcart, whatever her problem," Mr. Kelly said. "She's gonna have to pull up her socks. No doubt about it." He turned away from the game, and looked at Joanne. "You ready for tonight?"

"Of course," Joanne said, and grinned. "It's not like I can get knocked up now, is it?"

The two umps laughed uproariously. I didn't. Those two old coots always found Joanne a real cutup but I never had.

After she realized she'd rung all the laughter she could out of her bad joke, Joanne turned back to me. "So tell me," she said. "About the living girl who saw you."

"She plays for the Jolene Transport team," I said. "Right field. And she didn't just see me. She talked to me."

"Was she any good?"

"What do you mean?" I said suspiciously. There was no way I was playing straight man for Joanne. But all she did was glare at me.

"Was she any good at right field?"

"No." I shook my head, hard. "She got lucky a couple of times at bat, but I'm guessing she won't come back."

"Well, that would fix the problem, now wouldn't it?"

"Problem?" Mr. Kelly said, slowly turning in his seat to stare at Joanne. He'd been an ump for nearly thirty years, and had the bad knees and back to prove it. If he sat still for too long, he'd seize up like he was petrified. I would have found it funny if I wasn't secretly afraid that the same thing would happen to me someday.

Sometimes, the dead who had been here longest would freeze, staring out at the diamond, just like Mr. Kelly sometimes did, and then vanish. I was the oldest dead at the diamond. It hadn't happened to me yet, but I was afraid it would.

I didn't want to disappear. I just wanted to keep playing ball.

"Potential problem," Joanne said. "If this woman can actually see us—"

"And talk to us," I said.

"And talk to us," Joanne said, "she could cause us some trouble. You know. Like getting one of them psychics to come to the diamond and exorcise us all, or something." She frowned. "I don't think I'd like that, much."

I hadn't even thought of the possibility of her actually doing something to us. "So, what can we do?" I asked.

"Drive her off," Joanne said. "Make her life hell until she leaves us alone."

"And how would we do that?" Mr. Kelly asked.

"I don't think she'll come back," I said, weakly. "Like I said, she wasn't very good."

"Rita Danworth said that she moved a tea cup in her old house, once," Joanne said. "Scared the living shit out of her old man. Which he deserved, the son of a bitch. Maybe we can talk her into doing something like that to this Marie. Maybe?"

I couldn't see how moving a tea cup was going to frighten someone who could actually interact with ghosts, but the two umps grabbed onto the idea and wouldn't let it go.

As the game ground on in front of us, one error-filled inning after another, the three of them put their heads together and hatched a plan to drive Marie away from Diamond Two forever.

Unfortunately, most of the first part of the plan involved me. I tried to talk them out it but they would have none of it.

"This is going to work," Joanne said, as the living game finally finished, and the lights clicked off, bathing the shale in darkness. "But it's all up to you, Karen. You gotta figure out a way to be her friend and then the rest of us can take care of her."

I stared at the three of them but could think of nothing that would talk them out of their horrible little plan.

"I'll think about it," I finally said. "Now can we just go play ball, please?"

As I kicked off my platform sandals and headed out on the diamond to warm up with the rest of the dead, I knew that somehow their plan would blow up in our faces. Especially mine. I just wanted to play ball, dammit. Why didn't anybody understand that? I just wanted to play ball.

Marie:
Missing Girls and Metal Cleats

IT WAS TWO in the afternoon, and I was finally alone in the office. James had scurried off to his second appointment of the day after firing the Bensons as clients—"Because you are both too stupid to live." His words.

The Bensons had left the premises twenty minutes earlier, but their loud cries of "We'll sue, see if we don't," were still ringing in my ears when the desk phone rang. That was probably why I answered it before checking the caller ID.

"Jimmy Lavall, Private Investigations. How may I help you?" My voice flattened appreciably by the time I got to the end of my usual salutation, because I'd seen Sergeant Worth's name in the display. EPS—short for Edmonton Police Service—followed it.

I nearly slammed the phone down before she had a chance to answer. But I didn't. That would have been rude, and the last thing a receptionist could be was rude. Especially to a cop who took as much of an interest in my life as Sergeant Worth did.

"Marie." She sounded tired, but then she always sounded tired. "How did ball go last night? What do you think of Greg, the coach? Nice guy, huh?"

"Hi," I replied, and nearly snorted unamused laughter when I noticed that my voice now sounded as tired as hers did—even though I'd had a pretty good night's sleep. Over three hours, and that hadn't happened in a long while, if I was going to be honest.

"The game was good. Good. And Greg seems nice. So do the girls on the team."

"How did you do?"

I frowned. "How did I do what?"

"In the game," Sergeant Worth said. A hint of frustration etched her words in acid. "How did you do?"

"Oh!" I said, and regrouped. "It went fine. Just fine."

There was a small expectant pause from Worth's end and when she spoke irritation fought impatience in her voice. "What position did you play?"

"Right field."

"And?"

"I never caught one ball," I said. Might as well be honest. "Not even one."

"Oh well," Worth said. "You'll catch on. It's like—"

"Riding a bike," I said. "Yeah. It's been mentioned."

"Did you get on base?"

The batting part of the game had actually gone quite well for me, so I told her about the two balls I'd hit, and how I'd even managed to get to first base once.

"That's wonderful!" she said, sounding like I'd cured cancer or something. "I knew you'd fit in."

Now, I didn't know if I'd call what I'd done the evening before fitting in, but I thanked her for her almost-compliment anyway. "Even James had a good time," I said. "And he made a friend. One of the dads. Or a grandad or something. He looked pretty old, anyhow."

"Ah, they'll all seem old to you two," Worth said. "You young pups."

I didn't respond. I was pretty sure she was only ten years older than us, but whatever. She acted like she was ready for retirement, so maybe James and I did seem like young pups to her.

"The guy's name is Andy something," I said. "He said he knew you."

"Oh." She stopped for a moment, obviously thinking. "Probably Andy Westwood. He's a bit of a pain in the ass, but nice enough, I guess." She was silent a moment more, and I wondered if there was something James and I needed to know about Andy Westwood.

"He shows up for most of the games," she continued. "His daughter used to play for the Blues, I think. But not anymore."

"But he's okay?"

"Yeah, he's fine." She chuckled, shortly. "Don't worry. James can handle someone like Andy Westwood."

"Good," I said. "And thanks for finding me a team to play for. I had a good time."

"I'm glad," she said. "I thought about telling Reg Meyers to give you a call—he's the manager for the River Rats, a Division Three team—but you seemed too competitive for Div Three—"

"What do you mean?"

"Division Three is more like a beer league. Have a few laughs, smack the ball around, but no real competition in any of the teams. Not like Division One."

"Division One?" I asked. Why did it feel like she was speaking a completely different language?

"Yeah. Jolene plays Division One," Sergeant Worth said. "If you all do well enough, you could even go to Nationals. Greg must have told you. He loves going to Nationals. I think they're in—"

"What?" Now that her words had turned into English, I couldn't believe what she was saying. A beer league sounded perfect. "Why didn't you tell me about the River Rats before I committed to Jolene?" I asked.

She stopped talking for a second. "Don't you want to go to Nationals?" she finally asked. She sounded surprised.

"It isn't about Nationals," I replied. "I'm not that good. I'd probably do better in a lower division. You know?"

"That's not what James told me," she said.

"Why would James have an opinion about where I should play?" I asked, rather snippily.

"Well, he said he talked to your dad when you two were in Fort McMurray, and your dad said you were good. Really good. So, I thought that Div One would be better for you." She fell silent, as though waiting for me to respond. When I didn't, she spoke again, but her voice sounded wary, like she'd finally realized that perhaps there was a problem. "You're okay with Jolene, aren't you?"

"Yeah," I said. "I guess."

"Good," she said. As she nattered on, she acted like I wasn't upset—which probably showed just how good my receptionist skills were. I didn't give a thing away as I did a mini freak out about the fact that not only had I inadvertently committed to a Division One team, but I'd already played against a Division One team. Specifically, against a Division One pitcher.

I still had nightmares about the last Division One pitcher I'd watched back when I was twelve and Dad had taken me to a women's softball tournament in Fort McMurray.

"We're going to see the best of the best here," he'd said, leading me by the hand to a softball diamond with two teams already playing. The bleachers were packed, as were the fences along both sides of the diamond. But Dad managed to push us both through the throng so that we were sitting right behind home plate. And I got to watch Shelley Ness.

I came away from that game terrified. That woman could throw harder than most men, and the batter she hit with an errant pitch lost a couple of teeth and bled all over home plate as Dad whispered in my ear that he believed Shelley had done it on purpose.

"She doesn't make mistakes like that," he said.

For weeks my nightmares had my teeth spraying everywhere as a pitcher laughed like some kind of a ghoul.

Luckily, the pitchers I'd faced when I played hadn't been able to throw that hard, or that accurately, so I'd grown less afraid of them. That was why I'd stuck it out for three years, when I'd played the first time. But here I was in Division One, playing against pitchers just like Shelley Ness. For real this time.

"Maybe you can give me the name of that other coach," I said, riding roughshod over her words. "The coach for the River Rats."

"Why?" Sergeant Worth's voice grew wary. "I thought you said everything went well—"

"Well, yeah, it went fine, but I bet Greg'll try to find better players," I blathered. "You know, so they'd have a chance at Nationals or whatever. I don't want to sit on the bench. Maybe the beer league would be better for me."

"Oh Marie, don't worry so much," Sergeant Worth laughed, her voice back to just sounding tired. "If you hit Rachel Wellington's pitching, you can hit just about anybody. Except for the Blues pitcher, of course." She laughed, and it sounded real, like she wasn't taunting me. "I heard that Miriam Kendel is back. Nobody can hit her."

"Oh." A faint vision of spraying blood and teeth flashed before me, and I felt sick. "Well, that's okay then."

"Yeah. It'll all be fine. And if you want to learn how to play the game for real, talk to Greg. He's always willing to give players a couple hours of his time for a practice. He knows his stuff."

"Oh. Maybe I will." I waited a moment, but she didn't say anything. "Do you want to speak to James?" I finally asked.

"No," she replied. "I was just calling to find out how things went for you last night."

"Oh."

"Because, well, I did set you up with the team, now didn't I?"

"Yeah, you did," I muttered. Wondered what her game was, and then I thought about the dead girl at second base. I needed to find out more about her.

"Who would I talk to about a missing woman?" I asked.

"A missing woman?" Sergeant Worth's voice snapped to attention, and I imagined her sitting ramrod straight and staring at the phone like she could see into my soul or something. "Why? Did James pick up a case?"

I thought about telling her the truth for about a microsecond, and then regained my sanity. "Yes. That's it exactly. Just wanted to check and make sure that the parents called the police, and you know, reported her missing, before we start beating the bushes."

"Oh," Sergeant Worth said. "A missing person case. Those sometimes don't turn out so well, you know. They could be dead. Or not want to be found."

I thought about the girl on the softball diamond. Maybe Sergeant Worth was right. "I think James believes it's a good case," I said. "Who do I speak to?"

"Call Missing Persons. Here's the number." She listed it off, and I wrote it on the back of a handy envelope. All right, so I wasn't the perfect receptionist with a pad of paper always at the ready. But at least I had the number of someone who worked in Missing Persons.

Now all I had to do was call and see if anyone there would let me look at the records. All of them. Without wanting to check with the good Sergeant to make sure my research was on the up and up.

"Thanks," I said, staring at the number and wishing she'd end the call. "This should help a lot."

"Glad of it," she said. "I better let you go. Sounds like you're busy."

I looked at my mostly clean desk and shrugged. A teeny white lie wouldn't hurt. "Yeah," I said. "Worked off my feet, ha ha."

"That's good," she said. "Well, I'll see you next Tuesday."

I frowned. "Next Tuesday?"

"Yeah," she said, and laughed. "We play against each other."

Fabulous.

"See you then," I said.

But as I hung up the phone, I seriously considered taking next Tuesday off. The last thing in the world I wanted to do was see Sergeant Worth recreationally.

Cops, I thought as I punched the number for the EPS missing persons department into my phone. *They can be a pain in the ass.*

THE CONVERSATION WITH Missing Persons didn't go quite as well as I had hoped it would. I guess that me wanting to see all the files from 1970 to 1999 was a bigger deal than I thought.

True, the EPS dealt with nearly 1500 missing persons files a year, but still. I thought that going back a few years would make it easier.

"Check our website," I was told. "We have some of the history up. You might get lucky."

I went to the website. I knew I wouldn't get lucky, because I never got lucky. But I got lucky. There she was. Simple as that.

Her name was Karen Dubinsky and she was nineteen years old when she dropped off the face of the earth. She had been missing since April 14, 1974.

1974. That explained the clunky sandals, the peasant shirt, and the godawful skirt. I guessed that she'd stayed on the "hippie" side of things, as opposed to the disco rage that seemed to have swept the entire world around that time.

I glanced at the rest of the short article but there wasn't much to go on. She'd disappeared, her case was still considered open, and if anyone had any information please call.

Karen stared out from the school photograph that had been used on the website. She wasn't smiling. Just staring, as though waiting for something—anything—to happen. Her hair was shorter than it had been when I saw her, but it was straight, with the part dead centre on her head, same as she'd worn it at the diamond. She looked like she was trying to emulate the chick from the ancient TV show, *Mod Squad*, but she wasn't pulling it off. Not really. She just looked average. Like someone no one would look at twice. But she did look like she'd lost weight since the photo was taken—quite a bit of weight—and she was far from fat in the school photo.

She looked like she was wasting away before she disappeared.

I wondered if she'd been sick. Wondered if that was why she died. I scoffed and clicked off the computer. Humans didn't go out into the woods to die. Animals did that. Humans ended up in the hospital, surrounded by their family. So, she probably had not been sick. Something else had been eating away at her.

I wondered what it was.

"Hey, you ready to go?"

James burst into the reception area of the Jimmy Lavall Detective Agency just after four, looking like he'd been to hell and back. His shirt sleeve was ripped at the shoulder, and I saw a few drops of blood on his cheek.

"What happened?" I gasped. I threw open the topmost drawer of my desk where I kept the first aid kit. I was always surprised at how many times we'd had to use that kit since I took the first aid course a few months before. I had the feeling other PIs didn't need as many band aids and finger splints as we seemed to.

"Oh, nothing," James said. "Mr. Comox decided to take umbrage with the fact that I was photographing him with his girlfriend as they left the motel."

"How did he even know you were taking photos?"

"I got out. To stretch my legs, you know. And then there he was, with the girl on his arm, laughing his ass off on his way out of the motel room. So—" James shrugged. "I snapped a couple of shots. And he saw me."

"You didn't hit him, did you?" I asked. We didn't need an assault charge now that the agency was actually bringing in some cash.

"No," James said. He touched the ripped shoulder of his shirt, sighed, unbuttoned it, and pulled it off. I noticed a bruise starting to form on his ribs, which took away a bit of my pleasure at seeing him half-undressed. Not all of the pleasure, of course. But enough. "He was trying to get the camera away from me. That's all."

"But you saved the camera, right? Please tell me you saved the camera. Those things are so expensive."

"Absolutely," he said. "Couldn't have him wrecking our equipment, now could I?"

He walked to the closet door next to his office and opened it. Pulled a shirt off the hanger, and quickly dressed. I watched his face to see if he flinched in pain as he pulled on the shirt but saw nothing.

Maybe he was telling the truth about not being too badly hurt.

"And you got the money shot," I said. "Right?"

"Pretty close," he said. "Yeah."

We smiled at each other. Closing a case was seriously satisfying even if he did get a bit beat up to do it.

"So, let's go get you some cleats," he said. "To celebrate."

For a second I thought about saying no. I could finish invoicing and writing up the report for the case. But then I thought, what the hell. The paperwork could wait until the next day and shopping seemed like a great way to celebrate a win.

Even if it was for cleats.

I'D NEVER BEEN to United Cycle before, which wasn't surprising. The store in the Old Strathcona area of Edmonton was all things sporting, and I was not. However, James knew his way around, and soon I was standing beside him up on the second floor wishing I'd worn heavier socks.

He had three pairs of cleats chosen, and the shoe boxes were sitting on the bench, waiting for me. They all looked the same as far as I was concerned. Spiky running shoes you couldn't wear anywhere but on a softball diamond. And they were expensive. I pointed to the bottom shelf of the display wall.

"What about those?" I asked. They were half the price and looked like they'd do the job.

"Those are soccer cleats," James said shortly.

"Oh." I looked closer and saw that he was right. "Well, crap. Why are softball cleats so expensive?"

"I guess because people will pay," James laughed. "Now sit down and try them on."

I tried on the first pair, which was the least expensive of the three. They pinched everywhere but I tried to make them work. But even as I minced about in front of the full-length mirror, trying not to let the metal spikes nailed to the bottom of the shoes dig into the carpet and trip me up, I knew they weren't the ones.

"Maybe I can try a size bigger," I said hopefully. "They aren't that bad . . . "

"Try on the other ones first," James said. "And quit thinking about the price."

I sighed, heavily, and set the cheap pinchy pair aside. Pulled the next pair out of their box and tried them on. They were better. Much, much, better. They moulded to my feet like they'd been built for me. One spot on the right heel pinched but I figured I could work that out because they were one hundred dollars less than the third pair sitting on the bench beside me.

One hundred dollars.

"These are great," I said. "Let's take them."

"Try those on, first," James said, pointing at the last pair.

"No," I said. "These are good enough. Really."

"Try them on," James said again. "Or we aren't leaving."

Reluctantly, I pulled the second pair off my feet and dropped them back into their box—this last pair was going to have to be something pretty special to beat them.

Of course, they were. They slid on my feet, and I felt like I was coming home. No pinches, no pokes; it felt like my feet were being caressed and massaged by someone who really knew their business, with every step I took.

"Holy crap," I whispered. "These feel amazing."

The grin on James's face let me know that no matter how hard I tried to convince him to get me the second pair, the cleats on my feet were the ones I was taking home.

"Thank you," I said. "These are wonderful."

"Great," he said. "I'm glad to you like them. Now let's go find you some sweats. And maybe a couple more pairs of socks. And a bat. Would you like your own bat? That purple bat looks a little heavy for you . . ."

I didn't have to answer him because he'd wandered off down the aisles of sporting goods to find me everything I'd need to play softball for the next hundred years, I was sure.

I TOLD JAMES about figuring out who the dead girl was as he was paying for everything.

"Her name is Karen Dubinsky," I said. "And she's been missing since 1974. She was nineteen."

"Nineteen!" His brow furrowed. "She was so young."

"Yeah," I said.

"But now that you know her name that should make it easier to talk to her so you can move her along," James said. "Right?"

I stared for a shocked second at the cashier, but she wasn't paying a bit of attention to our conversation, so I glared at James and then grabbed the bags and walked out of the store.

He followed after a few moments. "What's wrong?" he asked.

"We do not talk about moving the dead on in front of the living," I said. "Did you forget that?"

"Sorry," he said. But he didn't look sorry. Not at all. "I figured it was all right since you started the conversation." He grinned at me. "Because you did start the conversation, didn't you?"

He had me. "Yes," I hissed. "I did."

"So it's all right for you to talk to me about the dead in front of the living, but not the other way around. Is that Rule 10?"

"It's rule 54," I snapped, "Which lets me know you haven't been taking any of my rule suggestions seriously at all."

He laughed. "All right. No more talking about ghosts in front of people, even if you start the conversation."

"And I'll try to remember my own stupid rules." I said.

We got in the car and headed out of the parking lot. "It's not called moving along, is it?" he finally said.

"No," I said. "It's moving her on." Then I fell silent. Moving the spirits on was what my mother had called what we do. I touched her old Timex on my wrist and wished, one more time with feeling, that she would magically appear in the back seat of the Volvo complaining about there being no space for her in amongst all the boxes and bags from United Cycle and offering advice on the best way to make the girl on the diamond move on so I could get my sunshine and exercise in peace.

She probably would have talked about how all ghosts deserve to move on to the next plane of existence and how the girl on second base was no different.

"Just get to know her," she would have said. "The rest will fall into place."

She couldn't tell me that, of course, because she was no longer with me. Thinking about her put my mood in the basement. "I don't know if Karen will even speak to me," I said. "So maybe I'm wasting my time. Maybe it would be better if I just—"

"What? Ignore her?" James said. He shook his head. "That worked for one game, but it won't help in the long term and you know it. Eventually, you're going to make it to second base, and then you'll be face to face with her. Better that you try to talk her into moving on—or at least convince her to vacate the premises while you play your games."

"That's actually a good idea," I said, my mood lightening.

"If she can leave the area, that is," James continued. "Do you think her body's around there somewhere?"

"I doubt it," I said. "City maintenance has worked on that diamond a ton over the years. Somebody would have found her."

"Well then, why is she there?" James asked. "If she didn't die there, why would she be hanging around?"

"I don't know," I said. Maybe I should find out.

JASMINE TEXTED ME as we were heading to the batting cages, wondering if I was coming home for supper.

I made chicken, she texted. *Why don't you invite James, too?*

I looked over at James. "You hungry?"

"Yeah, kinda," he said. "Maybe we can pick up a burger or something after practice."

"Jasmine's made her chicken," I said. "And she told me to invite you. But they're eating now."

James was absolutely in love with Jasmine's Curry Chicken Surprise. I could almost hear his mouth water as he glanced over at me.

"You have to practice batting," he said.

"I know," I said. "But, James. Chicken."

All right, so I loved Jasmine's chicken even more than James did. And I felt exhausted after our shopping spree. I just wanted to head home, eat, and then curl up on Jasmine's couch and watch one of her "stories" on TV.

James thought things over for about a second and a half, then turned the car and headed in the direction of Jasmine's house and her succulent chicken.

"Tomorrow," he said. "You'll practice tomorrow."

Absolutely, James. Absolutely.

Karen:
Making Friends with the Devil

WE HAD A meeting after the game, and Joanne convinced everyone that her grand plan, her big scheme to drive the girl who could see ghosts away from Diamond Two, would actually work.

"If she can see Karen she can probably see all of us," Joanne said. "Which means we can mess with her head. You know, scare the crap out of her so she goes home and leaves us all alone."

Rita Danworth, who could actually move physical objects and who figured large in Joanne's big plan, wasn't so sure it would work the way Joanne thought.

"What if it just brings her back," Rita said. "With her psychic friends? To . . . What did you call that, Joanne? What they could do to us?"

"Exorcise us," Joanne said.

"She doesn't do that, I don't think," I said. Exorcising was something that was done to demons by Catholic priests. None of us were demons. We were just the dead, out for a few laughs.

"Well, I saw *The Exorcist*," Rita said. "Scared the heck out of me. I don't want that to happen to me." She shook her head vigorously. "I think we should come up with a better plan."

"There isn't a better plan," Joanne snarled, instantly ready to do battle, as usual. "If we don't get rid of this girl, she'll wreck everything for us. I just know it."

Everyone sat back and thought things through for a few

minutes. I could see pink tingeing the edge of the horizon and knew that everyone would soon drift off to wherever they went during the day and we would not have a plan.

"What about us not playing on Tuesdays and Thursdays?" I asked, hopefully. "I mean, just until she quits."

"No!" This time it wasn't just Joanne, but the two umpires who yelled. I knew they'd put up a stink about that idea. They came to the diamond every night, without fail. They would not want their routine messed with, even if it was for the good of all of us. "We are not giving up half the season just because of that girl!"

"We need to get rid of her," Joanne continued. "My plan's the good one." She pointed at me. "You just do your part. Got it?"

I could see that the rest of them had fallen into line behind Joanne and, more importantly, behind the two umps. Nobody would even consider crossing them. Not if they wanted to have a close call ever go their way again.

"Got it," I said.

As soon as I spoke, the rest of them started to drift away on the light spring breeze. No sitting around and discussing the minutia of the first game of the season like they usually did. Just everyone floating, like dandelion seeds, to wherever they went when they weren't here.

Soon, I was the only one left. I went to second base and waited for that Marie to come back so I could put the first part of Joanne's plan into action and make her my friend.

I stared at the sun as it tiptoed over the horizon and wished that it could burn out my retinas so I didn't have to go through with Joanne's stupid scheme.

But dead eyes don't work like that. More's the pity.

I WAS STANDING at second base watching the Monarchs warm up when Marie walked up to her team's dugout. It didn't look like the guy who'd come with her for the first game was with her this time, and I hoped that this meant she'd decided to quit and was just dropping off her uniform.

She didn't go into the dugout where the other girls were chatting but sat on the lowest bench of the bleacher behind the dugout, disappearing from my view. When she reappeared, she was wearing her uniform, plus brand-new socks and cleats.

So, she was staying. And she was playing. Great.

She stepped into the dugout and everyone stopped talking until Greg grabbed her in a quick bear hug and welcomed her back.

"We're gonna have a good game tonight," he said. "I can just tell."

Marie smiled and nodded, looking supremely uncomfortable, but the rest of the team loosened up, and the chatting resumed.

There was some bitching when Greg held up the batting order for all of them to see.

"She only played one game," Jamie Riverton, the back catcher, said. "Why does she get to bat cleanup?"

Batting cleanup was a prime spot. For power hitters, mostly. The first three batters were usually fast, and could get on base with some regularity, but the fourth batter was expected to hit it far out in the field, every time, so the rabbits on base could scamper home.

Jamie had been the cleanup batter for two years, and she obviously wasn't happy about losing her spot. But Greg put paid to her griping double quick.

"She got on base twice last game," he said. "And you didn't, Jamie."

"Once," Marie said. "I only got on base once."

"Your second hit—that was a lucky catch," Greg said. "One in a million kind of a thing. You got the touch, girl, so you're batting cleanup. Congratulations."

He looked like he was going to give her another hug, but she stepped out of his range. "All right," she said. "Thanks."

"Now let's warm up," Greg continued, pointing out to the diamond. I looked around and realized that the Monarchs had vacated the premises, and soon I was going to be face to face with Marie.

I watched her grab her glove and follow the fielders out to centre field, where they were expected to shag some fly balls. Putting Joanne's plan into place had to happen now.

I jogged out to centre field and stood beside her, smiling in what I hoped was a fairly friendly fashion. Marie saw me but didn't say a word. Just tracked the ball Greg had hit to her, caught it, more or less, and threw it back.

She went to the end of the line of fielders, and then she stared at me. Now was my chance.

"Hi," I said. "Your name's Marie. Right?"

"Right," she whispered. She leaned over, pretending to tie her shoe. "And you are Karen Dubinsky. Right?"

She knew my name.

I froze, that stupid, insipid smile stuck on my face while I tried to think of something to say. Finally, the obvious popped out of my mouth. "How do you know that?"

"Missing Persons," she whispered. The centre fielder lined up behind her, and she stopped talking until she'd fielded another fly ball and taken her place at the end of the line again. "We need to talk."

"Stay after the game," I said. "We can talk then."

"All right," she said. And then she stared at me, hard. "Do you want me to help you move on? I can do that. If you're ready."

I had no idea what she was talking about, and I shook my head. "I just want to talk softball. You know, give you some pointers, so you can play right field a little better."

"Oh." She looked surprised. "Oh. All right, I guess."

It was her turn to field a fly ball again so she turned away from me. But after she threw the ball in she turned and stared at me long and hard.

So, I did the only thing I could think of—I turned my back on her and watched the infield warm up. But the whole time I stood there I could feel her eyes on me, like she was trying to read my mind.

She didn't want to be my friend, or take advice from me. She wanted to move me on. Whatever that meant.

Maybe Joanne was right. Maybe we did have to scare her so badly she'd just leave us all alone.

HER TEAM WON, seven to six, and I heard Greg say, "Let's go for a beer to celebrate." Since Marie had hit in the winning run, I was certain she would go with her team and felt a wild burst of relief. I was off the hook.

I watched them pack up their gear and vacate the premises. Marie left with them, and as I watched her drag her bag to the parking lot and dump it in the trunk of her car, I tried to think up an excuse for Joanne and the rest. We'd have to come up with a better plan than swarming Marie and scaring her off. Thank goodness.

The relief dissolved as I watched Marie wave good-bye to the rest of her team and come back to the diamond. She scrambled up the bleachers and parked herself halfway to the top. My heart fell. She was staying.

I could see her looking around. Looking for me. I was still by the fence that separated the diamond from the parking lot, out of her sight, and I wished I could just stay there for the rest of the night. Forget watching the second game. Forget my own game, even though I'd never missed even an inning before. Just let it all go so I didn't have to go through with Joanne's ridiculous plan.

I'd committed, though. I turned away from the fence as the last of Marie's team drove out of the parking lot and went to talk to her.

"You're here," she said, rather unnecessarily, I thought, as I trudged up the bleachers and sat beside her.

I didn't answer her. Just watched the two teams out on the field warm up as the last of the sunset pink washed away leaving nothing but grey and blue and black. The huge lights on either side of the diamond were on and they washed away any chance of seeing the stars. I knew they wouldn't be visible until the lights were off and all the living were finally gone.

I loved playing softball under the stars. The darkness wrapped itself around us as we played, like a warm blanket. The light that emanated from us gave us enough light to follow the ball when it was hit and the players as they ran the bases.

It was actually kind of weird the way we could track the ball even in the dark, but after a while, we quit trying to figure out the why of it all and just played. The women that played before they died used to give the umps a real hard time about their eyesight being even worse now that they were dead, but that wasn't the truth. They could track the balls and strikes better than they ever could alive, and they hardly ever missed a play.

Actually, the bright lights the living played under hurt my eyes a little, and sometimes I wished the living could figure out how to play in the starlight. It was a much nicer game, under the stars. But, that was never going to happen. I knew it as well as anybody else.

"You said you wanted to talk," Marie said, a little louder this time, as if she thought maybe I was deaf. I glanced over at a couple of the living—Miriam Kendel's mom and dad—parked at ground level in two lawn chairs, blankets and coats keeping their old bones warm, but they didn't react to Marie's words. Which was good. The last thing I needed was more attention from the living.

"Keep your voice down," I muttered, pointing at the two figures wrapped in their blankets. "We'll talk when the game starts."

Marie glanced at them, and her mouth snapped shut. She nodded and faced forward, watching the two pitchers warm up.

Mr. Kelly and Mr. Middleton, the two dead umps, trundled up into the bleachers on the other side of the diamond from us. What were they doing? This was not part of the plan. I silently cursed and glanced at Marie to see if she'd seen them. She did not react.

She was concentrating on the pitcher closest to us. It was Miriam Kendel, and her rise ball was really working.

"She's the best in the league," I said. "Nobody can hit her."

Marie nodded. "So I heard," she whispered. "She looks pretty good."

I snorted something close to laughter. "Wait 'til you see her in the game," I said. "Wait until you face her. You'll do well not to wet yourself the first time."

I couldn't read Marie's face. All she did was shrug and continue to watch Miriam as she threw rise ball after rise ball, harder and harder, until the ball was hard to follow. Just a yellow blur from Miriam's hand to the catcher's glove. A slow throw back, and again, the blur.

Joanne showed up, followed by Rita Danworth, of tea cup moving fame. They carefully scrambled up the bleachers furthest from us and sat with the two umps. Damn them. I thought the plan was to wait out of sight until this game was over and then jump Marie as she was heading to her car after the living were gone.

I was sure that was the plan.

"Excuse me for just a moment," I said. "I gotta check something out."

"You'll be back, right?" Marie frowned at me for a moment then went back to watching Miriam. She seemed hypnotized by the ball.

"Yeah. Just give me a second."

I scrambled away but kept my eye on her. She didn't appear to notice where I'd gone. Just watched the ball go from Miriam's hand to the catcher's glove and back. Over and over.

I ducked behind the bleachers and pelted over to the far side where the umps were sitting. Of course, everyone was there, milling around under the bleachers. Their nervous energy translated into light, so it was like somebody had set up a couple of spot lights under the bleachers. I knew most people couldn't see us, or the light, but I was willing to bet that Marie could see both.

"You guys can't stay here," I muttered. "You'll scare her off."

"But we want to watch the game," Charlotte, who'd died in 1993 and played on my team, said. "Why can't we do it from here?"

"Because she can see you," I snapped. I pushed my way past them all and to the far side of the bleachers where the umps and Joanne and Rita were sitting.

"What are you doing?" I asked. My voice was louder than it should have been, and I glanced around the bleachers to see if I'd disturbed Marie. She hadn't moved.

"We want to watch the game," Mr. Kelly said. "We took a vote and decided it would be all right. Just so long as it's just a couple of us up here." He pointed at the wood beneath his feet. "The rest have promised to stay below. Nice and quiet."

"That was not the plan," I whispered. "You were all supposed to stay away until after the game. I was supposed to chat her up and keep her here so you could show up and scare the crap out of her. After the game."

Joanne answered. With a sneer, of course. "The living are stupid," she said. "We won't have a problem. Just go back and do your job."

I looked at Mr. Kelly and Mr. Middleton, beseechingly, but got nothing but a shrug from either of them.

"Fine," I said. "But you watch. She'll see you, and then your stupid plan will fall apart. Seriously."

"I doubt it," Joanne replied, and then turned away from me. So I clambered my way down the bleachers to Marie.

"I'm back," I said, rather unnecessarily, as I plunked myself down beside her. I sat on her right side hoping it would keep her from looking at the far left side of the bleachers. "It should be starting soon."

She was still focused on Miriam's pitching. "I think I have her figured out," she said, distantly.

"She's just warming up," I said. "She's different in the game. You'll see."

"Maybe," Marie murmured. She watched Miriam's last two throws, then leaned back and frowned up at the sky. "Maybe."

I didn't say anything, content for the moment to have her looking anywhere but at the other end of the bleachers. Miriam's team, the Blues, took the field, and Miriam took her time cleaning up the pitcher's rubber, which meant that she very carefully kicked dirt all over it. Made it harder for the umps to tell if her back foot was actually touching the rubber when she pushed off for her pitch. Classic Miriam trick. Then the rest of the team gathered around her, and every one of them touched her glove hand. No one touched her pitching hand. No one would dare.

"Why does she do that?" Marie asked.

"Do what?"

"Keep her pitching hand away from everyone like that?"

"Oh." I glanced at Marie. "You saw that, huh?"

"Well yeah. What's her deal? Is it a good luck thing?"

I shrugged. "She licks her fingers before every pitch," I said. "She doesn't want the germs, or something."

Marie snorted. "That ball is rolling around in the frigging dirt," she said. "It's filthy."

"Yeah," I said. "But hey, it's her deal."

"Hmm." Marie looked like she was tucking that bit of information away, and it was my turn to snort laughter.

"Don't think you'll throw her off by grabbing her hand," I said. "She'll just go wash up, and then she'll make your life hell for the rest of the game."

"Oh," Marie said, but she didn't look like she believed me. Hey whatever, chick. It's your funeral.

The game started, and I tried colour commentating to give Marie background on the players and reasons they were playing the way they were. I was all ready to explain the rules to her—just to make sure she was up to speed—but she shushed me.

"I just want to watch for a while," she said.

I shut my mouth even though that was the last thing I wanted to do. Chatting was my way of "becoming her friend" so she'd stick around after the living were gone. Also, I wanted to keep her from noticing the rest of my people as they crowded under the bleachers. It was getting darker by the moment, even with the lights, and their glow was getting really bright.

I got more and more uncomfortable as the innings went on, but Marie didn't notice anything. She just watched the game in silence.

I was blowing it. So, I decided to talk to her about her play. Just to get the conversation started.

"You want some pointers for right field?" I said. "You looked kinda lost out there. Know what I mean?"

I felt her stiffen, and then she slowly turned toward me. "I haven't played in a while," she said. "That's all."

I was going to say something like, "Oh yeah, I know, but I can give you some stuff to work on," but that didn't happen because she looked past me and frowned.

"What the hell is that?" she asked.

I turned to see what she'd seen.

It was the rest. The ones who were supposed to stay carefully hidden under the bleachers. It appeared that they'd decided that watching the game was much more important than staying out of Marie's line of sight. They'd lined up along the right field fence, and even though the huge lights washed the fence in light, they could still be seen.

The ones who'd decided to park themselves a bit further back on the grass lit up the darkened area like beacons. They wavered and glowed as they leaned toward each other, talking. Worse than that, I could see other spirits coming toward the diamond from the opposite side. Wavering lights, meandering their way over.

They were everywhere.

I tried to keep up the façade that everything was hunky dory. "What?" I said, knowing I sounded like an idiot. "I don't see anything."

Marie pointed past me to the left field fence. "Are those what I think they are?" she asked.

I followed her finger and looked out at all the dead idiots who had decided not to follow Joanne's ridiculous plan.

"I don't know what you mean," I said, weakly.

"Shit," Marie said. Her face tightened, and she grabbed her belongings and stood. "Shit, shit, shit."

"Oh," I said, trying desperately to save the situation. "You mean the dead."

"Yes," she said. "I mean the dead." She glanced over my shoulder again and looked horrified. "How many of them are there?"

"Two teams," I said. "We have enough for two teams."

That brought her up short. "Teams?" she asked, then shook her head. "Never mind. I don't want to know. I'm out of here."

She headed for the bottom of the bleachers, and I looked over at Joanne and shrugged. Joanne didn't take that particularly well.

"You idiot!" she yelled at me. "You absolute idiot!" Then she turned to the left field fence and bellowed, "She's getting away!"

I looked over the end of the bleachers and watched Marie stomping her way to her car, the dead hot on her heels. If she didn't hurry, she wasn't going to make it to safety. And for a second, I felt quite sorry for her.

I really did.

Marie:
Exorcisms and Poltergeists

I PELTED AROUND the right end of the bleachers toward the gate, preparing to throw myself into James's car and get the hell out of there as quickly as I could.

There were ghosts everywhere. And they were all streaming out of Diamond Two after me.

"Crap!" I cried, and tried to scramble away from them. I tripped and almost fell, but managed to regain my footing and ran as fast as I could for the car.

I pulled the keys from my pocket and jangled through them as I ran. Why oh why did James have so many keys? I finally found the car key and held it like a weapon as I flew the final few feet to the car. But, before I could get the key in the lock the first of the ghosts caught up to me, and I was quickly surrounded.

I was ready to lose my mind—I'd never had so many ghosts all together in one spot before—but I realized they had stopped in a rough circle around me.

"So, go ahead." I recognized Karen's voice and glared at her. She ignored me, though, and concentrated on the two old men who'd arrived. "Do it if you're going to."

That didn't sound good.

"Thanks a ton," I said. She had the decency to look embarrassed.

"It's nothing personal," she muttered. "Just protecting our

turf."

"Quit talking to her!" the angry ghost cried. "Get her!"

And then, she ran at me, into me, and I had to endure some bad moments as she flailed around. But in her anger, I could feel fear, and I stopped my attempts to get her out of my space.

"Why are you so scared?" I asked.

"Get her!" the angry scared ghost said again, but I noticed that none of the other ghosts had moved. Only the angry one had stepped into me. I figured I could handle one.

"Tell me," I said. "Why are you so afraid?"

A latecomer jogged up to us, and accidentally stepped into my space. For a crazy second I had two of them in me. One angry and afraid, the other more confused than anything else.

In fact, despite the confusion, the second ghost felt normal. Which confused and disconcerted me more than the fear and anger of the first. I'd never run into a ghost whose emotions and reactions seemed healthy. What the hell was going on?

"Get out of me!" I yelled.

"Oh, sorry," the second ghost said, and obligingly took a step away.

"What are you doing, Lisa?" The angry ghost who was still flailing around in my space stopped and stepped away from me, which was a relief. "Get back in there with me!"

"But she doesn't like it," Lisa said.

"Of course she doesn't like it!" the angry ghost said. "That's the whole point!"

"I'm not going to," Lisa said, fairly stubbornly, I thought. "It's not nice."

"To hell with you and your being nice!" the angry ghost shrieked. She stepped back into me, and her anger quotient had jumped up a ton. My chest suddenly felt hot, and it was hard to breathe. I could have kicked myself. My mother had taught me how to keep ghosts from invading my space, but I'd been so overwhelmed I hadn't even tried using the defence she had helped me come up with. All I had to do was think of wings of steel—like in the ancient Batfink cartoon—but I couldn't do it with the ghost in my space. I just had to deal with her until she stepped away. Luckily for me, it was still only her.

The rest of them stood in a rough circle around us, staring, and for a second I wondered what it looked like to them. Could they see the angry ghost inside me, flailing around like an idiot?

"Stop that," Karen finally said. "Joanne, just stop. We aren't going to help you hurt her."

That brought me up. I hadn't thought about them trying to hurt me. Aggravate me to death maybe, but not hurt me.

That many ghosts could have caused me some emotional damage if enough of them were truly angry spirits, and they certainly would have made my next visit to the shrink interesting, but even though Joanne was angry and afraid she was not the worst ghost I'd dealt with. Not by a long shot. And she was not a poltergeist. Of that, I was sure.

"You can't hurt me," I said. I wasn't sure if I was telling the absolute truth but figured that it was close enough for this bunch. "Now, step out here so we can talk like two—"

"Human beings?" one of the ghosts asked. "Too late, I'd say."

A couple of the ghosts tittered nervous laughter, and Joanne's anger quotient went up. A ton.

"All you can do is joke?" she screamed. "This is not a joke! She'll destroy us!"

She stepped out of me, and the heat of her anger quickly faded.

"I'm not going to destroy you," I said. "Why do you think that?"

"Well, you *can* see us," one of the old men standing to one side said. I nodded. He had me there.

"She'll exorcise us!" Joanne screamed. "We talked about this!"

Exorcising? Seriously?

"I don't do exorcising," I said. "Honestly."

"Sure," Joanne said. "She says that now. But watch. Someday, she'll just start exorcising all of us, and there won't be a thing we can do about it. We gotta get her out of here!" She turned to a tall, thin ghost with a high, tight ponytail. "Come on, Rita," she said. "Do something to her. Hurt her!"

"I—I don't know if I can do that," Rita said. She tugged at her ponytail, looking uncomfortable. "It was just a teacup, before. She's so big."

"Do it!" Joanne cried, and then whimpered as though she was about to break into tears. "You promised me. You promised us all."

Rita gave her ponytail one more tug and took a step toward me.

"Leave me alone, Rita," I said. I thought about wings of steel, like my mother taught me, to keep her from entering my space the way Joanne had. Hoped it would be enough to stop her.

"I'm sorry," Rita said, and put a tentative hand to my arm.

For a second, I thought I could feel something touching me, then her hand slid through my arm and out.

"How did you do that?" I asked. "How did you touch me?"

"I'm not sure," Rita said. She sounded winded, like she'd run a mile, and she slowly slid to the ground. "I moved a tea cup once—"

I stared at her. My first official poltergeist. "That's cool," I finally said.

"Thank you," she muttered, looking completely exhausted.

"Is that it? Is that all you got?" Joanne looked disgusted and turned away from Rita, who was still lying on the ground by James's car. A couple of other ghosts squatted on the ground beside her, offering her whispered words of encouragement.

"Don't listen to Joanne," one of them said. "She's just jealous."

"Jealous of that?" Joanne spat. "That was pathetic. You've done nothing." She whirled, glaring at the ghosts who had encircled her and me. "None of you have done anything. And you promised."

"Joanne, let it go." Karen spoke, and I noticed that the rest of the ghosts' lights wavered. Then, as one, they all took a step back, widening the circle around Joanne and me appreciably. "This isn't going to work."

"Thank you," I said.

"They were afraid," Karen said to me. "When I told them about you."

"Why?" I asked. It struck me as funny that ghosts would be afraid of me, but I tried to keep any hint of a smile from my face. I didn't need to upset them further.

"Because we just want to be left alone," Karen said. "We figured if you realized we were here you'd do something to make us go away. That exorcising thing. And we can't have that. We just want to be left alone. You know?"

"Well, that's all I want, too," I said.

"Really?" Rita asked. She'd pulled herself up to sitting, and gave her ponytail a quick tug to tighten it. "You wouldn't lie to us, would you?"

Dying on Second

"No," I said. "I'm not lying. I won't bother you if you don't bother me."

"Now, Missy, you have to understand that we like to watch the early games," one of the old guys said. "We are not giving up on them just because you can see us."

"The early games?" I asked.

"He means the living games," the other old guy said. "The ones just before our games."

"Your games?"

Both of the old guys looked at me like I was being thick. Which, I guess, I was. Hadn't Karen said something about there being enough ghosts for two teams?

"You play softball," I said.

"Yeah," Karen said. "We play softball."

"You're telling her our secrets!" Joanne yelled, then burst into tears. "She'll ruin us all!"

"She said she wouldn't," one of the old guys said. "And she doesn't look like a liar to me."

The rest of the ghosts nodded, muttering softly. Joanne pushed through them and ran across the parking lot, her iridescent tears pattering to the ground around her. She disappeared when she hit the road, and we all watched her tears slowly disappear.

"She'll be back," one of them, I think it was Rita, said. "Won't she?"

"She better come back," another ghost said. "She's catching for me tonight."

The circle around me broke up into clumps of ghosts, standing close together, as if for comfort. They all stared at me, silently. Like they were waiting for me to say something.

So, I blurted out the first thing that popped into my head. "How do you play without equipment?"

"Oh!" Rita again, looking very much recovered from her poltergeist experiment. "It's easy!"

She started talking, and then others chimed in, and they stepped closer to me, all wanting to tell me how they played softball without equipment, and without the ability to pick up or move anything corporeal, past a tea cup. Their proximity was making me a bit uncomfortable—but the most interesting thing was, I felt no anger or fear or anything close to disturbed from them.

"One at a time, please," I said, taking a big step away from all of them. "I can't understand you."

"Maybe you need to watch," Karen said.

They all stopped talking and stared at her. "Are you sure you want that, Karen?" one of the old guys finally asked.

"Yeah, I think so," Karen said and turned to me. "You doing anything tonight?"

I stared at Karen, my mouth open. The last thing in the world I ever thought I would have been doing after playing softball was watching the dead play softball. But here I was with an invitation.

"I'm not doing anything," I said, and put the keys to James's car back in my pocket.

"Good," Karen said.

As one, the ghosts turned to the diamond.

"We gotta see how Miriam does in her game," Rita said. "We got a pool. We figure she'll strike out everybody this season."

"Everybody?" I scoffed. "I don't think so. She looks hittable."

"You haven't seen her in a game," Karen said. She took a few steps toward the diamond, then turned back to me. "So, you coming or what?" she asked.

"Right behind you," I said, and pulled my phone from my pocket.

Time to call Jasmine to let her know I'd be late. And James to let him know I was going to get his car back to him a few hours later than we'd planned because I had two more ball games to watch. A live one, and then a dead one.

Good grief.

Karen:
The Post-Swarming Talk

I DIDN'T QUITE know how Marie was going to be after the attempted swarming, but she seemed to have taken it all with a great deal of good humour.

I watched as she talked for a few minutes on her little mobile telephone and went up to her when she pulled her keys out of her pocket.

"You going?" I asked, surprised that I felt a little let down.

"Just going to get a coffee," she said. She was as good as her word and came back a few minutes later carrying three paper cups. She stopped beside Miriam Kendel's parents and handed each of them a cup.

"Why thank you," her mother, Rosa, said. "I thought you were gone."

"I decided I wanted to catch the end of the game," Marie said. She worked her way up the bleachers, sitting at the seat she had vacated when we rushed her.

I couldn't decide if I should go up and sit with her again. She'd have some tough questions for me, and I didn't know if I wanted to answer them.

Luckily, we were warming up for our game so the decision was taken out of my hands. We carefully distributed the equipment. Three balls and one bat for our team. The other team had two balls, two bats, and one glove. The glove was a bit of an affectation, because we no longer needed the protection, but hey, somebody got buried with a glove so it was going to get used.

We lined up just off the first base line close to the living right fielder, and began throwing the balls back and forth. Working out the kinks of a winter of—well, nothing, for some of us.

I was awake all winter and just hung around the diamond waiting for spring. But some of the dead didn't do the same. Some of them went to sleep, waking a few weeks before ball season started, and slowly making their way here. The rest didn't talk about what they did, and I never asked. I never told them my business, and didn't want to know theirs.

As I warmed up, I looked around for any new arrivals. I was the unofficial dead greeter since I'd been here the longest.

"Anybody new?" Lisa asked. She'd shown up three years before and had easily fit in. She'd died at twenty-nine from complications of an appendectomy, which, as she said, had been a pretty big kick in the teeth. She'd played softball right up until the night she died. She'd brought the newest ball and bat with her, so her arrival had been greeted with glad hurrahs all around.

"Not that I can see," I said. "But they don't always make it for opening night."

"True enough," Lisa said. She tossed the ball, then turned and looked at me, hard. "Are you feeling as bad about what we did to that girl as I am?"

"Yeah. I am."

"We never run anyone off," Lisa said. "Not even the cranks."

"I know," I said. "But she's—well, she's alive. That kind of makes her not one of us. Doesn't it?"

"Just because she's alive doesn't mean we should treat her like dirt," Lisa said.

"I know," I said. "She hasn't done anything to us. She just came to play softball. Just like the rest of us." I glanced over my shoulder, at Marie. She was watching the living game, but would occasionally glance in our direction. "Maybe I should go talk to her. You know, apologize, or whatever."

"That would be a very good idea," Lisa said. "One of us needs to."

I waved to Charlotte, who I was playing catch with, and pointed at Lisa, indicating that she would continue warming up with her. Then I walked off the grass and onto the shale that edged the bleachers.

Marie was steadfastly ignoring me, but I went up to her anyhow. "Can we talk?" I asked. "Just for a minute?"

"I guess," she said, after a short uncomfortable silence.

I plunked down beside her and watched Miriam mow the next batter down with three quick strikes. Her father cheered as the batter walked off the diamond, and Miriam waved her glove at him. I thought for a second how lucky Miriam was to have a father who cared enough to watch her play.

My father never would have come to a softball game if I'd played when I was alive. He thought activities like team sports were a stupid waste of time and money.

He was wrong, of course. Softball was the only thing that had kept me sane over all these years. But I was dead, so I guess he wouldn't have seen it as such a waste of my time, if he'd known.

And I wondered, for the first time ever, if he would have been proud of me. Wondered if he would have come and watched me if he'd known that it was the only way he'd ever see me again. Shook it off, because there was no point in thinking that way. I was dead, and he couldn't watch me even if he wanted to. Even if I wanted him to . . .

"You said you wanted to talk," Marie whispered, pulling me out of my reverie. "What about?"

"About—about what happened by your car," I said. "It was stupid, and I'm sorry. We shouldn't have done anything like that."

"Why did you?" Marie had turned back to the game, but I could see she was frowning even in profile. "I didn't do anything to you—wouldn't have done anything to you. What was the deal?"

"We—we were afraid that you'd try to make us leave," I said, miserably. "For some of us, this is all we've got. You know? We were afraid that you'd—"

"Exorcise you all?" Marie whispered. She sounded sarcastic, and her frown deepened.

"Well yeah," I said. "Something like that."

"You do know that exorcising doesn't work like that," she said.

I shrugged. "Joanne seemed to think that it was something you could do. I thought maybe that 'moving on' you talked about was the same thing."

I looked at her, and she briefly closed her eyes and shook her head. "Moving on has nothing to do with exorcism," she said. "And if you don't want to move on, I can't make you." She looked at me. "Would it be better if I quit?" she asked. "Just went away and never came back?"

"Maybe," I said, then glanced down at Lisa, who smiled and waved when she saw me looking at her. I turned back to Marie and shook my head. "No," I said. "That wouldn't be fair to you."

"Hmm," she said, after another long silence. "What about the one who attacked me? Joanne. She seemed pretty set on getting me to leave."

"Oh, that's just Joanne," I said. "She's always angry. But she might come around when she sees you're not going to do anything to mess with our games."

"She wasn't just angry," Marie said. "She was frightened, too." She glanced at me then back to the game. "What's her deal?"

"That's a good question," I said, and laughed uncomfortably. Joanne would have a fit if she knew I was about to talk about her. And to someone living, to boot. "She got here fifteen years ago. She rolled her car on the way to a tournament, out on Highway Two, and she was an emotional wreck when she first got here. Could barely stay for the games. Kept flipping back to where she died, sometimes mid-game. It was aggravating, but she was a good back catcher so we put up with it. Over the years she calmed down. Mostly."

"So, she died in a car crash?" Marie asked. "Any chance she meant to roll the car?"

"You mean did she commit suicide?" I shrugged. "She never said anything but maybe. I shouldn't be telling tales out of school, though."

"Telling tales?" Marie looked confused. "What do you mean?"

"History doesn't matter much, here," I said. "Most of us have gotten past how we died. The how and why we're here doesn't matter. We're all here for the same thing."

"To play softball."

"Yep. Exactly."

We both watched the game in silence for a while. I felt tense knowing that Marie would have a ton more questions. I suddenly didn't feel up to answering them.

"Look," I said, "I gotta get back. We're going to be playing soon. I just wanted to say sorry, you know, for before."

"Apology accepted," Marie said. She grinned at me, and I felt relief so strong my light momentarily flared. Marie squinted.

"Thanks," I said and left.

I was half expecting her to leave after the living game ended, but she didn't. Just sat in the bleachers, with her black hooded jacket pulled tight around her to keep out the cold, as all the rest of the living left.

Rosa Spears waved good-bye to her as she and Jerry packed up their stuff, and Marie waved back. Then, the only living people left were the two guys on the maintenance crew as they raced around on their little tractor raking the infield so that it looked perfect. Eventually, even they were gone and the lights cut out, leaving Marie sitting all by herself in the dark.

Of course, our fans started showing up just a few minutes after that, so Marie was never really alone. Not really.

IT WAS ODD, seeing a living human in the stands, watching our game. She was surrounded by a dozen other ghosts—the ones who showed up to watch our games—and didn't look that comfortable, but after a while I forgot about her. Forgot everything but the game.

We won handily because Joanne hadn't come back and that put the other team at a serious disadvantage. Jane Rogers stood in for her as back catcher, but she wasn't very good, and all the passed balls pissed off Robin, the pitcher, to the point that she glared at me a time or two as though it was my fault that they were losing. But I didn't care. It was nice to have all my people around me again, and I probably cheered the loudest when we finished the game ahead seven to five.

I looked up at the stands and saw that Marie was gone. Wondered if I was going to see her again and then decided not to care.

This was, after all, the dead's turn to play.

Marie:
Ribs and Advice

JASMINE WAS WAITING for me when I got back to her place. I was surprised, because it was kind of late for her to be up. After all, she had a full-time job and three kids to look after, which was actually another full-time job. She must have been exhausted all the time. I would have been.

"You hungry?" she asked. "I have some leftover supper, if you want."

"That would be fantastic," I said, suddenly starving. "And I'll make some tea. I'm freezing. Want some?"

She nodded, so I set to work making tea as she pulled the leftover meal out of the fridge. Ribs, mashed potatoes, and a bunch of cut up vegetables. Soon we had a nice little picnic going, and I dug in enthusiastically.

"So, how did the baseball game go?" Jasmine asked. "Did your team win?"

"It's called softball," I said, and then frowned. The night had gone on so long, I couldn't remember whether we'd won or not. "I think we won," I said, and then remembered. We'd won seven to six.

"Did you have fun?"

The question gave me serious pause. Did I have fun? I guess while I was playing I had some fun, but all the ghosts showing up after hadn't been that much fun. And the swarming—that hadn't been fun at all.

"It was all right," I finally said. I held out the teapot. "You want some more?"

She nodded, so I poured, and we drank in silence.

"I—I don't know if I'm going to keep playing," I finally said. "I don't know if it's really my game."

"Oh," Jasmine said. "That's too bad. I told Ella, and she said she wanted to come watch sometime."

Ella was Jasmine's scary smart daughter who spent more time doing homework than most girls her age spent online. I was pretty sure she just tolerated me living with them.

"Well," I finally said. "Maybe I can play a few more games. For her."

"Oh God, don't tell her that," Jasmine chuckled. "She isn't really into people doing things 'just for her.' Know what I mean?"

"I guess," I said, and laughed a little myself. Sounded a bit like me, truth be told.

"Now, tell me why you're thinking about quitting," Jasmine said. "I thought you were going to really give this a go. You know—sunshine and fresh air. What happened?"

I looked over my teacup at her and tried to think of something that would sound normal but realistic. Jasmine didn't know that I could see ghosts. I hadn't been able to figure out a way to tell her—not with all the other foolishness that seemed to have swirled around me—and I didn't want to lose her as a friend because of it.

"I—I just don't play as well as I thought I'd be able to," I said. "I think I'm holding the team back."

"But you guys won," Jasmine said. "Doesn't sound like you're doing much damage."

"Yeah, I know," I said. "It's just—it's been a long time since I've played. I don't know if I can actually get better."

"Does that matter?" Jasmine asked.

"Well, of course it does," I said, then looked at her. She was shaking her head.

"I don't know about that, Marie," she said gently. "You're just out there for a few laughs. You don't need to be the best. Do you?"

I chuckled. "No chance of that, my friend," I said. "There are some women who can really play. Miriam Kendel, for example. She pitches for the Blues. They played after our game, so I stuck

Dying on Second

around to watch. She's really good. People were actually making bets that she'll strike out everyone this year."

Then I shuddered, because the people who'd been talking about taking bets had been the ghosts. Jasmine poured me more tea.

"Still cold?" she asked.

I shrugged but accepted the tea. We sipped in silence for a few minutes.

"So maybe you can practice," she finally said. "You know, with James—"

"Ah," I said, and laughed. "Did he talk to you?"

"Well, he might have," Jasmine said. She smiled. "A little practice can't kill you, though, can it?"

I sighed. "I guess not."

"So, practice with him."

"I might." I stood, picking up my cup and plate. "But I think right now, I'll go to bed. Thanks for the late supper. It was fabulous as always."

"You are welcome, my friend." But Jasmine didn't smile. "When do you go see Dr. Parkerson again?"

"Tomorrow. Why?"

"Maybe you can ask her about quitting. You know, get her perspective on the whole thing."

Jasmine had been one of the ones who had convinced me to go to therapy, mostly because of my nightmares after I came back from Fort McMurray. The nightmares were the usual. Dealing with my dead stalkery ex-boyfriend—and his equally stalkery girlfriend. My mother dying and leaving me alone. Absolutely alone. Dr. Parkerson was helping, as much as she could. But I hadn't told her about the ghosts. No need to end up in a nut house, after all.

"Yeah, I guess." I knew she would tell me to keep playing. That it was doing me good. All that fresh air and exercise would help straighten out my chemistry so the nightmares and everything else would finally calm down, and I could live a normal life.

Yeah. Right.

"Promise me," Jasmine said, and looked at me with those "mother" eyes that did not allow me to say no.

"All right. I promise." I grinned at her, in spite of myself. "You're a bit of a hard ass, my friend."

"Back at ya," she replied, then caught me in a brief hug. "Sleep well."

I went down to the basement. It was a little rugged down there—mostly unpainted Gyproc and cement floors—but I had managed to set up a bit of a nest for myself. I had a bed and a desk, with an old—and I mean ancient—computer on it.

I stripped down, carefully putting my ball equipment to one side so I could find it all again, and then fell into bed. And, more or less instantly, to sleep.

That lasted a blissful hour and a half, until I had another one of my nightmares. It was an oldie but a goody about popping the eyeball of a drug dealer who was trying to kill me. Then I was wide awake. So, I got up, fired up the computer, and decided to do a little investigating.

I'd met a lot of ghosts the evening before. A shit ton, if I was going to be honest, and I felt like maybe I needed to know who I was dealing with. So, I wrote down as many names as I could remember, and Googled them all.

Some of them had died of natural causes. Some in accidents. But some of them had disappeared. I found Charlotte on the Missing Persons website, along with Jane Rogers. Both missing and presumed dead.

"No presumed about it," I whispered as I wrote the last of their information in a cheap scribbler Ella had given me. "All I have to do is find out where their bodies are, and I could really help the cops clean up their cold cases."

I looked up and sighed when I saw the pink of the sunrise touching the little window above my desk. Another night with little sleep.

Whatever. I'd been without enough sleep for so long, I wasn't sure I remembered how it felt to get a full eight hours any longer.

I looked at the little alarm clock on the wooden crate that served as my nightstand. Five in the morning. I could either get a couple more hours sleep or get up for real. So, I got out of the plastic folding chair that I used as a desk chair and headed upstairs.

At least I'd be able to have the first shower. In this house, that was a bit of a miracle all on its own.

JAMES WAS WAITING for me at the front entry way of "Casa del

James," when I drove up. He had Millie the comfort dog with him. I was late, and Millie was displeased. She let me know it by growling at me when I tried to pet her. James laughed.

"The dog's like a nasty little alarm clock," I said. "I'm only five minutes late."

"That five minutes puts us right in the middle of rush hour," James said. "And Millie knows that." He laughed out loud when I tried to pet the little dog one more time and got the cold shoulder.

"Good grief, did you train her to do that?" I asked. I slid over to the passenger's side as James got in the driver's seat and we headed off.

"Nope," he said. "She just knows her own mind, is all."

"Cranky old lady," I said. "That's what she is."

But Millie was right. The traffic downtown was terrible. James tried to talk to me about how softball had gone the evening before, but I felt like I needed a big cup of coffee before I told him what had happened. Surprisingly, he didn't push, and we drove in amicable silence. Even the dog was quiet, except for the occasional snort.

Finally, we arrived at the Jimmy Lavall Detective Agency, and Millie curled up in her little dog bed while James and I prepared ourselves for another day of detecting.

In reality, I listened to three voicemail messages while James handled emails. It looked like we'd have a couple more cases, if we decided to take them.

"What's our time like, James?" I called from my little receptionist desk at the front of the office. "Got room for another divorce case?"

Divorce cases were nasty things, generally speaking. Mostly it was one soon-to-be-ex-spouse trying to get the goods on another soon-to-be ex-spouse. Interestingly enough, though, they usually paid. Once I'd learned how to write up an air tight contract, that is.

"I think so," James said. "Let me look at the big book."

James's big book was an actual, physical book. A day timer—the biggest one he could find—that sat on the edge of his desk. Everything we had to accomplish was written down in it. First, in pencil, while we made certain we could do it. And then, in pen. From it, I filled my electronic calendar.

Seemed like a waste of a tree to me but he was the boss. What could I say?

"When do they want us to start?" he called.

"Looks like yesterday would have been good."

"Hmm." He was silent for a few moments more. "All right," he finally called. "We should be able to do it."

I made the phone call to confirm and set up a meeting with Lorraine Calloway, the extremely ticked off soon-to-be-ex of Randolph Calloway of Calloway Rentals.

Then I poured two cups of coffee and walked them both into James's office, so I could tell him all about the evening before. I wasn't certain how he'd respond to the ghost stuff, so I started with the game itself. He grilled me so hard about every aspect of it, I finally snapped.

"Next time come to the stupid game! I can't remember all that stuff, for heaven's sake."

All right, so he'd been working the night before but still, he sure knew how to get on my nerves. All he did was laugh and reach for my coffee cup.

"I'll get you a refill," he said. "Will that make things better?"

"Maybe," I said. He handed me the refilled cup—perfect, as always—and I was mollified. "Thank you."

"You are more than welcome," he said. "Now, tell me how it went with the ghost. Did she agree to stay away while you played?"

I flinched and put the cup on the edge of his desk. How to explain what had gone on after my game? I decided to ease into it.

"We didn't actually get to talk about that," I said. "But she did stay out of the way, more or less."

"That's good," he said. Then he stopped and stared at me. "What do you mean, more or less? What else happened?"

I looked up at him. "Well, she wasn't the only spirit there."

"What?" He sat straight in his chair and stared at me with all humour slapped from his face. "How many ghosts did you see?"

"I'm—I'm not sure," I said. My voice started to shake, so I picked up my coffee and took a quick sip to calm myself. "Lots."

"Lots?" He sat even straighter, if that was possible. "What does that mean?"

"It means lots," I said. I could hear my voice tighten up. That meant I was either going to yell or cry. At that point, I honestly couldn't tell which. "More than ten—probably twenty. Or so."

In all honesty, there had been more than forty ghosts hanging around that softball diamond if I included the dead in the stands, but the look on James's face kept me from saying that number out loud.

"Twenty?" he gasped. "Why—why would there be twenty ghosts at the ball diamond?"

"They were waiting to play," I mumbled.

"What?"

"They—they play softball. After the living games." I was mumbling so badly I could barely understand my own words, and took another big swig of my coffee just to get myself under some kind of control. "They've been doing it for years. Since the diamond was built, I think." I tried to smile. "Karen plays, too. Second base, of course."

"Of course," James said softly. "So what happened?"

"They—they swarmed me."

"They what?" James leaped from his chair and looked around frantically, as though he was certain that the ghosts were going to swarm him, too. Right at that very moment. "They swarmed you? My God, are you all right?"

"Yeah, I'm fine," I said, trying to smile, trying to show that everything was absolutely okey dokey even though my heart was beating trip hammer hard at the memory. "There were only a couple of them who tried anything. The rest mostly—watched."

"But why?" he asked. He was still standing. "Why would they do that?"

"They were afraid that I was going to make them leave. Or something."

"Aww Marie, I'm so sorry," he said. He came to me and pulled me into his arms. I barely had time to put my coffee cup down, otherwise we both would have been covered in the hot liquid. "That must have been horrible for you."

"It was a bit scary, at first," I said into his shoulder. "But there was only one who could actually touch me, so—"

"A poltergeist!" He practically shrieked out the word. "You met a poltergeist?"

"Well yeah," I said. "But she couldn't do much. Not really."

"Good God," he said again. "Well, it's a cinch you can't go back there. We'll have to find you something else to do for exercise. Maybe yoga—"

"I'm not quitting softball."

Now, up to that second, I hadn't decided how I was going to handle the softball spirits. I had promised Jasmine I'd stick it out for a little while longer—but she didn't know about all the ghosts. But I wasn't about to let James make that decision for me.

"They aren't going to do anything to me," I said. I really wasn't certain about crazy Joanne, but there was no way in the world I was telling James that. "And besides, my team is depending on me. At least until three of their players come back from college ball. You know?"

"I know," he said. "But still—"

"Don't worry," I said, and the smile on my face felt a lot more genuine. "I've got this handled. Really. I even Googled some of them to find out how they died. You know, to see if maybe I can help some of them move on."

"Oh?" James still didn't look convinced but at least he'd returned to his seat. "What did you find out?"

"There were two who are on the cop's Missing Persons website," I said. "So, I guess I'll talk to them. Find out what happened. You know, and offer them my services."

"You think you'll be safe?"

"Yeah!" I clicked my tongue at him like I'd been dealing with forty ghosts at a time forever. "No problem. No problem at all."

Luckily, Lorraine Calloway called at that moment, explaining why she couldn't possibly come to our office at two p.m.—the time she'd agreed to not a half hour before. James wandered out of his office as I tried to figure out when Lorraine actually was available, and when I was finally able to hang up the receiver, I saw that both he and Millie were gone.

He'd taken Millie for a walk without asking me if I wanted to go.

I was a bit hurt, but decided to get work done while they were gone. So, I Googled Karen's name again, and this time I went past the Missing Persons page.

I found out that Karen's family lived on the South side, close to Ninety-Ninth Street, when she disappeared. It looked like they still lived there. I even found a "She's been gone 40 years" article in the local rag from the year before. I stared at the photographs they'd used for the article for a long time. A close-up shot of Karen—looked like another school photo—her long hair wild around her face and over her shoulders. The second photo was of the front of Karen's parents' house.

The article gave me the names of Karen's mom and dad—Ethel and Rupert Dubinsky. It didn't take me long to get their phone number. I stared at it for a long time, trying to decide whether I should call and set up a meeting.

The anniversary article convinced me. They'd been looking for their daughter for a long time. They deserved to know what happened to her . . . as soon as I figured it out.

I looked at James's schedule. He had nothing for the rest of the day, so I decided what the heck, and picked up the receiver. If he had a problem with the meeting he could skip it. All he needed to do was lend me his keys. And the car, of course.

It didn't take James long to walk Millie. I'd just hung up the phone when they came in.

"Glad you're back," I said. "I phoned Karen's folks and set up a meet. Today."

"Karen?" James cocked his head—hilariously looking much like Millie, who'd done the same thing. "Karen who?"

"Karen Dubinsky," I said. "The dead girl on second base."

"Ah," he said. He bent down and unclipped Millie's leash from her collar. She stood on her hind legs and licked his chin, then walked over to her bed, ignoring me completely. "I thought you were going to leave her alone," he said. "What are you doing?"

I blinked. Talking to her parents had seemed like the logical next step, to me.

"Didn't Karen tell you she doesn't want to move on?" he continued.

"Yes, but I don't think she knows what it means." I snorted. "She thought that I was going to exorcise her."

James frowned. I couldn't tell if he was going to continue arguing with me or explain, in horrible detail, what an exorcism really was.

"I just want more information," I said. "Before I tell her the options. Her real options. That's all."

"Hmm," James said. "So you're not just being snoopy?"

I stared at him, then laughed. "Well," I said. "There's a bit of that going on, too. Here's the deal. Lorraine Calloway needed to change her meeting. She's coming in tomorrow morning. It's in your day timer, but not in pen yet. Since you're now free this afternoon, I thought you'd want to come with me. Help me figure out this little mystery." I shrugged, theatrically. "Hey, I can go alone, if—"

"No," he said. "I'll come with you. And maybe we can go to the batting cages after Mrs. Calloway finally comes in for her meeting."

"Fine," I said, though I didn't know if it was fine or not. I wrote the address on a scrap of paper and tucked it into my pocket. "We taking the dog?"

"No," James said. "She needs a nap." He reached down and patted Millie on the head. She licked his fingers, and settled back into her bed in a tight ball, the tip of her nose tucked into her tail. She glared at me as I walked by, as though daring me to pet her. I didn't. Just closed the door and locked it, then ran down the stairs after James.

My heart pounded a little harder as I got into the passenger seat. This was my first real case if I didn't count the dog park girl. "I'm going to ask the questions, right?" I asked.

James backed out of the parking stall and pulled onto the street. "Absolutely," he said. "Unless I think you need help. You know?"

"I know," I replied. "Just don't jump in unless I really, actually need help. All right?"

"All right," he said.

He headed south. Karen's parents lived just off Ninety-Ninth Street, and it was only a few minutes before we were parked in front of their nondescript bungalow with two dying birch trees out front.

"How did you convince them to let you come and talk to them?" James asked.

"They still don't know what happened to their daughter," I said. "I think they'd like to think that someone still gives a crap after all this time."

"Hmm," James replied. "You're not going to tell them she's dead, are you?"

"Not without proof," I said. "Without the body, I have no proof. I need real information, and I'm going to start here."

He didn't look convinced, but I didn't care. I threw the car door open and walked up to the front door without waiting for him. I needed some information about Karen and her life. Not the bits and pieces I could find online.

I knocked, and the door opened almost instantly, like the person on the other side of the door had been waiting for me. I was certain it was Rupert Dubinsky, Karen's father. He looked ancient. Beaten to a grey shrivelled pulp by too much grief.

"You Marie Jenner?" he asked.

"Yes," I said, and tried to smile. My heart was hammering so hard against my rib cage I was certain he'd be able to hear it. "And this is—"

I turned, preparing to introduce James, but he was still by the car, locking up. "Hurry up!" I hissed, then turned back to Karen's father and smiled. "That's my partner," I said. "James Lavall."

Rupert watched James run up the walk to the front steps with no change of expression. "What is it you want?" he asked. "We haven't heard from the police about Karen for years. Years." A faint twitch shuddered around his eyes, as though he was thinking about crying but couldn't muster the energy. Then he frowned. "Who are you with? You're not reporters, are you? Because we don't talk to reporters anymore."

He hooked his hand on the door, preparing to close it. I stared at him, wanting desperately to say, "No, we're not reporters and we're not cops," but it was like my tongue was frozen.

Luckily, James sprang into action. "We aren't reporters, Mr. Dubinsky," he said. "The police have asked us to look into some of their cold cases and Karen's on our list. We just have a few questions, to confirm the information in her file."

Rupert's face whitened at James's words. "Why are the cops looking at her file—" His lips twisted around the word as though it tasted poisonous in his mouth. "Have they found her?"

"No sir," James said. "As I said, the police have asked us for help with cold cases, including your daughter's."

"Oh," Rupert said. He clutched the door jamb like he was about to fall down.

"Are you all right?" I asked, afraid that he was having a heart attack or something. "Do you need to sit?"

"I'm fine," he said gruffly. He took in a deep breath, and let it out. "What do the cops need from us?"

"Just confirmation on the facts of the case, sir," James said.

"Can we come in and talk to you?"

He turned away from the open door. He hadn't invited us in exactly, but the door was still ajar, so we silently followed him into the house.

"Working with the police?" I mouthed at him. "Are you crazy?"

"Just go with it," he whispered.

The kitchen was spotless and sun soaked. I almost felt like I needed sunglasses, everything shone so brightly.

"I suppose you want coffee," Rupert said.

"That would be great," James said. "Marie?"

"Yes," I said, and managed to plaster a smile on my face.

A door clattered open somewhere down the hall behind us, and Rupert jerked to attention, looking like he'd been caught in some sort of indiscretion. "That's the wife," he muttered. "She can't know why you're here. Say you're insurance people, will you? She can't know—"

He fell silent when his wife—who looked remarkably like an old, worn-out Karen—walked through the door. She did not smile. "Who are these people, Rue?" she asked, without looking at either James or me. "And why are they in my house?"

"They're—they're—" Rupert started speaking, but his voice suddenly failed him. I guess he found it a little harder to lie to his wife than we did to him. Luckily, James jumped into the breech.

"Mrs. Dubinsky, my name is James Lavall," he said, leaning past me, and holding his hand out to the woman. "And this is my associate, Marie Jenner. We are with Whitehall Insurance, and we're here to talk to you about your insurance needs."

"Oh God," Ethel Dubinsky said. "Are you kidding me?" She turned on her husband and snarled. "You let these leeches into our house. Our house?"

"It's just to insure the stuff in the garage," Rupert said weakly. "I have to get it covered, Ethel. You know that. They'll only be here for a moment. Just a quick cup of coffee and a talk and then they'll be gone. Promise."

"You know how I feel about insurance agents," she said, and her mouth quivered. "In my house."

"It's only for a minute," Rupert said again. He took her gently by the arm and led her out of the kitchen. "I promise."

We heard him get her settled in another room and then shut the door. He walked back into the kitchen looking years older than he had when he left, if that was possible.

"I thought she'd sleep through your visit," he said. "Sorry about that." He walked over to the cupboard and pulled out a jar of coffee. "I only got instant," he said. "Hope you don't mind."

"Would it be better if we came back at another time?" I asked.

The real reason I suggested rescheduling our meeting was that I wanted to get the heck out. I could feel Ethel's crazy oozing from every pore of that house and was having trouble dealing. But Rupert shook his head.

"No," he said. "You're here. We might as well get this over with." His eyes grew cold. "But you are not talking to my wife. Understand?"

"Yes," I said. "We understand."

James gave me the "what the hell are you saying" look, but I ignored him. I wasn't going to do anything to alienate Karen's father. Not when we were so close to getting some actual information about her and her life.

The house was so silent, I could hear a clock tick-tocking in another room. I jumped when Rupert turned on the faucet to run water into the kettle. He set the kettle on the stove and turned on the burner. The gas hissed and the ignitor click-clicked until the gas finally lit with a small whomp. He opened the old-fashioned cupboards and pulled out three cups. Two had Santa Claus embossed on them, and the third was covered in a photograph of Rupert, "Looking good at sixty" embossed in black beneath.

I glanced at James, hoping he'd be able to telepathically give me some good opening questions, but he was staring intently through the door into the next room. I tried to see what he was looking at, but couldn't tell what had caught his attention so completely.

The kettle began to sing, and Rupert turned it off. He poured the hot water into the cups and handed us each one. "Dope it as you see fit," he said, pointing to the middle of the kitchen table.

The instant coffee, sugar, and fake cream sat before us. I smiled, trying to make it seem as real as possible, under the circumstances. "Thank you, Mr. Dubinsky."

"It's no bother," he said gruffly. He held his cup—the one with his image on it—tightly in his work worn hands, as though warming them. "Now, what do you need to know?"

I opened my mouth to speak, not at all certain what was going to pop out, but James beat me to the punch.

"When was the last time you saw Karen?" he asked. I snapped my mouth shut, not certain whether to be angry at him for continuing to take over, or happy that I didn't have to think of the first, hard question.

Rupert looked over our heads for a long moment. I realized he hadn't added anything to the hot water in his cup. Just held it in his hands, warming them. "It was May fourth," he said. "The afternoon of May fourth. My wife's birthday. Almost a year to the day after she moved out of our place and got her own apartment." Rupert's mouth twisted. "And they fought—Ethel and Karen. About that damned job of Karen's, as usual." He looked up at us, and his eyes were so full of pain I felt sick. "Ethel doesn't celebrate her birthday anymore."

I couldn't think of one thing to say to that man. I glanced at James, and for once it looked like he was struck as dumb as I was.

"Isn't that all in her file?" Rupert said. "I—I don't think I want to go through everything again."

"I'm sorry if this is painful for you," James said. "But we need to corroborate the information. See what needs to be updated." He didn't look down at the file. "Where did she work?"

"The Coffee Factory," Rupert said. "We used to be friends with the owner and his wife—Len and Carol Wesson." He pulled his cup to his lips and slurped. Swallowed and sighed. "They gave her the job after she finished school. We thought she could work there while she took some time to think about things. You know."

"I understand," James said. I didn't, and frowned.

"What did she need to think about?" I asked.

"What she was going to do with the rest of her life," Rupert said. "Things kinda blew up for her, after graduation."

"How?"

"She decided that plans needed to change," he said, after a small silence. "That's all."

"Thank you," James said, then threw a glance at me.

"Do you have anything from her apartment?" I asked. "Anything you've saved?"

James blinked, and Rupert jumped as though I'd stuck him with a cattle prod. "Her stuff?" he finally asked.

"Yes," I said.

Rupert stared at me for a long moment, then shook his head.

"No," he said shortly. "Ethel got rid of everything after the reporters were here. For that article they wrote, last year."

The article I'd found online. About the fortieth anniversary of Karen's disappearance.

We sat for a moment. Then James pointed past Rupert and into the next room. "That photograph," he said. "When was it taken?"

Rupert swung his big frame around in the chair, causing it to creak. "That's her grad picture. A year before she—disappeared."

"Who's the person in the picture with her?" James asked.

By that time, I was burning with curiosity. "Do you mind if I have a look?" I asked and stood.

"Go ahead," Rupert said. "Just keep it quiet. The wife's room is down that hallway."

"I will, I promise," I said. I walked up to the doorway and looked into the living room. Old-fashioned furniture was scattered about, with an equally old-fashioned CRV television parked against the far wall, but I paid it very little attention, because I couldn't take my eyes away from the photographs on the wall above the overstuffed couch.

They were all of Karen. Karen as a baby. Karen as a little girl, playing with a small black dog. Karen sitting unsmiling on Santa's lap, cheeks bright red from crying. Karen as a gawky teenager, staring into a huge bonfire, wearing the most godawful striped shirt and blue jeans with huge, billowing bottoms. *Bellbottoms*, I thought. *They were called bellbottoms*.

But it was the photograph of Karen in a long dress, hair pulled back with flowers in her hair, that caught my attention. She was half smiling, but it didn't touch her eyes, and she was leaning away from the boy standing next to her. He had a big goofy grin on his face and was wearing an incredibly ugly bright green velvety-looking suit.

I guessed that was the photograph James had been asking about. It was much larger than all the others, framed in an ornate but cheap-looking gold frame.

"Yes," I said. "Who is that with Karen?"

"It's Bobby. Bobby Kimble," Rupert said. "At their graduation. They were going to get married after, but it didn't work out."

Wondering just how their relationship hadn't worked and whether that had anything to do with Karen being stuck at a softball diamond on Edmonton's south side, I reached out to touch the frame. Well, straighten it, really. It was just off kilter, and it was driving me crazy. But I didn't get a chance to touch it.

"Get away from that!" Ethel screamed. She'd crept out of her room while I was staring at the pictures. She ran down the hallway and grabbed me hard by the arm. "Get away from her! Now!"

"I'm sorry," I said, trying to figure out a way to get her to disengage without damaging her. I'd learned how in those defence classes I'd taken, but most of them involved breaking fingers and such, and I really didn't want to hurt her. She'd been hurt enough. "Please let me go."

I jerked my arm away from her hand, flinching when her nails scratched across my bare skin.

"Get out of my house," she shrieked. "Both of you, now!" Then, she burst into tears and threw herself on the overstuffed couch.

"I think it's time for you to go," Rupert said. He sounded suddenly and absolutely exhausted. "If you need any more information, give me a call."

"I will not allow them to call this house," Ethel cried from the living room.

"Understood," he said. He pointed to the front door and then followed us out.

"Call my cell," he whispered, handing James a business card. "If you find out anything."

"Will do," James said. "And I'm sorry we upset your wife."

"Having our daughter drop off the face of the earth upset my wife," Rupert said. "And it's not going to get any better until we find out what happened. So, no matter what, give me a call if you learn anything."

"Will do."

"Anything at all."

"Understood."

He shut the door, but we could still hear Ethel sobbing into the big overstuffed pillows of the old-fashioned couch. I almost felt like asking Rupert if he wanted to come with us, just to get him away from all the pain. But I didn't.

"God," I said as we drove away. "That was horrible."

"What did you expect?" James asked.

"I thought—I don't know what I thought . . . " My voice

winnowed down to nothing. Karen's parents didn't know that she'd died. Didn't know where her bones were. Hadn't had a chance to put her to rest. They'd been living in limbo for over forty years. And it looked like limbo was their own personal form of hell.

"Karen has to know that her family needs closure, so they can finally move on even if she isn't willing to."

"With any luck we'll be able to give them some," James said. He put the car into gear and drove away from Karen's family home. "But first, we have to find that guy in the photograph."

"The guy in the horrible green velvet suit?" I asked. "Bobby Kimble?"

"That's the one," he said. "I think we need to find out what he knows."

I HAD TO see my shrink, so James dropped me off in front of Dr. Parkerson's building.

"You want me to pick you up?" he asked.

"Nah," I said. "I'll take the bus and catch up with you at the office."

I headed into the office building and up to the fourteenth floor. My appointment was at 4:30, and at 4:18 I was sitting in her waiting room, waiting.

I was by myself which did not surprise me. To be honest, it would have shocked me if anyone else had been there. I was supposed to have her attention, solely and completely, for fifty minutes, starting at 4:31.

Someone else in that waiting room would have meant that I had to share my time—share my shrink—with someone else. When I first started, I thought it would have been just fine to share her with someone else, so her focus wasn't so absolutely and completely on me, but I found that I had those thoughts less and less.

She was mostly non-threatening. Distant, which was probably for the best, but approachable enough that she hadn't scared me off in those first few visits. It would have been easy for her to do, because I was a wreck after my mother died, and I got worse when she didn't come back to me.

I couldn't tell the shrink that, of course, because that would have made her think I was crazy, and I wasn't crazy. I was deeply in grief and suffering from PTSD, due in no small part to being kidnapped and then having to save my kidnapper's life after she tried, unsuccessfully, to blow her brains out in front of me.

Dr. Parkerson had offered me a whole array of drugs on my first visit. Antidepressants, sleeping pills, the works. I told her no thank you.

"I want to work this out drug-free," I said.

"It will be easier with the drugs," she'd replied, but hadn't pushed. Not really.

She'd ask me how I was sleeping. About the nightmares, and the panic attacks, and the headaches. I'd say they were getting a little bit better, and then she'd offer me the pills. And I'd say no thank you.

Then, there was the experiment with IRT.

IRT. Imagery Rehearsal Therapy. She'd suggested it as a course of treatment soon after I started going to her. I was supposed to come up with better endings for my nightmares, and then replay them, over and over, until the nightmares didn't have any power over me.

I'd tried it once, thought it was stupid, and didn't do it again, even though she suggested a few times, ever more strongly, that I really needed to give it a chance.

I think I surprised her when I actually took her advice about exercise seriously. First with the self-defence classes, and then with softball. But throughout, she kept offering the drugs. And I'd say no every time, even though not sleeping and the nightmares when I did were getting old. Really old.

I picked up a magazine and stared at the cover without seeing it, waiting for the door to open and her to say, "Come on in, Marie. I'm ready for you now."

I looked at the time on my phone and then shut it off. I tucked it into the pocket of my hoodie, then sat with the magazine in my lap, forgotten, thinking about nothing until it was my turn to spill my guts all over her beige Berber carpet.

But nothing about ghosts. Never anything about ghosts.

DR. PARKERSON CONVINCED me to stay in softball, just like Jasmine said she would. I said I would. I think she was so pleased that she didn't offer me drugs. Just set up my next appointment in two weeks' time and asked me to reconsider the IRT. One more time. Please.

    I said I would, but forgot about it by the time I reached the bus stop.

Karen:
Making Joanne Feel Better, for Some Reason

JOANNE SHOWED UP at Diamond Two the next day, looking like hell. She stood by the edge of the diamond and stared at me until I reluctantly walked over to her.

"What happened to you last night?" I asked. "Kelly caught, so you can guess how the game went."

"Sorry," Joanne said. She stared down at her feet. "I just couldn't take being here while that—person—was hanging around, staring at us. You know?"

She spat out the word person like it was the worst possible swearword she could think of. Maybe it was.

"You coming back to play?" I asked.

"I don't know," she said. "We gotta do something about—"

"Marie," I said shortly. "Her name's Marie."

"Whatever," Joanne said. "Just as long as we run her off, for good this time—"

"I don't think that's going to happen," I said. "She didn't cause us any problems last night—"

"You mean to tell me she stayed?" Joanne's voice wound up, tight and angry, until it was almost out of hearing range. "She stayed, and watched, and got to know everyone . . . "

"She didn't get to know everyone," I snapped. "She just watched the game. Like everyone else. What the hell is your problem with her, Joanne?"

"I told you!" she cried. "She's gonna exorcise us all. We'll be gone. Gone!"

"She's not going to do anything like that," I said.

"What, did she promise that she wouldn't?" Joanne snapped. "Fuck, you're as stupid as everyone else. You can't trust the living. Why can't you get that?"

"Whatever, Joanne," I said, and shrugged. "Does this mean you won't be playing anymore?"

"What?" Joanne looked stricken. "I never said that. I just said—"

"Marie's going to stay," I said. "And the rest of us are going to play. If you can't handle that, then I guess you're done."

"But—"

"Done." I turned away from her so I didn't have to see the anguish on her face. I watched the two living men cut the grass and waited for Joanne to disappear.

It took her a long time. I could almost feel her eyes on me, but then the air lightened, and she was gone.

I hoped Mr. Kelly and Mr. Middleton would show up early, because I needed to talk to them. Joanne was going to be a real problem, and I figured they were the only two who could get her under control.

It was going to be a long day. Of that, I was certain.

Mr. Middleton showed up just before the second living game started and hunched his way up into the bleachers, settling directly behind home plate, so he could see every pitch.

"Karen!" he called, when he had himself properly settled. "Come up and keep an old man company."

I glanced up to see if Andrew was still in his seat. He was. Thought for a moment about asking Mr. Middleton to come to me and then let it go and went up and sat beside him. For a while, we just stared out at the diamond as the living warmed up.

"Did they rake the infield?" he asked. His usual question.

I nodded. "And they pulled some of the weeds by the backstop."

"Good. It was starting to look unkempt." He glanced over at me. "So, what about the Joanne situation?"

"Right to it," I said and smiled. "She showed up today."

"That's good," he replied. "She needs to get back in the game.

It's good for her well-being."

"Joanne's well-being?" I snorted laughter. "She doesn't have a ton of that, even when she does play."

"She's better than she was, Karen. You remember what she was like when she first showed up?"

"I do," I said, and shook my head. "She was a real mess."

"That she was," he said. "And now—"

"Now, she's still trying to run off a living human being, just because she can see us," I said. I could hear the anger in my voice and tried to tone it down. Mr. Middleton did not respond well to anger. "I mean, what are we supposed to do with that?"

"We can be understanding," Mr. Middleton replied. "And give her the space to get over whatever's bothering her."

"Marie's bothering her," I said. "And Joanne won't get over anything until she's gone."

"Any chance of that?" I could hear the hopefulness in Mr. Middleton's voice and sighed. It wasn't just Joanne who continued to be shaken by Marie's presence at the ball diamond.

"I don't think so," I said.

He sighed and shrugged. "So we have to come up with another plan. Something that will mollify Joanne. Get her back on the diamond, and playing."

"Are you and Mr. Kelly still betting on the games?" I asked, half-joking. "Is that why you want her back?"

"She's a good ball player," Middleton said, his voice stiff. "You know that."

"So you are," I said. "Betting, I mean."

"What of it?" he said, then laughed. "All right, so you caught me. But you know the games are better when she's playing."

He was right about that. No matter how crazy she was, she was a good back catcher. "So what do we do?" I asked.

"We convince her that there is nothing to fear," he said.

I stared out at the empty diamond. "How the hell do we do that?" I finally asked.

"Watch the language, girl," Middleton said.

"Sorry. What can we do?"

"We'll talk to the rest of the players and come up with a plan," he said. Then he frowned and pointed at the pitching rubber. "Does that look crooked to you?"

That let me know that the Joanne conversation was over for

the moment. But as I discussed with him whether or not the chunk of rubber nailed to the ground that the pitchers used to push off when they threw was crooked—and it was—I knew that we weren't finished. Not by a long shot.

THE DEAD DRIFTED in as the live game slowly played out. I saw Joanne by the far fence, talking with Rita Danworth. She pointedly ignored me, looking everywhere but in my direction.

Mr. Middleton called the meeting before the game, assembling everyone behind the bleachers as the last of the living left the diamond and the lights blinked dark.

"We need to talk," he said. "About the Marie situation."

"Damn straight we do," Joanne said. "Gotta get rid of that bitch, pronto." She glared at me, the first time she'd looked at me since her return. "Just because some of us have gone soft on the living, doesn't mean we need to take any more chances."

"She hasn't done anything, Joanne," I said. "She just wants to play ball."

"All right, that's enough," Mr. Middleton intoned, holding his hands out for silence. "We have to decide—as a group—how to deal with this—person."

"Well, the swarming idea didn't work at all," Lisa said. "It was just embarrassing."

"Rita thinks that she might be able to do more damage with a little more practice," Joanne said.

"That's not what I said," Rita mumbled. Joanne ignored her.

"I think we need to try again," she said. "And soon."

"Oh, this is ridiculous!" I cried. "She isn't going to do anything to us. Can't you understand that?"

Voices raised all around me. Some agreed with me, but many of them didn't. Joanne's fear was infecting them again. I could tell.

"That's enough!" Mr. Middleton yelled. "Be quiet, all of you!"

That stopped the noise. Even Joanne's mouth snapped shut, though she looked like she was ready to start foaming at the mouth.

"You are not going to swarm her again. Do you hear me? It didn't work, and nothing will convince me that a repeat will help." He turned, and glared at Joanne. "You hear me?"

"I hear you," Joanne said. Her voice sounded strangled, like she was choking on her words. But the rest, those who had agreed with her, quieted.

"I've been giving this situation some careful thought," Middleton continued. "And I believe I may have a solution. I say we shun her."

"What?" Joanne's voice sounded high and tight. I glanced at her and estimated about two seconds before she completely blew her top. "What?"

"Shun her," Middleton said again. "My guess is, she'll tire of us, and eventually go away." He clicked his tongue. "I hear she's not that good, anyhow. Probably won't last the season."

"I don't know about that," Lisa said. "I watched her last game. She has good instincts. Just needs a little direction."

"Well, she's not getting that from us," Mr. Middleton said. "In fact, she'll get nothing from us. Any of us." He stared at me for a long, long moment and then looked at Joanne.

"What say you, Joanne?" Mr. Middleton asked. "If we shun her, will you come back and play ball?"

"I guess," she said. "I don't think it will work, and I think we'll need a backup plan. But I'll do my part, Mr. Middleton. You can count on me."

"I knew I could," Mr. Middleton said and smiled at her. There was genuine warmth there, and I wondered what it was about Joanne that he found so endearing. "So ladies, are we all agreed?"

A chorus of "Ayes!" from everyone except me. I looked at them, surprised. They'd all talked to Marie after the swarming. Treated her decently enough. Why were they going along with this plan?

Then Mr. Middleton looked at me. "Do you agree, Karen?"

There was total silence all around me as I stared at him and then at the others. No one would make eye contact with me, and I realized that they wanted Joanne to stay more than they cared about the living. I had the feeling that they blamed me for the situation we were all in. After all, I was the first one to see Marie. Interact with her. I guess that made it my fault, somehow.

I still felt badly about what we'd done to Marie, and about what we were going to do to her, but I needed softball more than I needed her.

And who knew? This might be exactly what Marie wanted. For us to just leave her alone. All alone.

"All right, Mr. Middleton," I said. "We can try it. But everyone else has to do it, too. Including you." I pointed at Joanne, and she snarled at me like she wished she could tear me apart.

"We'll all do it," Mr. Middleton said. "And now, if we are all agreed, it's about time we play a little ball."

Everyone cheered and broke for the diamond, and soon the game was on.

I don't know about the rest, but it felt good to be playing again. I didn't have to think about anything. Could just concentrate on the ball and the base runners. Just be a little faster, a little smarter, than the other team, for seven innings.

I knew once the game was over, I'd have to think long and hard about what we'd all agreed to, because I didn't mind Marie. It was going to be hard, shunning her. But I'd do it. I'd agreed to the plan, after all. And these were my people. My family.

Not Marie. She was alive. Not one of us.

I had to remember that.

Marie:
Sergeant Worth Wants to Talk

OVER THE NEXT couple of days, James worked on his own cases and when I had the time, I worked on the Karen Dubinsky file. Wrote out some notes from what I remembered of meeting Karen's father. Considered, briefly, calling Missing Persons to see if they had any more information they were willing to share, but decided against it. They'd talk to Sergeant Worth, and she didn't need to know what I was up to. As far as I was concerned, she was as involved in my life as she was ever going to be.

Then, I called Bobby Kimble to set up a meeting with him for the next day.

"Call me Rob," he said. "I haven't gone by Bobby in years." Then he asked the question I was starting to dread. "Do you have news? About Karen?"

"No," I said. "We're working on cold cases. Karen's is one of them."

"Oh," he said. "I was kinda hoping."

"I'm sorry," I said. And I was. I was raking up all this old pain, and for what? Closure for her friends and family? Was it going to be worth it for them? After all, there was no happy ending to this story.

I might have started out just wanting to get her out of my way, but now, after talking to her family, I realized I had to talk to Karen and let her know just how much her family was still suffering because of her disappearance. Maybe, even if she didn't want to move on, she could be convinced to tell me where her body was. That would be something for her family, at least.

I can talk to her at the next game, I thought. *Start the process.*

I should have realized that wasn't going to be as easy as that. Whatever is?

I CONVINCED JAMES not to come to my game that night. My team was going to be playing the Chimo Angels—Sergeant Worth's team—and I decided it would be better for me if the two of them did not interact at my game. As far as I was concerned, it would be better if they never interacted, but Worth had taken an interest in James's agency, so it was hard to keep them apart. But I could do my bit at my game, at the very least.

James was a little hurt since he had no work that night, but said he understood. Millie the comfort dog looked pretty happy, though. She settled on his lap in front of the TV as I left, so I decided not to feel too terrible about not letting him come. There were lots of games left in the season. Missing one wouldn't kill him.

The game was at seven and I did everything I could to get to Diamond Two without a minute to spare. I didn't want to chat with her beforehand, or anything else. She got me on the team, but that didn't mean we were going to be friends or anything.

Funny, actually. I wasn't as worried about the ghost on second base as I was about a living person on the other team.

Karen looked surprised to see me and maybe a little disappointed, like she'd hoped that perhaps I wouldn't have bothered coming back. Then she turned away from me, and stared at the opposition's dugout.

It was obviously going to be harder to talk to her than I'd hoped.

I saw Sergeant Worth and waved weakly at her as I dove into my dugout and pulled on my cleats.

"You're late," Greg said.

"Sorry." I whacked my glove against my thigh a couple of times to get rid of some of the dust. "Had to work late."

"Well, I don't have enough players to sit you. Get out there, but know I am displeased."

He didn't sound particularly angry, but I still felt a twinge of guilt. "I really am sorry," I said.

"Really?" He looked surprised, then smiled and patted my arm. "Forget it," he said. "That's just something I say. Trust me, nobody else on the team worries about being late."

"Oh, we do," Jamie the back catcher said. "We just don't let you know. Otherwise you'd use it against us. You know, to get us here on time."

"Or to practice," Lily, the pitcher, said. "You'd probably want us to practice."

"Practice would actually be good," Greg said wistfully. "Do you know how much better you'd be as a team if you—"

"See, this is the reason we act like we don't care," Jamie said. "We can't allow you to use guilt on us."

"All right, fine," Greg sighed. "Get out there, and make me proud."

"One for the Gipper?" Lily laughed.

"Sure," Greg replied. "What the heck. One for the Gipper."

THE GAME WENT well, all things considered. I got on base twice and didn't screw up too badly in the outfield. Sergeant Worth got on base once, but didn't make it past second. Seeing her stand beside Karen gave me the heebie-jeebies.

Karen steadfastly ignored her, the way she did most of the live players. Just watched the game from her spectacularly good seat and ignored us all. Me included.

After the game, my team talked about going for a beer and a chat, and I was trying to figure out a nice way to say no when an oh too familiar voice floated into the dugout.

"Marie?" Sergeant Worth called. "Marie Jenner. You still here?"

She knew very well I was still there. I thought about ignoring her, felt every one of my team mates staring at me, and sighed.

"Hi," I said. I threw my glove into my outsized bag and zipped it closed, hoping it sounded decisive.

"Can I talk to you for a second?" she asked.

Yay.

More stares and a few whispers as my team tried to figure out what the deal was while I studiously avoided their eyes, because it was none of their damned business.

"Sure," I said. I pointed to the doorway of the dugout. "Meet you by the gate."

I threw the bag over my shoulder and pushed my way through the gaggle of women. "Gotta go," I said, as lightly and fluffily as I could. "See you next week."

"So no beer?" Stacey asked. She almost sounded sorry that I wasn't coming with them.

"Sorry," I said. "I gotta talk to her, and then I have to go back to work."

A small lie about work, but whatever. Stacey shrugged.

"Maybe next week," she said. "Because we do beer and a chat after most games. Just so you know."

I smiled at her, and she smiled back. Seemed genuine.

"I'll remember," I said, and then I was free.

Well, not really free. I still had to run the gauntlet that was Sergeant Worth.

SHE WAS LEANING on the fence, staring out at the ball diamond as two more teams warmed up for the late game. She snapped to attention when I shuffled up to her and dropped my bag at her feet.

"Good game," she said. "Looks like Greg likes you."

"Thanks," I said. I leaned against the fence beside her and watched the pitcher warm up. Miriam Kendel and her wicked rise ball. "I don't know how much he actually likes me, though. I think it's more that he only has the nine players most of the time."

"Oh no," Worth said, shaking her head. "He looks happy."

I blinked as I thought about that, because to be honest, the coach looked more like a chronically depressed basset hound than anything else to me. "That's happy?"

"As happy as he gets," Worth said. She turned and looked at me. "So, you enjoying yourself?"

I thought for a second and then nodded.

"Good," Worth said. "I'm glad."

She was silent again, so I went back to watching Miriam warm up as I waited for her to tell me what she really wanted to talk about. It wasn't ball. I knew that at the very least.

But she said nothing. Just stared, silently, into the outfield.

Jesus. I realized that if I didn't get things going conversation-wise, we'd end up standing here the whole night, watching another game.

"So, you wanted to talk to me?" I sounded a little snarlier than I should have, but I needed to get the conversation moving. I didn't want to stay at the diamond too long. Didn't want to get sucked into watching another dead game, to be honest, because I still wasn't sure how I felt about all the ghosts. "What about?"

I played out a bunch of different scenarios in my head as I waited for her to answer. "Let's be best friends." Or, "I've decided you shouldn't be playing softball anymore." Or the more than famous, "We need to talk about your mother." But it wasn't any of that.

"Got time for coffee?" she asked. "I have a problem, and I think you can help me."

I so dearly wanted to say no. Tell that little white "I have to go back to work," lie. But I didn't. All I said was, "Is Tim's good enough?"

She said yes.

"Want a ride?" I asked.

"No. I'll follow you. I only have a few minutes. I have to go back to work. But we really need to talk. You're the only one I know who can help me."

Huh.

THE TIM HORTONS was a couple of short blocks away from John Fry Park, and it was always busy on the nights softball played. Sergeant Worth and I both managed to find a couple of parking spaces and then stood in line, uncomfortably silent, as we waited for the line to snake up to the counter so we could order.

I considered trying some small talk, but shook off the fleeting thought as foolish. I didn't do small talk very well at the best of times, and small talking with Sergeant Worth was definitely not the best of times. Luckily, the line moved quickly, and soon we were seated at a table surrounded by chattering families and groups of old men all enjoying the hell out of their Tim Hortons experience.

Me? Not so much.

I played with the top of my to-go cup as Worth mucked around with her herbal tea—dunking the teabag and staring at the hot water, then dunking again—until I thought I'd lose my mind.

"What do you want to talk about?" I asked. "You said you didn't have much time."

"Yeah." Worth sighed and pulled the teabag from her cup. She took a sip and looked very much like she wanted to spit out what was in her mouth.

"What's wrong?" I asked.

"I hate this crap," she said. "But my blood pressure's through the frigging roof right now, so my doctor's cut me off coffee."

I stared down at my cup, trying to imagine a world without coffee. Looked back up at her. "That sucks."

"More than you can possibly know," she said, and pushed the herbal tea away. "At least my head doesn't feel like it's going to explode all the time now, though. So, I guess that's good."

She didn't look like she thought it was good. She looked like she thought it sucked lukewarm crappola. Which it did.

We sat for a couple of uncomfortable minutes, then she sighed, and looked at me. "A friend of mine from Calgary called me looking for people to play in a tournament," she said. "Is it all right that I gave them your name?"

This was what she'd dragged me to Tim Hortons to talk about? Playing for another team?

"I suppose," I said. "But I'm not very good."

She looked at me intently and almost smiled. "I think you have exactly the skills my friend needs," she said. "She'll call you about it, soon."

"All right," I said. "Thanks for thinking of me." I pushed my coffee cup back and prepared to stand.

"Oh, we're not done," Sergeant Worth said. "Not even close." She glanced around, as though checking to see if anyone was listening to our conversation, then looked back to me. "I have a problem," she whispered. "And I want you to help me with it."

I honestly thought she was going to try to talk me into doing something edging toward illegal for her through the detective agency. You know, James and I breaking into some place and getting some information for her to help her solve a big case, or something.

Was I ever wrong.

She whispered, so low I could barely make out what she was saying. "I'm being haunted. And I want you to help me."

I couldn't have heard her right. "You're being what?"

She looked suddenly furious and glanced around again. When she turned back to me, I could see a vein pulsing in her forehead.

"I am being haunted," she said again. "You know? Haunted?"

It was my turn to look around. This was not a conversation I wanted to be having in a crowded coffee shop. To be honest, it was not a conversation I wanted to have with Sergeant Worth at all.

"Did you say you're being haunted?" I whispered back.

"Yes," she hissed.

"By a ghost."

"Yes. Jesus. Keep your voice down." She looked around a third time, the vein pulsing harder.

"Maybe we should go outside. You know. Away from all these people."

"No." She wiped her forehead and took in a gasping breath. "No, this is fine. Just keep your voice down."

"'Kay."

Another brief silence as we both thought about things. The things I was thinking about included getting up and running away, but before I could act on it, Worth leaned forward again, her face haggard.

"I know about you, and your mother. About your abilities."

"Did Officer Tyler tell you that?" I asked, my voice high and tight. He was a cop from Fort McMurray. He had known my mother, thought he knew me, and he never could keep his mouth shut. "He's full of crap, just so you know."

"All he did was confirm what I knew. Word got around, before. About your mother. She helped someone from our department—a cold case—and that's how I heard about her. And you. So, you can drop the act. I know you can work with ghosts."

I figured I had two choices. Get up, flounce out, and then change every aspect of my life that this woman knew—which was absolutely everything—and start over again. That would be exhausting, and might not even work, what with her being a cop and all. So, I decided to pick choice number two. Act like an adult for once and hear her out.

"Tell me what happened," I said.

She smiled. I think she was trying to look triumphant, but she just looked sad. "I figured fate dropped you in my lap," she said. "Rory—a guy I was close to—died a couple of months before I met you. At first, he was just gone. You know? But then, he showed up. At my apartment."

I stared at her, shocked. The exhaustion, the low-grade sadness that seemed to permeate her very soul suddenly made sense. She was being haunted. Of course.

"You mean his spirit," I said.

"What?"

Jesus, now I was whispering so softly she couldn't hear me. We deserved each other, we really did.

"His spirit showed up in your apartment," I said.

"Yes."

"And you can see him?" Doubtful, but I had to ask.

"No."

"Then how do you know it's him?"

"Because I can smell his aftershave." She shuddered. "The apartment gets cold, and then I can smell his aftershave. He never shows up when my kids are there, thank God, but he's there when I'm alone." She shook her head and grabbed her cup of tepid herbal tea. Took a huge gulp and swallowed. "It used to be nice. Like I still had him with me. But now. Now, I hate going home."

"I take it Rory didn't die there?"

"No." She looked at me, her eyes hard. "Why?"

"Usually spirits stay close to their place of death. Or to their bodies." I tried to smile, but stopped when I caught a reflection of myself in the huge window behind Worth. I looked like I was having some sort of spasm. I really did. "You don't have his ashes, do you? Because you might be able to get him to leave if you bury them."

"No." Her face tightened. "He wasn't cremated. His parents took him—home. To Saskatchewan. Somewhere. They buried him there."

"Then he probably feels he has something to tell you," I said. "That's another big reason for a spirit to cling to a person or a place."

"Jesus," Worth said. Her voice sounded full of something like awe. "You really do know this stuff, don't you?"

"Yeah," I said, and sighed. "Yeah, I really do. When can I come over?"

"What?"

"If I'm going to move his spirit on, I need to meet him," I said. "That means me coming to your place. When can I come over?"

She looked down at the table top for a long, slow moment. That was when I realized that the coffee shop had grown quiet, as though every person in the place was listening to our conversation.

"Would Saturday night be too soon?" she asked. "I gotta work every other night this week."

I tried to remember if I had anything planned for Saturday evening but I'd left my phone in the car and wasn't about to scamper out to get it. It would be too easy to drive away.

"Sounds good," I said, deciding on the fly that I could move whatever else was on my schedule. Besides, getting this over with sooner rather than later was the best I could hope for. She gave me her West-end address. I wrote it down on a slightly used napkin and tucked it into my pocket. "Seven o'clock all right?"

"That'll be fine," she said, and then frowned. "Do you need me to pick up anything?"

I blinked. "Like what?" I finally asked.

"Oh hell, I don't know," she said. "I just thought maybe you needed like incense and stuff. For the process. Maybe a Ouija board? Want me to get my sister's? So you can communicate with him?"

"You didn't try using a Ouija board, did you?" I snapped.

"No," she said, shaking her head far too emphatically. She was lying.

"Really?"

"Well, once. It didn't work. My sister brought it over and we tried it out, but nothing happened." She shook her head and laughed guiltily. "We drank a lot of wine, though, so we might not have done it right. Do you think that's what happened? That we didn't do it right?"

"Jesus." Most times those boards were nothing more than a children's game or a parlour trick, but if there was a spirit already present they could be turned into beacons for other stray spirits. Especially when drunken idiots open the lines of communication. "Get rid of it, tonight."

She looked confused. "I think my sister took it home with her."

"Call your sister. Tell her to burn it."

"Really?" She looked incredulous and I didn't blame her. To be honest, I wasn't sure burning the thing would actually help but I wasn't taking any chances. I was dealing with enough ghosts as it was.

"Seriously. She has to burn it or I will not help you."

Worth's face spasmed. "Understood."

We were both silent a moment more, and I was relieved to hear that the noise level in the coffee shop had returned to normal.

Nothing to see here, folks. Move along.

"You going to want something to eat?" Worth asked.

I blinked. "Now?"

"No," she said, impatiently. "I meant Saturday night. You going to want supper or something?"

The last thing in the world I wanted was to have a meal with this woman. "No," I said. "I won't need to eat."

"'Cause if you do, just let me know," she continued as though she hadn't heard me speak. "I'll pick up a pizza or something."

God. She wanted to have a meal with me.

I sighed. "No," I said as gently as I could.

"Are you sure?" Her need was so great, it practically oozed from every pore. "Are you sure it'll really be all right?"

"Yes." I got up and grabbed my mostly full lukewarm coffee. A large to go, absolutely wasted. "Yes, everything will be all right. I'll see you tomorrow."

I left. When I pulled the car out of its parking spot, I could see her, still at the table, her cold herbal tea sitting before her, forgotten.

I forgot about going back and talking to Karen. Forgot about everything except getting as far away from there as I could.

What the hell had I just agreed to?

JAMES HAD COFFEE waiting for me when I brought his car back to his apartment.

"Tell me everything," he said.

So I did. Of course, I didn't tell him about the ball game, which was what he was expecting. I told him about Sergeant Worth's ghost.

"So now she wants me to go over to her place—her place, James!—and get rid of her old boyfriend. Just because Officer Tyler couldn't keep his frigging mouth shut about my mother. And me." I set down my cup and looked at him. "What am I going to do?"

I was hoping he'd tell me to drop it. "Just call her up and tell her that you can't help," I desperately hoped he'd say. "You have a job. A paying job. Leave the ghost foolishness to others."

He didn't, of course. He grinned like a maniac.

"Wow," he said, and shook his head. "Wow wow wow . . ."

"You're not helping," I snapped. "I couldn't think of an easy way to let her down, so now I'm committed. What should I do?"

"I guess you should go to her place and meet this ghost," he said. "Can I come?"

"What?" I glared at him. "No! What's wrong with you? You can't come."

He looked disappointed. "Are you sure? It could be fun."

"None of this is fun, James."

"Some of it is."

"No. It's not."

"All right. Quit yelling."

I snapped my mouth shut when I realized he was right. I was yelling.

"Sorry," I said. "This is just so inconvenient, you know?"

"They do seem to find you, don't they? First, all the ghosts at the ball diamond, and now this."

I sighed. "They sure do."

"Maybe this is the beginning of something good for you," he said.

I stared at him. "What do you mean?"

"Well, if the ghosts are coming to you, maybe there is an opportunity here that you're not seeing." He leaned forward and smiled. He still looked fairly maniacal but at least he wasn't saying "wow" anymore. "A business opportunity, if you know what I mean."

"What business opportunity? There are just a buttload of ghosts—"

"All right, so maybe the ghosts at the ball diamond aren't helpful—"

"Helpful? Helpful?"

Millie barked once, from her dog bed. A warning to me that I was yelling again.

"How do you think any of this is helpful, James?" I asked, my voice still high and tight, but not quite as loud as it had been a moment before.

"Well, maybe there's a way for you to be compensated for your time," he said. "What if you tell Sergeant Worth she has to pay you to get rid of her dead boyfriend. Think that would work?"

That stopped me. I leaned back and stared at him.

"Are you going to start yelling again?" he asked. "Because you look like—"

"No." I considered. "Pretty sure I'm not."

"Good." He smiled. "So, what do you think? Want to charge Sergeant Worth for getting rid of her dead boyfriend?"

"That might be an idea," I said. "If I tell her I'm going to charge her, I don't know, like a thousand dollars or something, maybe she'd let me off the hook."

"What?" The smile faded from his face. "No. No. That's not what I meant. I meant—"

"I know what you meant," I said, and smiled. "But this is better. I'll tell her that she has to pay me a thousand dollars, or I can't help her. She won't want to pay that much. Heck, nobody would. She'll drop it, and I'll be off the hook. Jesus, James, that might work. Thank you!"

He blinked. "You're welcome, I guess."

I stretched, and the tension in my shoulders eased. I yawned, and my jaw cracked. "I'll give her a call in the morning, before I head out to see Bobby Kimble."

"Who?"

"Bobby Kimble. Karen's ex-boyfriend. I called him and set up a meet. You don't mind if I borrow the car again, do you?"

"Sure," he said. "Want me to come with?"

"I'd love it, James," I said. He was much better at questioning people than I was, and I could use all the help I could get.

"Great." He picked up our empty cups and carried them to the sink. "So, am I taking you to Jasmine's now, or can I convince you to stay here?"

"I think you can convince me to stay."

"Good." He walked back to the table and took me by the hand. "Very good. That'll give me time to grill you about the ball game."

"Seriously?" I stood and stepped into his arms. "That's all you can think of? The ball game?"

"No," he said, and pulled me close. "But I can multi-task."

He was right. He could.

Dying on Second

THE PHONE CALL to Sergeant Worth the next morning didn't go quite the way I'd hoped it would. I mentioned money and she said how much. I said a thousand dollars—because in the light of day it still sounded like a huge sum of money—and she said yes without a second's thought.

"Are—are you sure?" I asked, hoping she'd back down. Hoping she'd tell me to forget it. That a thousand dollars was too much. That it was all a joke. A horrible, horrible joke.

"Absolutely," she said. "See you Saturday."

Then the line went dead. She'd hung up on me, and now I was really, truly committed.

"Crap," I whispered, and dropped the receiver of the office phone. "Crap, crap, crap."

"I told you she'd go for it!" James called from his office.

Shut up, James. Just shut up.

Marie:
Meeting Bobby Kimble

LATER THAT AFTERNOON, James and I drove up the driveway to the farm just outside Edmonton where Bobby Kimble—Karen's boyfriend from high school—lived. The house looked old, like it had been there forever. Next to it was a newer bungalow, and next to that was a garage. A garage like a mechanic would use.

James shut off the car, and we heard banging and crashing from within the garage.

I looked at James. "Think it's safe?"

James laughed. "Not all garages are dangerous, you know."

I thought back to the garage where I'd escaped from the drug gang. Felt like that had happened a million years ago. But still, I jumped with every metallic bang.

"Sometimes they are," I muttered. James's face stilled.

"Yeah," he said. "Sometimes they are. Want me to go in? You can wait here if you'd rather."

"No, no," I said. Just having him tell me I could opt out made me feel brave enough to face whatever was going on in that building. In control. "I'll come with you. I want to meet this guy."

Bobby Kimble was hammering a dent out of the door panel of a big old three-quarter ton truck that had obviously seen a lot more actual work than any of the trucks roaming around the streets of Edmonton. The years had been pretty good to him. His hair was mostly grey, of course, but he was really built—all muscle under his blue jeans and lumberjack-looking shirt. He either worked hard every day or he worked out. A lot.

He swung the rubber mallet with precision. The muscles of his arm flexed like rope under his skin.

"Hey!" I cried. I caught him just as he hammered the side of the truck again so he didn't hear me. Of course.

"Bobby," James said in a quiet moment between mallet strikes, and Kimble jumped and turned, holding the mallet like a weapon for the briefest moment, his face hard. Then he smiled at me and set the mallet aside.

"I take it you're Marie?" he asked. He held out his hand, and when I took it, I could feel the callouses. He shook my hand once, perfunctorily, then dropped it and looked at James. "And you are?"

"James Lavall," James said and pointed at the truck. "What did you hit?"

"Oh, it wasn't me. One of the grandkids took it to the back creek. Smacked a tree." He shrugged and smiled. "What're you gonna do though. Kids."

"Yeah." James smiled like he knew exactly what he was talking about, even though he had nothing to do with kids unless he came over to Jasmine's house and hung around with hers. "Doesn't look too bad."

"That's after an hour," Kimble said. "You shoulda seen it before."

Both he and James laughed. I almost felt like joining in, just to be part of the conversation, but before I could more than titter nervously Bobby stopped laughing and turned to me.

"You wanted to ask me about Karen," he said. "What, are the cops actually gonna reopen her case?"

"Something like that," I said. I didn't want to lie to the guy, but I also didn't want him to get all hung up on the idea that the cops were actually reopening old missing persons cases. "I just wanted to ask you a little bit about what happened. According to Karen's parents, you two were going to get married. What happened?"

Kimble looked around. "I thought we were going to get married, too," he finally said, his voice low. "We'd dated through high school, and I figured it was a done deal, you know. So, I asked her to marry me the night we graduated. After the dance.

"We'd gone back to her house, to change for the grad party. I figured that'd be the best time to ask her. You know, so she could tell all her friends. Show 'em the ring. All that crap girls like to do."

His face closed, and he looked around the garage again, like he was expecting someone or something to leap out at him. "But it didn't go quite the way I expected."

"Why?" I asked.

"She turned me down. Flat," he said. "Said she hadn't decided whether she was ever going to settle down. She wanted to travel, she said. See the world."

"That must've hurt," I said as gently as I could. I didn't want him to stop speaking. Not if he was about to confess to anything.

"It did," he said. "No doubt about it. And for a minute, I thought she was kidding me. You know, like a nasty joke. So I said, 'Well, we gotta get going on having our kids, don't ya think?'"

"What did she say?"

"She said she wasn't ever going to have kids," he said. His face spasmed at the memory, as though it hurt him as much now as it had forty years before.

I glanced at James, wondering if he was putting Kimble at the top of the "probably killed Karen" list the way I was, but all I saw on his face was sympathy. Seeing that look gave me pause, I must say.

He and I had never talked about whether either of us wanted kids. Not once.

True, life had kind of been full of "Oh God, I think I'm going to die" moments for us, generally speaking. But, even when life had slowed down and we'd grown closer, we had never talked about kids.

Maybe we needed to.

"That's when I knew she wasn't kidding around," Kimble said. "So, I stuck the ring in my pocket and headed out to the grad party by myself."

"What happened to her?"

"That night? She stayed home and watched a movie. Didn't even tell her parents what she'd done. And then, she got that job, and decided to turn it into a career. At least, that's what her mother said." He shook his head. "I don't know what kind of career she was gonna have, working at that coffee place. But she seemed happy enough, I suppose."

"So, you saw her again?"

"Once. To get all my stuff."

"Stuff?"

"A box of stuff I'd given her over the years. She gave it all back. Said she didn't feel right keeping it when we weren't gonna be together anymore."

"You still have it?"

"Nah," he snorted. "I burnt it. Box and all."

"Why?"

"Because I'd already met Freida by that time. I didn't want to upset her. Still don't. She's a good old gal. Wonderful mother and grandmother—and a good hand on the farm."

He smiled. "Guess I'll always have a soft spot in my heart for Karen, though. She was my first, if you know what I mean."

He turned away from both of us. Pulled a handkerchief from his pocket and blew his nose, noisily. "It'd be good to know what happened to her, though," he said. "I hope she got to travel, like she always wanted to."

Nope, I thought. *She didn't*. But all I did was smile and nod. "We hope so, too," I said. "Can you think of anything else about that last year? Anything at all?"

"Like I said, I lost track of her, so I didn't hear much. Her parents got real cold to me, after we broke up." His face tightened. "I think they thought it was my fault she left. So, I didn't hear much."

"I understand," James said. He put out his hand and shook Kimble's. "Thanks for giving us the time," he said.

"No problem. And hey, you'll let me know if you find her," he said. "Just so I know."

"Will do."

James took me by the arm and led me out of the garage. I waved weakly at Kimble, and he waved back, then I saw him reach for the rubber mallet. As we got into the car, the banging resumed.

"I don't think he did it," James said. "Sounds like he got his heart broken and then moved on."

"I suppose," I said. I wasn't sure if I was quite so ready to let him off the hook as a potential suspect. It seemed to me that Karen had hurt him badly. So badly that maybe he'd decided to exact revenge on her.

Unless he really was as over her as he said. Did he have an alibi?

"Stop the car," I said. Before James properly had the chance to stop, I leaped out of the car and peeled back to the garage.

"Bobby Kimble!" I yelled. He stopped hammering and turned. I couldn't read his expression. "When did you get married?" I asked. "To Freida, I mean?"

"In '75," he said. "In early May. Before we started seeding." He smiled. "Like I said, Freida's a good egg. She understood that the farm and the kids came first. Always did. And, nobody calls me Bobby anymore. It's Rob."

"Thank you," I said, and left for the second time.

James looked at me inquisitively when I got back into the car. "I think you might be right," I said. "I don't think he did it."

"Why?"

"Just a feeling," I said. "Let's go."

Karen:
Why Shunning Is Bad. For Real

SO, WE TRIED the shunning thing. At least, I did, because I was the only one at the living game. Not even Mr. Middleton showed up, which seemed like a pretty chicken shit move on all their parts. But, it seemed to work. Marie looked at me funny a few times, but for the most part, she ignored me too.

I can't say that it made me feel all right, because it didn't. I remembered being treated like that in high school a couple of times and then there was the whole shunning thing I went through after I broke off my engagement with Bobby Kimble.

That was worse than horrible. All my friends cut me out of their lives without a by-your-leave or anything. I'd tried talking to my mother about it, but she told me, basically, that it was my own fault.

"You didn't really think your friends would go along with these wild ideas of yours?" she'd said. She was frosting a cake, with her back to me, but I could tell by the set of her shoulders that she was angrier with me than she'd ever been before in her life. "You said you were going to marry Bobby," she said. "You broke his heart. What did you expect?"

I guess I'd expected her to think that having a life that did not involve marriage and kids right out of high school was a good idea, but I was wrong. And my friends from school were as angry at me as my mother. So they froze me out. All of them.

Hell, the way things turned out, maybe they were right.

Dad hadn't noticed how Mom was treating me, of course. He seemed to be of the opinion that just as long as he put food on the table and kept a roof over our heads, he didn't need to bother with the rest. That was Mom's department. So, it was anger and hurt in that house every day.

Luckily, I got the job at the Coffee Factory. I had no experience, but Len and Carol gave me a chance. They started me off at the University coffee shop then moved me to Ninety-Ninth Street, to the actual factory, a few months later.

At first, I worked front counter. Answering phones, taking orders, and everything else that went on in that little place. I took every advantage of it. After all, I had told everyone—yelled it from the rooftops, really—that I wanted a career. Looked like it would be with coffee.

There wasn't much to that gig that turned my crank at first, but I made sure I was there on time, every day, and that I treated everyone I dealt with as well as I could. Usually that meant a quick smile and then fighting off the idiot salesmen who seemed to flock to the place, but after I learned how much they made doing their jobs—because they were all quick to tell me, hoping that the big numbers would impress me enough to go out with them—I thought for that kind of money, I could do what they did, probably better.

I started sending out my résumé and quickly found out that getting a job like that was a lot harder than it should have been. I researched every business top to bottom when I applied, but my résumé were met with disdain. If I was lucky.

"Are you sure you want to try something like this?" they'd say if I was lucky enough to get an interview. "You wouldn't rather start in the front office with the other girls?"

"No," I'd say, trying to keep the smile on my face. "I'd rather be a salesman."

"Well, you can hear the problem right in the name," they'd say. "Sales man. Get it, little girl?"

If I had the guts to say, "I can do the job as well as any man," they'd say, "That may be, but you're young. You'll want to have kids, won't you?"

If I said yes, they'd gleefully reply, "Then you'll just leave and we'll have to train somebody else." If I said no, they were instantly concerned that perhaps I was going to turn into a nun or something. But the gist of every rejection was, "You'll leave and we'll have to train somebody else. Somebody male." So none of those jobs ever panned out.

At least I had the Coffee Factory job through all that. And it got better when Les decided I could begin learning to roast the beans. Learn the business, from the ground up.

It didn't take me long to save enough money to finally rent an apartment of my own. All right, so it was a basement suite, but still, I had my own place. Then I started thinking about travelling. Seeing all the places where the coffee that I roasted came from. Really making coffee my career.

And then, I made the mistake of my life. I went on a date.

ANYHOW, EVEN THOUGH I hadn't spoken to Marie through the whole game, I'd watched her play. She was getting better, she really was. Which meant she wasn't about to quit. Which meant I was going to have to deal with her twice a week for the rest of the season.

Even if the rest of the chickenshit ghosts were going to stay away from the living games, I couldn't. I was stuck there. Which meant that Marie and I were going to be face to face. And I wasn't going to shun her anymore.

To hell with Joanne. We needed another plan.

Marie:
Ella Comes to my Game

"You guys ready to go?" James called from Jasmine's living room at 5:54 pm on Thursday evening. "Marie's going to be late!"

Jasmine had finally talked me into letting her daughter, Ella, go to one of my ball games. Which meant, of course, it wasn't just Ella who was going, but the whole family. Getting Jasmine's family anywhere on time was next to impossible, even with James's help. So, there we were, six minutes away from me being officially late, and we weren't even close to getting into the car.

"Just give me a second," Jasmine called, somewhere from the bowels of her house. "I have to find hats for the boys, and I'm sure I have some of those foldable lawn chairs—"

"Jasmine, I told you! There are bleachers," I called. "Come on, get your rug rats out to the car. I can't be late!"

All right, so I wasn't even half ready myself. I thought I'd washed both of my ball socks, but could only find one, so I was tearing my room apart as I gave her a hard time. Then, as if by magic, there was my sock. Covered in dust from under my bed, and mostly red from the shale at the diamond, but I had it. Rammed it on and grabbed the big, black bag that held my glove, hat, and cleats, and bounded up the stairs two at a time.

I beat Jasmine to the car by a step and a half and helped her load both boys in the back seat. "It's going to be a bit tight back here," I said, rather unhelpfully.

"Well, I couldn't find a sitter, so here we are," Jasmine said. She pointed to the middle seat. "Ella, get in. I'm not sitting beside those two. Seriously."

Ella rolled her eyes, but climbed into the seat beside her two brothers.

"Too bad this car wasn't a bit older," Jasmine said. "With a bench seat in the front. I'd sit up there with you."

"But it isn't, so you can't," I said. Again, unhelpfully. "Tuck in. There's enough room."

To be honest, I didn't think there would be, but Jasmine somehow managed to get everyone belted in and strapped down.

"Let's go," she said. "Before I change my mind about this whole adventure."

"Do we have enough time to pick up some snacks before we go to the diamond?" James whispered.

"No," I whispered back. "I am going to be seriously late as it is. But maybe you can pick up some stuff after you drop us off?"

He smiled, unbelievably good sport that he was, and nodded. "Anything for the lovely Jasmine and her three wonderful children," he said, loudly enough for Jasmine to hear.

"And you better not ever forget it, my man," she said. Ella tittered into her hands, and Jasmine gave her a sideways glance. "It's no laughing matter, Ella," she said. "If that man wants me to continue to cook him the best meals in this city, he better treat me with the respect I deserve."

We all laughed at that. Even the two boys, who weren't paying any attention to any of us. But James laughed loudest of all.

"I will treat you like a queen, just as long as I get more meals," he said.

"Wouldn't hurt," Jasmine replied. Then she laughed herself. "Maybe not a queen. Don't know if I could take all the bowing and scraping."

"As you wish," James said, which cracked everyone up all over again. We'd watched *Princess Bride* the night before, and everybody had been "as you wish"-ing ever since.

"All right, enough," Jasmine said. "Everyone calm the heck down."

"As you wish!" everybody carolled. Then we all laughed and it was suddenly okay that I was late. This was going to be fun.

That thought surprised me a little. I didn't generally think in terms of something being fun. I was usually so certain that things were going to go badly that I managed to squeeze the fun out. But there I was, giggling like a kid and not even noticing the traffic or the clouds or anything.

This was going to be fun.

OF COURSE, THE first person I saw was Karen, standing on second base. She was watching my team warm up, but she looked at me—directly at me—when I walked up into the bleachers with the rest of my crew. And then, she waved.

So, no more ignoring. That was going to put a bit of a kink into the whole "having fun" thing, to be sure. I handed James my watch and said, "Wish me luck," to Ella.

Ella looked briefly confused, like she couldn't figure out how luck entered into the equation, but, with a little prodding from her mother, she nodded and smiled. "Good luck," she said.

The boys chorused "good luck" too, so I ruffled their hair and then walked down to the dugout. Karen waved at me again, but I ignored her. Turnabout being fair play and all that.

"Sorry I'm late, Greg," I said before the coach had a chance to open his mouth. "The family decided to come. What can I say?"

"Well, that's a nice thing," he said. "Having family here. Those kids yours?"

"No!" I gasped, and glanced over at Jasmine, who was doing her best to get her crew under some kind of control. I didn't see James at first, then realized he'd gone to the other bleacher to talk to the guy he'd met at the last game. Andy. Didn't know if I blamed him, because I imagined it was getting pretty loud around Jasmine. "Nope. No kids."

"Not yet," Greg said. I shook my head, pretty emphatically, but all he did was smile. "Nearly everybody has a kid, Marie," he said. "Eventually. Don't look so stricken."

"I'll try."

"And now," he continued, "you better get ready. Rachel couldn't make it, so you're playing second base today."

"What?" My fingers froze on the zipper of the big black bag. "I don't play the infield, Greg. And I don't have a clue how to play second base. Pick somebody else."

"Sorry, Marie." He didn't look sorry, though. "Nobody else left. Besides, I think it's time you give the infield a go. Suit up."

Jesus, not second base. That would put me right beside Karen for the whole freaking game. How would I be able to concentrate with her there? Wanting to talk . . .

I sighed and put on my hat, glove, and my cleats, silently hoping that I'd turn an ankle or something on my way out of the dugout and out onto the diamond.

That didn't happen, of course.

First base—I was pretty sure her name was Stacey—smiled at me as I walked toward second.

"Want me to throw with you?" she asked. "Just to warm you up a bit?"

"Thanks," I said. I stopped walking, but she shook her head impatiently and gestured toward second base. My base. Where Karen was waiting.

"Go to your bag," Stacey said. "I'll throw to you."

So, I did. Karen looked supremely shocked and even shuffled over a step or two to give me room. "Are you playing second?" she asked.

I didn't answer her, of course. I had to concentrate on the throw that was coming and the people in the stands—my people—who had come to watch. Didn't want to embarrass myself in front of them right off the jump.

"Ah," she said. "You're giving me the cold shoulder. I guess you owe me, after your last game. I am sorry about that, but—"

The ball flew at me just as I glanced in Karen's direction and flicked off the top of my glove. Of course. I glared at Karen and ran fifteen feet into the outfield to retrieve the ball.

"Sorry," Karen said, and finally shut her mouth.

I ran back to second and tossed the ball to Stacey. It seemed to take forever for it to get to her, and she frowned. "Throw with authority," she said. "I'm not made of glass."

At least she hadn't given me a hard time about the missed catch. She bounced the ball on the ground in my direction, and I ran, gathered it up, and threw, almost without thinking. The ball made a very satisfactory "thwack" when it hit the pocket of her glove, and Stacey smiled.

"Better," she said and gestured me over. "Have you played second base before?" she asked.

"No."

She closed her eyes for a second, as though she was trying to

Dying on Second

gather her strength. "All right, " she said. "Here are the three things you have to remember. If there is a runner on first, the ball will be coming to you, so you can make the out. It is up to you to make that out and then throw to me—hard—so we can try for a double play. Right?"

"Gotcha," I said. I couldn't believe she was even suggesting I try for a double play, but hey, whatever. "And what else?"

"Try not to let a grounder get by you," Stacey said. The umpire signalled that the game was about to start, and she tossed the ball, underhand, into the dugout. "And remember, if they bunt, you have to cover first."

"I have to what?" I asked. Well, to be honest, I kind of squealed the words out like a terrified dolphin.

"You have to cover first," she said and punched her glove open. "Got it?"

"Got it," I said. I took two big steps away from second base and ended up standing right beside Karen.

"Don't worry," she said. "I'll tell you what to do."

Exactly what I needed. A ghost giving me instructions.

"Just be quiet," I whispered. "I got this."

"Are you sure?" Karen asked. "I've been playing forever—"

"I said I got this," I said. Too loud, because Stacey gave me that strange look usually reserved for someone caught talking to themselves. I smiled at her—at least, I hoped it looked like a smile—and said, "You caught me. Just psyching myself up!"

"You'll be fine," Stacey said. She smiled back, but it looked as fake as mine felt. Luckily, the first batter stepped up and I could drop all pretenses of a smile. Time to concentrate on the game.

Okay, the lesson I learned in that first inning? The game moves a lot faster in the infield than it does in the outfield.

The first batter hit a slow grounder to second base—to me— and I waited for the ball to come to me.

"Go to the ball!" Karen yelled.

"Go to the ball!" Stacey screamed.

So, I ran for the ball, scooped it up, and threw it to first. I missed the runner by two full steps.

Dammit.

The second batter hit the ball out to left field. The left fielder let it bounce and then threw to the short stop. By that time, both runners were safe on first and second.

A bad start, and everyone infield looked angry. I tried to keep calm but my heart started pounding so hard I was afraid I was going to have a heart attack or something.

"Play's to third!" Jamie the back catcher called. Finally, some softball basics came back to me. Remember to throw ahead of the lead runner. I wanted to get the lead runner out. It was vital to get the lead runner out.

I took my position. Karen was still beside me but she kept her mouth shut so I was able to concentrate. The third batter set herself in the batter's box, and I got up on my toes so I could move quickly in either direction if I needed to. Lily threw the first pitch, and the batter fouled it off to the first base side. To my side.

Shit.

I glanced back at the girl playing my old position out in right field. She took a step or two closer to the right foul line, looking nervous. I knew exactly how she felt.

I set myself and watched Lily pitch a fastball to the outside of the plate, trying to force the batter to hit to the left field and keep the ball away from all the newbies on the right side of the field. The batter didn't bite and let the pitch go by, but it was a strike. Strike two.

I could see the batter's feet as she reset in the box. She was going to hit it to right field to take advantage of a neophyte second base person and an untried right fielder.

Fine. If that was the way it had to be, then fine.

The back catcher signalled for another outside pitch. I set and concentrated on the batter. The pitch came in fast. Just a little further inside than the second pitch and the batter jumped all over it. She hit a line drive back at Lily, who waved at it as it screamed by. She managed to get a teeny bit of her glove on it and changed the trajectory of the ball a hair. Right over to second base.

I was within a step of second base when the ball slapped into my glove. Nearly tore it off, to be honest, but I squeezed it closed. Took a step and touched the runner—the lead runner, who had been momentarily frozen by the speed of the hit. I pulled the ball from my glove, and threw at first. Hard.

The runner threw herself back toward first base but Stacey was waiting for her, foot on the base, and the ball in her glove.

"You're out," the umpire intoned. Then he said, "That's three."

"A triple play," Karen said. She sounded dumbfounded. "You pulled off a triple play."

I didn't have a chance to answer her, because, well, as they say, the crowd went wild.

THE REST OF the game was a happy blur. I hit a couple of times, once for extra bases, and actually made a couple more pretty decent outs. Didn't embarrass myself too badly, in any case. We won the game three to nothing, and I even got an "Atta girl," from Greg.

"Looks like I don't need to worry about second base," he said, as he patted me on the back. "If Rachel has to miss another game, I mean."

"Rachel's going to crap her drawers when she hears about this game," Stacey said. Then she laughed, and clapped me on the back herself. "Nice work out there."

"Thanks for the help," I replied.

She shrugged in a "I didn't do a darned thing" kind of a way. "You coming for beer?" she asked.

I shook my head. "I got family here," I said, and pointed up to the bleachers at James and Jasmine. "The kids, they gotta get home."

"You have to come one of these times," she said. "Promise you will."

I blinked. "Oh," I said. "All right. One of these times."

Stacey laughed. "I'll hold you to it," she said. Then she turned away, and I was free. Well, mostly free. I could see Karen waving at me.

"Can we talk?" she called. "Just for a minute?"

Yeah, like I was going to stand out on second base all by myself and start chatting. I was pretty sure that Stacey's "Let's go for a beer sometime," offer would disappear if I did that.

So, I turned toward Karen, pointed to the right field fence, and held up ten fingers in front of my chest. Low, so nobody but her would be able to see.

"See you in ten," she called, then turned and wandered through the lush outfield grass to the fence.

Jasmine and James had the kids all collected and ready when I finally changed my shoes and walked to the bleachers.

"So, what did you think of the game?" I asked Ella, as her

brothers whooped and ran around us in dizzying circles.

She smiled. "That was actually pretty cool," she said. "Especially that triple whammy thing you did. I didn't get it at first, but James explained it to me. Thanks for letting me come."

"You are more than welcome," I said. "Any time."

Jasmine shook her head. "I think that will be it for the season," she said. "It's a lot of work getting us all here, and I don't think—"

"She could come with James and me," I said, impulsively. "We'd look after her. Wouldn't we, James?"

"Absolutely," James said.

"So it's settled," I said, and smiled at Jasmine. "If you think it's okay, that is."

Jasmine nodded. "If Ella wants to." She looked at her daughter. "Do you want to?"

"Sure," Ella said nonchalantly. "Could be fun."

Not exactly a screaming recommendation, but hey, whatever.

"We were talking while we were waiting for you," James said, a big grin on his face. "And we think we all need to go get some ice cream. To celebrate your win."

"I wish I could," I said. "But I can't. Sorry."

"Oooh!" Billie, Jasmine's youngest, cried. "That's not fair!" He looked like he was just about ready to burst into tears which meant his brother would probably start crying too. Dammit. I didn't want to wreck the evening.

I looked over their heads at James. Stared at him, willing him to understand. "I have to have a meeting with the coach," I said. "He said it was important. You know? But maybe you can take them for ice cream and then come back and get me?" Please please please.

Jasmine shook her head. "I have to get these two home and to bed," she said. "We'll have to forget the ice cream."

James was quick on the uptake. "I'll take you all for ice cream, take you home, and then come back for Marie," he said to Jasmine. When she nodded, he picked up Billie and grabbed the hand of his brother. "Go have your meeting," he said to me. "We'll be just fine without you. Won't we, boys?"

"Yep," Billie said. And as quick as that, it was arranged.

"I'll pick you up in an hour," James said. "That long enough?"

"That'll be perfect," I said. "And I owe you."

I gave everyone a quick hug and then turned back to the

dugout. Saw Stacey still standing nearby, talking to a couple of other girls from the team, and wheeled back around and grabbed Ella by the hand.

"I'll walk with you," I said. "And put my equipment in the car."

She looked a little confused, but I walked them to the car, stuffed my bag in the trunk, and waved good-bye as they drove out of the parking lot, and away.

When they were finally out of my line of sight, I headed to the other side of the ball diamond. I snuck around the back of the bleachers, behind the opposition dugout, and down the left field fence to the outfield.

The next team was on the diamond warming up, but no-one gave me a second look as I scurried down the fence and around the corner, following the fence that encircled the outfield. I could see Karen's weak glow at the far right end of the field. It looked like she was watching the warm up.

"Karen," I whisper-called. I didn't want to catch her off guard, because sometimes ghosts act badly when they are frightened.

"I hear you," she replied. She didn't say anything more as I scurried over to her, and I was actually quite glad. I didn't have a clue what she would want to talk to me about. Maybe the game? After all, she liked softball enough to spend her afterlife here.

"So, what did you think?" I asked.

"The what?" she asked. She didn't look at me. Just stared at the brightly lit infield as the two teams threw balls around to warm up. "What?"

"Don't you wanna talk?" I asked. I pulled to a stop beside her and hung my arms over the fence. Stared at the infield, and tried to see it the way she saw it. "You're the one who called this meeting, not me."

"Yeah," she said. She took a deep breath and let it out slowly. I would have chuckled, because ghosts don't need to breathe, but she looked spooked, so I didn't. She looked at me for a moment, but couldn't seem to keep her eyes from the infield.

"The guy with the black hair," she said. "The one who sometimes gives you a ride."

"James," I said. "What about him?"

"He should maybe watch who he talks to here," she said. "I saw he was hanging around with a guy." She stopped speaking, but continued staring at the infield as though mesmerized.

"Yeah," I said. I was starting to feel just a little bit aggravated, which usually meant I'd turn mean in a second or two. "James met him a couple of games ago. What about him?"

"He's—he's not a nice guy," Karen said. "Maybe tell James to watch himself around him. And don't let him near your friend's little girl."

That set off my alarm bells, big time.

"What, is he some kind of a pervert?" I asked. "Have you seen him bother girls here?"

If he was a sicko who hung around the ball diamond trying to harass the girls, I could make sure that James and I made his life a living hell. Or I'd tell Sergeant Worth. She'd make short work of him, no doubt about it.

"No," Karen said. "No. Nothing like that." She stopped speaking, but her mouth worked, like she couldn't decide whether to keep talking or not. "He has a temper," she finally said. "Just tell James to watch himself."

"All right," I said. "I'll tell him."

Karen tore her eyes from the brightly lit infield where the game was now playing, and stared at me, hard. She still looked spooked, and for a ghost, that was something. "I wanted to talk to you about something else, too."

"What's that?" I heard the crack of bat, and watched the right fielder drift over to catch the lazy pop up. Things certainly moved more slowly in the outfield. It almost looked like she was moving in slow motion.

"I want to tell you about a crappy, crappy plan my friends came up with."

"Are these the same friends who decided that swarming me was a good idea?"

"The very same."

"I thought *that* was a pretty crappy plan."

"This one's worse," Karen said. She smiled, briefly. "If you can believe it."

"So what is it?" I asked.

"They decided we had to shun you."

"Shun me?"

"Yep. Shun you. I guess they were hoping that you'd quit coming to ball or something. You know?"

I thought of the last game, and Karen steadfastly looking every way but in my direction. Acting like I wasn't even there. "I seem to remember you doing something like that," I said.

"Look, you're not going to do anything to us, are you?" she asked. Her smile was gone, and she was half as bright as she'd been moments before. "Like make us all leave, or something. Are you?"

"I already told you I wouldn't do anything like that," I said. "Remember?"

"Yeah, I remember," she said. "But the rest of them aren't so convinced. And I also remember you talking about moving us on. Me on. What is that, exactly?"

"I have the ability to help spirits move to the next plane of existence," I said. "But only if you want me to. I can't do it without your say so." I looked at her, hard. "You understand?"

"I guess," she said. Then she shrugged. "It might be hard to convince the rest of them that you won't hurt them. Some of them were pretty badly hurt in their lives. So, it's understandable why they'd doubt that the afterlife would be any different. You know?"

"Like that Joanne girl you told me about. Right?"

"Right." Karen sighed out the word and her brightness dropped another lumen. "You promised me you wouldn't talk about her."

"What, I can't even talk about her to you?" I asked.

She shook her head a couple of times, then stared. "I—I don't know," she finally said.

"Just so I know the rules," I said. I was being a bit of a bitch, but hey, she was the one who'd gone along with the whole shunning thing.

"This is all just so—uncomfortable," she finally said. "I mean, we're all here for the same reason. So we can all play ball. Right?"

"Right."

"So, let me talk to them. Tell them the shunning thing is over as far as I'm concerned. Then, can we start again?"

I looked at her and snorted unamused laughter. "You mean you want us to be friends or something?"

"Well, maybe," she said. She smiled again, but it was genuine this time. "And then, when we're friends, we can talk about that amazing triple play you pulled off."

I smiled, and it felt genuine, too. "That was something, wasn't it?"

"Amazing was what it was," she said. "Pretty freaking amazing. You *have* to have played second base before."

"Nope," I said. "I never did."

And then, I told her about my dad teaching me to play softball, and playing for those three seasons.

I'd never told anyone everything like that before. Not my shrink. Not my mom. Not even James. And it felt all right, letting someone in, just a little bit. Even if she was dead. Maybe because she was dead. Who knew?

An interesting thing happened, though. After that, we just talked and the hour that I had to wait for James to come and get me absolutely flew by. When I finally saw him I felt a twinge of regret. It would have been nice to have stayed a little while longer. I'd actually had some fun.

I GUESS THAT'S why I didn't tell Karen that I'd been talking to her family and her old boyfriend. Why I didn't ask her where her body was buried, so I could find out, once and for all, what had really happened to her, and why she was stuck at second base on Diamond Number Two.

Karen:
My Turn to Call a Meeting

I HOPED MARIE listened to me about Andrew. I'd watched him weasel his way into other people's lives at the diamond. Lots of times, those families—those girls—disappeared. I didn't know if they'd just stopped coming to softball, or if the girls had actually disappeared, but I didn't want to see Marie's family hurt. They had to stay away from Andrew.

It didn't take long, after Marie left the diamond that night, for the rest of the dead to show up. I told them, tersely, I wanted to have a meeting.

"Not another one," Rita Danworth said. "This is starting to get boring, you know."

"I don't care, Rita," I replied. "We need to have a meeting. Behind the bleachers. Ten minutes. Make sure the rest know, including Joanne."

"She's not going to like it, either," Rita said. "You know."

"I don't care," I repeated, forcefully. "Get 'em all there, Rita. Ten minutes."

I scrambled down the bleachers without looking back at her. I didn't want her to see how that small interaction had shaken me. I needed to seem strong. To make them go along with me.

I had to.

THE LIVING GAME was long done when Joanne finally appeared,

and it was obvious to everyone there that she'd been trying to show up just for our game. Probably hoped she'd miss the warm up and just step into the game with no small talk. Instead, she'd walked into a meeting.

"What the hell?" she said. "I thought we were going to play tonight. What's this?"

The huge overhead lights clicked and whomped to darkness, but our light kept the area behind the bleachers bright enough.

"I called the meeting, Joanne," I said. "We gotta talk."

Joanne whirled to face the two old umps who were standing off to one side and looking a little pissy. "Mr. Middleton?" she called. "Are you okay with this?"

"Any player is entitled to call a meeting," Mr. Middleton said. He sort of looked like he was choking on the words, but he said them. "That's the rule, Joanne."

"Maybe it's time to change the frigging rules, then," Joanne said. "Because this is bullshit. We got a plan. For Christ's sake, we voted on it and everything. Didn't we?"

"Even if we did vote," I said, "we made a mistake."

"A mistake?" Joanne squealed. "A frigging mistake? We voted, bitch!"

"I don't care," I said.

That stopped them all, including Joanne. I didn't usually say those sort of things out loud. Mr. Middleton shuffled forward, looking old and worn out. Surprised me, seeing him change like that. Normally, the dead don't change.

I guessed that what was going on here really wasn't normal.

"You okay, Mr. Middleton?" I asked. "Want to sit down or something?"

"No," he said. "Karen, we did vote. The shunning must continue."

"Oh yeah, easy for you to say," I said, more angrily than I intended. I waited a second for Mr. Middleton to tell me to act like a lady, or shut my mouth, or whatever he usually said when one of us swore or tried to start a fight during a game. "None of you showed up for either of the living games. Just left me alone. All alone. I had to face her myself, and that wasn't fair."

Mr. Middleton still didn't say anything, but he looked embarrassed.

"So, if all of you are going to stay away from the diamond

whenever Marie's here, then I will not shun her," I said. "Because I don't think she's a problem."

There was a small silence as we all thought about what I'd just said. Of course, it was Joanne who broke first.

"If you can't follow orders," she said. "Then maybe we'll all shun *you*, Karen." She said my name like a curse. Guess in her mind, it was. "What would you think of that?"

The anger I felt—the ugly, painful spurt of anger—ran through me like poison. "If any of you try that," I said, "I will make this whole thing stop."

That shut them all up. Rita stood, her hand to her mouth, her eyes blinking like she was trying to signal for help by Morse code. The rest looked just as shocked. Except for Joanne. Of course.

"You can't stop anything," she said. "We can do whatever we want. Right, girls?"

She turned to the rest of them but no-one answered her. Not even Mr. Middleton, who stared at me as though he was afraid if he looked away I'd disappear. I wondered if he was afraid that if that happened he'd disappear next. They'd all disappear. All of them.

Rita had told me once, a long time ago, when it looked like we might be friends, that something had drawn her to the diamond the first time. And she thought it was me.

"I knew there was someone here," she said. "Not all of these people, of course, but one, for sure. And it was you. I could feel you. It was like you were calling me."

I'd told her she was crazy, of course. No-one could have that kind of power. It was softball that pulled everyone here, not me. But deep down, I'd wondered if maybe she was right. If I was calling them all to this place somehow. Allowing them to collect here every spring and summer, for a few good months, every year.

I'd never asked anyone else if they'd felt compelled to come to the diamond, but I'd watched them when they first wandered in. They'd always looked at second base. At me.

After that, the welcome wagon, which included Mr. Middleton and Mr. Kelly, took over, and the newbies were welcomed with open arms. But in those first few minutes before the old umps swooped in, every ghost looked for me on second base.

Now, I didn't know if I really could make the whole thing stop.

But I figured no-one else knew either.

They'd have to call my bluff.

"All right, Karen." That was Mr. Kelly, old, half-blind and still for some reason one of the best umps, living or dead. He was the one who brought calm when things got too crazy. Apparently, he'd decided that things had veered into "too crazy" territory. "Maybe we can talk about the shunning."

"She's going to win?" Joanne screeched. "You're going to let her win, just because she was the first one here? She doesn't have that much power, for God's sake!" She turned to Mr. Middleton, beseechingly. "Come on, Isaac, make her do the right thing for all of us."

I wondered when he'd told her his first name.

Mr. Middleton acted like she hadn't even spoken. Like she was invisible. Like maybe, just maybe, she was the one who was going to be shunned.

"Yes," he said, looking at me. Not Joanne. Me. "Maybe we went too far, shunning Marie."

"Isaac—" Joanne stammered, but Mr. Middleton cut her off.

"You will call me Mr. Middleton," he said, without looking at her. "And I think we should vote again."

AFTER THE VOTE, Joanne yelled that maybe she'd blow the whole thing up herself—and then she disappeared.

"Don't worry," Mr. Middleton said to me. "We'll talk to her. Get her back."

Even though I didn't care if I ever saw her again, I nodded. "Sounds good," I said. "Can we play ball now?"

"Yes, of course," said Mr. Middleton, a big smile on his face like it was his idea. But the rest of them looked a little afraid, and I realized they were actually waiting for me to make the first move to the ball diamond.

So, I led the way. Hey, why not? I'd won the vote and I wanted to play as badly as the rest of them. Maybe more.

As we settled into our game, everyone stopped acting weird around me. Even when I missed an easy grounder and yelled "Shit!" as I chased after the ball, Mr. Middleton called out, "Karen! Language!" just like always.

Maybe it would be all right, after all, and I could talk to Marie without the rest of them treating me like a traitor. I had things I wanted to tell her. Not about myself, of course. No way she was getting all my deep dark secrets. I had them buried, and that was the way it was going to stay. But I could talk to her about softball. After all, I'd been at this game for over forty years.

A small voice in the back of my head whispered, "You took such a chance. You never did anything like that before. Why did you do it now?" But I ignored it.

I didn't have an answer for the small voice. So, I shunned it. Just the way they'd all tried to shun Marie.

Marie:
The Coffee Factory, and Millie's Pee Dance

THE NEXT DAY, James and I had a free couple of hours between appointments, so we headed over to the Coffee Factory, where Karen had worked. According to the research I did online it had been in the same spot forever. The same owners and the same location. Everything the same. There was a chance that some of the people who were there when Karen worked there could still be around. Maybe.

At the very least, I hoped they'd be able to give me contact information for people who had been working at the same time as Karen. But it had been a long time.

"Do you think we'll have any luck?" I asked James.

He shrugged. "Not really," he finally said. "But hey. You never know."

Great. Not even James thought this was a good idea.

"Well, why didn't you tell me that before I made the phone call?" I asked, rather nastily I belatedly realized, and tried to smooth it over. "What I mean is, I don't want to waste your time."

"Hey, any time I get to spend with you isn't wasted," he said. "And besides, it's better to check for facts than assume. You know?"

"I guess." I glanced out the passenger window and saw we were back on Ninety-Ninth Street. "This seemed to be her hangout, didn't it?" I asked. "She lived on this street, worked on this street—"

"And probably died on this street," James finished. "Yeah, I noticed."

We turned up 77th Avenue, heading toward the railway line that bisected that part of the city. That railway line was the reason, primarily, that Ninety-Ninth Street on the east side was for houses, and on the west side was for businesses. It must have made for some uncomfortable cheek by jowl living.

The buildings down that small street were, generally, run-down looking, so the Coffee Factory stood out, like a little, clean, living gem. There were flower pots—with living flowers—on either side of the door, and the grass outside was close cropped.

"Looks nice," James said as he stopped the Volvo in front of the building. He opened the car door and smiled. "Smells even better," he said.

The smell of roasting coffee hit me, and I closed my eyes and revelled in it for a second. It smelled the way I imagined the best coffee in the world would taste. I wanted to sit there in the car with the windows open so I could enjoy the smell for the rest of my life.

"You coming?" James asked.

"Of course," I said, and threw the passenger door open. We walked through the front door and up to the counter. I rang the bell next to the cash register.

"Be with you in a second!" a man cried from the back of the building. So, I took that second to look around the front end of the Coffee Factory.

It was small, but clean. Lining one wall were rows of bags of coffee. Dark to light roast, something for everyone's taste. Along the far wall were coffee machines of every different size and shape, and down the window wall were cups and other coffee related bric-a-brac. And everywhere, that intoxicating smell of freshly roasted coffee.

"I could live in this place," I whispered. To James, I thought, but another man answered.

"Thank you," he said. "We try."

I whirled and felt my face heat. I tried to think of something to say and failed, but luckily James picked that moment to step in and take over.

"My name is James Lavall," he said. "I believe we have an

appointment?"

"Ah." The man's face stilled, and his smile slowly disappeared. "You're here to talk about Karen."

"Yes," James said. "We are."

"It's been a long time," the man said.

"Forty years," James said. "Were you working here at that time?"

"Well, I own the place," the man said. "So yeah."

"Mr. Wesson," I said, finally pulling myself together enough to get involved. "I'm the one who called you."

"Ah," Mr. Wesson said. "Why now?"

"What?"

"Why are you bothering with this now?" he asked. "It's been—"

"Forty years," James said again. He stared at Mr. Wesson's face for a long moment, as though measuring him. Then he went into our "we're helping clean up cold cases," spiel.

"So, you're not doing this for the family?" Wesson asked.

"No."

"Oh." His face fractured as he tried to smile but couldn't pull it off. "I thought maybe her parents hired—"

"No," James said. "This is through the police."

"That surprises me," Mr. Wesson said. "The police didn't seem to take Karen's disappearance very seriously at all at the time. I mean, they came here and talked to us, but it was only once." He shrugged. "I guess that's all the time they had to spare."

"It could be that the police had decided, at that time, that there was no reason to reinterview any of you," James said. "However, we are talking to everyone who had contact with Karen in the days before her disappearance. Are you okay with that?"

"No problem here," Mr. Wesson said, and his face softened. "She was a wonderful girl. I still don't believe that she just walked away from her family—her whole life. You know?"

"Yes," I said. "We know."

"So, what do you want to know?" he asked.

We hit him with the usual questions. Was there anyone left in the business, besides himself, who had worked with her? No. What did she do, when she worked here? Cashier, but she was showing an interest in learning how to roast coffee.

"I couldn't believe she wanted to do the heavy work—she was such a little bit of a thing," Mr. Wesson said. "But she had an affinity for it. She'd even joked with me, a time or two, that maybe someday she'd take over the business."

"Would you have considered it?" I asked.

"Oh, she was only with us a year or so," Mr. Wesson said. "I'm sure she would have found something else to do with her time. But she did have big dreams. She talked about going to Columbia, way down in South America, to find the best coffee. Things like that." He shrugged. "I think what she wanted was to travel. But back in the seventies, Columbia was not the best place for a woman to travel to alone. Still, it impressed me that she even thought about it."

"Did you ever socialize with Karen outside work?" James asked.

Mr. Wesson shook his head. "Not really. She came to our Christmas parties with her parents for a few years before she started working with us, but that was about it."

"So you and your wife were friends with Karen's family?"

"It started with the wives, Christina and Edna," he said. "They met at some group they joined. Knitting, I think, and became fast friends. Which meant Rupert and I became friends, too, even though they were older than us. We hadn't even had Patty—our daughter—when we first met them. They already had Karen, so, we watched her grow up." His lips tightened. "We stayed friends with them until Karen disappeared."

"Why didn't you remain close after that?" James asked.

"We tried to stay in contact," he said, "even though it was hard as hell to watch them fall apart. But after a while, they stopped returning our calls. To be truthful, it was almost a relief. And then, Christina got sick, and I didn't have the energy—emotional or otherwise—to try to keep in contact with them."

I could tell by the look on his face that his wife had not survived and was trying to think of a way to tell him how sorry I was, when James spoke.

"Can we speak to your wife?" he said. "Just to confirm what you've told us."

Both Mr. Wesson and I turned and stared at him as though he had suddenly lost his marbles. "My wife died," Mr. Wesson finally said. "Cancer."

Damn cancer.

"I'm sorry for your loss," James said, though to be honest he didn't sound very sorry. "Is there anyone else we can talk to who can corroborate the facts?"

Mr. Wesson's face closed. "Maybe her parents, if they'll talk to you."

"Other employees?"

"Not from that long ago," he said. By his tone, he was evidently finished with us, but unfortunately for him, James wasn't done with him.

"What about customers?" he said.

"From forty years ago?" Mr. Wesson asked. Then he stopped. "Actually, I might be able to give you some of those names. Christina and Karen set up a database when she started working with us, so we could keep in contact with our customers. You know, mail them flyers and the like. I haven't sent out mailers in a few years, though. Just Christmas cards." He smiled. "Christina loved Christmas."

A database, I thought. *Even something put together forty years before should be accessible—*

Mr. Wesson pointed at a bank of old-fashioned card file holders. Like the ones that libraries used to use, before they became computerized. "They're all there," he said. "In alphabetical order, of course."

I tried to smile. "So, all your customer data—"

"Is written down on index cards," he said. "I thought about getting it all on computer, but I couldn't bear to. You know."

"Because your wife built it," I said.

"Exactly," he said, sounding relieved that I understood.

"Any chance you could get me a list of your customers?" I asked. "With contact information?" He had to have that computerized. After all, nobody wanted to look up every name and address, every Christmas—

"I'm sorry," he said. "I'm the only one working here full-time anymore. Just a couple of part-timers to help me."

"Oh."

"And I don't have the time to go through all the cards for you," he said.

Damn.

"But if you want, you can do it," he continued. "Just promise me you'll put everything back exactly the way you found it."

I glanced at James, and he shrugged. This wasn't his deal. Not really. It was mine. If I wanted to take the time to do this, I could.

"Can I come back tomorrow?" I asked.

He finally smiled. "I open the doors at seven," he said. "And coffee will be on."

"YOU DO REALIZE that tomorrow is Saturday," James said as we walked back to the car. "And you have to go to Sylvia Worth's place. To meet her dead boyfriend."

"I know," I said, and sighed. "Looks like tomorrow's going to be busy."

I STAYED WITH James that night, and we talked about whether I would use his car the next morning. I was starting to feel guilty about how much I was using it, but he scoffed.

"You gotta get around," he said. "And I don't mind a day off."

"Can you actually afford that?" I asked. I knew he had three jobs on the go and needed to go to the office, even though it was Saturday. "I'll bus it to the Coffee Factory—and maybe cab it to Sergeant Worth's."

I didn't much like the idea of taking a cab to Sergeant Worth's because that meant when I was done, I'd have to wait at her place for the cab to return. All that time, waiting. Small talking. With her.

"Maybe I can use the car for Sergeant Worth," I said. "But honestly, I can bus it in the morning."

"It's up to you," he said. "But remember, I offered."

We retired and I tucked myself around him on his little bed. He'd talked about getting something bigger but I didn't want him to do that. Didn't want him to change too much about his life for me. Besides, I liked how protected I felt wrapped in his arms as he slowly settled and relaxed. I could listen to his breathing, steady and slow, and go along with it. My own breathing would slow. My heart would slow. My muscles would relax, and finally, finally, my brain would slow. And then, I could sleep, wrapped in his warmth and safety.

Nobody needed a big bed for that.

Four hours later, the nightmares kicked me awake. This one was "crazy girlfriend part two" and was a real scorcher. Watching someone shoot themselves was hard to take, even eight months after the fact. I managed to keep from waking James, but when I walked into the living room covered in sweat, Millie was waiting for me. Good old Millie the comfort dog. She stood by my feet, waiting.

"Hi, girl," I said. I reached down and scratched the top of her head, then straightened and went to the sink. I got myself a glass of water and drank it, hoping that that would be enough, this time. That I'd be able to go back to sleep this time. But it wasn't and I couldn't.

Millie curled up in my lap as I sat at James's computer, playing games so I didn't have to think about just how little sleep I was getting. Again.

After thirteen games of solitaire, I rechecked how long it would take me to get from James's house to the Coffee Factory by bus, looked at the clock hanging on the wall above James's desk, and sighed. It would take me just over one hour, which meant I would catch the bus at 6 am. I still had a couple of hours before I had to be at the bus stop.

"Should I try sleeping a bit more?" I asked Millie. She stared at me with her big brown eyes like she was actually thinking about answering me, then huffed and jumped off my lap. She walked to the door, then turned her head and stared at me, expectantly.

"Need to go out?" I said.

Her look seemed long-suffering. Like she couldn't believe the idiots she had to deal with. Of course, I have to go out, her look said. Unless you'd rather I pee on the carpet.

I glanced down at what I was wearing. One of James's old tee shirts, and a pair of shorts. Good enough. I rammed my feet into my sneakers, scooped the keys from the bowl, grabbed her leash and collar, and hustled her out.

The moon was huge and hung above the horizon like a staring eye. It kind of creeped me out, to be honest. I didn't want to follow Millie to her usual pee spot, but dogs are nothing if not routinized, so she won, and I stepped around the corner of the apartment building into total blackness.

I felt my nightmares slink and slither back into my brain and clutched the leash tightly as Millie walked and sniffed in order to choose that perfect spot.

"Please hurry," I whispered.

She ignored me, of course. Just kept sniffing and circling,

without a care in the world past the fact that she needed to pee in a very particular spot.

The nightmare wormed its way from my head to my chest and tightened until I felt like I could not breathe.

"Jesus, hurry up," I grunted, trying to pull air into my quickly freezing lungs. "Please, Millie."

But she ignored me. Just circled and sniffed until I thought I'd lose my mind. Then the voice of my shrink, Dr. Parkerson, whispered, "Remember the routine."

Ah yes. The routine. Breathe. Reconnect with the present. See. Touch. Smell.

I tried to belly breathe but my chest was still so constricted I couldn't do much more than gasp. So I looked around. Saw the edge of the apartment building, black on my side, and light on the other. The wall looked like it was made of cement. I took a step toward it, dragging a fairly pissed off Millie with me. She'd just found her perfect spot, and I was taking her away from it.

"Tough luck, dog," I wheezed and took two more steps so I was within touching distance of the wall.

Millie restarted her pee search dance as I stared at the wall. Specifically, at the edge of the wall where dark turned to light. I tried taking another belly breath. Had a little more luck and the nightmare began to uncoil from my chest.

I reached out the hand holding the leash. Touched the wall. Felt the roughness of the concrete under my fingers and took another breath in and out. The nightmare loosened its grip on my chest even further so I leaned forward and smelled the concrete of the wall.

You wouldn't think a wall would smell like anything, but it does. Sunshine with a hint of something sharper. Chemical. I tried to remember if the apartment complex had been painted recently. Breathed again, and felt my chest loosen even more. Smelled urine and glanced at the dog but it wasn't hers. Someone had peed on this wall. I took a step away, and at the edge of the wall that cut through dark and light, I could see the stain just below waist height.

Men. They could be as bad as dogs.

Millie barked once, as if she'd read my mind.

"Sorry, girl," I said. "I didn't mean it."

WHEN WE GOT back into James's apartment I took off Millie's collar and leash and she trotted to her little bed. Looked like comforting was over for the night, but I knew I wasn't going back to sleep. So, I made a pot of coffee and waited for the sun to rise.

AT THE COFFEE Factory, it took me two hours to gather all the information I could from the myriad index cards in Mr. Wesson's antiquated data base. Since they were all in alphabetical order with no indication of a start date I chose them based on the handwriting and the yellowing of the cards. The older, yellower, ones had been written by a woman—or perhaps, two women. I was fairly certain that Mr. Wesson's wife and Karen had written down the information about the Coffee Factory's customers on the index cards that appeared to be the oldest, the edges stained. I wondered which ones Karen had written.

When I left I had thirty-five names plus one pound of freshly roasted, freshly ground Columbian coffee.

Mr. Wesson tried to talk me into buying whole beans and a burr grinder, saying that the beans stayed fresher than the ground, but I resisted. The grinder was expensive, and I didn't want to have to carry the thing home on the bus.

"Think about it," he said as he walked me to the door. "You'd really like how fresh the coffee tastes. Believe me."

He was probably right about that—I loved the way the smell of freshly ground coffee surrounded me as I hopped the bus, heading downtown to the office. It was like wings of steel, protecting me from all the other nasty smells that hung out on a bus.

THE DOOR WAS unlocked when I got to the office, and Mille was in her little office dog bed. She barely glanced at me when I walked through the door. *Ungrateful whelp*, I thought. *I walked you at three in the morning.*

"That you, Marie?" James called from his office.

"It is," I said. "And I come bearing gifts."

He walked into the reception area and smiled when I held up the bag of coffee. "I figured you'd buy some," he said. "Shall we give it a go?"

We did. The wonderful smell filled the office as the coffee brewed, then we drank the elixir of the gods at my desk and went through the information I'd gathered from the index cards.

"Hmm," James said, pointing to a name in the middle of the list. "Will you look at that."

I looked at the name to which he pointed. Dianna Westwood. Nothing twigged.

"Somebody you know?" I asked.

"That guy," he said. "The one I met at the ball diamond. His last name is Westwood. I wonder if this person is related to him."

I blinked. This was the man Karen had warned me against.

"Didn't you say he was married?" I asked.

"Yeah," he said. "Maybe this is his wife. Now that would be a coincidence, wouldn't it?"

"Would you think it was still just a coincidence if I told you that Karen—dead Karen—told me to tell you to watch yourself around that guy?"

James looked at me. "Are you serious?"

"As a heart attack," I said. "She told me after the game. Said we had to watch him around Ella, too. I asked her if he was some kind of pedophile, but she said no. Just that he had a temper. Does this feel like more than a coincidence?"

"Yes," he said. "Yes, I think it's much more than that."

WE DOVE INTO Andrew Westwood's life as we drank the last of that wonderful coffee. Well, we tried, anyhow. There honestly wasn't that much that we could find online. Born and raised in the city. Graduated from Jasper High school in 1970. Married to Dianna Felix the next year. Went to university for a couple of years, but didn't finish his degree. Looked like he had a kid—his daughter—about the time he dropped out of school. Got a summer job with the city but only lasted a couple of months. Went to work out of town for a few years, then got on with EdTel, and later with Telus. He was still with the company but it looked like he'd be retiring within the next couple of years.

All in all, it looked like he had led a completely ordinary life. We couldn't even find a traffic ticket. All right, that wasn't the truth, he got a few of those, but still, they appeared to be the only blemish on his record. He even paid his taxes on time. Every year.

"He doesn't look like a bad guy," I said. "I wonder why Karen was so spooked by him?"

"I think that's something you are going to have to ask her,"

James said. "The next time you see her."

I felt a pinch of guilt. I was going to speak to her at the last game, but I hadn't. Now, I would have to explain to her that even though I told her I wouldn't, I was digging around in her life. She was not going to be impressed.

"But you can't do it now," he said. He pointed at the clock on the wall. "It's nearly time for you to go to Sylvia Worth's place."

Oh, even better. I had to go and meet a ghost. Dig around in his life and maybe piss him off. Just because Sergeant Worth knew about my mom and me.

Marie:
Meeting Rory

SERGEANT WORTH'S APARTMENT building was a nondescript four-storey walk-up in a nondescript neighbourhood in West Edmonton. Far enough from the Mall to be quiet, but close enough that she could walk over and join the rest of the merrymakers looking for fun and not-so-cheap crap, if she so chose.

My guess was she didn't choose to do that very often at all.

She opened the door to her apartment and let me in. Her place looked like an Ikea showroom.

As I took off my shoes at her front entrance, I wondered if she'd gone to the Ikea store, found a mock-up of an apartment with the same square footage as hers and said, "I'll take it. As is."

It was catalogue neat and looked unused. Was this Sergeant Worth trying to prove to everyone she was living a normal life, right down to the knickknacks on the coffee table? The dust on the Billy book cases said yes.

"Nice place," I said. I pulled off my hoodie and tossed it over the back of a dining room chair. Looking around I saw more dust at the edges of nearly everything. "How long have you lived here?"

"Fourteen months," she said. "Since my divorce." She looked around, like it was the first time she'd looked at it in a long time. "It's a nice neighbourhood."

"Good." I didn't know what else to say. I stood by my hoodie, draped over the dining room chair, and thought seriously about grabbing it and leaving Sergeant Worth to her Ikea catalogue apartment and her ghost.

Ah yes. The ghost. The reason I was there. That was a place to start.

"Rory," I said. "When does he normally show up, Sergeant?"

Worth blinked and stared at me as though she couldn't quite understand what I was saying. She looked exhausted, as usual. "Call me Sylvia, please," she said.

"All right," I replied, though I didn't want to. First names implied an intimacy I didn't think I wanted. Not with a cop. "When does Rory show up, Sylvia?"

"Usually at night," she said. "But then, he worked nights when he was alive, so—"

"That makes sense," I said. To be honest, I didn't know if it made sense or not. I hadn't noticed that ghosts followed the old patterns they'd developed in their lives. Not the ghosts who realized that they were dead, anyhow. "Can you tell me how he died?"

She turned away from me and pointed at the open concept kitchen that the open concept dining room where we were standing backed onto. "Want some coffee or something?" she asked.

"Sure," I said.

She was silent as she busied herself making the coffee, then pulling the cups—two cups, I noticed—from the cupboard by the fridge.

"You take cream?" she asked.

"Yes."

She opened the fridge and peered inside. "All I got is milk," she finally said.

"That's fine."

She took out the carton, opened it, and sniffed cautiously. Half-smiled. "All good," she said, and poured a dollop into my cup. Hers remained black.

"I thought you weren't supposed to drink coffee," I asked. "Blood pressure and all that."

"One won't kill me," she said. "Besides, if I have to drink one more cup of frigging herbal tea, I will lose my mind. Don't tell my doctor, though. He'd be pissed."

"Your secret's safe with me," I said.

"Good." I could tell by the look on her face that she wasn't just talking about the coffee. She was talking about the rest. The ghost, the mostly unused apartment, all of it.

Hey, you keep my secret, I'll keep yours, I thought.

She handed me the cup then walked back into the safety of her open concept kitchen. Picked up her cup and drank deeply, like she was dying of thirst. Closed her eyes and sighed. "Not bad," she said.

I took a sip of mine. It wasn't as good as the Coffee Factory coffee but, like she said, it wasn't bad. I set the cup down on the counter and turned back to Sylvia.

"How did Rory die?" I asked again. "I need to know."

"Of course you do," she said. "I'm sorry. It's hard, though. Talking about it. You know?"

"I understand," I said. "Would you feel more comfortable sitting down?"

I gestured at the table but she shook her head. "I'm okay here," she said. "Let's just get this over with, all right?"

She looked like she was ready to jump out of her skin, and I suspected her doctor was right. She probably needed to stay away from the coffee.

"He had a heart attack," she said. Whispered, really. Like she was afraid Rory would hear her telling his secrets. "He went out for a run, and he had a heart attack. Died before anyone even found him. It was horrible."

"I imagine," I said. Heart attacks weren't a bad way to go, all things considered.

"He was only forty-four," she said. "And he looked after himself." Her lips quivered. "It wasn't supposed to be this way."

"I know."

"She isn't telling you everything." The man's voice came from somewhere behind me, and I was turning when Sylvia gasped.

"He's here," she said. "I can smell his aftershave. He's here, I'm sure he's here."

I could smell it too. Nautica. Rory had used Nautica aftershave. I recognized it, because I'd tried to convince my stalkery ex-boyfriend to use the same scent in my life before.

He'd said no, of course. Said it smelled like something a faggot would use. Said he wouldn't be caught dead using something like that.

Of course.

I turned and looked at the silvery figure standing by the television at the far end of the living room. "Rory?" I asked.

"You can see him?" Sylvia's voice sounded strangled. "You can really see him?"

"Yes," I said. "Be quiet now, Sylvia. He and I need to talk."

Rory was shorter than I thought he'd be. Sylvia Worth looked like the type of woman who would pick someone six foot four, with blond hair and Viking heritage. Someone who could turn Berserker at a moment's notice.

Rory was the opposite of all that. Short—not more than five nine—and compact. Dark hair and eyes. He also looked haunted, but being dead could do that to you.

"What isn't she telling me?" I asked.

"I'm telling you everything you need to know," Sylvia said. Her voice roughened, but I couldn't tell if it was from anger or fear. "You asked me how he died, and I told you."

"Ask her about the last case I was working on," he said. He glanced at Sylvia, and his face softened. "And ask her why she looks so tired. She doesn't sleep, you know. She's going to kill herself. Nobody can go without sleep. No-one."

"Tell me about Rory's last case," I said to Sylvia. I kept my eyes on Rory, so I could see how he reacted to her answer. "He was a cop. Right?"

"Yeah," she said. "He worked vice but went over to the drug squad a couple of months before he died." She swallowed, and I could hear her throat click. "He was working the Ambrose Welch case."

I blinked. That was the guy from the drug house who had killed Eddie Hansen, a ghost I'd moved on the year before. Ambrose Welch had tried to use me to get out of that drug house, through all those cops. I'd taken his eye out when I'd escaped. He featured in my nightmares, too.

Jesus.

"Is that everything?" I was asking Rory but Sylvia answered.

"Yes," she said. "That's everything."

Rory shook his head.

"What else?" I asked.

"There's nothing," Sylvia said. She grabbed the coffee pot, poured more coffee into her cup, and drank deeply.

"That stuff's gonna kill her," Rory said. "I can hear her heart beating from here."

"Just relax, Sylvia," I said, as gently as I could. "I'm talking to Rory now. I need to get his truth. Not yours."

"Truth's truth," she said. She sounded angry.

"Nope," I said. "He'll know things not even you knew. Just let me find out what he knows. Please. There's a reason he came to you. Let's find out what it is. All right?"

"All right." I heard the coffee cup hit the counter. "Fine."

"Rory?" I asked. "What else?"

"I was undercover," Rory said. "I told Sylvia I'd only been with the drug squad for a couple of months, but that wasn't exactly the truth. I'd been working undercover with them for a while longer."

"How much longer?"

"A year." He shook his head. "I was deep in with that crew for that year. Did things—"

"What things?"

"I did everything!" he roared. He flared, briefly, setting that end of the living room awash in his light. "I did everything."

"Drugs?" I asked.

Rory looked at me. Smiled. "That was the least of it," he said. "The very tip of a mountain of shit that I did, getting close to Welch. And then, after all that, my bosses pulled me."

"Off the case?" I asked.

"Yep." He snorted derisively. "They said I had become unstable. That I needed some R and R. It was okay, they said. I'd done a good job and they'd get him without me." He shook his head. "But you know how that rolled out, now don't you?"

I blinked. "What do you mean?"

"Well, you were the reason they finally got into the Fortress," he said. "You were the one who put that asshole in jail."

"How did you know about me?" I asked.

"She told me," he said. "When she came home at night. She told me everything."

Huh.

I decided to forget that, for the moment. Sylvia could work that out in therapy or something. I had to concentrate on Rory.

"So, you were trying to get your life back together when you died?"

"Yeah." He sighed. "But the drugs . . . "

"Drugs?"

"Coke, mostly." He snorted unamused laughter. "I kept telling myself I could quit anytime. You know. Like every other addict in the world. But I couldn't seem to leave the coke alone. I figured that if I exercised and ate better doing the occasional line wouldn't kill me." He shook his head. "Was my face red."

"And Sylvia didn't know?"

"Sylvia didn't know what?" Sylvia asked.

I turned to her, touched my forefinger to my lips, and watched her face tighten. Turned back to Rory.

"Did she?"

"I never told her," he said. "Like I said, I thought I could quit." He shook his head. "It took me a couple of months after I died to figure out what the hell was going on. I would come to on that running trail in the river valley, and then feel a punch, right in the middle of my back, and then black. Over and over, until I finally figured out that I was dead. Dead."

I cocked an eyebrow. Addicts didn't normally snap out of that fugue state by themselves. He was one tough guy.

"And then?"

"Then, I looked for Sylvia. I had to tell her everything. She had to understand . . ."

"She had to understand what?"

"That I didn't mean to leave her alone," he said. He put his hands to his face, briefly, then dropped them by his side. "That was never part of the plan. I knew how much she'd sacrificed for me—"

"Her marriage, you mean," I said.

"And losing her kids. Yeah." He finally looked past me, to Sylvia. "Tell her I'm sorry. Please."

"I will," I said.

"And tell her to stay the hell away from Ambrose Welch," he said. "I think she's digging around—"

"He's been arrested," I said, quickly. "They got him for murder."

Rory snorted. "You mean Eddie Hansen?" he scoffed. "Welch won't do a day for his death. Guaranteed."

I felt a shiver down my spine. That was bad. Not just bad for

Sylvia, but bad for me.

"Is there anything that he can be arrested for?" I asked, then shook my head. *Forget yourself*, I thought. *Focus on Rory.* "Sorry," I said. "You don't have to worry about any of that, anymore. You do understand that, don't you?"

"But Sylvia—" he started. I shook my head.

"She has to worry about her life now," I said. "All you have to be concerned with is your death and what you'll do now."

I honestly expected him to argue with me. Tell me that I didn't understand. That he could help. All he had to do was stick around, and he could make Sylvia all better—

"I'm doing this to her, aren't I?" he said. He pointed at Sylvia, still cowering by the coffee maker. "The no sleeping and the high blood pressure. It's me, isn't it?"

"You're not helping," I said.

"But what can I do?" he asked. "I jump between the trail and this apartment. Nowhere else. When she's here, I get pulled here. When she's gone—I'm back at the trail." He shook his head. "I can't figure out how to make it stop."

"You need to let go," I said. *And Sylvia needed to let go*, I thought. *But first, you.* "You're a helping kind of a guy, I can tell. But this isn't helping her. Maybe it did at first, but now it isn't. She has to move on—which means you do, too."

"How do I do that?" he asked.

As I rolled the options out for him, his light dimmed, and then guttered. For a moment, I thought he was going to disappear. I hoped he'd hang on because I really didn't want to have to go to the running trails in the river valley to try to find him. But he pulled himself together, and his light steadied. He even gained a lumen or two.

"So, I just have to choose?" he finally asked.

I realized I could hear Sylvia sobbing, but Rory didn't respond to her. Was totally concentrating on me. This was going to be easy—

"Stop!" Sylvia cried. "Just stop! Please!"

Rory looked at her, devastated. "Look at her," he said. "God, just look at her. I can't leave her like—" And then, in mid-sentence, he was gone. Blasted back to the walking trail where he died, no doubt. Just what I needed.

I whirled and glared at Sylvia but she didn't notice. She was sobbing hard, with the end of a roll of paper towels pressed to her face. She pulled a bit more of the paper towel to her and the roll tottered toward the edge of the counter, and then fell. I watched as it rolled out across the carpet. When it reached the cardboard tube in the middle, it stopped.

"What are you doing, Sylvia?" I asked. "I thought this was what you wanted. That you wanted him gone—"

"I don't know!" she wailed. "This feels wrong. Like I'm turning my back on him. I don't think—I don't think I can do this without him."

"Do what?" I asked.

Please don't say your life, please don't say your life.

"My life," she whispered.

Shit.

I ENDED UP spending the rest of the night with her. First, it was to calm her down, pull her off whatever emotional cliff she was on. Then, I stayed so I could explain the whole situation to her. What Rory was doing to stay here, and what she was doing to keep him here. And how wrong it was for both of them.

He had to move on, and she had to let him. No matter how much it hurt.

She finally fell asleep on the couch in the living room. I found a blanket—a kid's blanket on a small Ikea bed in one of the bedrooms—and covered her. Thought about staying until she woke, but I was starving, and I needed some sleep myself. Besides, the sun was finally coming up. She wouldn't be in the dark when she woke.

She'd have to get through the day by herself. Make some hard decisions, and stick to them. She could call me when—if—she was ready for Rory to move on. Until then I was done. I was done.

Oh, and that thousand dollars I was overcharging her to move Rory on? It wasn't enough. Not by half.

Karen:
Marie Opens Up

I WATCHED MARIE'S Thursday game from the sidelines even though she was back in right field. She'd let me know that my presence on the diamond was a real distraction—meaning she kept throwing the ball to me, as opposed to the living second base person from her team who stood next to me.

I didn't want to be the reason that Marie blew plays, so I complied. It didn't take me long to see that she was right. She played much better when I wasn't muddying things up on second base. Her team won, six to three.

After her game and the never-ending meetings her coach Greg seemed to adore holding, Marie came over and sat beside me. In silence, of course, because there were other living hanging around watching the next game.

"You had a good game," I said. She didn't respond, but I hadn't expected her to. "We had a game, too," I said. "You missed it. It was good. Not triple play good, but good."

She held up her hand, her eyes glued to the diamond. I realized that Miriam Kendel was pitching, and Marie was watching her. Dissecting every aspect of every pitch.

"You won't be able to hit her," I said.

"I think I can," she muttered. "She has a tell when she's going to throw the rise ball. It's small, but it happens every time."

Then, she looked around at the living like she was

embarrassed that she might have been seen talking to herself.

"Don't worry about it," I said. "They're not paying attention to you. They're watching the game."

All she did was shake her head at me, a warning that I needed to shut my mouth. So I did. What the hell, it was fun watching Miriam take apart the batters, one after the other.

When the inning was over—and it didn't take very long—Marie got up and scrambled down the bleachers to the ground. She said hi to Miriam's parents, who were sitting in their usual spots beside Miriam's dugout.

"She's throwing good today," Marie said.

Miriam's mother, Rosa, nodded and smiled. "You going for coffee?" she asked. A preamble to asking her to pick them up a little something, but Marie shook her head.

"Just going to go stand by the fence," she said. "So I can watch her pitch from a different angle."

"We'll talk later, then," Rosa said, and turned back to the game.

Marie made good her escape from the living, and I followed her. She meandered around the fence surrounding the diamond, and finally stopped when she was standing between first base and right field. Far enough away for us to carry on a decent conversation.

"Can I tell you about my game now?" I asked when we were settled.

"Sure," she said.

So, I told her about the game throwing in all the details that make anyone who doesn't play wish they could die of boredom just to get out of hearing any more of the minutia.

Marie kept her eye on the game but asked all the right questions to let me know that she was listening to me. Hearing me.

I finally got to the happy ending of my story, because we won, then asked Marie how her weekend had been. I thought it was a fairly innocuous question, but she stiffened.

"It was fine," she finally said.

"So, what did you do?" I asked. Normally, I wouldn't have asked her, but she was acting queer. Like something untoward had happened.

She didn't answer. Just stared out at the diamond as centre

field drifted in to catch a lazy fly ball. Then the woman ran off the field, the ball still in her glove. She'd made the third out.

"Did something happen?" I finally asked. "You're acting like something happened." I was starting to feel creeped out by her silence. Then afraid. "What happened?"

Honestly, I thought she was going to tell me she found out that Andy had done something to the little girl who had accompanied her and her boyfriend to her last game.

She finally glanced over at me. "I met another ghost," she said.

I blinked. "Where?" I asked.

"At Sergeant—at Sylvia Worth's place."

"Who?"

"She plays for the Chimo Angels. First base."

I knew her. Or knew of her, at least. I'd watched her and her team through the years. She'd aged a decade in the past couple. Having a ghost might explain that.

"Who's the ghost?" I asked.

"Her boyfriend," Marie said shortly. Then she shook her head. "Never mind. Doesn't matter."

"It seems to be upsetting you, so I'd say that matters." I smiled at her. "Come on. Tell me about him. Maybe it'll help."

She shrugged. "All right," she said.

Then, she explained her process to me. Her process for moving on ghosts. I don't think she realized that's what she was doing, but she was.

"So, you can't move a ghost on unless they want to," I said.

"That's right," she said. "I thought I told you that, before."

"And he wants to go," I continued. "Move on. Isn't that what you call it?"

"Yes," she said. "It's Sylvia who's having the problem."

I frowned. "But I thought you said she was the one who asked you to help get him out of her place."

Marie shrugged. "There's the issue," she said. "She got upset, which set Rory—the ghost's name is Rory, did I tell you that?—off. He disappeared, probably back to the place where he died. I have no idea where that is, so now I have to wait for Sylvia to invite me back, and hope he shows up again." She clicked her tongue and shook her head. "I don't know why I bothered going there in the first place."

"If you didn't want to, then why did you?" I asked. Her face flushed an angry red, and I wished I could have taken my words back.

"Sorry," I said. "None of my business."

She took a deep breath in and let it out slowly. "No," she said. "It's a fair question. I went there because she's a cop, you see, and she knows about my—abilities. I guess I was afraid she'd make life hard for me, if I didn't."

"Oh, so you don't tell everyone about being able to see us?" I asked.

"I don't tell anyone," she said. "But she found out anyhow."

"Why don't you?" I asked. "Tell everyone, I mean?"

"Because people look at me like I'm crazy when they know," she growled. More anger, but I pushed anyhow.

"So, nobody but Sylvia knows about your abilities? No one?"

"Well, James figured it out. And my family knows, of course. Some of the people in my home town." She scowled. "But that's about it."

"Oh."

We were both silent as we watched the game and thought about things.

Personally, she'd given me lots to think about. Maybe I'd suspected some of what she'd told me. Maybe that's why I'd taken a chance with her.

She wouldn't tell anyone—except probably her boyfriend—about us. She was trying to protect herself, which meant we were protected.

"How did he disappear?" I asked.

"What do you mean, how did he disappear?" she asked. "It was just 'Poof!' and then he was gone, probably back to where he died. Come on, you can't tell me that you didn't know ghosts can do that."

"No," I said quickly. "Of course I knew they could do that. Otherwise, I'd be here by myself. I just thought—"

Then I stopped. I hadn't really thought about the fact that ghosts could disappear. That when they disappeared, they went somewhere else. For me, it was always the diamond. I hadn't thought—really thought—about the rest of them. Where they went. What they did when they weren't at the diamond. We didn't talk about that. We just talked about ball.

"Well, I don't care about that," I said, a tad defensively. "What makes ghosts move?"

"Compulsion, I suppose," she said. "If they really feel the need to attempt contact with someone, they can move. Temporarily, at least." She shrugged, then turned and stared at me. "You mean to tell me you've never moved?"

"Not once," I said. I tried for a light tone, but didn't think I'd pulled it off. "I guess I never felt compelled to contact anyone."

"Well, all ghosts are different," she said. "Some do, some don't."

"So I'm not unusual?"

She laughed. "Not really. For a ghost, you're pretty normal."

"Good," I said, though I wasn't sure how I felt about what she'd said. "Glad to hear it."

"I also got a call from one of Sylvia's friends from Calgary," Marie said. "Asked me to be a pickup for their team. There's a tournament down there in June. Sylvia told them I'd be perfect. That I have all the skills they need to win." She frowned. "Do you think she's trying to pull something?"

"Sylvia?" I asked.

"Yeah," Marie said. "For one thing, I am no good at ball. Not really. I play right field, for God's sake. And how many at bats have I had, really? A dozen? Maybe two? So, I got lucky and hit the ball a few times. What does that prove?"

"Are you kidding?" I asked. "You have a ton of natural ability, from what I've seen. You track the ball well, you figure out what the play is before the ball is hit—"

"Everybody does that. Don't they?"

"No. Most don't have a clue where to throw the ball once they catch it. If they did, the scores would be much, much lower." I glanced at her. "Are you telling me that you think the rest of the players on your team actually give a crap about figuring out the right play?"

"Well, yeah," she said. She looked confused. "Don't they?"

"No," I said again, more emphatically. "They don't. Which is why Sylvia probably told her friend about you. You have a better head for the game than most even if you haven't played much lately. Anyone with eyes can see that."

"Huh." She stared out at the grass of the outfield. In the glare of the lights, it almost glowed.

"All right," I said. "So maybe you don't have the best skills yet.

Practice will fix that. How many times a week do you practice?"

She looked embarrassed. "Well," she finally said. "The team hasn't gotten together for a practice yet, so the answer is zero."

"Oh, good grief," I replied and felt a twinge of something close to anger. "Just because they don't, doesn't mean that you shouldn't. Talk to Greg."

"Greg? You mean the coach?"

"Yeah. All you have to do is show even an iota of interest, and he'll help you as much as you can stand."

"Really?"

"Really." I looked past the diamond at the bleachers and saw Greg chatting with someone—looked like the coach of the team they'd just beaten.

I also saw Andy sitting at his usual spot, two rows down from the top of the middle bleachers, behind the backstop, so he could watch the whole diamond. Felt my whole essence tighten, and dragged my eyes away from him and back to Greg.

"He's here," I said to Marie. "You could talk to him now."

"About helping me practice?"

"Yeah."

"Just me?" She looked around, like she was trying to find a way to get out of the conversation. "I don't think he'd go for that. I wouldn't want to waste his time."

"He won't think it was a waste of time. Trust me. I've watched him, over the years. The man will do anything for his players. Anything." I pointed. "See? He's sitting right there. Go talk to him. And then call back that woman from Calgary and say yes to being a pickup for that tournament."

She grinned at me. "Did anybody tell you you're kind of pushy, for a ghost?"

"I'm not pushy," I said. "You're just very easy to push around. So, go."

She stepped away from the fence, then stopped. "I wanted to ask you something."

"So ask," I said.

"It's about that guy—"

It was Andrew. She was going to talk about Andrew.

"You know the one I mean. You told me to warn James about him."

"Andrew," I breathed. I suddenly felt cold.

"Yeah," she said. "That's the guy. So, what's your deal with him?"

"Deal?" I asked. I could not believe how cold I was. How afraid.

"Yeah." She glanced at me. "You okay? You look—sick."

"I'm fine," I said and tried to smile. "I just don't understand why you want to know about him."

"I want to know about him because you warned me to be careful around him," Marie said. She smiled at me, but her eyes were cold. "In fact, I Googled him."

"You what?" I asked, confused.

She laughed. "Oh yeah," she said. "Dead over forty years. Guess you wouldn't know about Google. I researched him. To find out what he's been up to."

"And what did you find?" I asked. The fear felt sharper now, like a small razor-sharp knife cutting through my skin. Maybe she found something bad that didn't involve me. Maybe she'd tell the cops and he'd be gone. Finally gone—

"Nothing," she said. "Looks like he's a fine, upstanding citizen. But there has to be a reason why you warned me about him. What is it?"

"It's—Well, it's because—" My voice trailed off as I tried to think. What was I going to tell her? The truth? I didn't think I could do that, because telling her that could be dangerous to my continued existence at the diamond.

"He's an old guy who's been hanging around the diamonds forever," I said, all in a rush. "Maybe his daughter did play ball once upon a time, but not for years now. I—I just don't trust him. He creeps me out."

Surprisingly, Marie laughed.

"What's so funny?" I snapped. "I wasn't trying. To be funny, I mean."

"It's just I don't hear many ghosts talking about being creeped out by the living," she said. "You know?"

"Maybe they are, and just don't tell you," I said, archly. "A lot of you are bad, you know."

Her laughter stopped. "Yeah," she said. "I know." She turned and looked me right in the eye. "Did you know that Andy guy when you were alive?"

I stared at her, wondering for a second if she had the capacity to read minds. "Why—why would you ask that?" I finally asked.

She didn't answer. Just stared at me like she was looking into my soul, until I turned away, unable to stand her awful gaze any longer.

"You're not going to answer, are you?" she asked.

"No," I said. "I'm not. Leave me alone."

"Then," she said. "At least tell me where your body is buried."

I glanced at second base, then jerked my eyes back to her face. "I'm not telling you that either. Leave me alone."

"Your family needs to know what happened to you."

"I gotta get ready for my game," I said, and walked away from her and her steel grey eyes that looked like they were trying to catch me. In a trap. In a lie.

I felt her staring after me until finally, finally, she turned away, walked to the bleachers, and sat beside her coach.

For a while, she said nothing, and I thought she was going to chicken out about asking Greg for help. Then, she began speaking. Barely looking at him, but speaking, none the less. Greg's face went from impassive to excited. He nodded and nodded, and then began talking himself, so quickly Marie couldn't get a word in edgewise. She finally quit trying and just sat there listening as he obviously took whatever free time she had and turned it into practice time.

IT STARTED TO rain as we were playing our game, but a little rain never stopped us before, and it didn't this time either. It came down harder and harder as the evening turned to night. Our game finished. My team lost, four to ten, and I made five errors.

Mr. Middleton asked if I was okay, so I lied and said I was fine. Just a little distracted by the rain. I don't think he believed me but it didn't matter. Soon enough everyone was gone, and I stood in the rain, just back of second base, and wondered where they all went. Wondered if I'd ask them where they went when they came back. Was pretty certain I wouldn't. It felt like an imposition. Like I'd be prying into their private deaths.

But that didn't stop me from wondering, as the rain fell around me—through me—in hard, driving, sheets.

Karen:
The Nightmare

THE NIGHTMARE WASN'T like the ones I used to have, with frightening regularity, just after my death. This one rolled out, inexorably, in real time. And it wouldn't stop, no matter how much I wanted it to. It just wouldn't stop.

I was on my last date.

I'd met him when I was working at the coffee shop at the University of Alberta. He was a student, he was nice, and I liked him. So, when he followed me from the University to the Coffee Factory on Ninety-Ninth Street, I just thought he'd taken a shine to me, and took it as a compliment. That was when he asked me out the first time. I said yes.

He told me he was married after we'd gone out for three months. He took me to a restaurant that night, a nice one, and then told me his dirty little secret. Probably hoped that I wouldn't cause a scene, and he was right. I made him take me back to my little basement suite before I started crying and told him we were through.

"Let me come in," he said. "So we can talk about this."

Stupid me, I let him in. Made him a coffee while he told me he was going to leave his wife, because he didn't love her anymore. "I love you," he said. "Just wait a few months, and I'll be free. And then, I'm all yours."

After he told me that, I quit crying. He drank his coffee and then we ended up in bed.

He was married, and I knew it, and we ended up in bed.

When he finally left, I felt sick and decided that the next time I spoke to him I'd do the right thing and break it off. But I didn't. When he called and asked me to go to the movies with him, I said yes.

For some reason, I said yes.

We went to the Twin, a drive-in on the north side of town. It had just opened for the summer, and two movies were playing that night. *Badlands* and *Amarcord*. *Badlands* played first, and it got him all jazzed up.

"I'm Martin Sheen and you're Sissy Spacek," he said. He pulled me into his arms. "Who do you want me to kill for you?"

"I don't want you to kill anybody," I said. "Jesus. You do realize that they're actors just playing characters in the movie, right?"

"Of course I do." He sounded hurt. "I just think it would be cool, being that free."

"Can't we watch the movie?" I asked. "Please?"

I tried to move to the other side of the car, but he wouldn't let me go. Pulled me even closer, and then grabbed my hand and rubbed it against his crotch. He had an erection.

"Touch me," he said. His voice was rough.

"No," I said. "I want to watch the movie."

But he insisted. Wouldn't let my hand go. Undid his jeans and pulled them down to his thighs. Then my hand was on him and he was hot. Throbbing and hot.

"Screw me," he whispered. "I gotta blanket in the back. No one would know."

"No," I said. But I couldn't seem to stop stroking him. Feeling the heat and the throb. All for me, if I wanted it.

He reached under my skirt. Grabbed my panties and I heard them rip.

"Don't," I whispered. "I like this pair."

"Take them off, then," he said. "Hurry."

I looked around at the other cars, to make sure no one was watching us. No one was. It was like we were on our own little island. No one would know. So I did.

He touched me between my legs and I gasped. "We can do it here in the front seat," he whispered. "Right here."

"But—" I looked around again, but he shook his head and grabbed me by the waist. He pulled me around so I was on my knees on the bench seat, facing him, and he hiked my skirt even higher.

"Fuck me," he said. "Right now."

The crude word cooled me. Not all the way, but enough so at least I could think. I shook my head to stop him, but he grabbed me hard between the legs and I groaned again. Before I knew what was happening he'd pulled me onto his lap. And then he was inside me and I rode him as the final credits rolled.

After, he offered to get me some more popcorn, because we'd knocked the box over, but I said no. Just pulled my ripped panties on and sat staring at the screen as the next movie started. *Amacord*, a Fellini film about Italy after the war.

I wanted to travel to Italy. And France. And Columbia. All over. The movie was weird, and my panties were ripped and wet, and I felt sick about what we'd done. And then I was crying, and he woke up, gave me a hug, and said he'd take me home.

"But let's eat first," he said.

I didn't answer him, because I'd turned into a huddled ball of self-loathing, but he didn't notice. He drove me across town to the Saratoga Restaurant.

"Order anything," he said. "Anything at all."

I had a Pepsi, and he ordered a burger and fries. "I'm starving," he said, and winked at me. "A good workout will do that."

We were silent as he ate. He didn't even seem to care that I wasn't talking. Just tucked into his food, a half grin on his face the whole time. When his plate was empty he pushed it away.

"Can you take me home now, please?" I asked. "I'm really tired."

"In a bit," he said. "I have something I want to show you." He threw some bills on the table and grabbed my hand, pulling me out of the booth. "Something I've been working on. You'll love it."

He drove out of the Saratoga parking lot and back onto Highway Two, the moon huge and full in the sky above us. As he headed back into town I wished I'd worn my watch—my almost new wristwatch that my parents had bought for me for my last birthday—because I had no idea what time it was, and it was starting to bother me. I had to call my parents first thing in the morning, to apologize for the scene I'd caused the evening before. I needed to make up to my mom for wrecking her birthday party, but I had to call early enough to catch her in. If I slept in, my plans would be ruined.

Besides, I didn't want to be in this car with this man—this married man—anymore.

"I'd rather go home," I said. "It's really getting late."

"Early, you mean," he laughed and grabbed my leg, pulling me closer to him across the bench seat of the Rambler. "It won't take long. I just want to show you something I've been working on."

He turned off the highway and headed east. I couldn't figure out where we were.

"I really want you to take me home," I said. "I have a lot to do tomorrow . . . "

He squeezed my thigh, hard, and shook his head. "I'll get you home," he said. "After I show you what I want to show you. Come on, be a good sport and do this for me. Didn't I show you a good time tonight?"

Thinking about the evening made me want to cry again, but all I said was, "Yes. You did," because I didn't want to fight with him. I just wanted to get home.

"All right then," he said. He pointed ahead at something in the dark. I couldn't tell what it was. "We're here," he said. "I told you it wouldn't take long."

He turned into what looked like an open field. The headlights flashed over a tractor and some other equipment, none of which I recognized.

"Where are we?" I asked.

"At the ball diamonds," he said. "The ones I've been working on, for the city. They're almost finished. I want you to see them, up close and personal."

He parked the car and shut off the engine. He got out, then stuck his hand inside and wiggled his fingers at me. I wasn't getting out of this, no matter how tired and heartsick I was. I took his hand and let him pull me out of the driver's side.

"See?" he said, and pointed. "Doesn't it look great?"

My eyes adjusted to the dark, and I looked at the ball diamond. I hoped that if I went along with him maybe I'd make it home before the sun came up.

It actually did look nice. I looked around and saw there were more, behind us. "How many diamonds are there?" I asked.

"One baseball diamond and four softball," he said. "We just put in the lights."

"Lights? On a ball diamond?"

"Yeah," he replied. "Three of them will have lights. It's all top shelf."

"Wow," I said, and walked to the fence surrounding the baseball diamond. "It looks really nice."

"Told you," he said. He led me away from the baseball diamond, but instead of going back to the car, he led me down a small path to the other diamonds. I followed him. *Just a few more minutes*, I thought. *Then I can go home.*

He stopped in front of the next diamond, and I stared at it.

"It doesn't look as finished as the first one," I said.

"It isn't," he replied. "The city wanted the baseball diamond finished first. But it won't be long before these are done." He pointed. "You can see the lights, and the bleachers. We just have to finish levelling the diamonds and putting the grass in the outfield, and they'll be done too. Quick as a wink."

The infield was nothing more than earth and sand. I couldn't imagine it looking any different than it did. But he could.

He looked excited and happy as he pointed at the spot where second base would be. "There were some problems with drainage. We had to tear this one up three times to get it right." He laughed, and pulled me through an opening in the fence so that we were walking on what would be the infield, whenever they finished it. "You know what they say, though. Third time's the charm."

"Yeah," I said. It was eerily pretty in the moonlight, and I shivered.

"You cold?" he asked. I nodded, and he pulled me into his arms. "I got a way to warm you up."

"I don't think so," I said. I tried to pull free, but he grabbed me harder.

"Come on," he said. "We had a good time, right?"

"Right," I said. I tried again to pull free, but he wouldn't let me go. He wouldn't let me go, and I felt the first hints of anger. Not fear. Not yet. "We did have a good time. But I have to go home. The evening's over."

"No," he said, and laughed. "No, I think you owe me a little more for this evening. Right here, under the stars. It was fun in the car, but this time I want to make you scream. And no one will hear you all the way out here."

And then, finally, I reached the end of my rope.

"Let go of me," I said. "And take me home right now. You hear me?"

I pulled away from him as hard as I could and broke free. I turned on the heel of my ridiculous platform sandals and stomped away from him. I was determined to get back to the safety and warmth of the car and then make him take me home.

It was getting easier and easier to imagine telling him we were through for real this time. He was acting like a jerk. His wife could have him. I was done.

"Don't you walk away from me!" he said. His voice sounded rough, and a twinge of fear wound its way into my anger. But not enough. Not by a long shot.

"I'm tired of this," I said. "I want to go, now. Take me home, or I'll calling your wife and tell her the truth about you. I really will."

I don't know why I said that, truly I don't. I knew it would make him angry, but I guess I hoped it would scare him, too. Scare him enough to finally, finally, do the right thing. But it didn't.

"No!" he roared, enraged. "You are not talking to Dianna. You're not telling her anything!" And then, he was after me.

Finally, I was more afraid than angry, and I ran.

My big plan was to get to the car, lock all the doors, and wait for him to cool off so he could give me that ride home he'd promised me. But my stupid sandals put paid to that idea.

I tripped and fell, and as I scrabbled around in the broken earth and sand, trying to regain my footing, he caught me.

And then that date that I never should have gone on turned into my last.

I saw his enraged face, his hands reaching for my throat. And then I was choking. I tried kicking him, scratching him, anything to get him to let me go. Let me breathe. But he was so big and so strong it was over before it truly started.

And then, I was dead.

I FLOATED ABOVE our bodies as he grabbed and groped me and

pulled at my clothes, whispering that he was going to leave his wife, I just had to trust him. That's why he'd gotten angry, because I was acting like I didn't trust him.

"Just put out a little bit more, baby, and all will be forgiven," he said. Then, his hands stilled as he looked—really looked—at my dead face.

"Fuck me," he muttered, and tried, more or less successfully, to pull my clothing back into place on my dead body. "What the hell?"

I would have screamed "You killed me you bastard!" if I'd known I could do that, but I didn't. Just floated and floated, watching as he freaked out and scrabbled back to the fence and through, running to his car. I thought he'd left me for someone else to find. But no, he came back with the blanket from the back seat of the Rambler and a shovel.

He dug a pit, just behind what was going to be second base. He sobbed and snivelled as he dug, and then, carefully rolled my body in the blanket, making sure he covered my face. He grabbed a big roll of thick plastic, and rolled me in it, too.

Entombed me in plastic.

Then, he dropped my body in the hole he'd dug and filled it.

Entombed me in dirt.

He even started the tractor and flattened out the top of my grave until it looked the same as the rest of the unfinished diamond. And then, as the sun finally edged its way up over the horizon, he ran to his car and drove away. He left me there, sitting on the unfinished bleachers at an unfinished softball diamond, all by myself.

WHEN I CAME to after the nightmare, I was standing right where I'd been buried, so many years before. Just behind second base. The rain had stopped, and the diamond had drained perfectly, as usual. It looked perfect. Pristine.

First, I cried. Then I screamed until my voice was gone. But no-one heard me, of course. Because there was no one there that could.

It had been a long time since I'd even thought about my death. For a second, I wanted to blame Marie for stirring all these old feelings up again, but stopped that crap quick.

I couldn't blame her. All she did was ask questions. I was the one who'd never done anything about what had happened to me. I'd just built up walls to make certain that no one knew my terrible secret. That I'd screwed a married man, even after I knew he was married, and then he'd killed me.

I felt like throwing up when I thought about all the girls who had stopped coming to the diamond after they met him. Had he hurt them? Killed them? I didn't know.

But I did know he had to be stopped.

"I've paid enough," I whispered. "Now, it's Andrew Westwood's turn."

Stage Two
Playing the Game

Marie:
Moving Rory On, and the Pink Invoice

JAMES LENT ME his car so I could go to Sylvia Worth's place again to move Rory on. Finally.

She'd texted me the night before.

I'm ready, the text read. *Be here tomorrow night. 7 p.m.*

No please or thank you. No nothing. Just the date, the time, and the fact she was ready. I decided right then that I would take her money.

I'd been throwing around the idea of telling her I'd changed my mind about charging her. My mother would not have approved of me charging her anything, and I felt kind of dirty when I thought about accepting that cheque. Until I got the text. Then, it felt like what I'd asked wasn't enough.

After work, I drove James to his apartment. "I don't know when I'll be done," I said.

"I know how this stuff works," he said. "You want something to eat before you go?"

"No," I said. "I think Sylvia's getting a pizza."

She hadn't mentioned a pizza in her oh so brief text, but I was too nervous to be hungry. I didn't want James to worry, though, and he would. So, I told him a little white lie. I figured he'd probably forgive me if he found out.

"Well, remember to pick up water," he said. "You know, for after."

I smiled. "Will do." I ran back to him and kissed him, a quick peck on the cheek. "Thanks for everything, James."

"Are you sure you can't come back to my place after?" he asked.

"I'm sorry," I said. "I told Jasmine I'd come home. I don't get there often anymore. I think she misses me. But can I come early for breakfast, before work?"

"I'd be hurt if you didn't," he said. "Good luck tonight."

"Thanks."

I patted Millie on the top of her little head on the way out the door. For luck, if I was going to be honest. And she let me. Probably could tell that I was nervous and needed all the luck I could get.

Then, I left. Early, but I was driving in rush hour traffic, after all, and I wanted to make sure that I got to Sylvia's before seven.

I GOT TO her apartment complex twenty-five minutes early, of course. A ridiculous amount of time to be early. I sat in the car, my knee jumping nervously, and listened to talk radio. Found some right-wing call-in show, the host working everyone who called in to a white hot froth about some possible tax increase that the provincial government was considering. I quickly got tired of his talking points and clicked it off. Then, I nearly jumped out of my skin when someone rapped hard on the passenger window.

It was Sylvia. She was still in uniform and she looked exhausted.

"What are you doing, sitting out here?" she asked. "Come on in."

"I—I was waiting for seven," I stammered.

"Oh, for heaven's sake," she said impatiently. "Come up."

She turned and walked back to the front door of the apartment complex, and I had to run to catch up with her. "Sorry," I said. "If I'd known you didn't care—"

"You could have texted me," she said, testily.

"Yeah, I guess." I followed her to her apartment. "Let's get this show on the road."

"Oh, he's not here yet," Sylvia said. "He never gets here before eight." She pointed at a pizza box sitting on the counter beside her fridge. "Want some pizza? I figured we could eat while we wait for him."

Looked like I hadn't white lied to James, after all.

THE HOUR AND fifteen minutes I spent with Sylvia before Rory finally showed up was easily the worst I'd ever tried to get through. Small talk was definitely not my strong suit.

She'd started off jittery and angry, talking in staccato bursts, like a machine gun. She peppered me with questions about James, and ball, and the rest of my life, like she was trying to drain every bit of information from me. Like she was interrogating me.

I mentioned the phone call I'd received about playing for the team in Calgary, the Thunder. That Henrietta Kendell was looking forward to meeting me.

"She said you've mentioned me before," I said, hoping she'd finally explain why she had even thought about me playing for this team.

Sylvia just looked at me strangely and finally said, "That's nice. They're a good team. You'll have fun."

I was going to push about why me, but she started the interrogation again, and I missed my opportunity. I finally shut her down by telling her I had to prepare for Rory's moving on.

"Please be quiet now," I said. "I must prepare."

That was bullshit, of course. No prep needed, but at least she was finally quiet.

Moving Rory on was easy. He was ready to go—he'd told me as much when we met—and now that Sylvia had decided to let him, it all went smooth as silk.

It was still dehydrating, of course, so I sat at her dining room table and drank four glasses of water. Drinking that much water takes time so we ended up talking. Again. Because she wanted to know what would happen next.

"What do you mean?" I asked. I drank more water, even though I'd already drunk so much I sloshed when I moved.

"I mean, what do I do now?" Sylvia asked.

"I guess you live your life," I said, putting down the glass. "Rory's gone, and he won't be back."

Sylvia stared at me hard. She was standing by the counter in her kitchen, and I realized I'd never seen her sit down. She was in her own apartment, and she didn't feel comfortable enough to sit down.

"Do you promise? It was hard to let him go. How can you be sure he won't come back?" She blinked. "Where did he go? Heaven or something?"

"I don't know. He didn't say."

"He didn't say? Are you trying to tell me he chose where he went?"

"That's the way it works," I said shortly. I pushed the glass to the middle of the table and stood. "I gotta go. My roommate's expecting me."

"Oh, you're not going back to James's?" she asked. Then she smiled, but it looked brittle, like it was ready to fall in shards from her face. "I thought you spent a lot of time there."

I stared at her, trying to remember if I'd told her that in that hour and fifteen minutes before Rory moved on. She laughed.

"Don't worry," she said. "I'm not having you followed or anything. James told me."

"Oh." James would have to learn to keep his mouth shut about our private lives. My private life. "I gotta go."

I walked to the door, then remembered the one thing I hadn't thought to tell her.

"Please don't tell anyone about me," I said. "About what I did for you."

She frowned. "Why not?"

"Because I don't want it getting around," I said.

"Oh. I thought this was your business. You know?" Then she gasped and snapped her fingers. "Dammit, I nearly forgot the cheque."

She walked back to the dining room table and picked up the plain white envelope sitting in the middle of it. I hadn't noticed it, even though my water glass was sitting not six inches away.

"Here," she said. "Your money. I didn't register the cheque. Did you want it registered? I can do that, if you want."

"No," I said. I pulled the envelope from her extended fingers. "This is fine. Thanks."

"Got an invoice for me?" she asked.

"A—a what?"

"An invoice. For my records. You know. So I remember exactly where I spent that thousand dollars."

"Oh." I hadn't thought of that. Hadn't thought of this being a transaction that needed an invoice. "Can I email it to you?"

"Yeah, that'd be fine," she said. Her mouth worked silently, and I realized she was trying not to cry.

"I gotta go," I said again, and turned to the door. "Try to get some sleep. You'll feel better in the morning."

"Promise?" she said.

I didn't answer her. Just opened the door and walked out. I heard her burst into sobs, through the door, so I walked away. Quickly. So I could stop invading her privacy anymore. I just hoped she'd return the favour and leave me alone now that this was done.

JASMINE'S HOUSE WAS dark when I finally got home. I half hoped that she was watching one of her shows, because it would have been nice to catch up even though I was exhausted, but she was already asleep.

I crept downstairs and found a Post-it note stuck to my pillow. *Greg Robertson called*, the note read. *He wants to meet you at the batting cages by the ball diamond at six o'clock tomorrow. Who is he? Did you hire a trainer or something? Tell all!*

I thought I'd told Jasmine the name of my coach then realized I really wasn't talking to her much about anything and resolved to fix that. Let her in, just a little bit more. Then, I tore off my clothes and threw myself across my unmade bed. I was asleep in seconds.

I WAS AWAKE exactly six hours later. I stared at my clock, willing myself back to sleep, then gave up, and got up. To be honest, I felt okay. Six hours was not too bad, and even though I'd moved Rory on the evening before, I felt refreshed. Maybe all I needed was six hours a night. And waking up this early did give me first kick at the shower.

But, as I stood in the shower, feeling the hot water wash away the night before, I realized that even though I felt all right, the nightmares every night were really getting old.

I decided I'd talk to Dr. Parkerson about them, when I saw her.

JAMES, SWEET MAN that he was, had breakfast waiting for me when I got to his apartment the next morning. He quizzed me about moving Rory on, and I answered his questions readily enough. Thought about how different it had been the night before, when Sylvia had interrogated me. Remembering that brought back the fact that James talked to Sylvia, a lot.

"Hey, you gotta quit talking to Sylvia about me," I said. "She was harassing me about staying at your place last night."

"Sorry," he said, but he didn't look sorry. He grinned. "I didn't realize I'm your dirty little secret. That's kind of cute."

"You're not my dirty little secret," I said. "I just don't want to talk to her about my private life. You know?"

"I guess," he said. He glanced at me, saw the look on my face, and nodded. "I won't talk about you to her. Not if you don't want me to."

"Thanks," I said.

Millie came up to the table and barked. Just once, but we both knew it was time to go. Millie the alarm clock.

"She's earning her kibble today," I joked as we got into James's car. "We should miss the worst of the traffic."

"She certainly is," James said.

Millie didn't say anything. Just curled up in the back of the Volvo and slept all the way to the office, obviously content with a job well done.

JAMES WAS BUSY with the Wellington divorce case, so I had time to work on the invoice for Sylvia. I thought for a second about just using James's invoice template, then stopped that foolishness. I was not tying his agency to anything to do with ghosts, even though he'd once joked about it being a viable second revenue stream.

So, I Googled "invoices" and built one. I sent it to Sylvia. Wondered how she was going to react to me using her work email, but she didn't seem to mind. Just replied with two words. *Thank you.*

James came in at two, looking a little worse for wear.

"What happened?" I asked. "Talking when you should have been listening?"

"No," he said. "Just a little case of road rage on the Whitemud. I thought the guy was going to kick the crap out of me, but I was able to talk him into calming down."

"Road rage?" I said. "Seriously?"

"Yeah," he said. He grabbed a cup and poured himself coffee.

I could see a rip in the armpit of his shirt when he reached up for the cup.

"And you were able to talk him into calming down? No violence, then?"

"Not a lot." He poured sugar into his coffee, too much, but he didn't seem to notice. "It helped that I was a foot taller than him."

I had a sudden vision of him pushing around a Hobbit on the side of the road, and snickered.

"It wasn't funny," James said. Then he smiled. "Well, maybe a little bit." He looked at my monitor. "What's that?"

"For Sylvia," I said. "She wanted an invoice."

"Why is it pink?"

I clicked the page closed. "The template I used was pink. I thought it looked okay."

"Yeah, it's fine," he said. He looked at me thoughtfully for a moment. Long enough to make me feel uncomfortable.

"What?" I snapped.

"Nothing," he said. "Remember to put that on your taxes. As income."

"Right," I said. "Can't forget taxes."

He went back to looking at me thoughtfully until I felt like screaming. But I didn't. Just composed myself, as much as I was able. "What is it, James?"

"I have been thinking about potential additional revenue streams," he said. "And I've come up with a pretty good idea but I'm not ready to talk to you about it, yet." He grinned. "Maybe when you get back from Calgary."

He'd been talking about additional revenue streams almost since the day he'd reopened his dead uncle's agency, so I didn't think much about his announcement, even with his grin. "Sounds good," I said. "Now quit staring at me."

"Was I?" he asked.

"Yes," I said. "You were."

He shrugged and dutifully turned his eyes away from me. But he didn't leave.

"Don't you have work to do?" I asked.

He didn't answer. Just tapped his upper lip as he pondered whatever the heck he was pondering. I decided to wait him out. Sometimes that was all I could do.

"You want to do something tonight?" he finally asked. "Maybe go to a movie or something?"

"You mean a date?" I asked. It had been forever since he and I had gone out like a regular couple. A movie sounded like fun.

"Yep. I thought, since you don't have ball tonight—"

"Oh damn," I said, remembering. "I'm meeting Greg at the batting cages tonight. And then I was going to watch the dead game, after. To talk to Karen. You know?"

"A practice?" he said. "That's great! Is it the whole team?"

"No," I said. "Just me. I asked him for some help. You know, for the Calgary tournament."

I felt bad for a second. James had offered to practice with me and I'd turned him down and now, here I was, practicing with my coach. I felt like I was being a practice two-timer. But it didn't seem to bother James at all.

"Want me to come with?" he asked. "Could be fun."

For a second I almost said yes, then remembered part two of my evening.

"I'm sticking around after to talk to Karen. After her game."

"And you don't want me there."

"I'm sorry," I said. "It's hard enough to get her to talk. I don't know how she'd react if you were there."

"Got it," he said. I was afraid he was going to get angry about me cutting him out, but all he did was smile. "What about this? I'll come with you to the practice, and then we can go out for something to eat. I'll drop you off at the diamond after, and you call me when you're done. I'll pick you up and you can stay at my place tonight. We'll watch a movie and eat popcorn. Pretend we're on a date."

The perfect solution. Of course.

"That sounds great," I said. "And thanks, James. For being so understanding."

"No problem," he laughed. "That's what I'm here for."

I PICKED UP a couple of big bottles of water before we went to the practice. I was pretty sure I was overdoing—but I was wrong. Greg hadn't been kidding what he said he was going to make me work harder than I ever had before in my life.

First, he put me in the batting cage.

"Hit the ball where I tell you," he said.

James hung off the fence that surrounded the cage. He waved

at me, and I heard a ball go by.

"Concentrate," Greg said.

So, I quit looking at James, who was laughing at me anyhow, and set myself, concentrating on the ball. Smacked the next one dead away centre. Greg nodded, didn't say anything, and sent another ball my way. I hit it, dead away centre.

"Hit to the left," he said. So, I tried. The ball dribbled off my bat to the left. "Again," he said, and sent another ball my way. Another grounder, a bit better than the first, but not great.

"Now right," he said. I did so, and the hit was better than to left. Greg nodded. "Looks like you're going to have to work on hitting to left field," he said. "Now, let's begin."

He had me hitting the ball for an hour straight. "Set your feet," he'd say. "Set your shoulders. Hands. Hips."

I hit ball after ball, until my arms felt like lead. When I complained, he said, "Ten more." And then ten more after that. Until I missed four balls in a row.

"Guess you're done," he said. "Good work."

I staggered out of the batting cage and downed one of the two bottles of water. The guy was a slave driver. We'd barely have time to go for something to eat—

"And now, let's do some fielding," he said, and grabbed a bat and a bucket of balls.

I glanced at James, half hoping he'd say, "She can't, we got a date," but he didn't say a word. Just set the bases out on the grass field by the batting cage, then grabbed the glove Greg offered him, and headed to first base.

"You take second," he said to me. "If you're going to play second base, there are a few things you need to work on."

I groaned, pulled on my glove, and walked to second base.

"What are we going to work on?" I asked.

"Throwing to first," he said.

For the next hour he hit grounders and pop ups and line drives at me, all the while barking directions about the position of my feet. My glove. My free hand.

By the time he finally stopped, I was missing more balls than I was catching, and I felt like my cleats weighed fifty pounds each.

I staggered up to him and dropped my glove. Grabbed the second bottle of water and downed it in one go.

"You trying to kill me?" I asked.

He laughed. Said no. "I'm just trying to make up for lost time," he said. "The season's going by, after all. You free tomorrow?"

"For another practice?" I gasped.

"Yeah."

"But we have a game," I said weakly. "Remember?"

"That's right," he said. "The day after, then."

I glanced at James, and he shrugged, grinning. Up to me.

"All right," I said. "Same time?"

"Yeah," he said. "We'll work on different scenarios. So you can be prepared."

Sounded like fresh hell to me, but I nodded. "Thanks," I said.

He looked at me like he was surprised. "You're welcome," he finally said. "That was fun."

He and James packed up the bases and balls and bats in the back of his crappy little car in the time it took me to take off my cleats. He waved good-bye and drove away while James helped me to my feet.

"That was a pretty good practice," he said. "How you feeling?"

"Like I've been to hell and back again." I looked at my watch, remembered it didn't work and turned to James. "What time is it?"

"Nearly eight o'clock," he said.

"We won't have time for dinner." I groaned. I was starving.

"There's Tim's," he said. "We can grab a soup and sandwich. Right?"

"Right." I sighed, wishing we could go somewhere better. Then I looked down at myself, covered in sweat and dirt. "Tim's is perfect," I said.

I WAS ABLE to scrape most of the sweat and dirt off in the Tim's bathroom and the soup and sandwich tasted great. By the time I got back to Diamond Two, I felt good. A little achy, but good.

Maybe better than good, if I was going to be honest.

"Text me when you're done," James said, and pecked me on the cheek. "I've got a great movie picked out."

"If I stay awake," I said. "I feel like I could sleep for a week."

He looked thoughtful. "That's good," he said. "That's real good."

Before I could respond sarcastically or something, he drove away. So, I walked to Diamond Two.

Dying on Second

I saw I was going to catch the end of the living game. Maybe if I found Karen, we could talk before the game, not after. Maybe I'd be able to get James to pick me up earlier than planned. Maybe I'd even be able to watch the whole movie with him. Finish our almost date like a real person, instead of falling into unconsciousness, like some sleep deprived zombie.

Of course, that didn't happen. I don't have that kind of luck.

THE LIVING GAME was in the final inning, and the dead were already warming up. I tried, half-heartedly, to get Karen's attention, so I could call her over. When she finally noticed me, she waved, but kept warming up. I wasn't going to be able to talk to her before. I'd have to wait, and catch her after.

Their game was good, all things considered. Karen made a couple of nice plays at second, and I noticed the position of her bare feet, of her ungloved hands, as she made the plays. Her glow made her easy to follow. Made them all easy to follow. Even the ball glowed.

I realized she was playing second base just the way Greg was teaching me. And it all seemed to work. Nice.

WHEN THE GAME was over, I went to talk to Karen. She was with her team. They'd finished their after game meeting, and now were just sitting on the grass kibitzing. A couple of the dead had already drifted away, disappearing when they reached the fence that surrounded John Fry. But Karen was in no hurry. After all, she'd just be walking to second base and then waiting for the next game.

For a moment, I felt a tinge of unease—it had not been very long ago that these ghosts had tried to run me off—but no-one even gave me a second look as I sidled up to Karen.

"Is it okay if I sit here?" I asked.

Karen stared at me for a long moment. "You're not going to interrogate me again, are you?"

I felt my face heat and shook my head.

"Good," she said, and glanced at the rest of the ghosts. "Should be all right. Joanne's not here, so you should be safe."

"Joanne?"

"She still has a bee in her bonnet about you," Karen said. "She'll get over it." She patted the grass beside her. "Sit."

"Good game," I said, and dropped down beside her. The muscles in my legs screamed, and I wondered if I'd be able to get up again.

"Thanks," she said. "You look like hell."

"Thanks," I replied, sarcastically. Then I laughed at myself. She was probably right. "I took your advice and asked Greg for some help. The first practice was tonight. I think he was trying to kill me."

"Try to talk some of the other girls from your team into coming," she said. "He won't be quite so focussed on you, then."

"It's actually not that bad," I said. "He really knows his stuff."

"Told you," she said. "Is he grooming you for second base?"

"Grooming me? That sounds kind of creepy," I said, and laughed. "But yeah, I guess he is."

"That's good," she said. "You should be playing that position."

I noticed that the chatting around us had stopped. Looked at the rest of her team, and realized they were all unabashedly eavesdropping on our conversation.

"Do you mind?" Karen said.

"Sorry," one of the women—I think it was Jane—said. Then they all moved away a couple of steps, and began talking among themselves again.

"That's better," Karen said. "Now, tell me. Have you seen that Rory guy again?"

I smiled. "Yes, as a matter of fact, I have." Then I told her all about moving Rory on and dealing with Sylvia. Even about having trouble with the pink invoice. When I finally shut my mouth, I realized one of the ghosts had hitched her way closer and closer to us. It was Jane, and she was hanging on my every word.

I stopped talking and stared at her. She looked embarrassed and tittered guilty laughter. "Caught me," she said. "I just wanted to know a bit more about that thing you did to that Rory guy."

"What about it?"

"He's dead, right?"

"Yes."

"And you helped him . . . uncouple from this world, or whatever. Right?"

"I helped him move on to the next plane of existence," I said. "That's right."

"Cool." Jane nodded her head, and I realized she was nervous. "Is that what you want to know about? How I moved him on?"

"Not really," she said. She looked around at the rest of her team, who were all studiously acting like they were ignoring us and our conversation, and then back at me. "I wondered if you could do that for anyone."

"Yes, if you want to, I can help you." I turned to Karen. "You don't mind if I talk to Jane about this, do you?"

She shook her head, her face stiff. "I don't mind at all," she said. But she was lying. I could tell.

Karen:
Blowing Up

I COULDN'T BELIEVE Jane wanted to talk to Marie at all, much less about getting moved on. But when Marie asked me if I minded, I said, "No. Doesn't bother me at all."

It did, of course. Jane played third base and if she did decide to let Marie move her on what would the team do for the rest of the season? We'd be screwed.

"I don't have to talk to her if you don't want me to," Marie said. "You look upset."

I tried to wave her off. Tried to smile. "I'm fine," I said. "Go ahead. Talk. I won't bother you."

I don't think she bought it, but I was as good as my word. I sat there silently and listened as Marie explained, in excruciating detail, what Jane would need to do before she would be properly ready to move on.

Jane looked afraid, at first. But as Marie walked her through the process she calmed down. Started asking questions—many of them the same questions I'd thought about asking Marie myself.

"Will it hurt?" Jane asked. "'Cause I don't want to be hurt. Not anymore."

"No," Marie said. "It won't hurt. But take your time. Think about things before you make your decision, because once you move on, it's final."

"And maybe wait until the end of the season before you bail

on the team," I said.

"I wouldn't bail on the team, Karen," Jane said. "You know that."

"I don't know anything," I said. The anger bubbled to the surface then. I was surprised at how supremely angry I was. "Just know that if you decide to be selfish, you'll wreck the season for everyone."

"I wouldn't do that," Jane said again. She stood and backed away from both of us. "I'm sorry, Karen," she said. "I didn't mean to make you mad."

"Don't leave," Marie said. "We're not done yet. I need to know where your body is—" But Jane shook her head, still staring at me. At my anger. My rage.

"We can talk another time," she said to Marie. "I—I gotta go." To me, she whispered, "I'm sorry," once more, then disappeared.

"What the hell's wrong with you?" Marie hissed at me. "You didn't need to chase her away like that. We were just talking."

"Yes," I said. "You were talking about her leaving the team. In the middle of the frigging season. I mean, how could you?"

"How could I what?" Marie asked.

I realized the rest of the team had stopped talking again. They were all silent, watching Marie. Watching me as I basically had a complete and total melt down.

"Talk her into leaving us," I said. "The games will be no good without her. You have to understand that."

Marie frowned. "I wasn't trying to talk her into doing anything," she said. "I was just—"

"Telling her to leave," I cried. I tried to stop my verbal diarrhea, but couldn't. It just kept spilling out of me in sickening waves. "She'll leave, and the rest of them will leave, and then I'll be alone."

"But—"

"I can't be alone!" I yelled.

And then, all was silent. I couldn't tell if it was because I'd somehow been struck deaf, or because the world had suddenly grown still. I gasped in the cold night air. Heard my gasp, and knew that it was the world, not me.

"I can't be alone," I whispered. "You can understand that, can't you?"

"Yes," Marie said. "I understand."

I looked at her and shuddered again. Because she did look like she understood me. All of me. Everything about me, even the stuff I'd never told her.

"Go," I said. "Please go. I don't feel well."

"All right."

Marie nodded and stood. Looked over at the other players on my team. "Make sure somebody stays with her for a while," she said. And then she was gone.

"Nobody needs to stay with me," I said. "I'm fine."

Then, dammit, I started to cry. Charlotte put up her hand.

"I'll stay," she said, and walked over to me. She stood closer to me than she ever had before, and I could see the marks on her arms where she'd cut herself when she was alive. I hadn't noticed them before.

Her light, her strength, washed over me. Calmed me, so I could finally stop crying.

"You don't have to stay," I said. "I'll be all right."

"I don't mind," she said. She even smiled at me a little. "We've never talked. Not really. I figure we can do it now. You know?"

She was right. We had never talked past discussing a play or a booted ball.

And then, I tried to remember when I'd last had a real talk with any of them. About anything that did not involve softball or Marie.

I couldn't think of one time. Not one.

AFTER THE REST of the dead dispersed we sat in the dark for a long time without saying anything. Charlotte turned and looked at me, her dead eyes staring, it seemed, right into my soul.

"So, what was with the breakdown?" she said. "I've never seen you lose it like that before."

I blinked in surprise. "Right to the point, huh?"

"I figure we might as well really talk," Charlotte said. "Good a time as any, don't you think?"

"I guess," I said. "But I—I don't even know where to start."

"Tell me what set you off," Charlotte said. "And we can go from there."

I sighed. "It was Marie. She was talking to Jane about moving on. She's not supposed to do that. I told her to leave us alone." I chuckled, miserably. "I think I was wrong about getting rid of her.

She's going to wreck everything."

Charlotte shook her head, and I stared at her. "What?" I said. "You don't think she's going to be a problem? What if she talks everybody into leaving?"

"People leave," Charlotte said. "New people come in and take their places, and we adjust. We've lost people before."

"Not in a long time," I muttered, but she was right, of course. People had left over the years. They'd get tired of the games, tell us they were done, and never come back. And we had adjusted. But we'd never had to deal with someone who could cause a wholesale desertion like Marie could. "I think she's dangerous."

"Pfft!" Charlotte cried. "You were right, before. She's not going to wreck anything and I think you know it."

"But—what if she convinces everyone to leave?" I said.

"She isn't convincing anyone to do anything. She's just talking to them. If they decide to go, then they go. And we adjust." She smiled. "Besides, I think you might miss her if she leaves. You two have gotten pretty tight over the season."

"I guess," I said. "She is easy to talk to, most of the time. It's just I don't think I could stand it if I was alone."

With Andrew.

I looked down at my hands and realized that they weren't glowing the way they usually did. "Do I look darker to you?" I asked.

"Yes, you do," Charlotte said. "Tell me what you're thinking about right now."

"I—I can't," I whispered.

Her face sharpened, and she frowned. "You better. Unless you want to be one of the ones to disappear. Lose all your light, so we can't see you anymore." She shook her head. "You don't want to be a ghost to us ghosts, do you?"

"Do you think that could happen?" I asked.

"I've never seen it, but some of the girls have," Charlotte said and pointed. "Out there, in the world. It really shook them up. All of a sudden, somebody's gone. With no forwarding address or anything, if you know what I mean."

I knew exactly what she meant. After all, that was the way I left the world of the living. I didn't want to do it again.

But that meant telling her—telling them all—about Andrew. What he'd done to me. And worse, what I'd done to get myself in that situation. I looked down at my hands and was horrified to see how dark they were. I was losing light by the bucketful. If I didn't say something, I could be gone before the night was out.

"All right," I said. "But you have to promise me that you won't hate me."

She frowned. "Why would I hate you?"

"Just because," I said. I tasted metal in my mouth, as though it was suddenly full of blood. And my hands were almost dark. "Promise."

"I promise," she said, impatiently. "Now talk."

So, I did. I told her the whole sordid story while I stared out over the darkened softball diamond, so I didn't have to look at her. At first, I was just going to talk about Andrew but once I started everything came out in a fetid rush.

"It was all right, before," I said. "Having him show up here every season. I could stand it, you know? But now, I've started having the nightmares again—and I don't think I can take it anymore." I laughed, but it sounded miserable, even to me. "If all of you leave, it would mean that I'd have to face him alone. And I can't. Not anymore. You know?"

"I understand," she said. I glanced at her, and she looked furious. Absolutely furious.

"I knew it," I whispered. "I knew if I told anyone that I'd gone to bed with a married man, that you'd hate me—"

"Oh!" Charlotte's eyes snapped wide, and then, she laughed. It wasn't a happy sound. "I don't hate you for sleeping with him. Jesus, we've all done something. No. It's not you."

"Why do you look so angry, then?"

"It's what that son of a bitch did to you," she said. "Of course."

Her words brought me to a full stop. I couldn't think of anything to say, and knew I probably looked like a fish, my mouth open and gaping.

"He can't get away with this," Charlotte said. "You know that, don't you?"

"But he did get away with it," I whispered. "I'm dead and he got away with it."

"What if you tell Marie?" Charlotte asked. "I know you're hating her right now and everything, but what if you tell her what he did? She could tell the police and he could finally answer for his crime."

I shook my head. "If I do, she'll want to know where I'm buried. The police will need my body, to prove the murder."

"And?" Charlotte asked. "That'd be a good thing. Right?"

"No," I said. "If the police move my body I'll follow it. And I won't be able to find my way back."

"Oh," Charlotte frowned and pursed her lips. Thought for a moment, then nodded. "Probably better that you don't tell Marie, then," she said. "So that means it's up to us."

"What do you mean?" I asked.

"We need to tell the others," she said. "And I think it's very important that we have a couple of conversations with the tea cup girl."

"Who?" Things were moving too quickly. I couldn't keep up. "Who are you talking about?"

"Rita," Charlotte said. "Rita Danworth."

I frowned. "Why do we need to talk to her?"

"Because she can move things in the living world," she said. "Remember the swarming?"

"Worst waste of time ever," I said, and rolled my eyes.

"Maybe," Charlotte said. "But I think the reason the swarming didn't work was because enough of us didn't know how to actually touch Marie. But think what could happen if we all learned. We'd be able to use it against Andy Westwood. We'd be able to make sure that the son of a bitch finally leaves and never comes back to your diamond. You know?"

Oh.

"Hey," she said. "We dead gotta stand together. Don't we?" Then she paused. "Can you imagine what crazy Joanne's going to be like if she actually learns to touch stuff in the living world? That'd be worth the price of admission, all on its own."

She laughed, and it didn't sound angry anymore. It sounded excited—almost alive.

"Come on," she said, and bumped me, showering me with her warm, wondrous light. "This is a good thing, Karen. It really is."

"I just can't believe it will work."

"We dead can do anything," Charlotte said. "Everything. All we have to do is want it bad enough."

I looked down at my hands. They were glowing their usual soft white. Maybe she was right. Maybe we could actually pull this off.

Charlotte stayed with me the rest of the night. Not because she had to, but because she wanted to. It was nice and I felt better than I had since I died. Maybe before that.

And I decided not to tell Marie anything about what we were planning.

After all, Marie was alive. She couldn't understand what it was like for the dead. Not really. Besides, we had a plan. And if we wanted it bad enough, it just might work.

Marie:
The "What If" Scenario

JAMES AND I didn't watch a movie when I got back to his place that night. We watched a couple episodes of the first season of a cable TV show he'd found on sale at HMV. I figured he was the last person in the known world that still bought physical discs anymore, but whatever. He'd picked a strange series, no doubt about it, about this crazy guy having delusions and trying to bring down the world with his computer hacking abilities. James liked it better than I did, to be honest, so once the popcorn was gone I went to bed.

James stayed up. "Just one more episode," he said. "And then I'll come to bed."

I could tell by the look on his face that he was probably in for an all-nighter, so I snuggled into bed. I was exhausted after my practice session with Greg, and hoped I'd be able to go right to sleep.

But of course, sleep refused to come. I kept thinking about Karen acting so wild when I was explaining moving on to Lisa.

I knew Karen wasn't interested in moving on. She'd made that absolutely clear to me the first time we met. But she caught me off guard, losing it on me—and Lisa— when all we were doing was talking.

And what was the deal with her being afraid of being left alone? I couldn't figure that out at all. She was surrounded—

literally surrounded—by ghosts, especially in softball season. They weren't all going to decide to move on all at once. In fact, I was willing to bet most of them would hang around for a few more years, at least. They seemed to like what they had, and didn't want to deal with their pasts, which was pretty much exactly what they had to do in order to move on.

"Jesus, it almost sounds like me," I muttered, punching my pillow as I tried, once more with feeling, to get comfortable enough to go to sleep. "I don't want to talk to my shrink about any of that stuff, either."

Then I sat upright and stared into the dark, all thoughts of sleep gone.

My shrink. Dr. Parkerson. She might be able to help me figure out what's going on with Karen.

Before, when I had a problem like this with a ghost, I'd just give my mom a call and she'd walk me through whatever part of the process I couldn't figure out. But my mom was gone to wherever she'd decided was her next phase of existence without even saying good-bye, so I could only bounce my ideas off James, who was sometimes helpful, but not often enough. I couldn't talk to Jasmine because she didn't know about the ghost thing. And Sergeant Worth—Sylvia! Why couldn't I remember her first name was Sylvia?—was on the no talk list too, even though she knew about me and ghosts, because she was a cop.

But my shrink. I might be able to use her.

I could tell her I was asking for a friend. Not a dead friend, of course, because there was no way in the world I was telling her about interacting with the dead. Just a friend, maybe on my ball team, who was showing some strange behaviours. And I'd ask her what I should tell my friend to do.

Now, I realized she'd probably think I was talking about myself, but I didn't care. She could think what she wanted. She might be able to give me some ideas about how to help Karen. Which would be great. Just great.

For a second, I tried to figure out why I cared so much about Karen getting angry at me. It wasn't like we were friends, or anything . . .

I laid back on my pillow and pulled the blanket up to my chin and stared at the hugely old-fashioned popcorn ceiling of James's bedroom as I thought about Karen. Maybe we were friends, sort of. Just softball friends, but still. Friends.

"She'd been through some shit that she doesn't want to talk about to everyone," I whispered. "And so have I. Wouldn't surprise me if we became besties, or something, if I can help her with her little overreaction problem." I snorted laughter at the thought of me being best friends with a ghost, then rolled over and closed my eyes.

Time to go to sleep for real this time. I hoped.

DR. PARKERSON'S OFFICE was mostly beige. The carpet, the walls, the art on the walls—all various shades of beige. I think she thought it was soothing, but it wasn't. Boring maybe, but not soothing. Not in that room.

She waved me in and pointed to the chair where I usually sat. No couch, thank God, because when I first started coming to her, I think that would have sent me running, screaming, into the night. Now I was just afraid I'd fall asleep, and she'd talk about sleeping pills again. Maybe insist this time. And I was afraid that I would take her up on them. Just to catch a few zees.

No. I'd catch a few zeds, I thought, and snorted laughter.

"You're in a good mood," she said.

I thought about it for a few seconds, and then nodded. "I'm feeling pretty good."

"Still playing that game for exercise?" she asked, then looked down at her notes. "The softball?"

"Yep. Still playing the softball," I said.

She stared at me, waiting, then made a note. Probably something like "her passive aggressive crap is really starting to tear me down. Maybe I'll start taking those pills I keep pushing on her." Or something.

"Actually, it's going well," I said. "I'm getting some extra help from the coach, so I'm improving. Even got picked up, by a team in Calgary."

She frowned. "Why?"

"To play in a tournament with them." I laughed, but felt uncomfortable. "Guess my name made it all the way to the city to the south."

"Well, that's good," she said, and made another note. "Sleep?"

I thought about making a joke, but let it go. "About the same. Maybe a little better."

"How much better?"

I thought about the five or so hours, on average, I slept. How that six hour sleep had felt like heaven. "Just a little."

"Headaches?"

"The same."

"Nightmares?"

I sighed. "The same."

"Is the IRT working?"

I jerked guiltily and couldn't look at her. She sighed. "You told me you'd give it a real try, this time," she said.

"I know." I shook my head. "I'm just having trouble coming up with a happy ending to being kidnapped. You know?"

"I didn't say it would be easy," she said. "But I'd like you to keep trying."

I remained silent. Didn't know how I could tell her I'd keep trying something that I thought was ridiculous.

"There's always the Prazosin option," she said.

Prazosin. A cheap, generic blood pressure medication that sometimes helps treat nightmares from trauma. Worked for war vets. No reason why it wouldn't work for me, too. That was her theory, anyhow.

"No drugs," I said. "I'll give the IRT another try."

"Every day," she said. "You have to replay the nightmare with the adjusted ending in your mind every day."

"I remember," I said.

I heard her pen scratch across her pad of paper. More notes. Probably about how impossible I was to help.

I was beginning to think that perhaps this was not the best time to ask her about my "friend with a problem." I wasn't giving her the answers that she wanted, and I didn't know if she'd be open to a "what if" scenario.

"I'll try," I said. "Really."

"I hope so," she said. "It can help you, if you let it. Because you have to sleep more. You'll feel better, in all ways, once you get a handle on the sleep issue."

"I know." I'd seen the research, online. She was right. It sounded dumb but it worked. Maybe it was time to give it another go. "I'll do it. Every day."

"Good."

Her pen scratched, and then we were both silent. I was trying to figure out how to segue into a dialogue about my "friend." I couldn't guess what she was thinking about.

"I'm getting to know my team mates," I finally said. "We go for beers after the games." I hadn't actually done that yet, but she didn't need to know. "And there's this girl. Karen. I think maybe she's suffering from PTSD too."

"Is she getting treatment?"

I thought of Karen, trapped on second base. "I don't think so," I said. "But she blew a gasket when we were just talking the other night."

We'd been talking about moving on spirits, but Dr. Parkerson didn't need to know that, either. No ghost talk. Not in this room.

"She reminded me of me, a few months ago," I said. "You know?"

Dr. Parkerson nodded. She knew. "What were you talking about?"

"Nightmares," I said. "And stuff. I told her I was having trouble sleeping. That I was having nightmares. She said she was too. I asked her what they were about, and she just blew up."

Now, this wasn't close to what happened, but I just needed Dr. Parkerson to give me a hint or two about how to get her to open up to me, so I could help her.

"How did it make you feel?" Dr. Parkerson asked. Her usual question.

"Pretty useless, to be honest. I didn't know what to say to her. I apologized, but it didn't seem to help." I shook my head. "What do you think I should do?"

"For her, you mean?"

"Well, yeah. I want to help her, but I don't know how."

I honestly thought Dr. Parkerson would be happy that I'd found people to talk to, to interact with. That was one of the reasons she'd suggested taking up a sport, after all. So I could make frigging friends. But she frowned.

"Marie," she said. "You shouldn't think about her in those terms."

"What terms?" I asked, confused.

"In terms of fixing her. Helping her."

"Why not?"

"Because you need to concentrate on helping yourself," she said. Scratch scratch scratch went her pen when I snorted derisively. Probably something about oppositional defiance disorder, or something.

She wasn't going to give me anything.

"Forget it," I said. "I'll figure it out myself."

Dr. Parkerson didn't respond, and I suddenly wondered if I'd even said the words out loud.

"Does she know you are in treatment? Your friend?" She looked down at her notes. "Your friend Karen."

"No," I said. "Why would I tell her that?"

"It might help her make the decision to help herself," she said. "If you show her that she's not alone. That you've found a way to help yourself." She looked at her notes again, then at me. "You do know that being in therapy isn't a secret, don't you? Lots of people are in therapy. You don't have to hide the fact."

I thought about that for a moment. Just a moment.

"I don't think I can do that," I said. "She doesn't seem like the 'go to therapy' type."

"Just like you thought about yourself, eight months ago."

She got me with that one.

"But here you are," she said.

"Yes," I said. "Here I am. So are you telling me that I can help her by telling her I'm in therapy?"

"In therapy for PTSD. Yes."

"But she'd want to know why."

"Why what? Why you are sharing, or . . ."

"Why I'm suffering from PTSD." I stared down at my hands. "She'll think I'm crazy."

"You're not—"

"I know!" I snapped. "I know I'm not crazy. But I don't think that her knowing all about me will help her."

"You have to open up to someone, Marie." Dr. Parkerson spoke softly, letting me know that I'd raised my voice.

"Sorry," I said. "I know. But I don't think I'll be opening up to Karen any time soon."

"Why not?"

"Well, she's dead, so I can't imagine—"

Dr. Parkerson sat bolt upright. "What did you say?" she asked.

I blinked. What had I said?

"I said she's damaged," I said. "And that—"

"No," she said. "No you didn't. You said she was dead."

My mouth went terror dry. "I didn't say that," I said. I could feel my lips catching on my teeth, my mouth was so dry, and hoped she didn't notice. "You misunderstood me."

"I don't think I did."

"Then it was a slip of the tongue," I said. I pulled my phone from my pocket and looked at it. Time had to be up. But all I saw was the blank screen.

"What time is it?" I asked. I turned on my phone, and listened to it tinkle awake. Felt horror when I realized that I'd only been there thirty-five minutes.

"Put your phone away," Dr. Parkerson said. "We need to talk about your slip of the tongue."

Jesus Christ almighty. What had I done?

IT TOOK ME the full fifteen minutes to convince Dr. Parkerson there was nothing to my Freudian slip. That it really, truly was just a slip of the tongue. She seemed convinced, anyhow. Even though she did offer me another drug to take, as I was gathering my stuff when I could finally leave.

"It's called Seroquel," she said. "It will help you sleep."

"I told you that I don't want drugs," I said.

But this time, she ignored me. Reached into her front drawer and pulled out her prescription pad. "I think you need this, Marie," she said. "That slip of the tongue makes me think that your lack of sleep is starting to affect brain function."

She quickly wrote the prescription, tore the sheet loose from the pad, and held it out to me. "Try it for a week," she said. "We can talk about how much better you feel when you come in."

I didn't want to take it, but she wouldn't put her hand down so I grabbed it and stuffed it into my hoodie pocket with my phone.

"I'll think about it," I said.

"Think hard," she said. "Your lack of sleep is—"

"Messing with my brain. Yeah, I get it," I said. I tried smiling, and I think I almost pulled it off. "You sure read a lot into a simple slip of the tongue, Doctor."

"That's what I'm here for," she said, and smiled back. It wasn't real, but at least she was trying. "So, I'll see you next week?"

"My next appointment is in two weeks."

"I just want to check how you are reacting to the Seroquel," she said. "Sleep-wise."

"Right." No smile this time. I couldn't have pulled one off, even if I tried. "All right then. I'll see you next week."

Then, after I'd escaped, I sat at the bus stop and tried to keep from puking all over the sidewalk. I could not believe I'd said that, in front of my shrink.

What the hell was wrong with me?

I GOT BACK to the office and Googled Seroquel. It was an anti-psychotic.

An anti-psychotic. She was trying to get me on an anti-psychotic, obviously because she hadn't believed me. She thought I was seeing dead people, and that I was crazy. I knew it!

Then I read a little further. *Seroquel—known for extreme sedation and sometimes prescribed for anxiety or sleep disorders* and I stopped freaking out quite so badly. Maybe Dr. Parkerson had given me that particular prescription because she actually believed that I needed help with my sleep, and nothing more.

Her telling me that my brain function was being impaired didn't mean that she thought I was crazy, exactly. It just meant that she thought I needed help with my sleep. Which I did.

I thought about telling James, then decided against it. He didn't need to know about the possible brain impairment thing. All I needed was a couple of good nights' sleep, and it would get better.

I even filled the prescription before I went to my softball game. But I hadn't decided whether or not I would take it. Just tucked it into my purse, away from prying eyes, and then went to my game, like nothing was wrong.

Yeah, right.

Marie:
Calgary Henry and the Old Man

THE NEXT WEEK was quiet, for the most part. James was working on two cases—more divorce, it seemed that was all that ever happened between married couples in this city—and so I was the one who had to walk Millie when she was at the office. She wasn't too thrilled about it. Just trudged out, did her business, and then trudged back and crawled into her dog bed.

She acted like I felt, to be honest. The office was a whole bunch better when James was there. But he had to work, so there Millie and I were, trudging through our days.

The evenings were better.

Greg set up more one-on-one practices for me. Focussed on the batting which was all right because I was actually starting to see some improvement. Plus James came to most of them, helping out, which made it all even better. And in our Thursday game Greg moved me up so I was batting fourth again. Clean up. And, for the most part, I did okay. We won that one, seven to three.

He left me in right field, but that was okay, too. I was effective there. Effective. Never thought it would happen, but it did.

Because of all the exercise I was getting I was sleeping more. Not a lot more, but some. So, I put away the bottle of Seroquel and decided to fire my shrink. I was not going to take the drugs, and the IRT still wasn't working. She wasn't helping me, so I decided it was better to let her go.

On the day that I was going to Calgary for the tournament,

James took Millie to the groomer so I had some alone time. I spent it carefully typing "it's not you, it's me" letters to Dr. Parkerson but none of them quite seemed right, so I blew them all away when James came back with a freshly coiffed comfort dog.

"She looks great," I said.

"I'm trying a new place," he said. "The groomer's nice. Millie seems to like her, anyway."

"That's good. And she looks cute with the little bow."

"She better," he said. "I spend more on her hair than I do on my own."

I laughed. "Your hair looks great, too."

To be honest, I liked his hair when he let it grow. It got all wavy and sexy and, well, I liked it. But I didn't think I'd ever tell him that. No ego boost from Marie. Not about his hair, anyhow.

"I thank you, Ma'am," he said. Then he glanced at the clock. "Isn't it just about time for you to go? You don't want to miss your bus, do you?"

"No," I said. "I wouldn't want that."

"Then let's go."

Even though I could have walked to the Red Arrow bus station, since it was just a few blocks from the office, James insisted on driving me. I figured he wanted to give me all the last minute advice he could.

"I wish I was coming," he said, for about the fourteenth time. "Come on. Let me. It'll be like a little holiday. We can get a hotel room—"

"What about the dog?" I asked. Millie, who was curled up in the back seat of the Volvo, lifted her head and whined. "See?" I said. "She doesn't want to go. She wants to stay here, with you."

"That whining is new," James said, glaring briefly into the back seat. "She started it on the way home from the groomer."

"Maybe you're going to have to find an even newer groomer," I said.

"Maybe." He sighed, Millie whined again, and I laughed. "It's not funny," he said.

"Yes, it actually is," I said. "Don't worry, she'll probably stop soon."

"I hope so," he said. "Because it's pretty grating, I have to tell you." He pulled the car over in front of the huge Red Arrow bus and parked. "All right, so you don't want me to come. Fair enough. Just promise me you'll call me when you get there."

"Will do."

"And after every game."

"Sure."

"And before you go to bed."

I turned to glare at him. Saw he was grinning, and grinned back. "I'll be fine, James. I told you. I'm staying with one of Sylvia's friends. She's driving me around and everything. There's nothing to worry about."

"You told me." He leaned forward and kissed me. "But I'm going to miss you, you know."

"You better," I said, and kissed him back. I grabbed my suitcase and the big black bag that carried all my equipment out of the back seat, being careful not to disturb Millie, who'd gone to sleep.

No good-bye from her. I didn't know whether that was a good sign or a bad sign. Decided it was good. That she knew, somehow, that everything was going to be hunky-dory. That I didn't need her comfort or support.

"I'll call you," I said to James, and shut the door. Stepped up to the bus, and as James drove away, got on board. Ten minutes later, I was on my way.

I was excited, if I was going to be honest about the whole thing. A little bit nervous, but mostly excited. I was pretty sure Millie was right. This weekend was going to be fun.

"Marie? Marie Jenner?"

Henrietta Kendall—no relation to the pitcher, Miriam Kendel—was waiting for me at the bus terminal when the bus pulled in. She was about the same age as Sylvia Worth, and just as fit. She didn't look tired, though, and she didn't look haunted. She just looked happy to see me.

"Call me Henry," she said, as she grabbed my suitcase and led me to her car. A late model Beamer with all the bells and whistles. "My dad named me. He chose Henrietta, after Henrietta Lacks, he said. But I don't like it much. It's so old-fashioned." She grinned. "However, it is hilarious when clients meet me for the first time, and finally figure out that they're dealing with me and not an old man, like they expected."

"That would be funny," I said. Pointed at her car. "Nice."

"What can I say?" she said as she tossed my stuff in the trunk. "Life's been good, down here in oil country."

"I thought Edmonton was called Oil Country," I said. "Isn't Calgary Cowtown, or something?"

"Only in July," she said. "The rest of the time, it's all about the oil." She pointed out her side window, at the city's downtown core. At all the towers, doing all that oil business. Then she laughed, her mouth open, wide, and her eyes sparkling. It put me off a bit, to be honest. I almost felt like she was trying to play me.

It didn't help that she looked nearly perfect. Her hair, cut short, was perfect, like she'd just come from the stylist. *Just like Millie*, I thought, and felt a teeny bit better. But only a teeny bit.

Her clothes were perfect, too. In fact she looked like she'd just come from working in one of those office towers, even though it was nearly eight thirty. And her shoes? They probably cost more than my entire wardrobe.

The only thing that gave me any hope about her was her fingernails. Someone like her always seemed to have perfect nails, acrylic or gel or whatever, but not Henry. They weren't perfect. Far from it.

Her nails were short, serviceable. Clean, of course, but it looked like she didn't use polish of any sort. Just like me.

"I'm going to take you to my place first, so you can drop off your suitcase," she said. "With any luck, you'll be able to meet the old man. Then, we're going out for drinks with the team. They can't wait to meet you. Sylvia's been singing your praises, let me tell you. Absolutely singing!"

I couldn't imagine Sylvia Worth singing anything, especially my praises. And what had Henry meant about meeting an old man?

"What old man do you want me to meet?" I asked.

"Why, the ghost, of course." She laughed again, showing me every one of her perfect, perfect teeth. "Didn't Sylvia tell you? My house is haunted, and I want you to get rid of the ghost for me."

The only thing I knew for sure, in those next few horrible minutes as Henry chattered on about the tournament and the bar where we would be meeting the rest of the team after I dropped off my stuff at her place and met the ghost that she wanted me to "expunge," was that I hated Sylvia Worth more than anyone else

in the whole world.
The whole world.

HENRY LIVED IN an upscale borough somewhere in Calgary. I never could keep directions straight in Calgary, even with the mountains to the West as a rough guide. The city was built on a four quadrant system that drove me crazy the few times I'd been forced to go there. But Henrietta—Henry—seemed comfortable as she and her crazy expensive car dipped and dove through the evening traffic. She never stopped talking the whole way.

Sometimes she talked about the sights we were blasting by at light speed, and sometimes about the ball team and the tournament. She never asked me a question, so I didn't have to even think about answering her. I just listened to her chatter and fumed.

Finally, she stopped in front of a two storey house with a built-in garage. It looked exactly like every other house on the block.

"I painted the front door red when I first moved here," she said. "Just so I could find the place." She laughed and pushed the single button of the remote clipped to her visor and waited for the double door of the garage to open. She pulled into the garage, which was empty except for a bike that looked really expensive and mostly unused. "Of course, that was against the rules. So I had to paint it black. Thank the good Lord for GPS, is all I can say."

She pressed the remote again, and as the door rattled closed behind us, hopped out of the car, popped the trunk, and pulled out my suitcase. "Come on," she said, and laughed again, whitely. Hugely. "Your stuff won't get itself inside!"

Then, she leaped up the stairs, unlocked the door separating the garage from the rest of her house, and disappeared inside. I could either sit in the car hating Sylvia Worth, or I could go inside and tell Henrietta—dammit! Henry—that she had been misinformed. I was not going to help her with her ghost. I'd just come to Calgary to play ball.

But first, I had to pee. That was a long bus trip, no doubt about it. I sighed, got out of the car, grabbed my suitcase, and trudged up the stairs into Henry's McMansion.

All I could think as I looked around, trying to get my bearings, was that my sister Rhonda would have loved this place. She really would. Every room I saw was tastefully decorated, and everything was so clean it positively gleamed.

Looked like Henry had a lot of people working to keep her world all neat and tidy while she did whatever she did every day.

Henry showed me to my room. It had its own ensuite. That bathroom was bigger than the one in Jasmine's little house that five of us used, and for a second, I kind of fell in love. Then I remembered that there was a ghost hanging around somewhere, and my mood went right back to glum.

I called James, because I'd promised I would, and told him I'd gotten there safely and that I was going to meet the rest of the team. But I didn't mention the ghost.

"Have fun," he said. Then he hung up, and I was back to being alone and feeling glum.

"You want to have a drink?" Henry called from the kitchen. "Before we go meet the rest of the team?"

"I don't think so," I called back. "Henry, we need to talk."

"About the old man, yeah, I know," she said. "I'm amazed that you're not all creeped out by him, but I guess if you work with ghosts all the time, you get past that, right?"

I didn't answer her. Just trudged out of the room with the fantastic ensuite and down the stairs to the huge kitchen where Henry was making a blender full of something green.

"Come on," she said, giving the green mess another quick pulse before she poured it into two glasses. "Nobody can say no to a margarita."

She wasn't going to back down, I could just tell. So, I took the proffered glass—a regulation margarita glass, I was sure—and put my lips to the salt encrusted rim. "Nice," I said. "Thank you."

"For business I drink martinis," she said. "But on the weekends, this is my poison of choice." She downed her drink and poured another without setting the glass on the kitchen counter. Marble, of course. I wondered if I was going to have to be the one to drive to the meeting with the rest of the team, but she only took a sip from the second glass, and then set it down with a small thump.

"I guess I have to talk business, even with the margarita," she said. "So, let's talk."

"Business?"

Her smile was nearly gone. Just a small shadow of her former toothy grin. It was unnerving. "Yeah," she said. "Business."

She pulled an envelope from a nearby drawer. "Sylvia said you charge a grand," she said. "I certified the cheque, hope you don't mind. Just to put your mind at ease." She almost smiled again. "After all, you don't know me from Adam, do you? I know I shouldn't be showing my hand like this. Paying you before you've done the job, but I want to demonstrate to you just how serious I am."

A wooden thunk sounded from the next room, but Henry didn't react. I wondered if she had a cat, or something. Wondered distantly how Millie would treat me if I came home smelling like a cat. Probably badly, I guessed. She hated it when one of us petted another dog, so a cat would probably be right off limits.

Another thunk, and then a crash and a tinkle. Henry sighed.

"I was hoping he'd wait until after the get-together with the team," she said. "But I guess he wants to meet you now."

I blinked. "Are you telling me that a ghost is doing that?"

"Yeah," she said. She picked up her glass and drained it. "It was hell, until I figured out not to put anything breakable anywhere in there. I even had to move the TV, even though it's the TV room, for heaven's sake. He hates TV. Well, CNN, anyhow. He was better whenever I turned it to CBC, but that was a no-go for me, so I moved the TV to the den."

"The ghost hates CNN?" I asked. My voice didn't really sound like my own. She had a poltergeist in the next room. A poltergeist throwing stuff around.

"Well, all the American channels, actually. But I mean, really. Have you tried watching Canadian programming? It's painful."

"I don't watch much TV," I said, distantly.

"Well, I gotta keep up," Henry said. Sloshed a thimble full of margarita into her glass. Offered me the jug, and set it down when I shook my head. "Clients love small talking about their favourite shows, after all." She gestured at the doorway to the next room. "Want to meet him?"

This was all moving way too fast for me. I was going to say no, but then there was a series of thunks from the next room. Thunk, thunk, thunk, thunk. Hurry up, the poltergeist in the next room seemed to be saying. Get in here, so I don't have to come to you.

"Dammit," Henry said. "He's really making a mess in there. Tina's gonna be pissed."

"Tina?" I asked.

"My housekeeper," Henry said.

Of course.

"Who is he?" I asked. "The ghost. Has he told you, yet?"

Henry snorted and shook her head. "I have no idea who he is," she said.

"But you've seen him—"

"No," she scoffed. "If I could see him, I'm pretty sure I could have convinced him to get the hell out, all on my own. No, I just have to deal with the mess."

I frowned. "How do you know he's an old man, then?" I asked. "If you've never seen him?"

"By the smell," she said. "That old man 'I forgot to shower for a couple of weeks' smell." She shuddered. "There is not enough Febreze in the world, when he gets wound up. Makes Tina crazy."

I tried not to roll my eyes. My guess was that Henry's housekeeper was the only one, really, who had to deal with the mess, as well as the smell. But that was not relevant. Not really.

"Does he go anywhere else in the house?" I asked. Like up to the spare bedroom with the wonderful ensuite bathroom.

"Sometimes," Henry said. "He will not leave the candles in my bathroom alone. They're always in the bottom of the tub. But mostly, he stays in the TV room." She clicked her tongue. "A TV room with no TV," she said. "What a frigging waste."

For a moment, I thought about demanding that she take me back to the bus depot. Forget the tournament, forget everything, I would just go home. No harm no foul, past having to explain to James why I hadn't stayed. He'd understand. He would.

But then, I thought of Sylvia Worth. I was fairly certain that she wouldn't be so understanding. That she could—and would—make my life a living hell if I didn't help her friend with her poltergeist problem.

That thought made me hate her all over again. Then I sighed, and set my mostly untouched margarita on the hugely expensive marble counter top.

"All right," I said. "I guess I better meet your ghost."

HENRY WAS RIGHT. Tina, her housekeeper, was going to be pissed. The TV room with no TV was a wreck. Everything that had been on the shelves surrounding the place the sixty inch flat-screen TV had been was on the floor. The two recliners that graced the wall furthest from the shelves had been moved as well. Shifted, so they faced the corner of the room, where someone would have put a big, fat, CRV television, back in the day.

The ghost sat in the recliner closest to the wall. He looked angry, which didn't surprise me at all. Poltergeists, generally, were angry. That was why they learned how to move things. Throw things. Smash things.

"Tell that bitch to move the TV back in here," he growled. "I'm missing the games."

"The games?" I asked.

"The ball games," he said. "Jesus, are you as stupid as her?"

"Probably," I sighed. "After all, I am standing here trying to have a conversation with a really nasty ghost. What I should be doing is kicking your butt out of here."

Now, I couldn't do that, as far as I knew, but at least I got his attention. The recliner snapped upright as he clambered out of it and stared at me.

"You do understand that this is my place," he said. "And she's just a damned squatter."

"And you understand that you are dead," I said. "Don't you?"

"Yes," he said. "Of course. I'm not stupid, you know."

"She owns the house, now," I said. "She bought it, after you died."

I watched him carefully, wary that he'd start throwing stuff again. But he didn't move. Just stared at the spot on the far wall that had probably once held a TV.

"I know she owns the house," he said. "But man, I am missing my sports." Before I could respond, he pointed at the chair. "And I miss my Barcalounger. That was a hell of a chair. Beats the hell out of this thing, even with the cup holders." He looked at me. "I'll make a deal with you. Tell her I'll leave her alone if she brings the TV back, with the sports package, and gets me a Barcalounger."

I was trying to think of a response to his deal, when Henry yelled, "We gotta go!" from the relative safety of the kitchen.

"Give me a minute!" I yelled, then turned back to the ghost.

"She's a pushy broad, isn't she?" he said.

No kidding.

"I'll tell her about your deal," I said. "But only if you promise to think about some things while we're gone."

He shrugged, then nodded, so I rolled out a quick and dirty version of "this is the way I can help you move on." Then, before he could react, I left. As I walked into the kitchen, I listened for crashing and banging, but there was only silence. So far, so good.

"Did you do it?" Henry asked. "Did you get rid of him?"

"Not yet."

She looked disappointed, which didn't surprise me. She seemed the type that would expect things to happen at light speed. Like the ghost had said, she was a pushy broad. But, whatever.

"I told him his options," I said. "And that we'd talk again when we got back." I looked down at my travelling clothes, which were, in reality, my every day clothes, but more wrinkled. "Should I change or something?"

"No," she said. "You look fine. And we gotta go. So, lets."

I SHOULD HAVE known Henry wasn't telling me the truth about the clothes, but there you go.

The bar she took me to was pretty upscale, and I could tell by the horrified glances that most of the other well-dressed individuals there thought I was probably a street person who'd inadvertently invaded their territory. But the rest of the team, crammed around two high tables littered with glasses, welcomed me with open arms.

"It's the triple threat!" one of them cried. She stuck out her hand. "My name's Carmen," she said. "Third base. Glad to finally meet you in the flesh!"

"Triple threat?" I asked. Carmen's hand shake was firm and cool. I glanced down at her fingernails and could tell they'd recently been done. But no gel, so she could probably play.

"Yeah," she said. "That's what Henry says Sylvia Worth calls you. Good defence, a better bat, and you can run off ghosts. Serious triple threat!"

I blinked as the rest of the team cheered. Then I turned to Henry, who was swilling back her third margarita of the night. "You told them?"

"Of course I did," she said. "Hell girl, you gotta get your name out, if you want to get business. Am I right?"

"Business?" I asked. I took the glass proffered by someone and guzzled. Sweet and green, but not a margarita.

"Absolutely. That ghost thing you got going on. That could really turn into something if you figure out the right way to brand yourself."

The rest of the team nodded enthusiastically, and for the rest of the evening talked more about branding me—which sounded truly horrible—than the upcoming tournament.

I felt like I was in hell.

Surprisingly, I managed to keep from drinking too much and at the end of the evening, it was decided, by Henry, of course, that I would drive her home.

I don't think she realized she'd said it that way. That I would drive her home. But she did. So, I felt a lot like a chauffeur as I mucked around with the GPS and finally got the Beamer on the road and back to her McMansion.

SHE GOT HERSELF to bed under her own steam, thank goodness.

"We gotta be up early," she said, from the top of the stairs. She stared myopically at the oversized wristwatch on her arm and clucked her tongue. "Really frigging early. Why the hell do we always seem to get the eight o'clock games?"

"No idea," I said. "Good night, Henry."

"Good night," she said. Then she was gone, and I was alone with the TV room ghost.

I could see his weak light emanating from the TV room. "Can I come in?" I asked, deciding on the fly that being polite was probably going to work with this guy.

"Sure," he said.

He was back in the recliner, staring at the wall. "I thought about what you said," he said. He glanced at me. "Did you talk to the bitch about the TV and sports package?"

"Not yet," I said. "But I will. Did you think about moving on?"

"I did." He stared at the wall. "Might be something to it," he finally said. "Because she's not going to go for the sports package, is she?"

"Probably not," I said. "She seems pretty set on having things her way. Know what I mean?"

"I do," he said. Then he chuckled. "She's like me, that way. I liked things the way I liked them, and didn't give a shit about what other people thought. You know?"

"I do," I said.

"You know, I built my house with my own hands," he said. "Did everything myself."

"Did you?"

"Yeah." He sighed. "I was going to retire here. Was gonna sit right here and watch all the sports I wanted. But that didn't work out."

I didn't say a word. Just waited to see the direction his dialogue would take.

"So now," he continued, "here I am, stuck here with a bitch of a woman that I didn't even marry. And no sports." He sighed again. "Doesn't seem quite fair, now does it?"

"Not really," I said. "But death rarely is fair."

"Yeah," he said. "You got that right."

And then he asked the question that the ghosts always ask. The one that let me know that he'd made his decision, even if he didn't yet know that he had.

"Does it hurt?" he asked. "This moving on thing. Does it hurt?"

"No," I said. "It doesn't."

HE DIDN'T MOVE on right away, of course. It's rarely ever that simple.

Henry's team, the Thunder, had three games the next day. I played second base and we won the first one quite handily. When we went back to Henry's McMansion, the ghost had a few questions for me. Apparently he'd decided he needed to make sure I was a decent human being or something before he made his decision.

When he found out I lived in Edmonton, he tightened up and got all cranky until I convinced him that I didn't cheer for the Oilers. Apparently, that could have been a deal breaker.

"I'll give you my answer in a couple of days," he said. "But remember to ask about the sports package, just in case."

"I will," I said.

And I did. I quizzed Henry, after game number two, which we lost three to four. Henry was cranky about the loss though, and snapped that there was no way in the world she was wasting money on a stupid sports package she'd never use.

"You tell him that," she snapped. "And find out what the hell his deal is with the candles in my bathroom. They were back in the tub again this morning."

"I will," I said.

This was starting to feel like one of James's divorce cases. Two people living in the same house and not communicating in any meaningful way whatsoever. Except for throwing things, and whining, of course.

All I can say is, James has a lot more patience than I gave him credit for. Divorce can get pretty nasty.

THE THUNDER HAD to play one more game on Saturday, which we won. And then it was decided, by Henry and Carmen, that we all had to go to the tournament dance that night, which was just an excuse for more drinking, as far as I could tell. I didn't drink anything stronger than water though, so I was the one who had to drive back to Henry's from Shouldice Park.

The ghost was waiting for me. He looked agitated.

"What's wrong?" I asked.

"She did it again," he said. "She left a candle burning upstairs. Jesus Christ, she's gonna burn this place to the ground if she doesn't stop lighting candles in that frigging bathroom."

Oh.

"I'll tell her," I said.

"Because I won't always be here to save her," he said. "You know?"

There it was. The real reason he was sticking around.

"I know," I said. "But you know that she's not your responsibility. Your only responsibility is making a decision about what you want to do now."

"I get it," he said. "But the house—"

"The house is hers," I said. "If she burns it to the ground, that's on her. Not you. Not anymore."

"Yeah." He looked sad, but relieved. As though I'd lifted a huge burden from him. "Yeah, I guess you're right. None of this is my responsibility any more." He shrugged. "I don't even miss the baseball and the hockey. Not really. It was just something I thought I'd be able to do. You know?"

"I know," I said.

And then, as easily as that, he made his decision.

"I guess I'm ready," he said. He flared bright white, and then clear. "Think I can come back as a baseball player?" he asked.

"Maybe," I said. "That will be up to you."

He laughed. "Good enough," he said. And then, in a sudden blizzard of white, red, and black light bees, he was gone.

When I told Henry about the candles the next morning, she had the good grace to look embarrassed. "Oh wow," she said. "So he's been trying to save me from myself all this time?"

"Looks like it," I said.

"Maybe the sports package would have been a good deal," she said. "I don't want to burn myself up."

"So buy some of those fake candles," I said. "Because he's gone. Your house is completely your own."

She blinked. "You know," she said, "I didn't think you'd actually pull this off."

"Could've gone either way," I said.

"What was his name?" she asked.

That stopped me, for a moment. "I don't know," I finally said. "He never told me."

"Oh." She was sombre, unsmiling, for the first time that weekend. I couldn't tell if she was hung over or upset about the ghost leaving. The problem was, we didn't have time for a debrief.

I pointed at the door. "You gonna drive?" I asked. "Or am I? We got a game."

We got knocked out in the semi-finals, which was a bit of a drag even though I was ready to go home. I did get a hug from everyone on the team, though. So it looked like they weren't going to use me as the scape goat for losing that last game.

"Girl, if you ever decide to move to Calgary," Carmen said, "remember that there will always be a place on our team for you." She smiled. "Always, Triple Threat."

Henry barely spoke as she drove me to the bus and dropped me off, but pressed the envelope with the certified cheque into my hand as I prepared to get out of her car.

"Thank you," she said. "Really."

"You're welcome," I said.

"And if you ever want help, you know, with branding and outreach for your business, just give me a call," she said. "I'd be honoured to set you up."

Honoured. Huh. That was kind of cool. But I shook my head.

"I don't need any of that," I said. "This isn't my business. I was just doing a favour for a friend. That's all."

As if Sylvia Worth was a friend. Sylvia Worth would be extremely lucky if I ever spoke to her again. Ever, ever again.

Marie:
That Good Old Second Revenue Stream

JAMES WAS WAITING for me when I got off the bus at 10:30. He ran up and grabbed me in a big bear hug, swinging me around like I didn't weigh anything at all.

"I'm so glad you're back," he said. "This is a pretty boring city without you. Did you know that?"

"Didn't realize," I said. I felt my face heat and tapped his arm. "Put me down. We're causing a scene."

He set me on the sidewalk, gently, and picked up my bags. "Let's get out of here," he said. "You gotta tell me exactly how that last game went. Man, I thought you guys were going to win it all."

"Getting to the semis wasn't bad," I said. "And I did get home early."

"Yeah, but still. Winning the whole thing would have been nice." He smiled at me, and unlocked the car. "Wouldn't it?"

"Yeah, actually, it would," I said. I reached into the back seat and patted Millie. She allowed me to, so I took that as a good sign.

Traffic was light so it didn't take us long to get back to Casa del James. I'd managed to tell James everything he decided he needed to know about the last game, and then all the games, and then about the team, and then about Henry.

I even told him about the ghost.

"It was actually pretty easy to move him on," I said, and held the cheque out. "And look what Henry gave me."

He glanced at it, and blinked. "Is that a thousand dollars?"

"Yes, it is." I tucked the cheque away. "It even has my name on it, and everything."

"Look at you," he said. "Developing that second revenue stream."

"Yeah," I said. I stretched, and the muscles in my back pinged. My legs were sore, and I'd gotten sunburned in the last game. Having a nice, long bath would be heavenly. "I'm like a financial genius. I have to tell you, though, I am going to kill Sylvia when I see her again."

"Why?" James asked.

"Because she told all of them about me. About what I could do. After I told her not to."

He frowned. "But didn't it all work out?"

"I guess, but now all those people know about me. And you know how I feel about that."

He blinked. "I thought, after you moved Sylvia's ghost on, that you were kind of loosening up about the whole 'I don't tell anybody about being able to see ghosts' thing."

I stared at him. "Whatever gave you that idea?"

"It was the invoice," he mumbled. "You made an invoice. You know, like a real business person."

"Trust me, that invoice meant nothing," I said. I stretched again. "It's going to be great to get back to your place. Maybe we can celebrate my almost win? After my bath, I mean."

"Yeah, okay," he muttered. "While you're bathing, I'll clean the place up, and then we can celebrate any way you want."

"Clean up?" I asked. "What, were you partying while I was gone?"

"No," he said. "I just have some—stuff—lying around. I thought you'd want to see it, but now I don't think you will."

"What is it? A surprise?" I smiled. "You have to give it to me. You know I love surprises."

He laughed, tightly. "You hate surprises. And I should have remembered that."

"Well, yeah," I replied. "But if it's a good one, I could learn to love them. What's the surprise?"

"Nothing," he said. "Just forget about it."

Forgetting wasn't in my repertoire, and when Millie decided she needed to pee when we got to Casa del James, I started guessing.

"Is it a new ball glove?" I asked. "Because that old one is okay, you know. At least to the end of the season."

"It's not a new ball glove," he said as Millie finally, finally squatted. "Please, forget about it. I'll show you sometime, just not now."

Millie finished and led the way to the front door, to the elevator, and finally, to James's apartment.

He opened the door and ushered me in. Dropped the bags and released Millie, who ran into the living room and stood beside a big—huge, really—whiteboard set on a pedestal. Emblazoned across it, in James's oh so boyish handwriting, was "Marie Jenner. Psychic."

"Don't look," he said. "Just go have your bath, and it will all be gone. Really."

How could I not look? "I'm not a psychic," I said, distantly. "James, what exactly am I seeing?"

"Please," James said. "I'm begging you. Forget everything you see here. Just go take your bath."

"I don't think I can do that." I stared at the white board. My stomach clenched. "I don't understand," I said.

"Fine," he said. He took my arm and pulled me to the couch. "Sit down, and let me tell you all about it. But you can't yell. Just let me explain."

There was a small bottle of champagne sitting on the coffee table beside two wine glasses, three file folders, and his portable computer. I pointed at the bottle.

"That for me making it to the semis?" I asked. Please. Please. Please.

"Nope," he said. He looked absolutely miserable. "It was so we could celebrate your newest revenue stream."

Oh my God.

He flipped open his computer, and the screen sprang to multicoloured life. "Here it is," he said. "My thoughts on the beginning of a new revenue stream for you. And remember, you said you wouldn't yell."

The mock-up of the website was as tasteful as a website for a psychic could be. There was a crystal ball up in one corner, and what looked like tarot cards fluttering, in a never ending stream, across the screen.

Marie the Psychic! it read. *Specializing in ghost removal! 98% accurate results, or your money back!* The phone number of the office blinked across the bottom in bright pink numbers. Under it, *Call now for an appointment!*

For a few seconds, all I could do was stare.

"There are a lot of exclamation marks," I finally said. "Aren't there?"

"Yeah, probably," James said. He sounded relieved, like he thought he'd passed a big test. "But I figured those were the details you could work on. Colour, too." He pointed at the pink flashing nightmare on the screen. "I used the pink because you made Sylvia's invoice pink. But it could be any colour, really. Maybe green would be better. Or blue. I like blue—"

I grabbed the bottle of champagne and popped the cork. It bounced around on the floor, and Millie chased it as I poured some champagne into one of the glasses and guzzled it.

"I probably shouldn't have started with the website," he said, and flipped open one of the file folders. "Here's the business plan—"

"The what?" My voice reached registers that only Millie could hear, I was sure. "The what? A frigging business plan?"

James looked down at the business plan, and I noticed that every page had a bright pink boundary. "You can do it, you know," he said. "You can actually make money off the ghost thing. If you work at it."

I grabbed the pages of the business plan. Looked at them. Blanched when I saw the five year projection. "Are you kidding?" I finally gasped. "I mean, really. Are you kidding me with this?"

"No, I'm not kidding." he said. He'd gone from miserable, to slightly pissed. He flipped open another folder. Inside were business cards. All bright pink. "You have a saleable skill, Marie. All you need is a push, to get things going."

I stared at the business cards. "This is a push?" I reached past them and flipped the last folder open. Looked at the flyers he'd made and the list of psychic conventions he'd typed up. There was an asterisk beside the one being held in Edmonton. I pointed at it and he shrugged.

"I bought you a table," he said. "A vendor's table. You know, so you could get out there and press the flesh. Let people get to know you, face to face."

"Face to face?"

"Yep," he said. "Face to face."

Silence reigned for a few moments, broken only by the sounds of Millie chewing the champagne cork and then puking it out on the rug.

Believe it or not, I decided to be tactful.

"I can see that you worked very hard on all this," I said, doing my best Vanna White impersonation as I gestured at the coffee table and the white board. "But honestly, James, this isn't going to work. It would be better if you'd suggested I find lost dogs. That, at least, pays."

"Marie, you only brought in one hundred and fifty bucks with the lost dog," he said. "You know that."

"I guess," I said. "But ghosts don't pay at all."

Honestly, I was thinking of Karen, trapped on second base. And my mother, who never charged anyone a penny. But James wasn't.

"You've made two thousand dollars from ghosts in the past three weeks," he said. "I'd say they pay a bunch better than lost dogs. All you have to do is get your name out there, so people can find you." He pointed at the pink bordered business plan with the five year projection. "It's called developing your brand, Marie. I have it all written out in the business plan—"

And then, the time for being tactful was over.

"I don't give a shit about your business plan!" I yelled.

"You said you wouldn't yell," James said. He looked furious.

Maybe I had said that, but sometimes yelling was needed.

"I'm not doing any of this!" I cried. I swept the folders with the business cards and the flyers and the business plan onto the floor, and then stormed to the door. "I can't believe you sprung this on me!"

"I told you not to look," he said, acidly.

"So, this is all my fault?" I said. "Screw you, James!"

I stomped out of his apartment. Slammed the door, and Millie barked crazily inside. I ran down the stairs to the main foyer and out into the dark, cold night.

I had to wait for half an hour for a cab, but James didn't come down. Didn't check on me, or anything. Which was just fine with me. Screw him and his business plan. I was out.

By the time I got to Jasmine's place I'd calmed down, a bit. Enough so that I was beginning to think maybe I'd overreacted, just a little. That maybe I should give James a call, and apologize, or something.

Jasmine was sitting on her couch in her pyjamas, and she looked pissed.

"Is everything all right?" I asked. "I—I didn't expect to see you."

"And I didn't expect to get a frantic phone call from James a half hour ago," she snapped. "But we don't always get what we expect, now do we?"

"Jesus," I said. "James called you?"

"Yes," she said. "He was worried about you. Said you left all in a lather. I'm supposed to call him, and let him know that you got here safely." She cocked her head and arched an eyebrow at me. "So, am I going to call him? Or are you?"

I sighed. "I'll call," I said.

"Good," she said. "And I'll make tea."

I pulled out my cell and stared at it as she disappeared into the kitchen. Water ran, and then the kettle clunked on the stove.

"Have you called him yet?" she called.

I stared down at my phone. "No," I said. "Maybe I'll text him."

"Call," she said. "He's waiting. And then, you can tell me why you ran out of his house in the middle of the night."

I sighed. This was going to be a long, long night.

James was good, of course. He apologized to me for hitting me with the whole second revenue stream idea the way he had, and didn't mention once that I was the one who'd pushed him to show me all of it. He'd warned me, and I hadn't listened.

"I shouldn't have showed you any of it," he said. "Until you were ready."

I was pretty sure I would never have been ready for his pink bordered business plan, but I told him that I'd think about everything he'd shown me and talk to him about it the next day.

"So that means you're coming to work tomorrow?" he asked.

"Of course," I said. Then my stomach tightened. "Why? Don't you want me to?"

"Good grief! Of course I want you to. I was afraid—"

"Afraid of what?"

"That you'd walk away from—everything. From the job. From me." He sniffed, and my stomach tightened even more. He wasn't going to cry, was he? Had I actually pushed him away so hard, hurt him so much, that he was going to cry? Had I?

"I'm not going to leave you, James. And I'm not leaving the business."

"Good," he said.

He still sounded choked up, and suddenly I felt like crying myself. What the hell was I trying to prove? All he'd tried to do was help me figure out a way to make more money. Didn't I bitch to him, every day, about how I needed more money so I could get my own apartment, and buy nice shoes and get a better haircut than Millie?

"I'm sorry if I made you think that," I said. My voice sounded stiff but my throat was so tight I could barely speak. I'd figure out a way to make it up to him. I had to. I could be such a jerk sometimes.

"It's just," he said, "that I love you—"

What?

"—And I want you with me—"

What had he just said?

"—For the rest of my life."

He stopped, but I couldn't make my mouth work, so he rushed on to fill the stupid ugly silent void. "Besides," he said, trying for light. "I think you should be as happy as I am. That's why I came up with the bloody business plan. So you could be happy."

Speak, that little voice in my head screamed. Speak to the man who had just professed his love for you. Right now!

"I am happy," I said, my voice a literal mouse squeak. "Really, I am."

"Well, good," James said. He sounded confused and I imagined him deciding I hadn't heard him. That he'd need to say those words again, louder this time. More clearly.

"Look," I said. "Can we talk tomorrow? Jasmine's making me tea and—"

"Oh," he said. "Okay. You want me to pick you up?"

"No," I said, quickly. "I'll take the bus."

"Oh. All right." Another silence as he digested what I'd said. And hadn't said. "So I'll see you tomorrow."

"Yep," I said. "You'll see me tomorrow."

And then, my phone went silent. He'd finally hung up.

Jesus.

"So, what did he say?" Jasmine called from the kitchen. "Did he fire your ass for treating him like crap even though he acts like you're a queen, or what?"

I gulped, and then the words flooded out of me in a rush. "He told me that he loves me," I said.

"What?" All tea making clatter in the kitchen stopped. "What?"

"He said he loves me."

Jasmine flew through the doorway into the living room, the tea pot forgotten in her hand. "What did you say?" she asked again.

"You heard me," I said. And then, stupid me, I burst into tears.

"Well, this calls for more than tea," Jasmine said. "A lot more."

THE SCOTCH TASTED good but didn't help me come to terms with what James had said. Neither did Jasmine who stated, bluntly, that if I didn't ask her to be my maid of honour she just couldn't be friends with me any longer.

"I'm not—we're not getting married!" I'd gasped. "Just get that thought right out of your head."

But she hadn't, and for the next hour pummelled me with even more crazy suggestions for the perfect wedding. When she said she thought camouflage bridesmaid dresses would be over the moon, I told her she had to go to bed. Then I helped her to her room.

She stopped at the door and stared at me.

"What?" I asked, afraid that she'd say she thought she was going to throw up or something. I'd had enough drama for one evening.

"Sergeant Worth called," she whispered. "She wants you to call her tonight."

"It's too late," I said. As if I was going to call her. I wasn't speaking to her ever again after the Calgary Triple Threat.

"Oh no," Jasmine whispered. "She's working tonight. She said you had to call her." She tried to wink, but ended up blinking like a half-cut owl. "Tell her about the wedding. I bet she'll want to get in on the ground floor of this shindig."

"Jesus, Jasmine, there is not going to be a shindig," I said.

"But you'll call her. Right?" She blinked again. "Don't make me a liar. I promised her you'd call."

I sighed, and pushed her gently onto her bed. "I will," I said. By the time I closed her door, she was asleep.

I walked into the living room and pulled out my phone.

"Might as well get this over with," I muttered. So much for no more drama.

SYLVIA WORTH ANSWERED on the third ring. She sounded exhausted, and I wondered for the briefest of moments if Rory, her old, dead boyfriend, had somehow fooled me and had come back to her. But her voice brightened appreciably when I said hello.

"Marie!" she said. "Good to hear you! I'm so glad you called."

"It kind of felt like a demand," I said. "But whatever. What do you want?"

My tone stopped her cold for a moment and the exhaustion crept back into her voice. "I wanted to know how the tournament went," she said.

"Oh." I knew very well she didn't want to talk about the tournament. She wanted to talk about her friend and the ghost. "Really?"

"Yeah, really," she said. "I talked to Henry. She said it went very well. That you played well, for them."

"Yeah," I said. "They loved me so much they want me to move down there, so I can play for them full time."

"Seriously?"

Her surprised tone pushed me to the edge, and then over it. "Don't sound so shocked, Sergeant," I said. "It isn't all about the frigging ghosts, you know."

"I know," she said. "I know that." Then she stopped, and I could almost hear the wheels turning. "What happened?" she asked. "With the ghost? Henry paid you, didn't she? She said she would."

I pulled the cheque from my hoodie pocket and stared at it. "Oh yeah," I said. "She paid me."

"Good."

"I just don't understand why you thought it was okay to tell her about me and the ghosts."

Silence again. Wheels still turning, I was sure of it. "Henry needed help," she finally said. "And you could help her. Why wouldn't I tell her about you?"

It was my turn to fall silent. How stupid was this woman?

"I told you not to spread it around," I said. "Remember that? After I helped you? It was the one thing I told you not to do."

I realized my voice was getting loud. Maybe so loud that it would wake Jasmine's kids, so I toned it down considerably. "Remember that?" I whispered.

"Yes, I remember," she said. "The thing is, I told Henry about you before you told me to keep my mouth shut."

"You could have given me the heads up, then," I said. "Before I went down there. She blindsided me with the whole ghost thing you know. Jesus!"

"Yeah, I probably should have," she said. "But if I had, you wouldn't have gone. Would you?"

"Don't you think that should have been my decision?" I asked, acidly.

"She's my friend, and she needed help," Sylvia said.

"That's beside the point," I snapped.

"No, that is exactly the point," she said. "You can help people this way. So you should. What the hell's wrong with you?"

"I want to be normal!" I yelled.

"Well, you're not!" she yelled back. "Can't you just get over it?"

"No!"

I hammered my phone off, then threw it more or less at the couch, so it wouldn't break. She was such a bitch!

Then, a thin cry echoed from somewhere in the back of the house. One of the boys was awake. Because of me.

I sighed, and trudged down the hall. The drama of this night was never going to end. I could just tell.

Karen:
Deciding What Was Right

I NOTICED MY team looked nervous when they came to the diamond. I couldn't blame them. After all, I'd really lost it before.

I was ready for the questions, the accusations, and the "Oh, he wouldn't have done anything like that! He's a great guy!" from the ones who knew Andrew before they died.

I was ready for all of it, but none of it happened.

Well, there was one question. And I didn't know how to answer it.

"Why didn't you tell us before?"

My excuses for hiding what had happened suddenly felt stupid. And I felt stupid for existing that way for so long. Luckily, Charlotte wouldn't let me dwell.

"She's told us now," she said. "And now, we have to do what's right. We have to run that son of a bitch off." She pointed at Rita, of teacup moving fame. "And she's going to help us."

"How am I going to help?" Rita asked. She looked confused, and I didn't blame her.

"You're going to teach us how you do that thing," Charlotte said. "That moving stuff thing. By the time you finish teaching us everything there is to know about how to move things in the real world, we are going to go after Andy, and we're going to run him off."

Even Joanne was on board. "Swarm him," she said. "Just like

we did to Marie."

"No," Charlotte said shortly. "We'll do it right, this time. Because we'll all be able to touch him. Hurt him. Give him exactly what he deserves."

They all nodded, even the old umps.

"So, what about it?" Charlotte asked Rita. "You ready to teach us all?"

Rita turned to me. "Is this really what you want?" she asked. "After all these years?"

"Yes," I breathed. "It's really what I want."

"Good enough for me," Rita said. Then everyone cheered, and we got to work. Didn't even play the game that night, but no-one seemed to care.

And through it all, all I could think was, we are really going to do this. Really.

WAY IN THE back of my mind, I wondered if I was making a mistake about not telling Marie about what Andy had done to me. There were all those other girls who had disappeared from the ball diamond over the years. They'd never come back. Had he killed them, too? Were they trapped in their own personal hells, just like I was?

I'd tell Marie after, I promised myself. But first, Andrew had to pay for what he'd done to me.

Marie:
The "I Love You" Conundrum and Miriam Kendel's Rise Ball

I WOKE UP and stared at the dusty open beams of the basement ceiling above my bed, and hoped that things that had been said the night before—by James—had been part of the nightmare, but they weren't. He'd said what he'd said to me. Really.

And I'd told Jasmine.

The last thing in the world I wanted from her was another pep talk about bridesmaid dresses, so I showered quickly and left before she and the kids got up. I arrived at the office two hours before James and pulled out a sheet of paper. Wrote "pros" and "cons" across the top but nothing more, because this was not really a pros or cons situation, was it?

I stared at the stupid piece of paper and tried to think.

James had said, out loud, that he loved me.

He loved me. Me.

Jesus, I couldn't even get my act together enough to get my own apartment. Didn't have the guts to call my shrink and break up with her. I felt closer to the dead ball teams than my own live one, for heaven's sake.

What the hell was wrong with him, falling in love with someone like me?

I crumpled up the paper and threw it in the trash can just as

James walked in.

Well, actually, Millie and James walked in. James didn't look at me as he uncoupled Millie's leash from her collar, and she didn't look at me as she trotted over and rolled herself up into a tight little ball in her bed.

Oh man. The silent treatment from both of them. This was not boding well.

As James hung Millie's leash on a hook on the wall just above her bed, I went through potential conversation openings in my head. I'd almost decided on, "James! So good to see you!" in my version of a high brow British accent that I'd heard on a TV show James made me watch once, when he turned to me and smiled.

"The coffee smells great."

"Thanks." I sounded almost normal, with no accent, thank God.

"You want some?"

I looked down at my shaking hands. "No thanks. I think I've had enough."

"All right." He poured a coffee for himself, doped it, then gestured at the chair in front of my little desk.

"Mind if I sit down?" he asked. "We need to talk."

Crap.

"Sure."

He sat, took a sip of coffee, then set the cup on the edge of my desk. "I owe you an apology," he said. "For last night."

I blinked. Took my own sip of coffee from the cold dregs left in my cup, and set it aside. "For what?" I asked.

"About the ghost business thing. I shouldn't have done what I did. I know that. It's just, I think you have something there. Something we can both work with. But I'll wait. However long it takes you to decide next steps, I'll wait." He smiled. "All right?"

What?

"You—you kind of said that last night," I said. "Didn't you?" And didn't you tell me that you loved me? Or had I actually dreamed that part?

"Well, I sort of apologized," he said. "But I wanted to make sure that you understood me. That I'll wait for you. No matter how long it takes."

Oh.

"This is about—the other thing you said," I whispered. "Isn't it?"

"Yes," he said. "It is."

Crap crap crap.

"I know I freaked you out last night," he said. "But I wanted to get it out there. So there was no confusion about how I feel. You know?"

"I don't know if I do," I said. I stared down at my desk top, too frightened to look at him in case I'd hurt him. Again. "I don't think you realize just how screwed up I am, James. Jesus, I'm going to a shrink!"

"I know," he said. "And I also know what you went through. Going to a shrink is the most sane thing you could do, right now." He smiled. "I wasn't kidding when I said that this city is boring without you. Stuff happens around you. Some of it is damned weird, and some of it is scary, but none of it is boring. And I want to be part of that. Part of your life, no matter how weird or scary it gets. I love you, Marie, I think I always will. And that's a fact."

As I tried to think of something to say, he stood and picked up his cup. "Guess we should get to work. After all, Mrs. Silverstein really wants to catch her no-good husband fooling around, doesn't she?"

"Yeah," I said. "I guess she does."

And, as easy as that, the whole "I love you" conversation was over.

I EXPECTED THE rest of the day—and my life—to be weird, but it wasn't. James and I worked. Took Millie for a walk. Went for lunch and talked about softball. About the quick batting practice I'd set up with Greg, and the game after. I kept watching James's face for signs that he was waiting for me to do something—say something—in response to his confession of love, but he wasn't.

It looked like he'd been telling me the truth. That his feelings were out there, in the open, just so I knew. I didn't have to do a darned thing about any of it. I just had to know.

It got a little bit strange when Jasmine kept sending me links to wedding planner websites, but I blew them away, telling myself that I'd have a serious talk with her about boundaries when I went back to her place. But it wouldn't be tonight.

Tonight, I had a game. I was batting against Miriam Kendel for the first time. And James was coming to watch.

"I BELIEVE MIRIAM Kendel is the only true rise ball pitcher in the Ladies League," Greg said. He soft tossed the ball to me and I tapped it out just past the mock second base James and I had set up in the field next to the batting cage. "She has great bottom to top spin, good speed on that spin, and fantastic pitch speed."

"How fast does she throw?" I asked. She looked fast when I watched her, but this would be the first time I'd be in the batter's box. All pitches looked faster in the batter's box.

He soft tossed another ball and I hit it with the bat as it was still going up. It sailed well out into left field.

"She throws close to seventy," he said. "Sometimes, on a really good day, a little higher than that."

Seventy wasn't fast. Seventy was slow . . .

"I'm talking miles per hour," he said. "In case you didn't get that."

Oh.

He tossed another ball, and I smacked it even further than the one before. I watched James run hell bent for leather to catch it, but it dropped to the ground and rolled to the fence.

"So she throws one ten or so," I said. "KPH."

"On average," Greg said.

"And why don't you think in kilometres per hour?" I asked. "You do live in Canada, after all."

"Because," he said, "I am older than dirt."

He tossed another ball, but I missed the rise and hit it when it was on its way down. The ball popped up in a lazy fly ball and James caught it easily. He grinned as he tossed it back to Greg.

"Concentrate," Greg said, "Or Miriam will eat you for breakfast." He tossed another ball for me to hit. Then twenty-five more, until I was covered in sweat but hitting the ball consistently, always catching it when it was rising.

"Good enough," he finally said, and looked at his watch. "Time to go. You have to eat before the game."

"Will do," I said.

We quickly packed up the equipment. James asked Greg if he wanted to join us for something to eat, but he shook his head. "The wife's got a meal on the table for me," he said. "I better not miss it." And then he left, in a spurt of dust and the smell of old oil.

Dying on Second

"Timmies?" James asked me as we stuffed my equipment into the back seat of the car with Millie, who looked miffed.

"Sounds good," I said.

"The usual?" he asked when we arrived, and I nodded.

He got in line as I ran to the bathroom to wash the dust and sweat from my face. The dust had spread a little further than just my face so by the time I got myself cleaned up he'd found a table for us, and was sitting, waiting, with my everything bagel—toasted with cream cheese—and two coffees. Beside his coffee were two plain Timbits.

"You're eating Timbits?" I asked.

"These are for Millie," he said. "I'll eat something later. Something a little less—"

"Timmies?"

"Yeah," he said, and laughed. "We've kind of been living here. Know what I mean?"

"I do," I said. Because we had. It seemed that since ball season started, we'd been eating nothing but Timmies. And he was right. It was getting a little bit old.

"Maybe we can go somewhere else after the game?" I asked.

"Yeah," he said. "That sounds nice."

I ate the bagel, and licked the extra cream cheese off my fingers. Glanced at the time, but we had twenty more minutes before I had to be back at the ball park. Then I remembered Karen. I had to speak to her, after the game. To make sure that she was okay.

I hadn't spoken to her since her blow up about me moving her friends on, and I didn't feel great about it. I needed to apologize or something. Make her understand that she had free will—but so did her friends.

Plus, it was time to confront her, once and for all, about where she was buried. Moving on the old man in Calgary had inspired me. What can I say?

I told James, and he nodded. "No problem," he said. "I'll just wait in the car. Me and Millie."

"God yes, Millie," I said. "I forgot about her. Maybe we should pick up something to go instead of going to another restaurant after the game. She'll be pissed if we leave her in the car."

"She really will," James said. "That's a good idea."

I glanced at the time. Ten more minutes, but I was ready to go.

Nervous energy building every time I thought about getting into the batter's box and finally facing Miriam Kendel. I glanced at James, and he nodded. Gathered up our garbage, tucked Millie's Timbits into his pocket, and ushered me out to the car.

It was time to play ball.

GREG WAS TELLING the truth about Miriam Kendel's rise ball. She threw so hard, with the right spin, that the ball momentarily overcame the downward pull of gravity as it crossed the batter's box.

Batters expect the ball to drop, just a bit. That's the natural order of things. Gravity happens to everything. Except the rise ball. It seemed to magically jump above the hitter's bat, every time.

It was mostly illusion, of course. The rise ball pitcher—in this case, Miriam Kendel—did whatever it took to have the pitch start lower than a regular fast ball, so the ball would go from low to high. So it would rise.

Miriam Kendel dropped her shoulder.

That was the tell I saw in her throw. She dropped her shoulder when she threw the rise ball. Every time.

But here's the real deal about a rise ball. Hitting it is hard, even if you know it's coming.

I learned that in the second inning of our game against the Blues. Miriam had gotten her usual three up three down in the first inning. Surprisingly, we did the same thing. Not strike outs, of course, but we did all right. Then it was my turn to bat. Fourth. Clean up. Cleaning nothing up, because, well, Miriam Kendel had cleaned up before I got there.

I stepped into the batter's box. Narrowed my focus until it was on Miriam's hand. The ball left her hand, and I could see the spin. Bottom to top, straight as an arrow. I swung, and watched the ball jump above the bat, as though by magic.

Strike one.

"Concentrate!" Greg yelled. He thought he was being encouraging. He wasn't.

I stepped back in. Focussed, but not quite as hard. And then I saw the tell. It surprised me, to be honest, and I was momentarily frozen as she threw. Miriam had missed the strike zone. Just. The ball was high and inside. I dove back, and the ball whizzed right by the spot where my head had been moments before.

"Good eye," Greg called.

Yeah, right. She'd almost hit me. My nightmare, in real time. But she hadn't. I'd seen, and reacted and saved myself.

I took a deep breath in and out, trying to calm my rapidly beating heart. I could do this. I could *do* this.

I stepped back in and Kendel went into her windup. I focussed. Concentrated so hard that just for a second, everything slowed down. Everything.

She threw the ball, and I watched it spin, bottom to top with no deviation. It was coming fast but I was faster. I swung, and felt the bat hit the ball, solid, and I watched it arc out between centre and left field even as I dropped the bat and ran as hard as I could to first base, and then to second. Safe.

I was safe. I'd hit Miriam Kendel's rise ball.

I'd hit Miriam Kendel's rise ball!

She tipped her hat to me, then turned to demolish the batter coming up after me. Looked like my hit pissed her off. I never got off second base, but I didn't care.

I felt like a god.

That feeling went away quickly, because it was like my hit woke her whole team up. They sprayed balls all over the diamond when they were up to bat, and Kendel walked me the next two times I came to the plate, leaving me stranded on first base every time. When the bloodletting was finally over, they'd beaten us ten to nothing.

All Greg said to the rest of the team was, "We'll get 'em next time." But he patted me on the back. "Keep practicing," he said. "You'll be unstoppable."

Nice.

JAMES TOOK MILLIE to the car, and I walked over to Diamond Two to talk to Karen. She stood in her usual spot on second base, but she wasn't paying any attention to the game going on around her. She was staring at the bleachers behind home plate. Staring at Andy Westwood, as he ate sunflower seeds and watched the game.

I had to walk to the backstop before I finally got her attention. She stared at me for a second, like she didn't recognize me, then shook it off and smiled. Pointed at the right field fence, and trotted over to it.

I turned to follow, and Andy called my name. I waved.

"I hear you had a good game," he said.

"Oh, we lost," I said. "Bad. But I did hit Kendel's rise ball. A legitimate hit too. Nothing flukey."

"Great," he said. "That's just great." He patted the seat beside him. "Come on up and tell me all about it."

I shook my head. "Sorry, Andy. I'm here to watch the pitcher." I pointed to the right field fence. Where Karen was standing, waiting for me. "From over there."

"Well, maybe we can do coffee sometime," he said. "And James, of course." He sniggered. "Wouldn't want everyone thinking we were doing anything untoward or anything, now would we? Dianna would never forgive me."

I tried to laugh because it was obvious he thought he was being funny, but I just couldn't do it. "Gotta go," I said. "I'll tell James about the coffee."

"You do that," he called after me. "Get him to call me. We'll set it up."

After I finally broke free of Andy, it took me a few minutes to get to where Karen was standing. People kept stopping me to congratulate me. Word had spread about my hit, and it appeared that I was having my five minutes of fame.

When I finally got to the fence, Karen's face looked pinched. I honestly thought she was still pissed about the last time we'd spoken, so I started my apology.

"Look, I'm sorry," I started. "I shouldn't have—"

"Why were you talking to him?" she asked, cutting me off in mid word. "I told you to stay away from him. Didn't I?"

"Well, yeah," I said. "But—"

"Didn't I?" Her voice rose, and she glared at me, her eyes hard.

"Yeah," I said again. "You did."

"So, why are you still talking to him?"

"I was just being polite," I said. "Besides, James and I checked him out—"

"You what?" Karen stalked up to me and stood, dead nose to nose with me. "Why?"

"Because you warned me about him," I said. "Of course we'd check him out."

That gave her pause.

"Oh," she finally said. "What did you find?"

"Nothing much," I said, and shook my head. "He seems like a regular guy. Normal. You know?"

"Yeah," she said, and laughed. "That's what he is. A regular guy."

"Well, if he's not regular, then what is he?"

She stiffened. "Nothing."

"What is he to you?" I decided to push. "I know he used to go to the Coffee Factory when you were working there—"

She gasped and her light dropped precipitously. "How do you know about the Coffee Factory?" she asked. "And how did you know I worked there?"

"Because we checked up on you, too," I said.

She stared at me, and her light dropped even further. Left her ash grey. I could barely see her.

"I'm sorry," I said. "I should have told you before."

"You think?" she asked. "Why did you do that after I told you to leave it all alone?"

"Because I had to know your deal," I said. "You wouldn't tell me anything. About your death, about where you were buried. Nothing. It felt—odd."

"Me not talking about my death felt odd to you so you thought that gave you permission to dig around in my life." Her voice was flat, like I'd punched all the emotion from her.

"Yep." I looked at her. "I'm sorry. But what I found out was that no-one knows what happened to you. That you just disappeared, over forty years ago. Without a trace. Until now."

She didn't say anything. Just stared at me with her ash grey face like she wished I'd disappear, too. I couldn't really blame her but, in for a penny, as they say. She had to hear everything.

"That's the reason I asked you where you died," I said. "At first, I thought you were like the rest of the dead ball players. That you came from somewhere else, maybe somewhere close, and just played ball here. It wasn't until I worked with the old guy that I began to suspect that maybe I was wrong."

"What old guy?" she asked.

So, I told her all about Calgary Henry's ghost. How easy it was for him to move on once he figured out that he didn't need to protect Henry—or the house—from Henry.

"He died in the house," I said. "That was probably why he was so attached to it. You know."

Karen didn't answer. Just stared at me.

"Kinda like you," I said. "Right?"

"What do you mean?"

"You died here, didn't you?" She stared at me, her eyes wide. "And you're still here, somewhere. Aren't you?"

That was when I saw Karen Dubinsky's tell. She glanced at the diamond, specifically at second base, and then back at me. She only did it for a microsecond, of course, but she did it. She looked at second base.

"I don't know what you're taking about," she said. "It's like you said. We come from all over. And we just come here to play ball. All of us."

I didn't bite. Just leaned in so she had to look me in the eye.

"You're buried at second base," I said. "Aren't you?"

"Just let it go," Karen said. She scowled, like she wished she could touch me. Hurt me, just to shut me up.

"And Andy Westwood had something to do with your death," I said. "Didn't he? That's why you stare at him all the time. Why you warned me about him. Because he did something to you. Didn't he?"

"I told you I'm not telling you anything," she said. Her voice was flat, but her light dropped even more, lumen by lumen, until she was a dark grey smudge on the grass in front of me. I was pushing her buttons, in a big way. Decided to push even more. She had to tell me the truth. She had to.

"I'm not going to let this go," I said. "Think about your family, Karen. Your friends. Don't they deserve to finally be able to know what happened to you? They need to put your body to rest. For their sake, if not for yours." I pointed at the bleachers behind home plate. At Andy Westwood, eating his sunflower seeds and thinking his life wasn't about to fall in great huge pieces around him. "If he did this to you, he needs to be brought to justice."

"Yeah," she said. Her voice burned like acid. "Sure. I tell you where my body is and who killed me. Then the cops dig up my body and move it, and you know what happens after that? Nothing. Digging my body up will do no good. Not for my family, and especially not for me. If my body is moved, I will disappear. Completely this time. And then I won't be able to play ball anymore. So, I'm telling you nothing."

Dying on Second

Oh.

"You won't disappear," I said. "Not if you don't want to."

"I don't believe you," Karen said. Her light flickered even darker, and for a moment, I was afraid that I'd pushed her too far. "I've never been able to move. Not like the others."

"But you can," I said. "Honestly. It'll be like everybody else on your team. Most of them have been buried by their families, but they still show up here every season because they want to play ball. It'll be the same for you. If that's what you really want."

"Can you guarantee that?" she asked. "One hundred percent?"

"Yes, I can," I said. "One hundred percent."

Her light came up a lumen, and I could almost see her face. "You better," she said. "Because you're right. My body is there." She pointed at second base. "Now tell the cops, so they can tell my family. But you better be here when they dig me up, 'cause I gotta be able to stay here, even with my body gone."

"I will be here," I said. "I promise. Now, tell me how Andy's involved."

"That I will not do," she said. She turned and walked away from me before I could respond. Stood at second base and went back to staring at Andy—at nothing—so I left.

I'd tell Sylvia that I'd located Karen's burial site, and then it was up to her and the cops to finally do the right thing. They could dig her up and CSI her body and figure out who killed her, if they could. I'd make Sylvia promise to call me when they were ready to dig up Karen's body, so I could help her stay where she wanted.

I suspected that Andy had had something to do with her death, but for whatever reason, she would not tell me. Didn't matter though. The evidence would out.

And we'd both be able to play ball.

JAMES HAD ORDERED a pizza for us to pick up on the way home, so we ate it as we watched another episode of the strange cable show he'd found. And I felt great.

I'd hit Miriam Kendel's rise ball, and I'd figured out where Karen's body was buried. I was batting a thousand. I really was.

Karen:
I Need More Time

WHAT HAD I done? What had I done, what had I done?

Marie had guessed everything. She'd guessed where my body was buried, and she'd guessed who killed me. And I'd confirmed it all. Well, almost all. She was going to tell the police where my body was, and I had to trust her to be here when I was exhumed so that I could stay.

Maybe she was right. The other girls could do it. Maybe I could, too. If I wanted it bad enough. And I did want it bad enough, and not just because of the ball games. I desperately wanted revenge.

We dead were all learning how to manipulate things in the living world from Rita, but I wasn't certain that we could hurt Andrew Westwood the way he needed to be hurt yet.

Marie was right. It was time for Andrew to pay. Out in the real world, where he lived. Eventually, I would tell her he was the one who killed me. But before that happened, I wanted to have my chance to hurt him. Hurt him, just like he hurt me.

I wanted to hurt him to death.

Marie:
Contacting Sylvia, Who I Hate

I PHONED SYLVIA Worth when I got to the office, first thing the next morning.

I didn't want to talk to her, because she'd really pissed me off with all her, "You can make a real difference in people's lives" talk. Plus her telling Calgary Henry all about me and my ghost interacting abilities, when I'd told her to keep her mouth shut. All right, so I told her after I moved Rory on, but still. She should have known better.

To make things even worse, not only did I have to talk to Sylvia Worth—who I hate—the timing was terrible. Provincials started tomorrow and I didn't want to have to miss them.

The provincial tournament was the biggest of the year. It was being held in Camrose, and teams from all over the province were going to be there, trying to win the tournament so they could represent the province at Nationals. Camrose was just far enough away for me to convince James we could turn it into a weekend getaway. And I'd convinced Jasmine and her kids to come, too.

We were all going. Even Millie.

But Karen's family deserved to know what had happened. Our weekend away wasn't more important than that.

So, I called Sylvia Worth.

She was in bed. Apparently she was still working nights and didn't appreciate me waking her up at that ungodly hour. I glanced at the clock on the wall, saw it was nine a.m., not really too ungodly, but didn't correct her.

"I have some news," I said. "About Karen Dubinsky."

"Who is Karen Dubinsky?" she asked. "And why can't this wait until a more decent hour?"

"Karen Dubinsky is an old missing persons case," I said. "She disappeared over forty years ago. She's dead, and I know where her body is."

"You what?"

It took me a few more tries to beat the information about Karen into Sylvia's sleep deprived brain. Then she put me on speakerphone, and I had to listen to her get dressed and do everything else that was involved with her morning ablutions.

To be honest, her brushing her teeth while trying to continue the conversation was the worst part of the whole ordeal. But not by much. And then she was in her car and on her way to her office in the main police station in downtown Edmonton.

As she drove I told her where Karen was buried.

"Diamond Two?" she said. "Are you sure?"

"Yes," I said. "Right behind second base. I'm absolutely certain."

"Well, that's going to screw with the rest of ball season," she muttered. I almost laughed, then didn't. I hadn't actually thought about that. If—when—the police dug up the diamond, we wouldn't be able to play there, probably for the rest of the season.

Sylvia moved on from the inconvenience of ball season quickly. "You're in contact with the deceased," she said. "Aren't you?"

"Yes," I said. I couldn't think of a good reason not to tell her that bit of truth.

"And did she tell you who killed her?" Sylvia asked.

"She won't tell me."

"Why the hell not?" she snapped.

"I don't know. She won't talk about it. But I have an idea. There's a guy who hangs around the ball diamond. Andy Westwood."

"You asked me about him before," she said. "What about him?"

"When we were checking out where Karen used to work—the Coffee Factory, do you know it?"

"I've heard of it," she said.

"Well, Karen used to work there. And Andy used to be a customer. At the same time. He still is. Or his wife is, anyhow. I couldn't tell when he stopped going. Their records aren't that good." I grimaced, thinking of the old index cards, in alphabetical order. "But I'd be willing to bet that it was shortly after Karen disappeared."

There was a small bit of silence as Sylvia mulled over what I'd just said.

"I imagine lots of people were the Coffee Factory's customers over the years," she finally said. "So what?"

"He's the only connection we found," I said. "Between Karen's life and—death."

Sylvia clicked her tongue. "It's pretty thin," she said.

"Maybe," I replied. Caustically, because she was really starting to piss me off. I'd found the body. What did she want me to do, wrap it up in a big pink bow? "But here's the thing. Karen was killed forty years ago, and no one—I mean no one— in the police department seems to have ever given one happy crap about that fact."

"If there was no body, there was nothing to move the case forward," Sylvia said, coolly.

"Well boo-hoo for the police," I said. "They've got a body now."

"You know, forty years is a long time," Sylvia said. Her voice sounded suddenly gentle, like she was prepping me for bad news.

"So?"

"There might not be much left. Of her."

That caught me off guard. What if Sylvia—and Karen—were right? What if they dug up her body, and there wasn't enough of her left to determine how she died and who killed her?

"Are you trying to tell me that you might not be able to identify her?" I asked.

"No," she said. "We should be able to do that. But prove who murdered her? That might be impossible." She paused. "I just wanted to prepare you for that possibility. You know?"

"I don't care," I said. "You have to do something. Apply pressure."

"To whom?"

"To Andy!" I snapped. "You guys can make people say anything once you get them in the box. So do that."

More silence as Sylvia thought. "What show have you been watching?" she finally asked.

"What?"

"You've been watching a TV show." She sighed. "It's always a TV show. Remember when *CSI* came out? Everyone thought that's the way we did things." She snorted unamused laughter. "As if."

"I have not been watching a TV show," I said. I realized my voice was starting to get loud. "I have had firsthand experience being interrogated by the police."

"Oh."

Another bit of silence as we both thought about what that meant.

"All right," she said. "This is what I can do. I'm at the station now, so I'll get the ball rolling concerning the remains. You bring over everything you've found out about the victim—"

"Karen," I said. "Her name is Karen."

"—About Karen," she continued, "and we'll examine it. And then, if we feel it's warranted, we will apply the appropriate pressure to Andy Westwood. All right?"

"All right," I said.

"But you have to promise me one thing," she said.

"What?"

"You have to promise me you'll stay away from him. No going and trying any of your Sherlock Holmes tricks on him to get him to confess, or anything. Leave him to us, now."

"Sherlock Holmes?"

"You know what I mean."

"All right," I said. "I'll stay away from him."

"Promise," she said.

Good grief.

"I promise. All right?"

"All right. Now I gotta go. But keep in mind this could take a few days to set up. Maybe longer."

"Really?" I said. A faint glow of hope touched my soul. Maybe doing the right thing wasn't going to mess up my weekend plans.

"We'll have to confirm that the body is actually there," she said. "They'll use ground penetrating radar or something, to confirm, before they dig up that diamond. My guess is that they won't do the exhumation until Monday."

"I have to be there," I said. "When Karen's body is dug up. I promised her."

"I'll give you a call, but like I said, it will be a few days," Sylvia said.

"I'm going to Provincials," I said. "With the family. We're leaving tonight. Should I cancel? Stay here, just in case?"

"No," she said. "It will definitely take longer than that. Heck, my team's playing too. I don't want to miss, either."

Oh.

"So, go," she continued. "Have fun. I'll keep you apprised, and if things move more quickly, I can give you a ride back to town. How does that sound?"

"Sounds good," I said, even though Camrose was sixty-six kilometres from Edmonton, and the thought of riding back with Sylvia Worth seemed like a truly horrible idea. She had given me a way to get back into town if Karen's body was exhumed, though, so that meant I could go to the tournament.

I walked into James's office. "Well, it's done," I said.

"You don't look happy," James said. "Why don't you look happy? Will I have to go to Provincials alone?"

"No," I said. "Sylvia said to go. She said she'd keep me apprised. She also said she'd be willing to give me a ride back if the timeline moved up. But that would mean that you could end up there, by yourself, with Jasmine and the kids. I'm sorry."

"I'm not," he said. "Don't sweat it. We'll be fine. Besides, if she says it will happen next week, I'd tend to believe her. So don't worry. It will all work out."

"I don't know about that," I replied. "She wasn't convinced that Andy is involved. She says they need evidence. Crap like that. And there might not be any when they dig up her body."

"Oh?" His face remained carefully neutral.

"Yes," I said. "So, I think we better get some evidence."

He frowned. "How would we do that?"

"By going for coffee with Andy, this afternoon, if possible, and pumping him for information."

James stared at me. "That doesn't sound like anything Sylvia would want us to do," he finally said. "We'd be stepping into their investigation. Because it is *their* investigation now, you know."

"I don't care," I said.

"We'll get into trouble," he said.

"No, we won't." Then, I grinned at him. "Only you will. I can't go, so you'd have to do it alone."

"Why?"

"Because I promised Sylvia I'd stay away from Andy. But you didn't."

James sighed. "No, I didn't, did I?"

"So you'll do it?" I asked. "You'll have coffee with Andy Westwood, and pump him for information about Karen Dubinsky's death? Today? Before we go?"

"Yes," he said. "I can't believe what I let you talk me into."

I laughed. "Sometimes, neither can I."

HE SET UP the coffee with Andy for six o'clock that evening.

"I thought you were going to meet him in the afternoon," I said. "We have to leave tonight, you know."

"I know," the ever-patient James said. "But he works. That means you'll have to take Millie and look after her until I come to get you all. Since you have me working, I might not get to Jasmine's until quite late." He grinned. "You're going to have to puppy-sit."

JASMINE'S HOUSE WAS happy chaos when Millie and I finally arrived. The boys loved Millie, even if she wasn't enamoured of them, but soon Ella whisked her up and took the dog to her room, and I joined Jasmine in the kitchen.

She stood in the middle of the welter of suitcases. "I can't believe I let you talk me into this," she said. "I even took a day off work and pulled the kids from school, for heaven's sake. I don't do that."

"I know you don't," I said. "You're the perfect mother."

"You better remember that," she replied. "When I'm beating my two boys to squishy little pulps for disturbing my sleep this weekend. Man, I should have made you get me two hotel rooms for all of us, not just one."

"The boys will be hanging around with James most of the time," I said, hoping I was telling her the truth. "And besides, we're at a hotel with a pool. Just send them there when you need a little quiet time."

"That's right," she said. She stared at the suitcases and frowned. "Did I pack their swim trunks?"

"Probably," I said. "Looks like you've packed enough for a month."

"Wait 'til you have kids," she said. "Then we can talk."

Luckily, I didn't have to respond to that comment, because Ella came out of her room, Millie in tow. "I painted our nails," she said. "In your team colours. For the tournament."

I looked at her hands and her carefully painted nails, alternating red and white. Then I looked down at the dog's nails, which were painted the same colours.

"How did you convince her to sit still for that?" I asked. I couldn't get her to sit long enough to put her collar on most of the time. Ella, uncharacteristically, giggled.

"She was a good girl," she said, looking down at the little dog. "Weren't you, Millie?"

Millie looked up at her adoringly, and I felt a little envious. That dog never looked at me that way. However, I'd never tried painting her nails. Maybe that was the secret.

"Have you finished packing, Ella?" Jasmine asked.

"Not yet," Ella said.

"Well, get to it."

"Will do." Ella twinkled a smile and ran back to her room, Millie on her heels.

"She's in a good mood," I said.

"She's practically delirious," Jasmine replied. "It's been a while since we've gone on a trip."

"Even if it is just to Camrose for a ball tournament."

"A trip is a trip," Jasmine said, and smiled. "Thanks for inviting us all."

"Thanks for saying yes," I said. "It'll be good having fans in the stands."

"If I can get those two out of the pool, that is." Then she frowned. "Did I pack their trunks?"

"You already asked me that," I said. "And I have no idea. Want me to check?"

"Don't touch." She knelt and opened the suitcase closest to her. "I have a system, and I don't want you screwing with it."

The boys' trunks were there, of course, and Jasmine closed the suitcase with a satisfied sigh. Then, she looked at me and I saw that a worry line had formed between her eyes. The boys usually ran when they saw that, and for a second, I knew how they felt.

"What's up?" I asked. "Did you forget your swim suit?"

"No," Jasmine said. "Dr. Parkerson called."

Crap. I'd forgotten to fire my shrink and she'd called my emergency contact. Jasmine.

"She wanted to know if everything was all right. She said she felt concerned, since you missed your appointment without calling her." The line deepened. "Why did you miss that appointment? You're not giving up on therapy, are you?"

"No, I'm not giving up on therapy," I said. "I just think I could do better than Dr. Parkerson. She keeps pushing drugs, Jasmine. She's driving me crazy with the drugs." I tittered nervous laughter, since Jasmine had been the one to help me find Dr. Parkerson in the first place.

Jasmine did not respond. Just stared at me. I'd seen her do that to her kids, too. Classic Mom move.

"I'll deal with it when I get back," I said. "On Monday."

"Promise?" Jasmine asked.

What was the deal with having to promise all the time?

"Of course," I said. "I promise. Absolutely."

"See that you do." She smiled, and gave me a quick hug. "You're so much better than you were when you came back, after your mother and everything," she said. "I just want you to be—"

"Sane?" I said.

"Happy," she said. "I just want you to be happy."

"I am happy," I said, and shrugged. "Well, happier, anyhow. And getting out of town with everybody? This is like—a family thing. It's going to be great."

Just as long as James got the information out of Andy Westwood the cops needed. But I didn't tell Jasmine that. She didn't need to know.

Stage Three
Winning the Game

Marie:
The Weekend Away

I THOUGHT THAT James was going to wreck everything before we left for Camrose, because he hadn't been able to find a good way to broach the Karen Dubinsky situation when he went for coffee with Andy "Womankiller" Westwood.

"I tried," he'd said, as we loaded the suitcases into the SUV he'd rented for the weekend. "I even brought up the Coffee Factory. Thought if I mentioned that we'd just started going there, he'd talk about being an original customer. You know, opening the door for some of your fairly in-depth questions. But he didn't bite. Not even a nibble. It's like he didn't even know the place." He frowned, rammed the last suitcase into the back, and slammed the door closed. "I didn't have anywhere else to go in the conversation, so we were done. You'll be happy to know he won't be at Provincials, though. He doesn't go to them. 'I just like hanging around John Fry,' he said. 'Watching the ladies play.' It creeped me out, the way he said it."

I was going to yell but Jasmine and the kids trooped out of the house so I didn't. We all just jumped into the van and headed off to our big adventure. Of course, we had to go back for Millie, but once we got her in the van too, we were off for real.

The weekend was great. My team made it to the semis, by the skins of our collective teeth, then lost a heartbreaker to the Chimo Angels—minus Sylvia Worth, which gave me a couple of bad moments, I must admit. I asked her coach where she was. He said that she'd been called to work that morning, so I texted her repeatedly, until she finally, grouchily, replied.

I'm working, she texted. *I told you I'd let you know about the exhumation. Nothing yet.*

So, we watched Miriam Kendel and the Blues win the tournament, and then we left.

The kids slept on the drive home. So did Millie. I was suffering badly from another sunburn and couldn't sleep even though I was exhausted, so as we drove back to Edmonton, James, Jasmine, and I made plans to do the same thing next year. Which meant I'd be playing ball next year. The idea didn't bother me at all.

We dropped Jasmine and the kids off at her house and I went with James and Millie back to his place. I was a teeny bit surprised at myself. After all, we'd spent the whole weekend together. I thought I'd want alone time, but I didn't. Then I thought James would. But he was happy I decided to stay with him, and later that night, when I was safe in his arms and almost asleep, I was too.

I thought, for a moment, that I should try Sylvia one more time, but I didn't. She was working and she would have called me if anything was going to happen on Diamond Two. She'd promised me she would. So, I slathered myself in sunburn lotion, and slept like a lamb, instead.

Karen:
Finding Me

THE POLICE SHOWED up at Diamond Two just as the sun was rising on Sunday morning. I watched two of them run out the yellow caution tape and wondered where Marie was. She said she'd be here when the police came so she could help me stay at the diamond.

The police—and there were a lot of police—brought in heavy equipment, including a little excavator, and in no time, they were tearing up the infield all around second base.

"The remains are in this area," the woman in charge said. I didn't recognize her. "The witness wasn't certain how deep the burial is, though. So be careful."

First the excavator tore up the shale. Nearly a foot deep, the shale was. When all of it was scraped away, humans with shovels replaced the machine.

They dug down two feet, then three.

"I don't think there's anything here," one of the officers said.

"Just keep going," the woman said. "And be careful. There won't be much left—"

She's talking about me, I thought. *About my body*. I felt myself tighten. Looked down at my hands, and they were grey. Dark grey, as though all the light was being sucked from them by the excavator and the shovels. I was so afraid.

They dug down a half foot further and the first feather of

plastic appeared.

"We got something," one of the shovelers announced.

"Stop," the woman said. She signalled to two other people who'd been standing by the backstop. They were dressed like surgeons, right down to the plastic gloves, and they carried boxes that looked like something a mechanic would use to carry his tools. "Get in there," she said. "We need everything. Everything."

The two jumped into the hole, and carefully scraped the earth away from the plastic. First they used small shovels, then trowels, and then brushes.

"We got a body," one of them announced, and soon my grave was surrounded by a horde of police officers including the woman in charge.

"The plastic looks new," one of the officers said. "No way this is a forty-year-old burial."

"Plastic doesn't break up underground," one of the people in the hole said and turned to the woman in charge. "Let's get it out of here and back to the lab."

The woman in charge waved the other officers away from the hole and, as they edged back, gestured to a vehicle idling beside the fence. Two men pulling a stretcher walked to my grave. I could see the black body bag and knew that soon my body would be encased in another roll of plastic. But this time, my body would be taken away.

"Please let me stay," I muttered, as I watched them carefully remove the dirty roll of plastic that held my body. I could see the tartan of the blanket within it. "Please let me stay."

Quickly and efficiently, the two men placed the plastic roll in the body bag and zipped it closed. They rolled the stretcher off the diamond and to the waiting vehicle. Then, the body bag was placed in the back, and the door slammed shut.

"Please let me stay," I said, as I watched the vehicle drive out to the parking lot. The parking lot was the furthest I'd ever wandered from the ball diamond, and my body, in more than forty years.

I felt the first pull as the vehicle turned onto the street, heading west. I resisted, or tried to, and for a moment or two, I thought I was going to be all right. But then the vehicle turned a corner and disappeared and it felt like I was suddenly trapped in a huge vacuum. Pulling me, tearing me away from the diamond.

"I want to stay!" I screamed, and fought the pull as hard as I could, but it was no use—I was being dragged, inexorably, to the vehicle that was taking my body away. I screamed, "Let me stay let me stay let me stay!"

That didn't happen.

Marie:
Losing Karen

SYLVIA TEXTED ME at nine on Monday morning, just as James was parking the car at the office. I was going to make a crack about her contacting me so early, but her brief text beat the humour out of me.

The exhumation was done on Sunday, the text read. *They didn't let me know. I'm sorry.*

"Oh my God," I cried. "I have to go to the diamond right now. They exhumed Karen's body yesterday. She's alone, James. I was playing ball, and she's all alone."

James didn't even blink. "Let's go," he said, and put the car in reverse.

WE DROVE HELL bent for leather to the ball diamond, but when we got there, the cops had the parking lot blocked.

"No entry," the cop said. "Contact the Ladies League if you're supposed to be playing today."

"We are part of the investigation," James said, brazenly. "Let us in."

"Name?" the cop asked.

"Oh, we aren't on your list," James said. "But Sergeant Worth gave us permission—"

"If your name's not on the list, you are not getting in here," the cop said. "Have—who did you say? Sergeant Worth? Have her put your name on the list. Then, I can let you in."

"Can't we look around?" James asked. "Just let us stand by the fence for a minute."

"No, sir, you can't," the cop said. "This area is off limits until the investigation is concluded. Unless your name is on the list."

"How long is the investigation going to take?" James asked. "Any idea?"

The cop looked around, sighed like he wished that James was talking to anyone else in the world, then looked back at James. "A day or two," he said. "At the outside."

"What are we going to do?" I whispered to James. "I have to get in there."

James shrugged and turned back to the cop. "A day or two isn't going to cut it. We have to get in there, now." He smiled. "Come on. Just let us in there for a minute."

The cop didn't answer, but his face tightened. It looked like he was going to start the whole "let me see your licence and registration" thing, so James finally gave up and backed out of the entryway.

I was ready to lose it, but James was cool and calm.

"There is more than one way to skin a cat," he said, and drove around the block to the other parking lot. Its entryway was blocked, too. But the two ball diamonds that lined the street, Diamond Four and Five, were not surrounded by the yellow tape. And they backed onto Diamond Three, which backed onto Diamond Two.

"Think this is smart?" I asked, fairly surprised that I was the one exercising any caution whatsoever, but James shook me off.

"You have to get in there," he said. "For the ghost."

He stopped the car by Diamond Four. I opened the car door and then stopped when I heard a strange noise. A keening, like wind through the branches of a dead tree. I looked at the poplar trees that edged the street, but none of them were moving. And I didn't feel any wind.

"Do you hear something?" I asked.

James shook his head. We walked quickly between Diamond Four and the outer fence of Diamond Three, hoping to skirt it and come in on the back end of Diamond Two's outfield.

Of course, we ran into another cop guarding the pathway that would have led to Diamond Two.

"This area is closed," he said.

"I need to use the bathroom," I said. "Before we practice." I waved back in the general direction of Diamond Four. "Be a pal."

"Sorry, Miss. No entry at this time." He pointed past Diamond Three. "There's a Tim Hortons on thirty-fourth. Maybe you can use the bathroom there."

"Thank you," I said to the helpfully unhelpful cop and turned away. Heard the noise again. Keening. It seemed to be coming from somewhere behind the cop.

"What is that?" I asked, turning back to the cop. "That noise?"

"I don't hear anything, Miss," he said. "Now, please, move along."

"All right," I said. "We will."

I grabbed James by the arm and led him back the way we'd come. Past the fence that surrounded the outfield of Diamond Three. That was when I saw the first dead ball player.

She floated down the path toward me, her mouth wide, her eyes awash in glowing tears. "Marie!" she called, when she saw me. "What have you done?"

Another ghost floated in from somewhere. And another, and another. They were all calling my name, and they all looked angry. No. Not angry. They looked completely undone.

"James," I said. "Go to the car and wait for me."

"I think if we try coming in a little further down," James said, completely ignoring my words. "We might be able to sneak past that guy—"

Four more ghosts floated in. One of them was Joanne, the crazy ghost. She saw me, and I swear her eyes almost glowed red.

"This is all your fault!" she screamed. "All your fault."

What the hell happened?

"James," I said, interrupting his break and enter plan. "You have to go to the car. Now."

"Why?" he said. Then he glanced around. "Oh, is Karen here? You know, you could talk to her in front of me. I won't make a—"

"Jesus, James!" I yelled. "It's not Karen. It's a bunch of them. And they don't look happy. I think I'm dealing with a situation here."

His smile dissolved, and he looked around like he would actually be able to see them or something. "I should stay," he said. "You know, protect you."

I snorted. "You can't protect me," I said. "Now go. Please."

He reluctantly headed back to the car. I was left alone with the undone ghosts. More had appeared in the time it had taken me to convince James to leave. Now, it looked like I was dealing with most—if not all—of the dead ball players. Except for Karen. I couldn't see her anywhere.

"Where's Karen?" I asked.

My question stopped them, momentarily. Then, as one, they began wailing again, and I finally realized what the keening sound had been. It was coming from the ghosts of Diamond Two.

"Where's Karen?" I asked again. I was starting to feel afraid.

"She's gone!" One of them—it was Joanne—had spoken and she was bearing down on me with her hands outstretched and her mouth open wide. "The police took her body and now she's gone! And it's all your fault!"

What?

"She can't be," I said. Joanne roared up to me, through me, and I put up my wings of steel to stop that foolishness. "Joanne, stop that."

She looked surprised, but she stopped, as did the others. They formed a rough circle around me and I could feel their anguish, their fear pressing down on me from all sides.

"She never left the diamond before," one of them said. "But now she's gone. She's gone!"

Another of them, it was Rita, I recognized her from their attempted swarming the first night I came to the ball diamond, walked up to me and put out her hand. Touched my shoulder. And I felt it. It was nothing more than a gentle nudge, but I did feel it. "You have to find her," she said. "Find her and bring her back."

Then another ghost walked up to me, and nudged me. And another and another. Finally Joanne whacked me, hard. When my head snapped back, she smiled.

"We'll do more to you than that," she said. "If you don't find Karen and bring her back to us. Now."

"I will," I said. "Don't hit me again." I wondered how they'd all developed the ability to touch things in the living sphere but figured I'd have to find out another time. Right now, I had to get away from these ghosts before they really hurt me.

"Find her and we'll stop," Rita said. "It's all up to you."

"I will," I repeated. I took a step in the direction of the car and they gave way, letting me pass. Once I was clear of them and their overwhelming feeling of loss and despair, I wanted to run, but I didn't. I walked to the car like I didn't have a care in the world.

When I got in, I turned to James. "Get me out of here, James," I said. "I have to find Karen. Now."

Karen must have followed her body wherever it had been taken. So now it was up to me to find her body, and her spirit. To convince her spirit to follow me back to the diamond, so that her crazed friends would quit hurting me.

Dammit. Dammit anyhow.

OF COURSE, JAMES was confused, and I yelled. Then I cried, dammit, but as we drove away from the diamond, I pulled myself together and called Sylvia Worth.

"Why didn't you call me before they started the exhumation?" I said. "You told me you would. For God's sake, they exhumed her on Sunday. Sunday!"

"I'm sorry," she said. "I was working another case, and I wasn't contacted about the exhumation. I texted you as soon as—"

"That wasn't good enough," I yelled. "Jesus, Sylvia you promised me!"

"I was at another murder scene," she said coldly. "I texted you as soon as I could. The body will be at the ME's office."

"I have to see it."

She gave me the address. "I'll let Dr. Remington know you're on your way," she said. "I'll meet you there."

Good, I thought as we drove across town. *You show up, Sylvia, and I can yell at you in person.*

THE OFFICE OF the Medical Examiner was in a nondescript building in a nondescript part of the city. If I had been behind the wheel I probably would have driven past it, but James didn't. We entered the building and spoke directly to Dr. Remington, who was waiting for us.

"Sergeant Worth will be here shortly," she said.

"I need to see the body that was brought in from John Fry Park," I said.

Dr. Remington's eyes flashed to James and back to me. "I think that would be unwise," she said. "At this time."

I was ready to start my yelling and crying thing again to get things moving but then Sylvia showed up, and soon we were on our way to the basement where the bodies were kept in cold storage.

I didn't actually need to see Karen's body, of course. I just had to get into the same room, to see if her ghost was there. Still clinging to the last bit of her meat and bones.

As Dr. Remington located the refrigerated drawer that held Karen's body, I looked around for her ghost. But, she wasn't there. She wasn't there, anywhere.

Karen's worst nightmare had apparently come true. Her body had been taken from the ball diamond but her ghost had not followed it. It was somewhere between the diamond and the medical examiner's office, which meant I was going to have to do a painstaking grid search for her spirit.

What was I going to do?

SYLVIA STAYED WITH Dr. Remington to discuss timelines and such. James led me back to the car and helped me inside. I figured I must have looked pretty pathetic if he was acting that way, which ticked me off. Of course. Then he suggested that perhaps I needed to eat something, which set me off again.

"You're hangry," he said. "All the signs are there. I'm getting you a burger."

"And then what?" I yelled. "How the hell am I going to find Karen's ghost?"

"We'll go back to the office and come up with a plan," he said. "But first, food."

He was right, of course. I was starving and wolfed down the burger. Didn't even share with Millie, who had been patiently sitting in the back seat of the Volvo the whole time.

Me not sharing made *her* hangry, so James gave her a corner of his burger. A big deal, because he didn't normally give that dog any people food past Tim Bits, but my guess was he'd decided he was not dealing with two hangry individuals at the same time.

Then, we headed back to the office to figure out what the hell to do next.

"We should use the big map of Edmonton that I have in my office," James said. "We can pin it to the wall out in the reception area, and use highlighters to determine the grid pattern." He put the key in the lock and turned it.

I was about to tell him just how ridiculous his paper map and highlighter plan was when I realized I could see light through the translucent glass of the door.

"Wait," I said. "Someone's in there."

The light wavered and wafted, like a candle flame in a strong breeze.

"Open the door," I said. "It's a ghost!"

Karen:
So Much for the Guarantee

I STARTED YELLING as soon as Marie, her boyfriend, and his little dog walked over the threshold of the crappy run down offices of the Jimmy Lavall Detective Agency. "You guaranteed me I'd be able to stay at the diamond!" I yelled. "One hundred percent guarantee! Do you remember that?"

The dog barked once, hackles up, then hid behind the boyfriend, whining. Marie looked more than surprised.

"What's going on?" the boyfriend asked.

"Karen's here," Marie said, staring at me. "And she's pissed."

"I wouldn't doubt it," the boyfriend said and scooped up his frightened little dog. "Are you in any danger?"

"No," she replied.

"Then Millie and I will wait in my office," he said. He walked through the door and closed it. Marie and I were alone.

"How did you get here?" she asked.

I could have told her about the nightmare ride in the back of the ambulance, with my dead body, to the medical examiner's office. Screaming at the medical examiner as she puttered about, getting paperwork in order. Calming down enough to read the paperwork, and seeing Marie's name down as person who had contacted the police about my body, with her work address and phone number written beneath. I could have explained about deciding to go to her instead of waiting for her to come to me. About not knowing if I could do it, but trying anyhow. Walking for hours, and feeling my body tugging at me, trying to pull me back to it, the whole time. Finally finding the crappy little office in the crappy part of downtown Edmonton and sitting down to wait. Clinging, with all my strength, to the place, so my body couldn't pull me back to it. Waiting, for what seemed like weeks for her to finally show up. I didn't tell her any of that.

"Where the hell have you been?" I yelled. "I've been waiting forever."

Marie had the decency to look embarrassed. "I'm sorry," she said. "I was assured I'd be called before they exhumed you. I did not get that call."

"You have a strange sense of what one hundred percent actually means," I said. "You know?"

"I know," she said. "And I'm sorry. I went to the diamond as soon as I heard. I honestly thought you'd stay there. You seemed so connected to the place."

"I am," I said. "At least I thought I was. But my body pulled me with it. I couldn't break loose."

Marie's frown deepened. "So, why weren't you stuck at the Medical Examiner's office, then? That's where your body is."

"I don't know!" I yelled. "Aren't you the big expert? You tell me!"

"Maybe it has to do with belief," Marie said. "You believed that if your body was removed from the diamond, you'd be compelled to go with it. So, that happened."

"Are you trying to say that this is my fault?" I cried.

"No," she said. Then she shrugged. "Well, yeah. But when you ended up at the Medical Examiner's office, you were compelled to find me. Probably because you were angry with me."

"Angry doesn't quite describe it," I said.

"Duly noted," she said. "However, you managed. To find me, I mean."

"I can still feel the pull," I said. "I feel like I have to concentrate hard, or I'll bounce back there." I pointed to a softball Marie had sitting on her desk. "I found that concentrating on that helped."

Marie picked up the ball and stared at it. Then looked at me. "What does it represent, to you?"

"It represents softball," I said. "Of course. So?"

"And you love softball, right?"

"Right."

"Above everything else."

"Yes." I frowned and thought through what she had just said. "So, you're saying that I am using this softball to keep me here?"

"Yes," she said, and smiled. "Like an anchor. That was clever of you."

"Well, thanks. But I don't want to be stuck here, now." I pointed at the ball. "Because of that. I want to get back to the ball diamond."

Marie frowned. "If you could find this office, you should have been able to find the ball diamond," she said. "Why didn't you just go there?"

I stared at her. "I don't know where it is."

She snorted. "What do you mean, you don't know where it is?" she asked. "You've been there for over forty years."

"But I never left before," I said. "I had no idea where the diamond is, in the city. And even if I'd known where it was, I would imagine that the city has changed somewhat in forty years."

Marie nodded.

"So, that's why I didn't even try," I said. "I was waiting for you."

"I think I'll be able to take you there," Marie said. "And we might be able to use the ball the same way when we get you back there."

"How?" I asked.

"I'll take it—and you—back," she said. "I'll bury it there, somewhere. So it will anchor you to the place."

She pointed at the closed door of the inner office. "Do you mind if I let James know everything's okay?" she asked. "He'll be worried."

"All right."

She walked to the door and knocked. "Karen's calmed down," she said. "Why don't you come out here so we can plan next steps?"

James didn't answer, and Marie frowned. Knocked again, harder this time.

"James!" she called. "Come on out."

There was still no answer, and she snarled, "What the hell," and threw the door open. James was on his little mobile phone and he held his finger to his lips, begging Marie for quiet. Then he pushed a button on the face of the phone and placed it on the desk top.

"Can you repeat, Andy?" he said. "I missed that."

And then, Andrew Westwood's voice crackled and sprang to life all around me.

"You gotta get a new phone," he laughed. "That thing is a piece of crap. I told you, I can get you a real deal—"

"I like this phone," James said, all the while signalling to Marie to keep quiet, please keep quiet. "But what did you ask me before it cut out?"

"I asked if you heard anything about Diamond Two," he said. "The cops dug it up. Do you know what they were looking for? What they found?"

I stared at Marie, who was staring at the phone on the desk.

"Why is he calling you?" I asked. My voice sounded weak, like somehow all my strength had sucked from me. "I told you not to talk to him."

Marie turned and shook her head. She couldn't speak. If she did, Andrew would hear her. Would know she was in the room with James.

"I didn't know that happened," James said. He leaned over the small mobile phone and didn't see Marie frantically shaking her head at me. Didn't even realize there might be a problem brewing. "We were at Provincials. Just got back. You don't know what the cops were looking for? Good grief. How badly dug up is the diamond? Are the girls going to be able to keep playing?"

"No clue," Andrew said. I could hear that he was trying desperately to keep his voice light. Like he didn't have a care in the world. "Provincials. I forgot. How did Jolene do?"

"Knocked out in the semis," James said. He'd looked up and saw that Marie was in distress. Looked around the room like he was trying to see me. When the little dog started whining he picked her up and held her in one arm as he gestured frantically at Marie with the other.

What's going on? He gestured.

Karen's losing it, Marie gestured back.

I'm not losing it, I thought. *Not yet.*

"Tell him to quit talking to Andrew," I said aloud. "Or I'll start screaming and I won't stop. Might not bother him, but I'm thinking you and the dog will hate it."

Marie turned to James and gestured frantically but before

James could respond, Andrew spoke again.

"Wouldn't doubt it," he said. "That Greg is not a great coach. I warned you about him. Marie's really starting to come around. You should get her involved with another team. Maybe the Blues. There's a winner—"

"Screw you, Andrew!" I yelled, and then I was standing beside James, swiping at the little mobile phone on the desk. On the second swipe I connected, and the phone bounded to the floor.

Unfortunately, I didn't wreck the thing.

"What's going on?" Andrew asked, as the phone bounced and clattered across the floor.

"Jesus," James said. Ran over and picked it up. "Sorry about that," he said. "I dropped my phone. Listen, I've got another call. I'll call you back."

"Don't bother," Andy said. "I'll call you."

Before James could answer, Andrew disconnected. James set the phone back on the desk and then glared at Marie.

"Tell me what is going on. Right now."

Marie didn't look at him, though. She looked right at me. "It appears Karen has learned how to move things in the physical world," she said.

"So, we're dealing with a poltergeist?" James asked.

"Apparently," Marie said.

Neither of them looked too happy at the prospect, but I didn't care. Personally, I was thrilled. I'd moved that phone a long way. A long way.

Imagine what I could do to Andrew, the next time I saw him. "You gotta get me back to the diamond," I said. "As soon as possible."

"We can't do that," Marie said. "The cops have it blocked off. No one in or out."

"Well, then what are you going to do?" I asked. "I gotta get back."

I thought about Andrew, and about my newfound ability. Thought of touching him the way I'd touched that phone. Pushing and prodding him, harder and harder. Inside and out, until I'd beaten him raw. Then giving him one more big push, right off the top of the bleachers. Maybe even to his death. After all, turnabout is fair play, isn't it?

"How did you learn to do that?" Marie asked, pointing at the phone.

"From Rita," I said.

"Looks like Rita taught that trick to more than you," Marie said. "I ran into some of your team mates when we tried to go to the diamond earlier this evening. They pushed me around, too."

James looked shocked. "Why didn't you tell me?" he asked.

"Didn't want you to worry," she said shortly, her eyes still on me. "Did Rita teach everybody that trick?"

"Maybe," I said.

"Why? Why did she teach you all how to manipulate things in the living world?" She pointed at the phone. "Is it because of Andy? Are you planning on doing something to Andy? Have you convinced your team to help you?"

I couldn't look at her. She sighed and shook her head. "Of course," she said. "That's the reason you didn't tell me about him. About what he did. You're planning on getting revenge."

"I never said that," I said.

"You can't do this, Karen," she said. "Revenge isn't the answer. It really isn't."

I shrugged. "All right," I said, offhandedly. "I won't do anything—to anyone."

"I don't believe you," Marie said.

"Oh, I can guarantee it," I said. "One hundred percent."

Marie closed her eyes and sighed then opened them and glared at me, but all I did was shrug. She was wrong. Sometimes revenge was the answer. The only answer.

Marie turned away from me and back to James. "Call Sylvia Worth," she said. "And convince her to get us on the diamond as soon as possible."

James nodded, picked up the real phone sitting on his desk, and was soon deep in conversation. He put his hand to the receiver and looked at Marie.

"Tomorrow morning early enough?" he asked.

"Tonight would be better," I said.

"Tonight would be better," Marie said at the same time, and then glared at me.

James spoke into the phone again, then shook his head. "Tomorrow morning is as good as she can do," he said.

"Great," I said, disappointed. "What am I supposed to do until tomorrow? Sit here by myself? Again?"

"I'll stay with you," Marie said "Here, at the office."

"I don't think that's a good idea," James said. "What if she does something to you?"

He was talking about me. He thought I was going to do something to Marie.

"She won't hurt me," Marie said. "Will you, Karen?"

I nodded. Just as long as she took me to the diamond, I had no reason to hurt her.

"And the cot's still here," Marie said. "If you bring me a change of clothes, I'll be fine."

"I can do that," James said. "If you're absolutely sure."

"I am," she said. "Absolutely."

THE DAY WORE on. I watched Marie and James work and tried to be patient. It felt like I'd been stuck at the office forever. I missed the diamond. I really did.

Marie and I talked for a bit after James finally left. Well, Marie talked. I listened and fumed.

She was trying to convince me that I was past things like revenge. That if I did what I was planning, I could turn into something not even I would recognize.

"I'm afraid that if you take revenge on Andy, you'll find others who you believe deserve revenge," she said as she pulled the small cot out of the closet and opened it.

I thought about some of the other women I played ball with. The ones who had been murdered, too. Marie was probably right. If they saw that I got the satisfaction of hurting Andrew—possibly to death—for what he'd done to me, I would imagine that they'd want the same thing.

But what would be so bad about that?

"You could get into the habit of seeking vengeance," Marie continued. "Which would make things difficult for you—and the other spirits that you help hurt the living."

"How could it hurt me?" I asked. "It actually sounds like a great way to spend my time. When I'm not playing ball, that is."

"One day you'll decide to move on," Marie said. "And at that time, you have to make peace with everything you've ever done. Living or dead."

I blinked.

"Being a revenging spirit is a pretty nasty thing to deal with."

"What if I decide never to move on," I said. "After all, I've been here forty years—"

"I'd be afraid that someday you won't have a choice. You could fade away so much that not even other spirits can see you. You'd disappear, again. I'd like to make sure that doesn't happen." She stared at me. "Don't you think you've suffered enough?"

"But he has to pay," I whispered. "Why can't you understand that?"

"I do understand," she said. "But it isn't up to you to make him pay. Not any longer."

WHEN MARIE FINALLY went to sleep, I sat at the window, staring out into the street in front of the office. It was empty, but I was certain it would soon fill with the living, all going about their days. Living their lives.

That depressed me more than all the years of standing on the ball diamond. There, at least, I wasn't surrounded by the living all the time. Pressing on me, reminding me of what I'd missed. What I no longer had. Staring out Marie's office window, I was reminded of all that, and more.

I never got to go to Italy, or France. Or Columbia. I never got to learn how to roast coffee. I never got to live my life.

"Andrew got to live his," I muttered. "After he took mine. And that's not fair. He has to pay, no matter what Marie says."

Marie:
Back to Diamond Two

THREE HOURS AFTER I'd finally fallen asleep, another stupid nightmare jerked me awake. I was looking for my mother and I couldn't find her. I was running through the streets of Fort McMurray, calling for her, but she didn't answer me. All I could hear were ghosts, calling my name. More and more of them, all calling my name.

I jerked awake covered in fear sweat, and tried to figure out where I was.

The office. I was at the office with Karen.

She was standing by the window, staring out into the dark. She didn't move as I threw the blankets back and dragged myself off the cot.

"Sounded like a bad one," she said without turning around. "You all right?"

"Sorry," I said. I wrapped myself in a blanket, then headed to the Bunn to make some coffee. "Didn't mean to bother you."

"Does that happen often?" she asked. She seemed mesmerized by whatever she saw out the window. "The nightmares?"

"Often enough," I said, then shrugged. "Guess both of us still have some stuff to deal with."

"Looks like," she said. "Want to talk about it?"

"The nightmare?" I said. "No."

"Are you sure?" Karen asked. "It really did sound bad."

"They usually are," I said, trying for a light tone. She didn't need to dig any further into my personal life. "But they fade, fast enough. You know?"

"Yeah," she said. "I know. I've had some experience with nightmares over the years."

"Maybe I can teach you a technique my shrink taught me—or tried to teach me—to lessen them," I said.

She looked at me, surprise on her face.

"You go to a psychiatrist?" she asked. "I—I thought psychiatrists were just for—you know—crazy people." She laughed. "Am I dealing with a crazy person?"

"No," I said, my voice tight. Why had I mentioned my shrink? "Maybe back in your day that's the way people thought of shrinks, but lots of people go for therapy now. The world's pretty—complicated. People need help."

"I imagine," she said, her voice carefully neutral. "So, what do you talk to this—shrink— about?"

"Stuff that's happening in my life," I said. I could have kicked myself for starting this conversation. "You know. Stuff."

"Like whatever the nightmares are about, I imagine," she said.

I thought about my latest nightmare. Trying to find my mother, and being pursued by ghosts. "Not always," I said. "Sometimes it's better to keep some of my—stuff—to myself." I laughed, hoping it sounded at least half real, and pour myself a cup of coffee. "I don't talk about ghosts to my shrink. It's not—helpful."

"I imagine," she said, looking at me. "When I was alive, if someone had told me they could see ghosts, I would have thought they were batty. I take it that attitude hasn't changed much in the past forty years?"

"You're right about that," I said.

"And that's the reason you don't tell your psychiatrist," she continued. "Because she couldn't possibly understand, having never experienced interacting with the dead."

"True," I said. "She says she can understand what I've gone through, but she can't. Not really."

"I get it," Karen said. "That's the way I feel about you."

I frowned. "What do you mean?"

"Well, you've never been dead," she said. "So you don't really know what it's like. You know?"

"It's not quite the same—" I started, but she cut off my words.

"After all," she said, turning back to the window, "until you've been murdered, you really don't have any real idea what it's like to be murdered."

"Wait—"

"And you don't know what it's like to have your murderer in front of you, every day. Living his life, every day, while you are dead." She turned and stared at me, her eyes glowing. "You know?"

"I do know how that feels," I said. "Honestly, I do. I had a stalker, and I would have done anything to get away from him. To keep him from me. But I didn't try to hurt him. I let the cops handle it." I thought for a second how that all turned out, but decided not to tell Karen. "Revenge isn't the answer, Karen."

"So you say," Karen said. Then she turned back to the window, and wouldn't speak to me anymore. I'd done nothing to convince her, and I could tell she was just biding her time until I took her back to the diamond. And I couldn't even blame her that much.

She had to be pulled from the path she was on, but I couldn't think with my nightmare still rattling around in my head.

I turned my attention to the computer. I hoped that stupid cat and dog memes would be enough to calm me, and maybe even jog my memory. Mom must have spoken about revenge. About how to keep a ghost from committing the act of vengeance even if they didn't want to move on. There had to be a way to do it. But I was running out of time.

Thanks for leaving me with all these unanswered questions, Mom. Thanks a lot.

My cell rang, just after seven in the morning. It was Sylvia, and for the first time ever, she didn't sound exhausted. She sounded jazzed. I guessed that finding Karen's body had given her a new lease on life.

"Sylvia," I said. "Give me good news. Please."

"You can get on the ball diamond," she said. "Anytime you want. How's that?"

"That's great," I said. "Fantastic. I just have to get James to pick me up and take me there, and then everything will be all good."

"I can get you there faster," Sylvia said. "If you want."

Oh lord, she was offering to drive me to the ball diamond. Just about the last thing in the world I wanted after a night filled with ghost babysitting and nightmares.

"You don't have to bother yourself," I said hastily. "It won't take him long—"

"Oh, I don't mean me," Sylvia laughed. "I can't drop everything for you. No, there's an unmarked car sitting outside your office—"

"How did you know I was at the office?" I barked. "You're not following me. Are you?"

"No," Sylvia said. "James called me, last night. Told me you were staying at the office with the ghost." I could almost see the word ghost in italics, but left it alone. "And he also told me that Andy had called him earlier. That he was pumping you guys for information about what we were looking for at the ball diamond." There was a small silence. "James told me neither of you told him anything. He was telling me the truth, right?"

"Of course he was," I snapped.

"Good," she said. "The problem is, he disappeared a short while after that phone call."

My heart tightened. "You *are* talking about Andy, aren't you?"

"Of course Andy," Sylvia said. "Who did you think I meant? James?"

"I guess not," I said, even though that was exactly what I'd thought.

"Well, it was Andy," she said. "He went off the grid. That's why I decided to put a car on you. Just to make sure. You know?"

I sighed. "How are you going to find him?"

"It won't take long," she said. "As soon as he uses a credit card or his bank card, we'll know where he is." I turned to Karen, who was still standing by the window.

"Did you hear?" I asked. "We can go to the diamond."

"About time," she said.

But as I pulled on my hoodie over my sleep wrinkled clothes, yanked on my shoes, and put the softball in my pocket, she turned back to the window. Watching something. The world, I guessed.

I CALLED JAMES, and he took us to Diamond Two.

"Do you want me to come in with you?" he asked, when we

slewed past the parking lot and right onto the grass next to the diamond proper.

I glanced in the back seat at Karen. She shook her head. "You need to talk to the rest," she said. "Remember?"

"No," I said to James. "I'll be all right."

He was going to argue. I could tell, so I pointed. "I'll be right there," I said. "On the diamond. You'll be able to see me the whole time."

"All right," he said reluctantly. "Just don't go out of my line of sight. Please."

"Don't worry," I said. "I won't go anywhere but right over there. Honest."

I got out of the car and Karen followed me to the torn up diamond. For the moment, we were alone.

"Look what they've done," Karen said. "Because of that man." Her eyes flared in the overcast light. "He wrecks everything he touches. Really, he does."

I pulled the softball from my hoodie pocket and stared at it. "Maybe I shouldn't do this," I said.

"What?" Karen called. She'd walked away from me, and was standing by the hole that used to be second base. "What did you say?"

"I said maybe I shouldn't leave you here alone," I said.

"I have been here over forty years," she replied. "This is like coming home."

"Not really," I said. "Your body is gone. Things are changing around here, fast. As soon as your identity is confirmed, your family will be here. Friends. You're going to see them all, for the first time in decades. I think you'll need my support."

"Maybe I will," Karen said. "In time. But it's going to take the medical examiner a while to prove that my body is mine. Right?"

"Well, yeah," I said. "But—"

"I think I heard something about it taking months," she said.

She had me there. It could take months to get DNA results. "Yeah," I said.

"That's when I'll really need you," she said. "In the winter, probably. When I'm all alone here." She looked at me and smiled. "But right now, I have my people. Or will, soon." She pointed at the right field fence, and I turned and watched one after another of the ghosts appear. "They can support me. You know?"

I thought about what their support meant and shook my head. "You gotta forget the revenge thing, Karen. I'm not kidding. It's dangerous—"

"Didn't you tell me that Andrew is in the wind?" she asked.

I nodded, reluctantly.

"And even he wouldn't be stupid enough to come back here," she said. "Since the police are looking for him and all."

I nodded again.

"So, there will be no revenge," Karen said. "Just let us finish our season, please. That's really all I want now. To finish my season in peace."

I stared at her for a long moment, but she did not look back at me. Didn't even acknowledge my presence. Just turned and watched as her people popped into existence at the fence line.

"All right," I said. "I'm going to trust you to do the right thing."

I walked to the hole that had held her body at second base. Jumped in and dropped the ball to the ground, then kicked dirt until it was covered. Scrabbled out, and brushed my hands as clean as I could.

As I stood, I saw that nearly all the ghosts had coalesced. I didn't know how they'd react to me being there—they'd been pretty angry, before. I thought that maybe it would be better if they had their reunion alone.

"I imagine James is getting impatient," I said. "I should go. Are you sure you're going to be all right?"

"Absolutely," Karen said. "I feel like I've come home. Besides, I'll see you tomorrow."

"Tomorrow?" I said, confused.

"You have a game," she said. "Or did you forget."

"That's right. I do." I nodded and felt like a bit of a fool. She'd be here when I got back, and if the softball didn't hold her, she knew how to find me.

Karen:
My Welcome Home

MY TEAM SHOWED up as Marie was leaving, and nearly lost control when they saw me sitting by the right field fence. They surrounded me and pressed in, as close as they could get without entering my interior space. I could feel their light, and it was wonderful. Like coming home, for real.

"We thought you were gone forever," Charlotte said. "That you'd disappeared."

"No chance of that," I said. "Marie brought me back."

"So she found you?" Rita asked. "We told her she had to, but I never thought in a million years she'd ever pull it off."

"Well, she did," I said. "And now, apparently, the police know about Andrew Westwood. What he did to me."

"Oh," Charlotte said. She sounded disappointed. "Does this mean that we're going to leave him alone?"

"Oh no," I said. "It just means the timeline is going to move up." I smiled. "Even though Marie's convinced he won't come back here now that the police are looking for him, I know him. He'll be back. He won't be able to stay away."

Like me, I thought. *We're both compelled to be here.* The thought made me angry and then I remembered prodding James's little mobile phone off his desk. I knew how to touch him, but I wasn't strong enough to hurt him the way he deserved. If I was right and he showed up here soon, I'd have to hurry.

"We need to keep practicing interacting with the living world," I said. "Because I believe that he'll be back soon, and we have to be ready for him."

"Ready for him?" Rita asked.

"Ready to make him pay," I said. "Before the living take over."

They all nodded. They understood.

Strangely enough, as we practiced, I was happy. This was like coming home and being with family. I hoped that after we'd dealt with Andrew, we'd feel the same way.

Marie didn't seem to think we would, but how would she know? We were dead, and she was not. And that was the truth of it.

Marie:
Handbills and More Fresh Air

AFTER WE GOT back to the office I wrapped my arms around James's waist. "Thank you," I said. "You really helped me keep it all together, with Karen and everything."

"You're welcome," he said. "Now, you help me get the Comox paperwork done, and we'll be square. Almost."

"What do you mean, almost?" I asked.

"When this is done," James said, "our work day is officially over. In fact, our work week is almost over."

"Seriously?" I looked at the day timer on his desk. He was right. We had nothing left for the day, and only one job James had to work on the next day—trying to get the money shot at another no-tell motel, for the Vickerson soon-to-be-divorce case. And that was it for the week.

"This is not good," I said. "You do have employees who rely on you, you know. You want me to try a little online advertising or something to drum up business?"

He grinned and pulled a pile of handbills from his desk drawer. "That sounds good," he said. "But let's stick to something local, at least for today. Are you up for a little exercise?"

Handbills. Good grief. But I smiled and nodded. Since I'd made it absolutely clear I was not ready to consider my own second revenue stream, I decided I'd better help him with his.

But handbills. God.

AT LEAST MILLIE liked the walk. Four hours later, the handbills were either tucked under windshield wiper blades or blowing in the wind, and we were on our way back to James's place with a large pizza. Millie was already asleep in the back seat and refused to open her eyes when we got home. I ended up carrying her which James found extremely amusing. Me? Not so much.

I hoped I'd be able to sleep as well that night, but even though I was exhausted, I only managed to keep my eyes closed for a couple of hours before the nightmare, huge and horrific, bounced me out of bed.

I'd found my mother, but all she did was point and laugh as the ghosts screamed for my help while they attacked me and tore me apart.

Apparently I'd been screaming too because James was staring at me, horrified, when I finally pulled myself free from the nightmare's talons.

"Are you all right?" he asked.

"No," I said, and then I started to cry. Of course.

James wrapped a blanked around me. I huddled under it, shaking like I was wandering the plains in the middle of winter or something, as he set me at his tiny dining room table and made me a cup of tea. "When do you go to see Dr. Parkerson again?" he asked. "I think your dreams are getting worse."

"Nightmares," I said. "I'm having nightmares."

"Yeah, right." He handed me the tea, then sat across the table from me, staring at me earnestly. "Have you told her how bad they've gotten?"

I stared down at my tea. "No," I finally said. "I haven't told her."

He frowned. "Why not?"

"Because I've decided to go to someone else," I said. "She's not working out."

"Oh." His face stilled. "I thought you liked her."

I shrugged. "I did, well enough. Until she started pushing the drugs again."

"Maybe you need them this time," he said. "To sleep."

"I don't," I snapped. I grabbed my cup but my hands were still shaking so badly I slopped tea everywhere. "I think they've gotten worse because I'm dealing with the ghost. With Karen. And it's not like I can talk to Parkerson about that problem, now can I?"

"Maybe she'd understand," James began, but I cut his words off with a look.

"She won't understand about ghosts," I said.

I managed to get the cup to my lips without spilling, and drank deeply. It tasted perfect, of course, and I smiled my appreciation at James. He did not smile back.

"How long has it been since you've seen Dr. Parkerson?"

"A couple of weeks," I said. "Don't worry about it."

I tried the smiling thing again, but it still didn't work. He was not appeased. "Have you found a new psychiatrist?"

I shook my head.

"Have you even looked for one?"

Crap.

"No," I said. "But I've been busy."

"Too busy to find someone who can help you with your nightmares and sleeplessness?" he asked. "Good grief, Marie. People can die from lack of sleep."

I scoffed. "I don't think so."

"It's documented," he said, pointing in the general vicinity of his computer. "Seriously."

"Quit doing medical research online, James." I tried to keep my voice light, but couldn't. "All you find is crap to scare yourself. Seriously."

"It did scare me," James said. He reached across the table and took my hand. "Please," he said. "Find someone you can trust and resume your therapy. Please."

I looked at the clock on the wall. It was two forty-five and I was exhausted. I wished desperately that I could go back to sleep, but knew it wouldn't happen. I was done for the night. Again.

"I will," I said.

"Promise?" he asked.

There was that word again.

"Yes," I said. "I promise."

When the sun was finally up, we got ready to go to the office.

"I'm going to call Mrs. Soon-to-be-divorced Vickerson," James said. "And tell her I can't work tonight. That something's come up."

"What do you mean?" I asked. I poured the last of the coffee into two metal take out cups, sloppily doped them, and secured the lids. "You have to go tonight. You signed that contract."

"She'll understand," he said. He looked tired and anxious, and I wished he hadn't stayed up with me all night. I was glad he'd done it, because having him with me helped, but it had done nothing good for him. "I don't think you should be alone."

I scoffed. "I won't be alone. I'll have Millie with me for the rest of the day, and while I'm at the ball diamond, I'll be with my team. I'll be fine."

"Well, you have to be able to get to the game," he said. "And I'll have the car."

"Don't worry about it," I said. "I've got it covered."

"How?" he asked, and then scoffed. "Somebody from your team picking you up?"

"Actually, yes," I said. The last time Stacey, the first baseman, had asked me to go for a beer with the team, she'd given me her number.

"Call if you need a ride," she'd said. So I had.

James looked surprised, and then pleased. "That's good," he said.

"See?" I replied. "I'm growing as a person."

To be honest, I didn't know how the drive to the diamond would be, with small talk and all that, but at least James would be able to go to work.

"Is she giving you a ride home after?" he asked.

The thought of small talking all the way back home didn't sound quite as great. "I hadn't talked to her about it," I said. "How about you come after you're done? Maybe you can catch some of the game."

He laughed. "I'll do my best."

"See?" I said. "All figured out. I'll be just fine, James. Everything's covered. You can do your job and I'll be just fine."

I thought we had it all decided, but when we got to the office, he tried one more gambit.

"Maybe I should put off my appointment," he said. "Just until tomorrow. I do like coming to your games, you know," He looked at me imploringly. He reminded me of Millie when she tried to get one more Tim Bit.

The look didn't work.

"You should be able to catch some of the game after work, and if you don't, I'll get Greg to phone you," I said. "He'll give you every detail. Promise."

Luckily, Sylvia Worth called, so James had to give the whole "I want to come to your game and protect you from the whole world," thing a rest.

"I have news," Sylvia said. "Big news. Is James there? He needs to hear this too."

I put her on speaker and we both bent over the phone as she gave us her news. Sylvia was right. It was huge.

The medical examiner had started the examination and she'd found something on Karen's body. Specifically, she'd found skin under Karen's fingernails.

"Karen fought back," Sylvia said. "She fought whoever killed her. The ME's office is giving the DNA tests top priority. Marie, I think we'll be able to prove who killed her, soon."

James and I looked at each other. James smiled, but I couldn't do that. Not yet.

In spite of everything I'd said to Karen, I had been sure that there was not going to be a hope in hell that the cops would ever be able to prove who killed her. Now, I could barely wrap my head around what I'd just heard.

Karen had done that. She'd been a fighter even when there was no hope, and now, the cops would be able to prove everything.

"I'll let her know," I said. "She'll be pleased."

I just hoped it would be enough for her.

STACEY PICKED ME up, just like she'd promised. I was afraid that me bringing Millie was going to be problem, but all she did was laugh hard when I dropped the dog in the back seat of her car.

"I'm used to kids on the bench, but we don't often have dogs," she said.

"She'll be good," I said. "I hope."

We spent the rest of the ride talking about her, and what a pain in the butt she would be at the game, which took care of the small talk situation quite nicely. Then we picked up burgers, scarfing them down in the front seat of the car when we parked at the ball diamond.

We were supposed to play our game on Diamond Two, but it was torn apart, so we'd been relegated to Diamond Four. Normally, the beer leagues played on Diamond Four, and the beat-up condition of the infield attested to that fact, but soon enough we were warming up, and the other team arrived, and then the umps. And then, we played.

In spite of very little sleep I had a hell of a game, if I do say so myself. I caught three fly balls and managed four more outs at first base in the first three innings. The other team got desperate after that, and never hit another ball out to right field, so mostly I had the best seat in the house for the rest of the game. When we were at bat, I hit every time. Mostly singles, but once I hit a triple, which was glorious. Almost as good as a home run. Almost.

After the game, Stacey nudged me with her elbow. "You better tell me you're coming for beer tonight. Since I gave you a ride here."

"Sorry," I said. "Can't make it. Besides, I've got Millie. They won't let her in."

I think she was going to argue, but subsided when I brought up the dog. Part of me wished I could have gone for a beer with the team, but I had business at the diamond, and I didn't want her to hang around for that. No matter how nice Stacey was, I had secrets and I wasn't ready to let her in.

But, I hoped James and I could go after the next game. I suspected we would have a good time.

I glanced over at Diamond Two, and saw a weak glow emanating from it. Karen was there, with her team. I needed to check in with her to make sure she was okay. And to tell her Sylvia's news about the DNA so, perhaps, I could talk her out of her vengeance scheme.

I gave James a call as I gathered the dog and my equipment. "The game's done," I said. "But I'm going to go talk to Karen. Tell her developments and what not. Want to come get me when you're done?"

"I'd be happy to," he said. "Almost done here. Give me half an hour. Maybe less."

"Get here as quick as you can and I'll tell you all about the game. Hey, maybe we can go for a beer with the rest of my team. They can tell you all about our big win."

"Sounds great," he said, and signed off.

Finally, I was alone.

I had thirty minutes to talk to Karen. I hoped it was enough.

Dying on Second

BOTH DEAD TEAMS were preparing to play. I dropped my equipment by the bleachers, tied Millie to the fence, and waved at Karen. She walked away from second base and the huge hole that had held her body for so long.

"You're going to play here?" I asked, pointing at the hole. "With that?"

She shrugged. "We'll make do," she said. "This is where we always play."

"Right." I looked at her. "You look good. Calm. You know?"

"Yeah," she said. "It helped to get back here." She pointed at the rest of the dead, most of whom were warming up. "And seeing them, too. It all helps."

"I get that," I said. "I have some news for you. I think it will help, too."

"Good news?" she asked.

"Very good news," I said.

I told her about Sylvia's phone call. About the skin found under her body's nails and how it could be used to convict Andy.

"You did that," I said. "When you fought him."

"And you'll be able to prove that it's him, from that skin?" she asked.

"Yes," I said.

I heard a gasp from the left side of the diamond, near third base. The dead woman standing there was staring at something in the dark, beside the bleachers.

I tried to see what had surprised her, and caught sight of someone walking around the bleachers next to the left field dugout. Looked like a man. Karen stared at the figure, and her light faded. "Jesus," she whispered. "It's him."

"Who?" I asked.

I shouldn't have had to ask, but I was honestly shocked when she said, "It's Andrew."

He walked between the backstop and the bleachers in my direction. The dead looked as surprised to see him as I felt. But not Karen. She looked resigned.

"I knew he'd come," she said.

"Well, I didn't," I replied. I pulled my cell phone free and called James.

"What, you want me to pick you up a coffee?" he asked. I could hear noise in the background. Sounded like he was driving.

291

"You're lucky. I haven't ordered yet."

"James," I said, "He's here. Andy Westwood is here. At the diamond."

"Has he seen you?"

I looked at the dark figure walking toward me. He waved. "Hey, Marie!" he called. "Good game tonight. Really good game."

I blinked, and took a step back. Stumbled over the lowest bleacher row, and scrambled to regain my footing.

"Yes," I said into the phone. "He has."

"Marie, get out of there!" James cried. "Get to the parking lot. Onto the street. Run west toward Parson's Road. I'll be there five minutes, tops. Do you understand?"

"I understand," I said. I tried to keep my voice calm, and almost pulled it off. "Just hurry, okay?"

"Five minutes," James said. "I'll call the cops. Just run. Now!"

"Hey, Marie," Andy called. "Can we talk?"

I turned away from him and scrambled past the bleacher to the gate. If I hurried, I'd make it out the gate and then it was a clear run through the parking lot to the street. I was much younger than Andy, and I was more scared. There was no way he'd catch up to me in time. No way.

"Marie!" he cried. "Don't run away! I have to talk to you!"

I heard him behind me. Right behind me. I squealed, hating the sound of fear, like a piglet about to be butchered, but he was faster than me. *Jesus*, I thought as I felt him grab the back of my hoodie and haul me back into his arms. *Jesus, he's going to kill me.*

"Let me go!" I cried. "The cops are on their way. Let me go!"

Andy whirled me around in his arms and shook me. "I just want to talk to you and you call the cops?" he cried. "What's wrong with you?"

I heard keening coming from somewhere. Everywhere. It sounded like sirens from more than one car. Ray must've called for backup.

"Hear that?" I said. "It's the cops. They're almost here."

"I hear nothing," he said, and shook me again. "I just want you to tell Sylvia Worth to stop this witch hunt. You're friends with her. Tell her to leave me alone. I've done nothing wrong. Do you hear me? I'm a model frigging citizen!"

He shook me with every word, and my head snapped back and

forth like I was a rag doll. God, he was strong.

I kicked at his legs and then some of my self-defence training finally popped into my head. Kicking was wrong. I needed to go for his nose.

I curled my fingers and jabbed the heel of my palm at his nose as hard as I could. My palm connected with his face, and I felt the bone snap. He screeched and let go of me to put his hands to his suddenly bleeding face.

"You bitch," he cried. "You broke my frigging nose. What the hell's wrong with you? I just wanted to talk."

I wheeled away from him, intent on heading out that gate, but before I took a step, he grabbed me by the hoodie again. He threw me to the ground and flung himself on top of me, straddling my waist. The worst position to be in. The absolute worst.

"Do everything you can to keep your attacker from pinning you," the dry voice of my self-defence instructor whispered in my head as I frantically writhed under him. "Everything."

I went for the nose again but he was ready for me this time and slapped my hand away. Then he pinned my arms beneath his legs, placed his hands on my shoulders, and leaned.

"I just want to talk to you," he said. "What don't you understand about that?"

"Let me go," I yelled. At least I tried to yell, but he was leaning on my chest and it was getting hard to breathe.

The keening I'd heard before Andy attacked me was louder now, and coming from everywhere. "It's the cops," I wheezed. "They're almost here. Run while there is still time."

"I don't hear any sirens," he said. He moved one hand, and then the other, to my throat. I tried to move, tried to stop him, but he had my arms pinned and he was sitting on my chest and his fingers tightened on my throat and all I could see was his angry, crazy eyes. "You should have listened to me," he said, tightening his fingers. "I told you."

The keening got louder. Sounded more like screaming than keening, and I could see flickering lights boiling over the bleachers toward us.

"You should have listened to me," I wheezed. "And run."

And then, the dead were on him, and he started to scream.

Karen:
Finally, Vengeance

ANDREW MOVED FAST which caught us all off guard. He'd seemed like such a slug all the years he'd sat in the bleachers watching the girls play ball that I didn't think he had the capacity to move quickly anymore. But he did.

"We have to stop him," I said. "He has her. He's going to kill her."

I stepped through the fence, realized I was alone, and turned back. The rest of the team were standing, staring at me.

"I can't do this by myself!" I cried. "I'm not strong enough! I need you!"

One by one, they came to me. Stood by me, so that our light coalesced and glowed stronger and stronger. Then we poured over the bleachers and down onto him and Marie.

He had Marie by the throat and was screaming into her face. Just like he'd done to me so many years before. That was when we all went crazy.

We swarmed him, scratching his arms and face and neck. We stuffed ourselves into him, as many as could fit, and tore at him from the inside. We bit him, everywhere. We gouged and gored and tore.

He screamed and threw his arms up to protect his face.

"What are you doing?" he cried. "What are you doing?"

"We're hurting you," I cried. "Just the way you hurt me." I grabbed him by the throat and tore at it, revelling in the rivulets of blood that mixed with the blood from his broken nose. "We're giving you everything you deserve!"

He was talking to Marie, of course, because he couldn't see us. As much damage as we were wreaking on his body, he could not see us. Didn't know that it was me doing this to him. Me. Finally me.

"Tell him!" I screamed at Marie. "Tell him it's me!"

Marie coughed and scrambled weakly, still trapped under Andrew's legs. We had to get him off her so that she could be free. Free of him. So she could tell him what I was finally doing to him.

"Lift!" I cried. "Lift him up."

The women outside grabbed him and lifted. The women inside him did the same. And, after a moment, he moved up. Just an inch, but he moved.

Andrew screamed again, and I could finally see terror in his eyes. I pulled at his eyelids, wishing I was tearing the very eyes out of his head, and he moved upward another inch, and then another.

Marie finally had enough room and scrambled away from his writhing body. She scrabbled back, against the fence, and grabbed at her poor bruised throat.

"Tell him it's me!" I cried. She shook her head so we lifted him a foot in the air, and then another. "Tell him it's me," I said. "I deserve this! You know I do!"

A siren blared from somewhere, and car lights flashed over the fence as a vehicle careened into the empty parking lot toward us.

"Put him down," Marie said, her voice a hoarse whisper. "He'll be brought to justice. I promise."

"No," I said. "Justice isn't what I'm after."

We dragged him up in the air, higher and higher, until he was level with the top of the bleachers. He screamed and flailed, and I felt such angry joy, I could barely contain myself.

"How are you doing this?" he cried. Still at Marie. And she finally answered.

"It's not me," she said. "It's the girl you killed."

"What?" he cried. He looked confused, and that infuriated me.

"My name is Karen Dubinsky!" I howled, and pulled him even higher in the air. "And this is for killing me!"

And then, I let him drop.

Marie:
The Season's Not Over

ANDY HIT THE ground and I heard something crack. As he fell silent, so did the ghosts. They floated above him, staring down at his unconscious face.

"Is he dead?" someone, maybe Joanne, asked. "Did we kill him?"

I pulled myself to my feet and walked over to his body. He was still breathing. "No," I said. "You didn't."

"That's too bad." Karen floated down beside me and stared at him. "Maybe we should finish the job."

"That's enough!" I cried. "You've done enough!"

A police car slewed to a stop at the fence and the cop leaped from his car, gun drawn.

"Please stop," I whispered to Karen. "The police will handle this now. Please."

Karen glowed so strongly, I could barely look at her. "Are you all right?"

"Yes," I whispered. "You saved me."

"Yeah, I did, didn't I?" Karen said. She looked up at the rest of her team, floating above her. "We all did."

"Police!" the officer yelled as he ran through the gate. "Don't move!"

I did exactly what I was told as he looked over the scene.

"Are you okay?" he finally asked.

"I think so," I said. My voice sounded like I was still being strangled, and my throat hurt. A lot. But at least I was alive.

"Is he?"

"I don't know."

"Just stay back for a second, ma'am," the cop said. He checked Andy for weapons, then touched his neck, looking for a pulse.

"He's alive," he said, then turned to me. "What did you do to him?"

"I protected myself," I said. My throat hurt so badly I could barely speak. "That's all. I just protected myself."

"Why didn't you run?" he asked. He couldn't take his eyes from Andy's unconscious body, from the scratches and punctures that covered his face, hands, and neck.

"I tried," I said. "But he caught me."

He snorted. "Looks like he should have let you go."

He quickly handcuffed Andy on the ground, then took me by the arm. "Come with me to the car," he said. "While we wait for the ambulance." He shook his head. "I'm still not sure how you did that."

"Did what?"

"Damaged him like that." He clicked his tongue. "That looked like he was at the bad end of a gang swarming."

"I took self-defence classes," I said. "What can I say?"

He led me to his sedan, and gently put me in the passenger seat. That's when I remembered Millie. I could hear her crying, still tied to the fence.

"My dog," I said. "Can you get my dog?"

He nodded and retrieved Millie. Handed her to me, then called for an ambulance.

I closed my eyes, and tried not to think of Andy's fingers on my neck. I must have made a sound, because Millie curled into my lap. She stared up at me with her big eyes, and laid her head on my chest. And that undid me completely.

I started to cry, and couldn't stop.

JAMES ARRIVED AT the same time as the ambulance. He threw himself out of the car, and then he was beside me, holding me, tight.

"You're hurting me," I said.

"I don't care," he mumbled into my hair. "My God, Marie. I

told you I should have come. I could have protected you—"

"I did all right," I said. "After all, he's the one being loaded into the ambulance, not me."

James looked over at the emergency crew as they loaded Andy onto a stretcher and put him in the ambulance. James frowned. "You did all that?" he asked.

"No," I said. "Karen and the rest were there. They stopped him. They did that."

"Remind me never to piss off a ghost."

Andy woke up as the emergency crew began loading him into the ambulance. I frowned when I realized he was screaming my name.

I grabbed for the door handle, but James held me. "Just let him go," he said. "The police will handle it."

"But he's telling them it was me," I said. "I have to tell them what really happened. I have to."

"Tell Sylvia," he said, and pointed as Sylvia's car drove into the parking lot. "She'll understand about the ghosts. I don't think the emergency crew will understand, or care."

James was right. I needed to talk to Sylvia.

As I told her everything that had happened I could see the ghosts standing on the top row of the bleachers, watching us. Karen was with them, and she glowed the brightest of them all.

I didn't know if that was good or bad and I was starting to hurt everywhere so badly that, for the moment, I didn't care. Karen wasn't going anywhere, after all. But it looked like I was. Sylvia had ordered me to the hospital to get checked out and have trace evidence collected from my body, since Andy had attacked me.

At least I wouldn't have to wait forty years for justice.

JAMES STAYED WITH me for the whole hospital experience. The doctors tried to run him off but he would have none of it.

"I'm never letting her out of my sight again," he said. Which was sweet but a little over the top. I tried to tell him to relax, that I wasn't in any danger any longer, but he wouldn't listen to me, either.

"I should have been there," he said. "At the diamond. I'm never letting anything like that happen to you again. I'm going to protect you from all that's bad in the world, even if you don't want me to."

"You're sweet," I said. He wouldn't be able to do it, but I liked the thought of him trying. That thought actually pushed me over the edge again, and I started to cry. He didn't freak out, though. Just held me until I finally quieted.

Then it was time for the professionals to do their jobs. They scraped under my fingernails, and I tried to remember if I'd scratched him. I didn't think I had, but hoped they'd find something besides dirt. They swabbed the blood from my hand, from Andy's broken nose. And then they took pictures of me. Of my face, and my neck, and my shoulders, and my arms. The bruises were starting to purple nicely, and I looked like I'd been through a war.

Sylvia told me we could talk tomorrow. "I want to talk to Andy first," she said. "And he won't be out of surgery for a couple more hours."

"Surgery?" I gasped. I'd heard something snap when he fell, but had never imagined that it would take surgery to repair it.

"He broke his leg in three places," she said. "He was suffering from osteoporosis. Guess that's what he gets for not drinking milk."

I tried to laugh, I really did, but I couldn't. I was too exhausted. I just kept thinking about Karen and the rest of the ghosts swarming him. Hurting him so badly that he needed surgery.

"Can I get out of here?" I asked. "I really want to go home."

"Sure," she said. She patted James's arm. "You look after her."

"You can count on it," James replied.

He helped me dress, so I could leave. "I'll get you home," he said. "And tuck you in bed."

"I can't go home yet," I said.

He looked at me and shook his head. "You have to see the ghosts," he said. "Don't you?"

"I do," I said. "You'll stay with me, won't you?"

"I told you," he said. "I'm not leaving your side again."

I FELT STRANGELY proud when I saw that more yellow caution tape and been draped over Diamond Two's fence. The police were still there, working the scene, and the cop standing by the gate started shaking his head before we even got within talking distance.

"You can't go in there," he said.

"But—" James started. He stopped abruptly when the cop held

up his hand.

"Not a word more," he said. "I know who you are. Sergeant Worth gave me strict instruction not to let you in here, no matter what you say. She says you need sleep more than you need anything else. Got it?"

"Yeah," I said. "I got it."

"So, what are you going to do?" James asked when we turned away from the officer.

"I'll get her to come to me," I said. I walked a few feet further, then put my hands to my mouth in a makeshift megaphone.

"Karen!" I called. "I need to talk to you now!"

"There's no Karen in there," the confused cop said. "I think you should do what Sergeant Worth suggested. Go home."

I ignored him. Called Karen's name again and watched the light in the diamond brighten. She'd heard me.

"Meet me in the parking lot!" I yelled. Then, before the cop could say anything more, I grabbed James by the arm and pulled him back to the car.

"They're coming," I said. And then we were surrounded by ghosts. Karen walked out of the brightness of their light and stood before me.

"You wanted to talk to me?" she asked.

"Yes," I said. "I do."

James's eyes did that glance everywhere thing when he realized that I was talking to a ghost.

"Andy's under arrest," I said. "And you've been avenged. Haven't you?"

Karen stared at me for a moment, then nodded. "I have," she said.

"Have you given any more thought to moving on?" I asked.

"I have," Karen said. "But we have the rest of the season to play. I'm not going anywhere."

"What about after?" I asked. "Do you think that maybe you'd consider it after the season?"

"Not right now," she said. Then she smiled. "But maybe talk to me in a few months. After I see my family. You know, when they confirm whose body they dug up."

"All right," I said. That was the first chink I'd seen in Karen's armour. The very first.

"I might want to do that," a voice said, behind me. I turned. It was Rita Danworth. "After the season's over."

She looked at Karen. "I'm sure Robin Vickers will show up next season. She can take my place. She's a much better utility player than I am, and you know it. Besides, I'm tired, and what we did to Andy—that scared me. I don't want to do anything like that anymore." She reached out and touched Karen's arm. "I get why you needed that, I really do. And there are others who probably feel the same way, but Karen, I think it's time for me to move on."

"I understand," Karen said. She looked around the circle of ghosts. "Any more of you want to talk to Marie? I won't cause a fuss this time, I promise. Just as long as you promise to stick around to the end of the season, that is. Otherwise, I'll figure out a way to haunt you. I really will." She glanced at me. "Could I do that?" she asked. "Haunt someone who's moved on?"

"I've never heard of it before," I said. "But I get the feeling you can do whatever you want."

"I want to do that moving on thing, too." Joanne pushed her way to the front, and stood in front of me. "I don't want to feel so angry anymore. I'm tired of it. Tired of everything, really. Can you help me?"

"I can," I said. "I can help you with everything." Then I smiled. "Once ball season's over, of course."

"Of course," Joanne said. "I owe it to the team."

They disappeared, after that. Drifted off in all directions, going to wherever they went when they weren't playing ball. Soon, it was just Karen and James and me left.

"So, I'll see you tomorrow?" I said.

"Of course," she said.

"And after the season's over—if you decide it's time—you'll be able to find me, right?"

"At the Jimmy Lavall Detective Agency?"

"That's right."

As she went back to her spot on Diamond Two, I turned to James.

"Can you take me home?"

"I'd love to," he said, and pulled me into his arms. "I would absolutely love to."

Marie:
Inquiring Minds Want to Know

I SLEPT THAT night, better than I had in months. Maybe longer. When I opened my eyes and looked at the alarm clock beside James's bed, I saw that it was five thirty. Five thirty in the morning.

"Maybe it was Karen," I whispered, then looked down at James's sleeping face. He jerked once and then opened his eyes and stared at me.

"Are you all right?" he asked.

I smiled and pointed at the clock. "I think maybe I am," I said.

He looked at the time, smiled, and pulled me into his arms. "How do you feel?"

"I ache absolutely everywhere," I said. "But other than that, I feel pretty good."

Actually, I felt better than that. I pulled myself loose and stood. "I think I'm going to make you breakfast," I said.

"Oh?" he laughed. "Toast and coffee?"

"Hey, I'm feeling so good I might even try to make bacon and eggs," I replied. "You know. Do the whole thing."

"I'm shocked, but pleased," he said. "I'm going to take a shower while you make this thing you call breakfast. Call if you need any help."

"You can be a bit of a smart arse, you know," I said, slapping him lightly on the arm. "I can make bacon and eggs."

I hoped.

JAMES WAS OUT of the shower and sitting at the dining room table watching me butcher basted eggs when my phone rang.

"Will you answer that?" I asked. "My hands are full."

"Are you sure you don't want me to do that?" he asked. He looked like he really wanted to take over, but I shook my head. I'd started. I would finish. Somehow.

"No," I said, and grabbed a fork. "Scrambled eggs would be all right, wouldn't they?"

"I guess," he said, and rolled his eyes. Then he answered my phone.

I hacked at the destroyed basted eggs with the fork, trying to break them up enough to be able to legitimately call them scrambled. Then I realized that the tone of James's voice had changed. Something was wrong.

"I'm sorry," he said. "She's not available for an interview. No. If you want information on the case, you should contact Sylvia Worth. That's right. Sergeant Sylvia Worth with the EPS."

"What's going on?" I asked as he disconnected. "Who was that?"

"A reporter," James said. "From the Sun."

I frowned. "A reporter?"

"He wanted to talk to you about what happened at Diamond Two," he said.

"Why would he want to talk to me?" I asked. "The cops handle that stuff, don't they?"

"Yeah," James said. "They usually do. But somehow the reporter got your name."

The phone rang again. James picked it up, and looked at it. "Global TV," he said. "You want me to—"

"No," I said, and grabbed the phone. "What do you want?"

"I just need confirmation," the silky smooth voice said. I thought it sounded like Ellis Wheeler, the talking head for the local news. "Were you the woman who was allegedly attacked by Andrew Westwood?"

"How did you get my name?" I asked.

"Andrew Westwood alleges that you attacked him," Wheeler said. "And that you told him a ghost made you do it. Tell me, Marie, did the ghost of the body the police dug out of Diamond

Two tell you to kill him?"

"What?" My heart was pounding so hard, it felt like I was going to have a heart attack. "What?"

"Hang up," James said.

"Just tell me your side of it," Wheeler said. "Inquiring minds want to know."

"Hang up!" James yelled. So I did. Too late, of course. Far too late.

"Westwood's telling the press that I attacked him," I said. I dropped into the nearest chair, feeling like I was about to puke. "And he's telling them about Karen. That Karen told me to do it." I gasped as my chest constricted. "Jesus, what am I going to do?"

"Don't talk to any of them," James said. "Not until we talk to Sylvia. She'll know what to do."

He grabbed my phone and called Sylvia as I took the burning eggs off the stove. I dumped them into the garbage and listened to James explain to her what had just transpired.

She spoke for a long time. At first James jumped up and tried to interrupt her, but then he sat back down, and just listened. Finally, he said, "I'm putting you on speaker. She needs to hear this."

"What do I need to hear?" I said. He shook his head, hit the button, and then put the phone in the middle of the dining room table.

"I'm so sorry about this," Sylvia said. "We think the ambulance driver talked to the press about Andy Westwood and his allegations. They've already run it on the morning news."

"Run what?" I asked.

"Your story. They're saying that you told Westwood a ghost convinced you to hurt him. Westwood's lawyer is involved, too. He told the media that you were the one who attacked Westwood, not the other way around. That you're crazy. He's trying to win this case through the media before it even goes to trial, Marie."

"But you know the truth," I said. "Just tell them the truth."

"Westwood passed a polygraph, Marie. He's telling the truth, or thinks he is."

"Jesus," I whispered. "What am I going to do?"

"Tell Marie about her psychiatrist," James said, his voice furious. "Tell her."

"Are you talking about Dr. Parkerson?" I asked. "What about

her?"

"She called my office. She saw the story on the morning news, and said she has grave concerns about you. About your ability to tell the difference between reality and fantasy."

I stared at James, hoping that he'd something—anything—that would stop Sylvia from speaking, but he looked devastated.

"She's my shrink," I said. "Don't I have patient doctor confidentiality, or whatever?"

"Not if she's convinced that you are a danger to yourself or to others. She says that you attacking Andy Westwood proves that. Marie, she wants you committed for thirty days. She feels you should be under observation, for your own safety."

"But—but she can't do that," I said. I stood and picked up the phone, holding it so tightly in my hand I was surprised it didn't break into a million pieces. "She can't, can she?"

"I'm afraid she can," Sylvia said. "The papers are being signed as we speak."

"You're going to get a lawyer," James said.

"I don't think a lawyer will help," Sylvia said.

"I don't care!" James roared. "I'm getting her a lawyer, and I'm putting a stop to this before it even starts."

"Once those commitment papers are signed, you have to go to the hospital," Sylvia said. "Come in now, and I'll make sure that everything's done properly. That you're treated decently. Until we can prove, beyond a shadow of a doubt, that Westwood is the one who attacked you."

"So it's all about the evidence," I said. The smell of burnt egg was overwhelming me. I needed to lay down for a minute. Or wake up from this nightmare, once and for all. "Isn't it?"

"Yes," Sylvia said. "It is. Come in, please. Now."

"Sure," I said, and clicked the disconnect before she could say another word.

"James," I started, then stopped. Tried to think, but nothing would come to me. Not one thing.

"I'll call Vinnie VanKlief," he said.

"But he's in Fort McMurray."

"I don't care!" he yelled. Then he took a deep breath in and out. "I don't care. I'll get him on a plane in an hour and he can put a stop to this whole business." He grabbed my hands. "And I'll get hold of Jasmine. I'll tell her what's going on. If she sees this on TV, it could freak her out."

"Please call Karen's parents," I whispered. "Tell them I'll be in contact when I can. To explain everything."

"I will," he said.

"And Greg," I whispered. My stupid throat tightened. "Tell him I might not make the next game."

"Will do," he said. "But first, I'll get you to Sylvia's office, just like she asked. We have to get ahead of this thing, Marie."

My phone rang again. Another TV station. I hit ignore and rose.

"Yeah," I said. "Take me to Sylvia's. But promise me you won't leave me."

"I'm not leaving your side again," he said. "I told you that."

I hoped he wasn't lying to me. But I suspected he was. Once I was in the nuthouse there was no way he could stay by my side even if he wanted to.

I WAS IN real trouble, this time. Real trouble. What was I going to do?

Acknowledgements

I've always wanted to write a novel about softball. This is it.

Softball is like baseball, but is played with a larger ball on a smaller field. The ball is pitched underhand, unlike baseball, where it is pitched overhand. It is also called fast pitch or fastball, but I call it softball, simply because I love the quip "there is nothing soft about it!" (Believe me. There isn't.)

I needed a lot of help this time, because I had to work out the history of a relatively little known part of Edmonton, John Fry Park, where the Edmonton Ladies Softball Association has played ball since the mid-seventies.

Thanks to Al Schwartz, president of the Edmonton Ladies Softball Association, and Michele Party at Softball Alberta, for helping me connect with Jane and Brian for the history.

Thanks to Jane Kornelson and Brian Jacobs, who were involved with the Association when it made the move to John Fry Park. They were wonderful enough to share their memories with me—and that helped me develop the timeline for this book.

Thanks to Patriyca Thenu, Media Relations for the EPS, for connecting me with Sgt. Steve Sharpe. And thanks to Steve, for giving me the words I needed for a vital scene in the book.

If there are mistakes, they are mine alone.

Thanks to Guillem Mari for the art and Lucia Starkey for the set up for another fantastic cover. I think this one is definitely the best!

Thanks to Ryah Deines for the layout. And to Rhonda Parrish for editing—you made the words sing! I'm so glad you still love this book. Makes me think I have something special here.

And, thanks to Margaret Curelas, my publisher, for letting me run with this whacked out idea and keeping me honest about how many games could be played in one day of a tournament. (That wasn't the only thing she kept me honest about, but it was important.)

My family is still standing behind me, and I can never thank them enough for all their support. Without it, I don't think I could have finished this one.

And to Buddy the border collie. Sorry, Millie's still the only dog in the series. (Man! He never forgets anything!) I hope another cookie will help ease the pain.

About the Author

E.C. (Eileen) Bell's debut paranormal mystery, *Seeing the Light* (2014) won the BPAA award for Best Speculative Fiction Book of the Year, and was shortlisted for the Bony Blythe Award for Light Mystery. The second book in the series, *Drowning in Amber*, (2015) was nominated for an Aurora Award for best novel. Dying on Second is the fourth book in the series, and she has plans for a fifth. In her spare time (!) she edits for *On Spec, The Canadian Magazine of the Fantastic*. When she's not writing or editing, she's living a fine life in her round house with her husband and two dogs. And yes, one of them is a step-on dog.

For more info, check out her website: www.eileenbell.com

CPSIA information can be obtained
at www.ICGtesting.com
Printed in the USA
BVHW08s0722260618
520065BV00001B/38/P